Praise for **Perfect Chemistry**
by *New York Times* and *USA Today* bestselling author
Simone Elkeles
RITA Award Winner for Best Young Adult Fantasy

"Elkeles sure hits her stride in this story of star-crossed lovers."
—*Romantic Times*

"Smoldering doesn't quite do justice to the romantic banter." —*SLJ*

"Elkeles pens plenty of tasteful, hot scenes . . . that keep
the pages turning." —*Kirkus Reviews*

"Teens with a taste for romance will eat this up like ice cream
on a hot day." —*BCCB*

"There isn't any teen girl that I can think of that wouldn't love
this story." —Read Space

"Three chapters in and I could NOT put this book down. To say the
two main characters had sparks is putting it mildly. I found myself
re-reading the same page over and over—it was THAT good.
I haven't done that since the Twilight series." —Chasing Heroes

"*All* teenagers should read this book and explore truths about first
impressions, first love, first loss, and first everything else.
Throughout *Perfect Chemistry*, it's easy to see a bit of screwed-up
Fairfield in every town, a bit of screwed-up Alex or Brittany in every
one, and a bit of the good sides of both of these everywhere in this
story that annihilates all stereotypes and exceeds all expectations."
—Reading Rocks

"It is the perfect beach read and definitely one to add to your summer reading list." —Lost Between the Pages

"The most amazing teen-romance book I've ever read." —J Is Looking for J

"Some parts of this book actually made me forget I was reading. I became so wrapped up in their lives. . . . If you enjoy YA and especially if you love a YA love story, this is an amazing tale." —J. Kaye's Book Blog

"This was the first book I have read by Simone Elkeles and I must say I will be looking for more books by her. I highly recommend this book." —A Passion for Books

"*Perfect Chemistry* is a wonderfully written, intense and emotional story that tugs at your heartstrings as you watch these two star-crossed lovers break down the social and racial barriers between their worlds, fighting for the happily ever after that they deserve." —Happily Ever After

Perfect Chemistry

Simone Elkeles

BHS SOUTH LIBRARY

WALKER & COMPANY

New York

For Moshe, who gave up so much for me

Copyright © 2009 by Simone Elkeles
All rights reserved. No part of this book may be reproduced or transmitted in any form or by any means, electronic or mechanical, including photocopying, recording, or by any information storage and retrieval system, without permission in writing from the publisher.

First published in the United States of America in January 2009 by
Walker Publishing Company, Inc., a division of Bloomsbury Publishing, Inc.
Visit Walker & Company's Web site at www.bloomsburyteens.com

For information about permission to reproduce selections from this book, write to
Permissions, Walker & Company, 175 Fifth Avenue, New York, New York 10010

Library of Congress Cataloging-in-Publication Data
Elkeles, Simone.
Perfect chemistry / Simone Elkeles.
p.   cm.
Summary: When wealthy, seemingly perfect Brittany and Alex Fuentes, a gang member from the other side of town, develop a relationship after Alex discovers that Brittany is not exactly who she seems to be, they must face the disapproval of their schoolmates—and others.
ISBN-13: 978-0-8027-9822-0 • ISBN-10: 0-8027-9822-5 (paperback)
ISBN-13: 978-0-8027-9823-7 • ISBN-10: 0-8027-9823-3 (hardcover)
[1. Social classes—Fiction. 2. Dating (Social customs)—Fiction. 3. Gangs—Fiction. 4. Family problems—Fiction. 5. High schools—Fiction. 6. Schools—Fiction.] I. Title.
PZ7.E42578Pe 2009   [Fic]—dc22   2008013769

Book design by Nicole Gastonguay
Typeset by Westchester Book Composition
Printed in the U.S.A. by Worldcolor Fairfield, Pennsylvania
14 15   (paperback)
4 6 8 10 9 7 5 3   (hardcover)

All papers used by Walker & Company are natural, recyclable products made from wood grown in well-managed forests. The manufacturing processes conform to the environmental regulations of the country of origin.

1

Brittany

Everyone knows I'm perfect. My life is perfect. My clothes are perfect. Even my family is perfect. And although it's a complete lie, I've worked my butt off to keep up the appearance that I have it all. The truth, if it were to come out, would destroy my entire picture-perfect image.

Standing in front of my bathroom mirror while music blares from my speakers, I wipe away the third crooked line I've drawn beneath my eye. My hands are shaking, damn it. Starting senior year of high school and seeing my boyfriend after a summer apart shouldn't be so nerve-racking, but I've gotten off to a disastrous start. First, my curling iron sent up smoke signals and died. Then the button on my favorite shirt popped off. Now, my eyeliner decides it has a mind of its own. If I had any choice in the matter, I'd stay in my comfy bed and eat warm chocolate chip cookies all day.

"Brit, come down," I faintly hear my mom yelling from the foyer.

My first instinct is to ignore her, but that never gets me anything but arguments, headaches, and more yelling.

"I'll be there in a sec," I call down, hoping I can get this eyeliner to go on straight and be done with it.

Finally getting it right, I toss the eyeliner tube on the counter, double and triple check myself in the mirror, turn off my stereo, and hurry down the hallway.

My mom is standing at the bottom of our grand staircase, scanning my outfit. I straighten. I know, I know. I'm eighteen and shouldn't care what my mom thinks. But you haven't lived in the Ellis house. My mom has anxiety. Not the kind easily controlled with little blue pills. And when my mom is stressed, everyone living with her suffers. I think that's why my dad goes to work before she gets up in the morning, so he doesn't have to deal with, well, her.

"Hate the pants, love the belt," Mom says, pointing her index finger at each item. "And that noise you call music was giving me a headache. Thank goodness it's off."

"Good morning to you, too, Mother," I say before walking down the stairs and giving her a peck on the cheek. The smell of my mom's strong perfume stings my nostrils the closer I get. She already looks like a million bucks in her Ralph Lauren Blue Label tennis dress. No one can point a finger and criticize her outfit, that's for sure.

"I bought your favorite muffin for the first day of school," Mom says, pulling out a bag from behind her back.

"No, thanks," I say, looking around for my sister. "Where's Shelley?"

"In the kitchen."

"Is her new caretaker here yet?"

"Her name is Baghda, and no. She's coming in an hour."

"Did you tell her wool irritates Shelley's skin? And that she pulls hair?" She's always let it be known in her nonverbal cues she gets irritated by the feeling of wool on her skin. Pulling hair is her new thing, and it has caused a few disasters. Disasters in my house are about as pretty as a car wreck, so avoiding them is crucial.

"Yes. And yes. I gave your sister an earful this morning, Brittany. If she keeps acting up, we'll find ourselves out of another caretaker."

I walk into the kitchen, not wanting to hear my mother go on and on about her theories of why Shelley lashes out. Shelley is sitting at the table in her wheelchair, busily eating her specially blended food because, even at the age of twenty, my sister doesn't have the ability to chew and swallow like people without her physical limitations. As usual, the food has found its way onto her chin, lips, and cheeks.

"Hey, Shell-bell," I say, leaning over her and wiping her face with a napkin. "It's the first day of school. Wish me luck."

Shelley holds jerky arms out and gives me a lopsided smile. I love that smile.

"You want to give me a hug?" I ask her, knowing she does. The doctors always tell us the more interaction Shelley gets, the better off she'll be.

Shelley nods. I fold myself in her arms, careful to keep her hands away from my hair. When I straighten, my mom gasps. It sounds to me like a referee's whistle, halting my life. "Brit, you can't go to school like that."

"Like what?"

She shakes her head and sighs in frustration. "Look at your shirt."

Glancing down, I see a large wet spot on the front of my white Calvin Klein shirt. Oops. Shelley's drool. One look at my sister's drawn face tells me what she can't easily put into words. *Shelley is sorry. Shelley didn't mean to mess up my outfit.*

"It's no biggie," I tell her, although in the back of my mind I know it screws up my "perfect" look.

Frowning, my mom wets a paper towel at the sink and dabs at the spot. It makes me feel like a two-year-old.

"Go upstairs and change."

"Mom, it was just peaches," I say, treading carefully so this doesn't turn into a full-blown yelling match. The last thing I want to do is make my sister feel bad.

"Peaches stain. You don't want people thinking you don't care about your appearance."

"Fine." I wish this was one of my mom's good days, the days she doesn't bug me about stuff.

I give my sister a kiss on the top of her head, making sure she doesn't think her drool bothers me in the least. "I'll see ya after school," I say, attempting to keep the morning cheerful. "To finish our checker tournament."

I run back up the stairs, taking two steps at a time. When I get to my bedroom, I check my watch. Oh, no. It's ten after seven. My best friend, Sierra, is gonna freak out if I'm late picking her up. Grabbing a light blue scarf out of my closet, I pray it'll work. Maybe nobody will notice the drool spot if I tie it just right.

When I come back down the stairs, my mother is standing in the foyer, scanning my appearance again. "Love the scarf."

Phew.

As I pass her, she shoves the muffin into my hand. "Eat it on the way."

I take the muffin. Walking to my car, I absently bite into it. Unfortunately it isn't blueberry, my favorite. It's banana nut, and the bananas are overdone. It reminds me of myself—seemingly perfect on the outside, but the inside is all mush.

2

Alex

"Get up, Alex."

I scowl at my little brother and bury my head under my pillow. Since I share a room with my eleven- and fifteen-year-old brothers, there's no escape except the little privacy a lone pillow can give.

"Leave me alone, Luis," I say roughly through the pillow. *"No estés chingando."*

"I'm not fuckin' with you. *Mamá* told me to wake you so you won't be late for school."

Senior year. I should be proud I'll be the first family member in the Fuentes household to graduate high school. But after graduation, real life will start. College is just a dream. Senior year for me is like a retirement party for a sixty-five-year-old. You know you can do more, but everyone expects you to quit.

"I'm all dressed in my new clothes," Luis's proud but muffled voice comes through the pillow. "The *nenas* won't be able to resist this Latino stud."

"Good for you," I mumble.

"*Mamá* said I should pour this pitcher of water on you if you don't get up."

Was privacy too much to ask for? I take my pillow and chuck it across the room. It's a direct hit. The water splashes all over him.

"*Culero!*" he screams at me. "These are the only new clothes I got."

A fit of laughter is coming through the bedroom door. Carlos, my other brother, is laughing like a frickin' hyena. That is, until Luis jumps him. I watch the fight spiral out of control as my younger brothers punch and kick each other.

They're good fighters, I think proudly as I watch them duke it out. But as the oldest male in the house, it's my duty to break it up. I grab the collar of Carlos's shirt but trip on Luis's leg and land on the floor with them.

Before I can regain my balance, icy cold water is poured on my back. Turning quickly, I catch *mi'amá* dousing us all, a bucket poised in her fist above us while she's wearing her work uniform. She works as a checker for the local grocery store a couple blocks from our house. It doesn't pay a whole heck of a lot, but we don't need much.

"Get up," she orders, her fiery attitude out in full force.

"Shit, Ma," Carlos says, standing.

Mi'amá takes what's left in her bucket, sticks her fingers in the icy water, and flicks the liquid in Carlos's face.

Luis laughs and before he knows it, he gets flicked with water as well. Will they ever learn?

"Any more attitude, Luis?" she asks.

"No, ma'am," Luis says, standing as straight as a soldier.

"You have any more filthy words to come out of that *boca* of yours, Carlos?" She dips her hand in the water as a warning.

"No, ma'am," echoes soldier number two.

"And what about you, Alejandro?" Her eyes narrow into slits as she focuses on me.

"What? I was tryin' to break it up," I say innocently, giving her my you-can't-resist-me smile.

She flicks water in my face. "That's for not breaking it up sooner. Now get dressed, all of you, and come eat breakfast before school."

So much for my you-can't-resist-me smile. "You know you love us," I call after her as she leaves our room.

After a quick shower, I walk back to my bedroom with a towel wrapped around my waist. I catch sight of Luis with one of my bandannas on his head and my gut tightens. I yank it off him. "Don't ever touch this, Luis."

"Why not?" he asks, his deep brown eyes all innocent.

To Luis, it's a bandanna. To me, it's a symbol of what is and will never be. How the hell am I supposed to explain it to an eleven-year-old kid? He knows what I am. It's no secret the bandanna has the Latino Blood colors on it. Payback and revenge got me in and now there's no way out. But I'll die before I let one of my brothers get sucked in.

I ball the bandanna in my fist. "Luis, don't touch my shit. Especially my Blood stuff."

"I like red and black."

That's the last thing I need to hear. "If I ever catch you wearin' it again, you'll be sportin' *black and blue*," I tell him. "Got it, little brother?"

He shrugs. "Yeah. I got it."

As he leaves the room with a spring in his step, I wonder if he really does get it. I stop myself from thinking too hard about it as I grab a black T-shirt from my dresser and pull on worn, faded jeans. When I tie my bandanna around my head, I hear *mi'amá*'s voice bellowing from the kitchen.

"Alejandro, come eat before the food gets cold. *De prisa*, hurry up."

"I'm comin'," I call back. I'll never understand why food is such an important part of her life.

My brothers are already busy chowing down on their breakfast when I enter the kitchen. I open the refrigerator and scan its contents.

"Sit down."

"Ma, I'll just grab—"

"You'll grab nothing, Alejandro. Sit. We're a family and we're going to eat like one."

I sigh, close the refrigerator door, and sit beside Carlos. Sometimes being a member of a close family has its disadvantages. *Mi'amá* places a heaping plate of *huevos* and *tortillas* in front of me.

"Why can't you call me Alex?" I ask, my head down while I stare at the food in front of me.

"If I wanted to call you Alex, I wouldn't have bothered to name you Alejandro. Don't you like your given name?"

My muscles tense. I was named after a father who is no longer alive, leaving me the responsibility of being the designated man of the house. Alejandro, Alejandro Jr., Junior . . . it's all the same to me.

"Would it matter?" I mumble as I pick up a tortilla. I look up, trying to gauge her reaction.

Her back is to me as she cleans dishes in the sink. "No."

"Alex wants to pretend he's white," Carlos chimes in. "You can change your name, bro, but nobody'd mistake you for anythin' other than *Mexicano*."

"Carlos, *cállate la boca*," I warn. I don't want to be white. I just don't want to be associated with my father.

"*Por favor*, you two," our mother pleads. "Enough fighting for one day."

"*Mojado*," Carlos sings, egging me on by calling me a wetback.

I've had enough of Carlos's mouth; he's gone too far. I stand, my chair scraping the floor. Carlos follows and steps in front of me, closing the space between us. He knows I could kick his ass. His overblown ego is gonna get him in trouble with the wrong person one of these days.

"Carlos, sit down," *mi'amá* orders.

"Dirty beaner," Carlos drawls at me in a fake deep accent. "Better yet, *es un Ganguero.*"

"Carlos!" *mi'amá* reprimands sharply as she comes forward, but I get in between them and grab my brother's collar.

"Yeah, that's all anyone will ever think of me," I tell him. "But you keep talkin' trash and they'll think that of you, too."

"Brother, they'll think that of me anyway. Whether I want them to or not."

I release him. "You're wrong, Carlos. You can do better, be better."

"Than you?"

"Yeah, better than me and you know it," I say. "Now apologize to *mi'amá* for talkin' smack in front of her."

One look in my eyes and Carlos knows I'm not kidding around. "Sorry, Ma," he says, then sits back down. I don't miss his glare, though, as his ego got knocked down a peg.

Mi'amá turns and opens the fridge, trying to hide her tears. Damn it, she's worried about Carlos. He's a sophomore and the next two years are either going to make him or break him.

I pull on my black leather jacket, needing to get out of here. I give *mi'amá* a peck on the cheek with an apology for ruining her breakfast, then walk outside wondering how I'm going to keep Carlos and Luis away from my path while steering them toward a better one. Oh, the fucking irony of it all.

On the street, guys in the same color bandannas flag the Latino Blood signal: right hand tapping twice on their left arm while their ring finger is bent. My veins fire up as I flag right back before straddling my motorcycle. They want a tough-as-nails gang member, they got one. I put on a hell of a show to the outside world; sometimes I even surprise myself.

"Alex, wait up," a familiar female voice calls out.

Carmen Sanchez, my neighbor and ex-girlfriend, runs up to me.

"Hey, Carmen," I mutter.

"How about giving me a ride to school?"

Her short black skirt shows off her incredible legs, and her shirt is tight, accentuating her small but perky *chichis*. Once I would have done anything for her, but that was before I caught her in another guy's bed over the summer. Or car, as it was.

"Come on, Alex. I promise not to bite . . . unless you want me to."

Carmen is my Latino Blood homegirl. Whether we're a couple or not, we still have each other's backs. It's the code we live by. "Get on," I say.

Carmen hops on my motorcycle and deliberately places her hands on my thighs while pressing against my backside. It doesn't have the effect she was probably hoping for. What does she think, that I'll forget the past? No way. My history defines who I am.

I try to focus on starting my senior year at Fairfield, the here and now. It's damn difficult because, unfortunately, after graduation my future will likely be as screwed up as my past.

3

Brittany

"My hair gets all frizzy in this car, Sierra. Every time I put the top down, my hair looks like I've walked through a tornado," I say to my best friend as I drive on Vine Street toward Fairfield High in my new silver convertible.

"Outward appearances mean everything." My parents taught me the motto that rules my life. It's the sole reason I didn't comment about the BMW when my dad gave me the extravagant birthday present two weeks ago.

"We live a half hour from the Windy City," Sierra says, holding her hand in the wind as we drive. "Chicago isn't exactly known for its calm weather. Besides, you look like a blond, Grecian goddess with wild hair, Brit. You're just nervous about seeing Colin again."

My gaze wanders to the heart-shaped picture of me and Colin taped to my dashboard. "A summer apart changes people."

"Distance makes the heart grow fonder," Sierra throws back. "You're the captain of the pom squad and he's captain of the varsity football team. You two have to date or the solar system would go out of alignment."

Colin called a few times during the summer from his family's cabin, where he was hanging out with his buddies, but I don't know where our relationship stands now. He just got back last night.

"I love those jeans," Sierra says, eyeing my faded Brazilian pants. "I'll be borrowing them before you know it."

"My mom hates them," I tell her, smoothing my hair at a stoplight, trying to tame my blond frizzies. "She says it looks like I got them at a used clothing store."

"Did you tell her vintage is in?"

"Yeah, like she'd even listen. She was hardly paying attention when I asked her about the new caretaker."

No one understands what it's like at my house. Luckily, I have Sierra. She might not understand, but she knows enough to listen and keep my home life confidential. Besides Colin, Sierra is the only one who's met my sister.

Sierra flips open my CD case. "What happened to the last caretaker?"

"Shelley pulled a chunk of her hair out."

"Ouch."

I drive into the high school parking lot with my mind more on my sister than on the road. My wheels screech to a stop when I almost hit a guy and girl on a motorcycle. I thought it was an empty parking space.

"Watch it, bitch," Carmen Sanchez, the girl on the back of the motorcycle, says as she flips me the finger.

She obviously missed the Road Rage lecture in Driver's Ed.

"Sorry," I say loudly so I can be heard over the roar of the motorcycle. "It didn't look like anyone was in this spot."

Then I realize whose motorcycle I almost hit. The driver turns around. Angry dark eyes. Red and black bandanna. I sink down into the driver's seat as far as I can.

"Oh, shit. It's Alex Fuentes," I say, wincing.

"Jesus, Brit," Sierra says, her voice low. "I'd like to live to see graduation. Get outta here before he decides to kill us both."

Alex is staring at me with his devil eyes while putting the kickstand down on his motorcycle. Is he going to confront me?

I search for reverse, frantically moving the stick back and forth. Of course it's no surprise my dad bought me a car with a stick shift without taking the time to teach me how to master driving the thing.

Alex takes a step toward my car. My instincts tell me to abandon the car and flee, as if I was stuck on railroad tracks with a train heading straight for me. I glance at Sierra, who's desperately searching through her purse for something. Is she kidding me?

"I can't get this damn car in reverse. I need help. What are you looking for?" I ask.

"Like . . . nothing. I'm trying not to make eye contact with those Latino Bloods. Get a move on, will ya?" Sierra responds through gritted teeth. "Besides, I only know how to drive an automatic."

Finally grinding into reverse, my wheels screech loud and hard as I maneuver backward and search for another parking spot.

After parking in the west lot, far from a certain gang member with a reputation that could scare off even the toughest Fairfield football players, Sierra and I walk up the front steps of Fairfield High. Unfortunately, Alex Fuentes and the rest of his gang friends are hanging by the front doors.

"Walk right past them," Sierra mutters. "Whatever you do, don't look in their eyes."

It's pretty hard not to when Alex Fuentes steps right in front of me and blocks my path.

What's that prayer you're supposed to say right before you know you're going to die?

"You're a lousy driver," Alex says with his slight Latino accent and full-blown I-AM-THE-MAN stance.

The guy might look like an Abercrombie model with his ripped bod and flawless face, but his picture is more likely to be taken for a mug shot.

The kids from the north side don't really mix with kids from the south side. It's not that we think we're better than them, we're just different. We've grown up in the same town, but on totally opposite sides. We live in big houses on Lake Michigan and they live next to the train tracks. We look, talk, act, and dress different. I'm not saying it's good or bad; it's just the way it is in Fairfield. And, to be honest, most of the south side girls treat me like Carmen Sanchez does . . . they hate me because of who I am.

Or, rather, who they *think* I am.

Alex's gaze slowly moves down my body, traveling the length of me before moving back up. It's not the first time a guy has checked me out, it's just that I never had a guy like Alex do it so blatantly . . . and so up-close. I can feel my face getting hot.

"Next time, watch where you're goin'," he says, his voice cool and controlled.

He's trying to bully me. He's a pro at this. I won't let him get to me and win his little game of intimidation, even if my stomach feels like I'm doing one hundred cartwheels in a row. I square my shoulders and sneer at him, the same sneer I use to push people away. "Thanks for the tip."

"If you ever need a real man to teach you how to drive, I can give you lessons."

Catcalls and whistles from his buddies set my blood boiling.

"If you *were* a real man, you'd open the door for me instead of blocking my way," I say, admiring my own comeback even as my knees threaten to buckle.

Alex steps back, pulls the door open, and bows like he's my butler. He's totally mocking me, he knows it and I know it. Everyone knows it. I catch a glimpse of Sierra, still desperately searching for nothing in her purse. She's clueless.

"Get a life," I tell him.

"Like yours? *Cabróna*, let me tell you somethin'," Alex says harshly. "Your life isn't reality, it's fake. Just like you."

"It's better than living my life as a loser," I lash out, hoping my words sting as much as his words did. "Just like you."

Grabbing Sierra's arm, I pull her toward the open door. Catcalls and comments follow us as we walk into the school.

I finally let out the breath I must have been holding, then turn to Sierra.

My best friend is staring at me, all bug-eyed. "Holy shit, Brit! You got a death wish or something?"

"What gives Alex Fuentes the right to bully everyone in his path?"

"Uh, maybe the gun he has hidden in his pants or the gang colors he wears," Sierra says, sarcasm dripping from every word.

"He's not stupid enough to carry a gun to school," I reason. "And I refuse to be bullied, by him or anyone else." At school, at least. School is the one place I can keep up my "perfect" facade; everyone at school buys it. Suddenly pumped about starting my last year at Fairfield, I shake Sierra's shoulders. "We're seniors now," I say with the same enthusiasm I use for pom-pom routines during football games.

"So?"

"So, starting right now everything is going to be p-e-r-f-e-c-t."

The bell rings, which is not exactly a bell because the student body voted last year to replace bells with music between classes. Right now they're playing "Summer Lovin'" from *Grease*. Sierra starts walking down the hall. "I'll make sure you have a *p-e-r-f-e-c-t* funeral. With flowers and everything."

"Who died?" a voice from behind me asks.

I turn around. It's Colin, blond hair bleached from the summer sun and a grin so large it takes up almost his whole face. I wish I had a mirror to see if my makeup is smudged. But surely Colin will date me even if it is, won't he? I run up and give him the biggest hug.

He holds me tight, kisses me lightly on the lips, and pulls back. "Who died?" he asks again.

"Nobody," I answer. "Forget about it. Forget everything except being with me."

"It's easy when you look so damn hot." Colin kisses me again. "Sorry I haven't called. It's been so crazy unpacking and everything."

I smile up at him, glad our summer apart hasn't changed our relationship. The solar system is safe, at least for now.

Colin drapes his arm around my shoulders as the front doors to the school open. Alex and his friends burst through as if they're here to hijack the school.

"Why do they even come to school?" Colin mutters low so only I can hear. "Half of them'll probably drop out before the year is over, anyway."

My gaze briefly meets Alex's and a shiver runs down my spine.

"I almost hit Alex Fuentes's motorcycle this morning," I tell Colin once Alex is out of hearing range.

"You should have."

"Colin," I chide.

"At least it would have been an exciting first day. This school is boring as shit."

Boring? I almost got in a car accident, was flipped off by a girl from the south side, and was harassed by a dangerous gang member outside the school's front doors. If that was any indication of the rest of senior year, this school will be anything *but* boring.

4

Alex

I knew I'd be called into the new principal's office at some point during the year, but I didn't expect it to be on the first day of school. I heard Dr. Aguirre was hired because of his hard-ass personality at some high school in Milwaukee. Someone must have pegged me as a ringleader, 'cause it's my ass sitting here instead of another Latino Blood's.

So here I am, pulled out of gym so Aguirre can puff up his chest and ramble on about tougher school rules. I detect him feeling me out, wondering how I'll react, as he threatens me, ". . . and this year I've hired two full-time armed security guards, Alejandro."

His eyes focus on me, trying to intimidate. Yeah, right. I can tell right off that while Aguirre might be Latino, he knows nothing about how our streets work. The next thing I know he'll be talking about how he grew up poor, just like me. He's probably never even driven through my side of town. Maybe I should offer to give him a tour.

He stands in front of me. "I promised the superintendent as well as the school board I'd personally be responsible for rooting out the violence that has plagued this school for years. I won't hesitate to suspend anyone who ignores school rules."

I haven't done anything besides have a little fun with the pom-pom diva and already this guy is talking suspension. Maybe he heard about my suspension last year. That little incident got me kicked out for three days. It wasn't my fault . . . entirely. Paco had this crazy theory about cold water affecting white guys' dicks differently than Latinos'. I was arguing with him in the boiler room after he'd shut down the hot water heaters when we were caught.

I had nothing to do with it but got blamed all the same. Paco attempted to tell the truth, but our old principal wouldn't listen. Maybe if I fought more he would have listened. But what's the use in fighting for a lost cause?

It's clear Brittany Ellis is responsible for me being in here today. You think her jerk of a boyfriend'll ever get called into Aguirre's office? No way. The dude is an idolized football player. He can ditch class and start fights and Aguirre will probably still kiss his ass. Colin Adams is always pushing me, knowing he can get away with it. Every time I've been about to retaliate, he's found a way to escape or rush to where teachers were in abundance . . . teachers who were just waiting for me to fuck up.

One of these days. . . .

I look up at Aguirre. "I'm not startin' any fights." I might finish one, though.

"That's good," Aguirre says. "But I heard about you harassing a female student in the parking lot today."

Almost getting run over by Brittany Ellis's shiny new Beemer is *my* fault? For the past three years I've managed to avoid the rich bitch. I heard last year she got a C on her report card but a little call to the school from her parents got it changed to an A.

It would hurt her chances of getting into a good college.

Screw that shit. If I got a C, *mi'amá* would smack me upside the head and nag me to study twice as hard. I've worked my ass off to get good grades, even though I've gotten interrogated more often than not about my means of getting the answers. As if I'd cheat. It's not about getting into college. It's about proving I *could* get in . . . if my world was different.

The south siders might be seen as dumber than the north siders, but that's bullshit. So we're not as rich or obsessed with material possessions or getting into the most expensive and prestigious universities. We're in survival mode most of the time, always having to watch our backs.

Probably the hardest part of Brittany Ellis's life is deciding which restaurant to dine at each night. The girl uses her smokin' bod to manipulate everyone who comes in contact with her.

"Care to share with me what happened in the parking lot? I'd like to hear your side," Aguirre says.

Not happening. I learned long ago that my side doesn't matter. "The thing this mornin' . . . total misunderstandin'," I tell him. *Brittany Ellis's misunderstanding that two vehicles can't fit in one spot.*

Aguirre stands and leans over his polished, spotless desk. "Let's try not making misunderstandings a habit, okay, Alejandro?"

"Alex."

"Huh?"

"I go by Alex," I say. What he knows about me is in my school file, a file so biased it's probably ten inches thick.

Aguirre gives me a nod. "All right, Alex. Get ready for sixth period. But I have eyes at this school, and I'm watching your every move. I don't want to see you back in my office." Just as I get up, he puts a hand on my shoulder. "Just so you know, my goal is for every student in this school to succeed. *Every* student, Alex. Including you, so whatever biases you have about me you can throw them out the window. *¿Me entiendes?"*

"*Si. Entiendo,*" I say, wondering how much I can believe him. In the hallway, a sea of students are rushing to their next class. I have no clue where I'm supposed to be and I'm still in my gym clothes.

In the locker room after I change, a song plays on the loudspeaker indicating it's now sixth period. I pull the schedule out of my back pocket. Chemistry with Mrs. Peterson. Great, another hard-ass to deal with.

5

Brittany

I turn on my cell and call home before chemistry to see how my sister is doing. Baghda isn't too happy because Shelley was freaking out about the way her lunch tasted. Apparently Shelley swiped her bowl of yogurt onto the floor in protest.

Was it too much to hope that my mom would take a day off from hanging out at the country club to transition Baghda? Summer is officially over and I can't be there to pick up where the caretakers usually leave off.

I should be focusing on school. Getting into my dad's alma mater, Northwestern, is my main goal so I can go to a college close to home and be there for my sister. After giving Baghda some suggestions I take a deep breath, paste on a smile, and walk into class.

"Hey, babe. I saved you a seat." Colin motions to the stool next to him.

The room is arranged with rows of high lab tables for two. This means I'll sit next to Colin for the rest of the year and we'll do the dreaded senior chemistry project together. Feeling foolish for thinking things wouldn't be okay between us, I slip onto the stool and pull out my heavy chem book.

"Hey, look. Fuentes is in our class!" a guy calls out from the back of the room. "Alex, over here, *ven pa'ca*."

I try not to stare as Alex greets his friends with pats on the back and handshakes too complicated to reproduce. They all say *"ese"* to each other, whatever that means. Alex's presence catches every eye in the classroom.

"I hear he was arrested last weekend for possession of meth," Colin whispers to me.

"No way."

He nods and his eyebrows go up. "Way."

Well, the information shouldn't surprise me. I hear most weekends Alex spends drugged out, passed out, or doing some other illegal activity.

Mrs. Peterson closes the door to the classroom with a bang and all eyes move from the back of the room, where Alex and his friends are sitting, to the front where Mrs. Peterson is standing. She has light brown hair pulled back into a tight ponytail. The woman is probably in her late twenties, but her glasses and perpetual stern expression make her look way older. I hear she's tough now because her first year teaching the students made her cry. They didn't respect a teacher who was young enough to be their older sister.

"Good afternoon and welcome to senior chemistry." She sits on the edge of her desk and opens a folder. "I appreciate you picking your own seats, but I make the seating arrangements . . . alphabetically."

I groan along with the rest of the class, but Mrs. Peterson doesn't miss a beat. She stands in front of the first lab table and says, "Colin Adams, take the first seat. Your partner is Darlene Boehm."

Darlene Boehm is co-captain of the varsity pom squad with me. She flashes me an apologetic look as she slides onto the stool next to my boyfriend.

Down the list Mrs. Peterson goes, students reluctantly moving to their assigned seats.

"Brittany Ellis," Mrs. Peterson says, pointing to the table behind Colin. I unenthusiastically sit on the stool at my assigned place.

"Alejandro Fuentes," Mrs. Peterson says, pointing to the stool next to me.

Oh my God. Alex . . . my chemistry partner? For my entire senior year! No way, no how, SO not okay. I give Colin a "help me" look as I try to avoid a panic attack. I definitely should have stayed at home. In bed. Under the covers. Forget not being intimidated.

"Call me Alex."

Mrs. Peterson looks up from her class list and regards Alex above the glasses on her nose. "*Alex* Fuentes," she says, before changing his name on her list. "Mr. Fuentes, take off that bandanna. I have a zero tolerance policy in my class. No gang-related accessories are allowed to enter this room. Unfortunately, Alex, your reputation precedes you. Dr. Aguirre backs my zero tolerance policy one hundred percent . . . do I make myself clear?"

Alex stares her down before sliding the bandanna off his head, exposing raven hair that matches his eyes.

"It's to cover up the lice," Colin mutters to Darlene, but I hear him and Alex does, too.

"*Vete a la verga,*" Alex says to Colin, his hard eyes blazing. "*Cállate el hocico.*"

"Whatever, dude," Colin says, then turns around. "He can't even speak English."

"That's enough, Colin. Alex, sit down." Mrs. Peterson eyes the rest of the class. "That goes for the rest of you, as well. I can't control what you do outside of this room, but in my class I'm the boss." She turns back to Alex. "Do I make myself clear?"

"*Sí, señora,*" Alex says, deliberately slow.

Mrs. Peterson goes down the rest of the list while I do everything in my power not to make eye contact with the guy sitting next to me. It's too bad I left my purse in my locker or I could pretend to look for nothing like Sierra did this morning.

"This sucks," Alex mumbles to himself. His voice is dark and husky. Does he make it that way on purpose?

How am I going to explain to my mother I have to partner with Alex Fuentes? Oh, God, I hope she doesn't blame me somehow for screwing this up.

I glance at my boyfriend, deep in conversation with Darlene. I'm so jealous. Why couldn't my last name be Allis instead of Ellis so I could sit next to him?

It'd be cool if God gave everyone a Do Over Day and you could yell "Do Over!" and the day would start new. This would definitely qualify for a DOD.

Does Mrs. Peterson actually think it's reasonable to pair the captain of the pom-pom squad with the most dangerous guy in school? The woman is delusional.

Mrs. Delusional finally finishes assigning seats. "I know you seniors think you know everything. But never think of yourself as a success until you can help treat diseases that plague mankind or make the earth a safer place to live. The field of chemistry plays a crucial role in developing medicines, radiation treatments for cancer patients, petroleum uses, the ozone—"

Alex raises his hand.

"Alex," the teacher says. "Do you have a question?"

"Uh, Mrs. Peterson, are you sayin' the president of the U.S. isn't a success?"

"What I'm saying is . . . money and status aren't everything. Use your brain and do something for mankind or the planet you live on. Then you're a success. And you'll have earned my respect, which not many people in this world can boast about."

"I got things I can boast about, Mrs. P.," Alex says, obviously amusing himself.

Mrs. Peterson holds up a hand. "Please spare us the details, Alex."

I shake my head. If Alex thinks antagonizing the teacher will get us a good grade, he's sadly mistaken. It's obvious Mrs. Peterson doesn't like smart-asses and my partner is already on her radar.

"Now," Mrs. Delusional says, "look at the person sitting next to you."

Anything but that. But I don't have a choice. I glance over at Colin again, who seems pretty content with his assigned partner. Darlene already has a boyfriend or I seriously would be questioning why she's leaning a bit too close to Colin and flipping her hair back too many times. I tell myself I'm being paranoid.

"You don't have to like your partner," Mrs. Peterson says, "but you're stuck together for the next ten months. Take five minutes to get to know each other, then each of you will introduce your partner to the class. Talk about what you did over the summer, what hobbies you have, or anything else interesting or unique your classmates might not know about you. Your five minutes start now."

I take out my notebook, flip to the first page, and shove it at Alex. "Why don't you write down stuff about yourself in my notebook and I'll do the same in yours." It's better than trying to have a conversation with him.

Alex nods in agreement, although I think I caught the corners of his mouth twitch as he hands me his notebook. Did I imagine that twitch or did it really happen? Taking a deep breath, I wipe that thought from my mind and write diligently until Mrs. Peterson instructs us to stop and listen to each other's introductions.

"This is Darlene Boehm," Colin begins, being the first to speak.

But I don't hear the rest of Colin's speech about Darlene and her trip to Italy and her experience at dance camp this summer. Instead, I glance down at the notebook given back to me by Alex and stare at the words on the page with my mouth open.

6

Alex

Okay, so I shouldn't have fucked with her on the introduction thing. Writing nothing except, **Saturday night. You and me. Driving lessons and hot sex . . .** in her notebook probably wasn't the smartest move. But I was itching to make Little Miss *Perfecta* stumble in her introduction of me. And stumbling she is.

"Miss Ellis?"

I watch in amusement as Perfection herself looks up at Peterson. Oh, she's good. This partner of mine knows how to hide her true emotions, something I recognize because I do it all the time.

"Yes?" Brittany says, tilting her head and smiling like a beauty queen.

I wonder if that smile has ever gotten her out of a speeding ticket.

"It's your turn. Introduce Alex to the class."

I lean an elbow on the lab table, waiting for an introduction she has to either make up or fess up she knows less than crap about me. She glances at my comfortable position and I can tell from her deer-in-the-headlights look I've stumped her.

"This is *Alejandro* Fuentes," she starts, her voice hitching the slightest bit. My temper flares at the mention of my given name, but I keep a cool facade as she continues with a made-up introduction. "When he wasn't hanging out on street corners and harassing innocent people this summer, he toured the inside of jails around the city, *if you know what I mean*. And he has a secret desire nobody would ever guess."

The room suddenly becomes quiet. Even Peterson straightens to attention. Hell, even I'm listening like the words coming out of Brittany's lying, pink-frosted lips are gospel.

"His secret desire," she continues, "is to go to college and become a chemistry teacher, like you, Mrs. Peterson."

Yeah, right. I look over at my friend Isa, who seems amused that a white girl isn't afraid of giving me smack in front of the entire class.

Brittany flashes me a triumphant smile, thinking she's won this round. *Guess again, gringa.*

I sit up in my chair while the class remains silent.

"This is Brittany Ellis," I say, all eyes now focused on me. "This summer she went to the mall, bought new clothes so she could expand her wardrobe, and spent her daddy's money on plastic surgery to enhance her, *ahem*, assets."

It might not be what she wrote, but it's probably close enough to the truth. Unlike her introduction of me.

Chuckles come from *mis cuates* in the back of the class, and Brittany is as stiff as a board beside me, as if my words hurt her precious ego. Brittany Ellis is used to people fawning all over her and she could use a little wake-up call. I'm actually doing her a favor. Little does she know I'm not finished with her intro.

"*Her* secret desire," I add, getting the same reaction as she did during her introduction, "is to date a *Mexicano* before she graduates."

As expected, my words are met by comments and low whistles from the back of the room.

"Way to go, Fuentes," my friend Lucky barks out.

"I'll date you, *mamacita*," another says.

I give a high five to another Latino Blood named Marcus sitting behind me just as I catch Isa shaking her head as if I did something wrong. What? I'm just having a little fun with a rich girl from the north side.

Brittany's gaze shifts from Colin to me. I take one look at Colin and with my eyes tell him *game on*. Colin's face instantly turns bright red, resembling a chile pepper. I have definitely invaded his territory. Good.

"Quiet down, class," Peterson says sternly. "Thank you for those very creative and . . . enlightening introductions. Miss Ellis and Mr. Fuentes, please see me after class."

"Your introductions were not only appalling, they were disrespectful to me and the rest of your classmates," Peterson says after class as Brittany and I stand in front of her desk. "You have a choice." Our teacher holds out two blue detention slips in one hand and two pieces of notebook paper in the other. "You can either serve detention today after school or write a five-hundred-word essay on 'respect' to hand in tomorrow. Which is it?"

I reach over and grab the detention slip. Brittany reaches out for the notebook paper. Figures.

"Do either of you have a problem with the way I assign chemistry partners?" Peterson asks.

Brittany says, "Yes," at the same time I say, "Nope."

Peterson sets her glasses on her desk. "Listen, you two better work out your differences before this year is up. Brittany, I won't be assigning you a different partner. You're both seniors and will have to deal with a plethora of people and personalities after you graduate. If you don't want to go to summer school for flunking my class, I suggest you work together instead of against each other. Now hurry to your next class."

With that, I follow my little chem partner out of the room and down the hall.

"Stop following me," she snaps, looking over her shoulder to check how many people are watching us walk down the hall together.

As if I'm *el diablo* himself.

"Wear long sleeves on Saturday night," I tell her, knowing full well she's reaching the end of her sanity rope. I usually don't try to get under the skin of white chicks, but this one is fun to rattle. This one, the most popular and coveted one of all, actually cares. "It gets pretty cold on the back of my motorcycle."

"Listen, Alex," she says, whipping herself around and tossing that sun-kissed hair over her shoulder. She faces me with clear eyes made of ice. "I don't date guys in gangs, and I don't use drugs."

"I don't date guys in gangs, either," I say, stepping closer to her. "And I'm no user."

"Yeah, right. I'm surprised you're not in rehab or some juvie boot camp."

"You think you know me?"

"I know enough." She folds her arms across her chest, but then looks down as if she realizes her stance makes her *chichis* stand out, and drops her hands to her sides.

I'm doing my best not to focus on those *chichis* as I take a step forward. "Did you report me to Aguirre?"

She takes a step back. "What if I did?"

"*Mujer*, you're afraid of me." It's not a question. I just want to hear from her own lips what her reason is.

"Most people at this school are scared that if they look at you wrong, you'll gun them down."

"Then my gun should be smokin' by now, shouldn't it? Why aren't you runnin' away from the badass *Mexicano*, huh?"

"Give me half a chance, I will."

I've had enough of dancing around this little bitch. It's time to fluff up those feathers to make sure I end up with the upper hand. I close the distance between us and whisper in her ear, "Face the facts. Your life is too perfect. You probably lie awake at night, fantasizing about spicin' up all that lily whiteness you live in." But damn it, I get a whiff of vanilla from her perfume or lotion. It reminds me of cookies. I love cookies, so this is not good at all. "Gettin' near the fire, *chica*, doesn't necessarily mean you'll get burned."

"You touch her and you'll regret it, Fuentes," Colin's voice rings out. He resembles a burro, with his big white teeth and ears sticking out from his buzz cut. "Get the hell away from her."

"Colin," Brittany says. "It's okay. I can handle this."

Burro Face brought reinforcements: three other pasty white dudes, standing behind him for backup. I size up Burro Face and his friends to see if I can take them all on, and decide I could give all four a run for their money. "When you're strong enough to play in the big leagues, jock boy, then I'll listen to the *mierda* flyin' out of your mouth," I say.

Other students are gathering around us, leaving room for a fight that is sure to be fast, furious, and bloody. Little do they know Burro Face is a runner. This time he's got backup, though, so maybe he'll stay to duke it out. I'm always prepared for a fight, been in more of 'em than I can count on my fingers and toes. I've got the scars to prove it.

"Colin, he's not worth it," Brittany says.

Thanks, mamacita. Right back at ya.

"You threatening me, Fuentes?" Colin barks, ignoring his girl-friend.

"No, asshole," I say, staring him down. "Little dicks like you make threats."

Brittany parks her body in front of Colin and puts her hand on his chest. "Don't listen to him," she says.

"I'm not afraid of you. My dad's a lawyer," Colin brags, then puts his arm around Brittany. "She's mine. Don't ever forget that."

"Then keep a leash on her," I advise. "Or she might be tempted to find a new owner."

My friend Paco comes up beside me. *"Andas bien, Alex?"*

"Yeah, Paco," I tell him, then watch as two teachers walk down the hall escorted by a guy in a police uniform. This is what Adams wants, perfectly planned to get my ass kicked out of school. I'm not falling into his trap only to end up on Aguirre's hit list. *"Sí,* everything's *bien."* I turn to Brittany. "Catch ya later, *mamacita.* I'm looking forward to *researching our chemistry."*

Before I leave and save myself from suspension on top of my deten-tion, Brittany sticks that perky nose of hers in the air as if I'm the scum of the earth.

7

Brittany

After school I'm at my locker when my friends Morgan, Madison, and Megan come up to me. Sierra calls them the Fairfield M-factor.

Morgan hugs me. "Oh my God, are you okay?" she asks, pulling away and examining me.

"I heard Colin protected you. He's amazing. You're so lucky, Brit," Madison says, her signature curls bouncing with each word.

"It wasn't a big deal," I say, wondering what the rumor is in contrast to what really happened.

"What exactly did Alex say?" Megan asks. "Caitlin took a picture on her cell of Alex and Colin in the hallway, but I couldn't make out what was going on."

"You guys better not be late for practice," Darlene yells from the end of the hallway. Just as quickly as Darlene appeared, she's gone.

Megan opens her locker, which is next to mine, and pulls out her poms. "I hate the way Darlene kisses Ms. Small's butt," she says under her breath.

I close my locker and we walk toward the practice field. "I think she's trying to focus on dance instead of obsessing about Tyler going back to college."

Morgan rolls her eyes. "Whatever. I don't even have a boyfriend so she gets zero sympathy from me."

"No sympathy from my end, either. Seriously, when is that girl *not* dating someone?" Madison asks.

When we reach the practice field, our entire squad is sitting on the grass waiting for Ms. Small. Phew, we're not late.

"I still can't believe you got stuck with Alex Fuentes," Darlene says quietly to me as I find an open spot beside her.

"Wanna switch partners?" I ask, although Mrs. Peterson would never allow it. She made that crystal clear.

Darlene sticks her tongue out in full gross-out mode and whispers, "No way. I never go slumming on the south side. Mixing with that crowd'll get you nothing but trouble. Remember last year when Alyssa McDaniel dated that one guy . . . what was his name?"

"Jason Avila?" I say in a low voice.

Darlene does a little shiver. "In a matter of weeks Alyssa went from being cool to being an outcast. The south side girls hated her for taking one of their guys and she stopped hanging with us. The confused little couple was on an island all alone. Thank God Alyssa broke up with him."

Ms. Small walks toward us with her CD player, complaining about someone moving it from her usual spot and that's why she's late.

When Ms. Small tells us to stretch, Sierra nudges Darlene over so she can talk to me.

"You are in big trouble, girl," Sierra says.

"Why?"

Sierra has "super" eyes and ears; she knows everything going on at Fairfield.

My best friend says, "Rumor has it Carmen Sanchez is looking for you."

Oh, no. Carmen is Alex's girlfriend. I'm trying not to freak out and think the worst, but Carmen is tough, from her red-painted fingernails all the way down to her black, stiletto-heeled boots. Is she jealous I'm Alex's chem partner, or does she think I reported her boyfriend to the principal today?

The truth is I didn't report him. I got called into Dr. Aguirre's office because someone who'd seen the parking incident and witnessed our confrontation on the steps this morning reported it. Which was ridiculous because nothing happened.

Aguirre didn't believe me. He thought I was too scared to tell him the truth. I wasn't scared then.

But I am now.

Carmen Sanchez can kick my butt any day of the week. She probably practices with weapons, and the only weapon I know how to use is, well, my pom-poms. Call me crazy but somehow I doubt my poms will scare off a girl like Carmen.

Maybe in a word war I would make a good showing, but definitely not in a fistfight. Guys fight because of some primal, innate gene that makes them prove themselves physically.

Maybe Carmen wants to prove something to me, but there is seriously no need. I'm no threat, but how do I let her know that? It's not like I'm going to go up to her and say, "Hey, Carmen, I'm not going to make a move on your boyfriend and I never reported him to Dr. Aguirre." Or maybe I should. . . .

Most people think nothing bothers me. I'm not going to let them know something does. I've worked too long and hard to keep up this facade and I'm not about to lose it all because some gang member and his girlfriend are testing me.

"I'm not worrying about it," I tell Sierra.

My best friend shakes her head. "I know you, Brit. You're stressing," she whispers.

Now that statement worries me more than the idea of Carmen looking for me. Because I try really hard to keep everyone at a distance . . . not really knowing what it's truly like to be me or what it's like to live at my house. But I've let Sierra know more about me than everyone else. I wonder if I should back off from our friendship sometimes, to make sure she's kept at arm's length.

Logically, I know I'm paranoid. Sierra is a true friend; she was even there when I cried last year about my mom's nervous breakdown but never revealed the reason. She let me cry it out, even when I refused to give her details.

I don't want to end up like my mom. That's my biggest fear in life.

Ms. Small has us get in formation, then plays the custom music made for our squad by the music department while I count off. It's a mixture of hip-hop and rap music, specially mixed for our routine. We've titled our routine "Big, Bad Bulldogs" because our team mascot is the bulldog. My body hums to the beat. That's what I love about being part of the squad. It's the music that pulls me in and makes me forget about my problems at home. Music is my drug, the one thing that makes me numb.

"Ms. Small, can we try starting in the broken T position instead of the T position like we previously practiced?" I say. "Then go into the low V and high V combos with Morgan, Isabel, and Caitlin moving to the front. I think it'll look cleaner."

Ms. Small smiles, obviously pleased with my suggestion. "Good idea, Brittany. Let's try it. We'll start in the broken T position, elbows bent. During the transition I want Morgan, Isabel, and Caitlin in the front row. Remember to keep your shoulders down. Sierra, please make your wrists an extension of your arms instead of bending them."

"Yes, ma'am," Sierra says from behind me.

Ms. Small plays the music again. The beat, the lyrics, the instruments . . . they all seep into my veins and lift me up no matter how low I feel. As I dance in sync with the other girls, I forget about Carmen and Alex and my mom and everything else.

The song is over too quickly. I still want to move to the beat and the lyrics when Ms. Small turns off her CD player. The second time around is better, but our formation needs work and some of the new girls are having a hard time with the steps.

"Brittany, you teach the basic moves to the new girls and then we'll try it as a group again. Darlene, you lead the rest of the squad in reviewing the steps," Ms. Small instructs as she hands me the CD player.

Isabel is in my group. She kneels down to take a drink from her water bottle. "Don't worry about Carmen," she says. "Most of the time her bark is worse than her bite."

"Thanks," I say. Isabel looks tough, with her red Latino Blood bandanna, three eyebrow rings, and hands always folded on her chest when she's not doing the routines. But she has kind eyes. And smiles a lot. Her smile softens her harsh appearance, although if she put a pink bow in her hair instead of a red Latino Blood bandanna I bet she'd actually look girly. "You're in my chemistry class, aren't you?" I ask.

She nods.

"And you know Alex Fuentes?"

She nods again.

"Are the rumors about him true?" I ask carefully, not knowing how she's going to react to my prying. If I'm not careful, I'll have a long list of people who are out to get me.

Isabel's long brown hair moves as she talks. "Depends on which ones you're referring to."

As I'm about to rattle off the list of rumors outlining Alex's drug use and police arrests, Isabel stands. "Listen, Brittany," she says. "You and me, we'll never be friends. But I have to tell you, no matter how much of a jerk Alex was to you today, he's not as bad as the rumors. He's even not as bad as *he'd* like to think he is."

Before I can ask another question, Isabel is back in formation.

An hour and a half later, when we're all exhausted and crabby and even I've had enough, we're dismissed from practice. I make a point of walking over to a sweating Isabel and telling her what a good job she did today on the routine.

"Really?" she asks, looking surprised.

"You're a fast learner," I tell her. It's true. For a girl who never tried out for poms the first three years of high school, she's caught on to the routine really fast. "That's why we put you on the front line."

While Isabel's mouth is still open in shock, I wonder if she believes the rumors she's heard about me. No, we'll never be friends. But I can tell we'll never be enemies, either.

After practice I walk to my car with Sierra, who's busy texting her boyfriend, Doug, on her cell.

A piece of paper is tucked under one of my windshield wipers. I pull it off. It's Alex's blue detention slip. Crumpling it up, I shove it into my book bag.

"What was that?" Sierra asks.

"Nothing," I say, hoping she gets the hint that I don't want to talk about it.

"Guys, wait up!" Darlene yells, running up to us. "I saw Colin on the football field. He said to wait for him."

I look at my watch. It's almost six and I want to get home to help Baghda make my sister's dinner. "I can't."

"Doug texted me back," Sierra says. "He's invited us for pizza at his house."

"I can come," Darlene says. "I've been so bored now that Tyler is back at Purdue and I probably won't see him for weeks."

Sierra is still texting away. "I thought you were gonna visit him next weekend."

Darlene stands with her hands on her hips. "Well, that was until he called and said all the pledges in the fraternity had to sleep at the frat house for some crazy initiation thing. As long as Tyler's penis is intact when it's all over, I'm happy."

At the mention of "penis," I search for my keys in my purse. When Darlene gets to talking about penises and sex, stand back because she never stops. And since I'm not one to share my sexual experiences (or lack thereof), I'm out of here. A perfect time to escape.

As I dangle my keys on my fingers, Sierra tells me she'll get a ride from Doug, so I'm alone during the drive home. I like being alone. Nobody to put on an act for. I can even blast the music if I want.

Enjoying the music is short-lived, though, when I feel my phone vibrate. I pull my cell out of my pocket. Two voice messages and one text message. All from Colin.

I call him on his cell. "Brit, where are you?" he asks.

"On my way home."

"Come over to Doug's."

"My sister has a new caretaker," I explain. "I have to help her out."

"Are you still pissed because I threatened your gangbanger chemistry partner?"

"I'm not pissed. I'm annoyed. I told you I could handle it and you totally ignored me. And you caused a whole scene in the hallway. You know I didn't ask to be partners with him," I tell Colin.

"I know, Brit. I just hate that guy. Don't be mad."

"I'm not," I say. "I just hate seeing you get all riled up for no reason."

"And I hated seeing that guy whispering in your ear."

I feel a headache coming on, full force. I don't need Colin to make a scene every time a guy so much as talks to me. He's never done that before and it left me open for more scrutiny and gossip, something I never want to happen. "Let's just forget it ever happened."

"Fine by me. Call me tonight," he says. "But if you can get out early and can come to Doug's, I'll be there."

When I get home, Baghda is in Shelley's room on the first floor. She's attempting to change her special leak-proof undergarments, but she has Shelley in the wrong position. Her head is usually where her feet are, one leg is dangling off the bed . . . it's a disaster and Baghda is huffing and puffing as if it's the most difficult task she's ever attempted.

Did my mom check her credentials?

"I'll do it," I tell Baghda, pushing her aside and taking over. I've changed my sister's underwear since we were kids. It's not fun changing the undergarments of a person who weighs more than you do, but if you do it right it doesn't take long and it doesn't become a big, drawn-out deal.

My sister smiles wide when she sees me. "Bwiee!"

My sister can't enunciate words, but she uses verbal approximations. "Bwiee" means "Brittany," and I smile back while situating her better on her bed. "Hey, girlie girl. You hungry for dinner?" I ask as I pull wipes from the container and try not to think about the task I'm doing.

As I slip new leak-proof underwear on her and slide her legs into a fresh pair of sweats, Baghda watches from the sidelines. I try explaining while doing the task, but one glance at Baghda and I can tell she's not listening.

"Your mother said I can leave when you got home," Baghda says.

"That's fine," I say as I wash my hands, and before I know it Baghda has Houdini'd on me.

I wheel Shelley into the kitchen. Our usually pristine kitchen is a disaster. Baghda hasn't cleaned up the dishes, which are now piled in the sink, and she didn't do such a hot job of wiping the floor after Shelley's earlier mess.

I prepare Shelley's dinner and wipe up the mess.

Shelley drawls out the word "school," which really sounds like "cool," but I know what she means.

"Yeah, it was my first day back," I tell her as I blend her food and set it on the table. I spoon soupy food into her mouth while I keep talking. "And my new chemistry teacher, Mrs. Peterson, should be a boot camp instructor. I scanned the syllabus. The woman can't go a week without scheduling a test or a quiz. This year isn't going to be easy."

My sister looks at me, decoding what I've told her. Her intense expression says she's giving me support and understanding without having to say the words. Because every word that comes out of her mouth is a struggle. Sometimes I want to say the words for her because I feel her frustration as if it's my own.

"You didn't like Baghda?" I ask quietly.

My sister shakes her head. And she doesn't want to talk about it; I can tell by the way she tenses her mouth.

"Be patient with her," I tell her. "It's not easy coming into a new house and not knowing what to do."

When Shelley finishes eating, I bring her magazines so she can scan them. My sister loves magazines. While she's busy flipping pages, I stick some cheese between two slices of bread for my own dinner then sit at the table to start my homework while I eat.

I hear the garage door open just as I pull out the notebook paper Mrs. Peterson gave me to write my "respect" paper.

"Brit, where are you?" my mom yells from the foyer.

"In the kitchen," I call out.

My mom saunters into the kitchen with a Neiman Marcus bag on her arm. "Here, this is for you."

I reach in the bag and pull out a light blue Geren Ford designer top. "Thanks," I say, not making a big deal about it in front of Shelley, who didn't get anything from my mom. Not that my sister cares. She's too focused on the best- and worst-dressed pictures of celebrities and all their shiny jewelry.

"It'll go with those dark denims I bought you last week," she says as she pulls out frozen steaks from the freezer and starts defrosting them in the microwave. "So . . . how was everything with Baghda when you got home?"

"Not the best," I tell her. "You really need to train her." I'm not surprised she doesn't respond.

My dad walks through the door a minute later, grumbling about work. He owns a computer chip manufacturing company and has prepped us that this is a lean year, but my mom still goes out and buys stuff and my dad still bought me a BMW for my birthday.

"What's for dinner?" my dad asks as he loosens his tie. He looks tired and worn, as usual.

My mom glances at the microwave. "Steak."

"I'm not in the mood for heavy food," he says. "Just something light."

My mom turns off the microwave in a huff. "Eggs? Spaghetti?" she says, listing suggestions to deaf ears.

My dad walks out of the kitchen. Even when he's physically here, his mind is still on the job. "Whatever. Just something light," he calls out.

It's times like these I feel sorry for my mom. She doesn't get much attention from my dad. He's either working or on a business trip or just plain doesn't want to deal with us. "I'll make a salad," I tell her as I pull lettuce out of the fridge.

She seems thankful, if her small smile is any indication, for the help. We work side-by-side in silence. I set the table while my mom brings the salad, scrambled eggs, and toast to the table. She mumbles complaints about not being appreciated, but I figure she wants me to listen and not say anything. Shelley is still busy looking at her magazines, oblivious to the tension between my parents.

"I'm going to China on Friday for two weeks," my dad announces as he comes back to the kitchen in sweatpants and a T-shirt. He plops himself down at his usual spot at the head of the table and spoons eggs onto his plate. "Our supplier there is shipping defective material and I've got to find out what the deal is."

"What about the DeMaio wedding? It's this weekend and we already RSVP'd."

My dad drops his fork and looks at my mom. "Yeah, I'm sure the DeMaios' kid's wedding is more important than keeping my business afloat."

"Bill, I didn't insinuate your business is less important," she says, dropping her own fork on her plate. It's a wonder our plates don't have permanent chips in them. "It's just rude to cancel these things at the last minute."

"You can go by yourself."

"And have rumors start because you're not accompanying me? No thank you."

This is typical Ellis dinner conversation. My dad saying how hard work is, my mom trying to keep up the facade that we're a happy-go-lucky family, and me and Shelley quiet on the sidelines.

"How was school?" my mom finally asks me.

"Okay," I say, omitting the fact that I got stuck with Alex as a partner. "I got a really tough teacher for chemistry."

"You probably shouldn't have taken chemistry," my dad chimes in. "If you don't get an A, your GPA'll go down. Northwestern is a tough school to get into, and they won't give you a break just because it's my alma mater."

"I got it, Dad," I say, totally depressed now. If Alex isn't serious about our project, how am I going to get an A on it?

"Shelley had a new caretaker start today," my mom informs him. "Remember?"

He shrugs because the last time a caretaker quit, he insisted Shelley should live in some facility instead of at home. I never remember screaming so much as I did then, because I'm never letting them send Shelley to a place where they'll neglect my sister and not understand her. I need to keep an eye on her. That's why it's so important for me to get into Northwestern. If I'm close to home, then I can live here and make sure my parents don't send her away.

At nine Megan calls to complain about Darlene. She thinks Darlene changed over the summer and now has a big ego because she's dating a college guy. At nine thirty Darlene calls to say she suspects Megan is jealous because she's dating a guy in college. At nine forty-five Sierra calls to tell me she talked to both Megan and Darlene tonight and she doesn't want to get in the middle of it. I agree, although I think we already are.

It's ten forty-five before I finally finish the respect paper for Mrs. Peterson and help my mom put Shelley to bed. I'm so exhausted my head feels as if it's about to fall off.

Sliding into bed after I've changed into my pj's, I dial Colin's number.

"Hey, babe," he says. "What're you up to?"

"Not much. I'm in bed. Did you have fun at Doug's?"

"Not as much fun as I would've had if you were there."

"When did you get back?"

"About an hour ago. I'm *so* glad you called."

I pull my big pink comforter up to my chin and sink my head into my fluffy down pillow. "Oh, really?" I say, fishing for a compliment and speaking with my flirty voice. "Why?"

He hasn't told me he loves me in a long time. I know he's not the most affectionate person in the world. My dad isn't, either. I need to hear it from Colin. I want to hear he loves me. I want to hear he missed me. I want to hear him say I'm the girl of his dreams.

Colin clears his throat. "We've never had phone sex."

Okay, those so aren't the words I expected. I shouldn't be disappointed or surprised. He's a teenage guy and I know guys are focused on sex and fooling around. This afternoon I pushed away the feeling in the pit of my stomach when I read Alex's words about having hot sex. Little does he know I'm a virgin.

Colin and I have never had sex, period. Phone sex or real sex. We got close in April last year at the beach behind Sierra's house, but I chickened out. I wasn't ready.

"Phone sex?"

"Yeah. Touch yourself, Brit. And then tell me what you're doing. It'll totally turn me on."

"While I'm touching myself, what'll you be doing?" I ask him.

"Choking the gopher. What'd you think I'd do, my homework?"

I laugh. Mostly it's a nervous laugh because we haven't seen each other in a couple of months, we haven't talked all that much, and now he wants to go from "hi, nice to see you after a summer apart" to "touch yourself while I choke the gopher" in one day. I feel like I'm in the middle of a Pat McCurdy song.

"Come on, Brit," Colin says. "Think of it as practice before we do the real thing. Take off your shirt and touch yourself."

"Colin . . . ," I say.

"What?"

"Sorry, but I'm not into it. Not now, at least."

"You sure?"

"Yeah. You mad?"

"No," he says. "I thought it'd be fun to spice up our relationship."

"I didn't know we were boring."

"School . . . football practice . . . hanging out. I guess after a summer away I'm sick of the same old routine. The entire summer I've been waterskiing, wakeboarding, and off-roading. Things that get your heart racing and blood pumping, you know? Pure adrenaline rush."

"Sounds awesome."

"It was. Brit?"

"Yeah."

"I'm ready for that adrenaline rush . . . with you."

8

Alex

I push the guy up against a sweet, shiny black Camaro, one that proba-bly cost more than my mom makes in a year. "Here's the deal, Blake," I say. "You either pay up now, or I break somethin' of yours. Not a piece of furniture or your fuckin' car . . . somethin' you're permanently at-tached to. Get it?"

Blake, skinnier than a telephone pole and as pale as a ghost, is looking at me as if I just handed him his death sentence. He should have thought about that before he took the Big 8 and bounced without paying up.

As if Hector would ever let that happen.

As if I would ever let that happen.

When Hector sends me to collect, I do it. I may not like doing it, but I do it. He knows I won't do drug deals or break into people's homes or businesses to steal shit. But I'm good at collecting . . . debts, mostly. Sometimes it's people, but those get to be messy affairs, especially be-cause I know what's gonna happen to them once I haul them back to the warehouse to face Chuy. Nobody wants to face Chuy. It's way worse than facing me. Blake should feel lucky I'm the one assigned to look for him.

To say I don't live a squeaky-clean life is an understatement. I try not to dwell on it, the dirty job I'm doing for the Blood. And I'm good at it. Scaring people into paying us what's ours is my job. Technically my hands are clean of drugs. Okay, so drug money does touch my hands quite frequently, but I just hand it over to Hector. I don't use it, I just collect it.

It makes me a pawn, I know. As long as my family is safe, I don't care. Besides, I'm good at fighting. You can't imagine how many people break down with the threat of their bones breaking. Blake is no different than the other guys I've threatened, I can tell by the way he's trying to act cool while his spindly hands are shaking uncontrollably.

You'd think Peterson would be afraid of me, too, but that teacher wouldn't fear me even if I shoved a live grenade into her hands.

"I don't got the money," Blake blurts out.

"That answer ain't gonna cut it, man," Paco chimes in from the sidelines. He likes coming with me. He thinks of it as playing good cop/bad cop. Except we play bad gang member/worse gang member.

"Which limb you want me to break first?" I ask. "I'll be nice and let you choose."

"Just smoke his sorry ass, Alex, and get this over with," Paco says lazily.

"No!" Blake shouts. "I'll get it. I promise. Tomorrow."

I shove him against the car, my forearm pressing on his throat just enough to scare him. "As if I'm gonna take your word for it. You think we're stupid? I need collateral."

Blake doesn't answer.

I eye his car.

"Not the car, Alex. *Please.*"

I take my gun out. I'm not going to shoot him. No matter who I am and what I've become, I'd never kill anyone. Or shoot anyone. Blake doesn't have to know this, though.

At the first glance of my Glock, Blake holds out his keys. "Oh, God. Please, no."

I snatch the keys out of his hand. "Tomorrow, Blake. Seven o'clock behind the old tracks on Fourth and Vine. Now get outta here," I say, waving my gun in the air for him to run off on foot.

"I've always wanted a Camaro," Paco says after Blake is out of sight.

I toss the keys to him. "It's yours—until tomorrow."

"You really think he'll come up with four G's in a day?"

"Yeah," I tell him, totally confident. "'Cause that car is worth way more than four G's."

Back at the warehouse, we give Hector the update. He's not happy we haven't collected, but he knows it'll happen. I always come through.

At night, I'm in my room unable to sleep because of my little brother Luis's snoring. By the way he sleeps so soundly, you'd think he didn't have a care in the world. As much as I don't mind threatening loser drug dealers like Blake, I wish to hell I was fighting for things worth fighting for.

A week later I'm sitting on the grass in the school courtyard eating lunch by a tree. Most of the students at Fairfield eat outside until late October, when the Illinois winter forces us to sit in the cafeteria during lunch period. Right now we're soaking up every minute of sun and fresh air while it's still decent outside.

My friend Lucky, with his oversized red shirt and black jeans, slaps me on the back as he parks his butt next to me with a cafeteria tray balanced on his hand. "You geared up for next period, Alex? I swear Brittany Ellis hates you like the plague, man. It's hilarious watchin' her move her stool as far as she can from you."

"Lucky," I say. "She might be a *mamacita*, but she ain't got nothin' on this *hombre*." I point to myself.

"Tell your mama that," Lucky says, laughing. "Or Colin Adams."

I lean back against the tree and cross my arms. "I had phys. ed. with Adams last year. Believe me, he's got *nada* to brag about."

"You still pissed off 'cause he trashed your locker freshman year after you smoked him in the relay in front of the entire school?"

Hell, yeah, I'm still pissed. That one incident cost me a shitload of money having to buy new books. "Yesterday's news," I tell Lucky, keeping up the cool facade I always do.

"'Yesterdays news' is sittin' right over there with his hot girlfriend."

One look at Little Miss *Perfecta* and my defenses go up. She thinks I'm a drugged-out user. Every day I've dreaded having to deal with her in chem class. "That chick has a head full of air, man," I say.

"I heard that *ho* was dissin' you to her friends," a guy named Pedro says as he and a bunch of other guys join us carrying either trays from the cafeteria or food they brought from home.

I shake my head, wondering what Brittany said and how much damage control I'll have to do. "Maybe she wants me and doesn't know any other way to get my attention."

Lucky laughs so hard everyone within a few yards stares at us. "There's no way Brittany Ellis would get within two feet of you on her own free will, *güey*, let alone date you," he says. "She's so rich the scarf around her neck last week pro'bly cost as much as everythin' in *tu casa*."

That scarf. As if the designer jeans and top weren't fashionable enough, she'd probably added the scarf to showcase how rich and untouchable she is. Knowing her, she had it professionally dyed to match the exact shade of her sapphire eyes.

"Hell, I bet you my RX-7 you can't get into her panties before Thanksgiving break," Lucky challenges me, breaking my wayward thoughts.

"Who'd want those panties?" I say. They're probably designer, too, with her initials embroidered on the front.

"Every single dude in this school."

Do I need to state the obvious? "She's a snow girl." I'm not into white chicks, or spoiled chicks, or chicks whose idea of hard labor is painting their long fingernails a different color each day to match their designer outfits.

I pull a cigarette from my pocket and light it, ignoring Fairfield's no-smoking policy. I've been smoking a lot lately. Paco pointed it out yesterday night when we hung out.

"So what if she's white? Come on, Alex. Don't be an idiot. *Look* at her."

I take a glance. I admit she's got it goin' on. Long, shiny hair, aristocratic nose, slightly tanned arms with a hint of muscle in her biceps to make you wonder if she works out, full lips that when she smiles you think world peace is possible if everyone had her smile.

I shove those thoughts from my mind. So what if she's hot? She's a first-degree bitch. "Too skinny," I blurt out.

"You want her," Lucky says, leaning back on the grass. "You just know, like the rest of us *Mexicanos* from the south side, that you can't have her."

Something inside me clicks on. Call it my defense mechanism. Call it cockiness. Before I can switch it off, I say, "In two months I could have a piece of that ass. If you really wanna bet your RX-7, I'm in."

"You're trippin', man." When I don't answer, Lucky frowns. "You serious, Alex?"

The guy will back down, he loves his car more than his mama. "Sure."

"If you lose, I get Julio," Lucky says, his frown turning into a wicked grin.

Julio is my most prized possession, an old Honda Nighthawk 750 motorcycle. I rescued it from a dump and turned it into a sleek ride. Rebuilding the bike took me forever. It's the only thing in my life I've made better instead of destroying.

Lucky is not backing down. Time to either back down myself or play the game. The problem is, I've never backed down . . . not once in my life.

The most popular white chick at school would sure as hell learn a lot by hanging with me. Little Miss *Perfecta* said she'd never date a gang member, but I bet no Latino Blood ever tried to get into those designer pants.

Easy as a fight between Folks and People—rival gangs on a Saturday night.

I bet all it'll take for Brittany to come around is a bit of flirting. You know, that give-and-take wordplay that heightens your awareness of the opposite sex. I can kill two birds with one stone: get back at Burro Face by taking his girl and get back at Brittany Ellis for having me called into the principal's office and dissin' me in front of her friends.

Might even be fun.

I imagine the entire school witnessing the pristine white chick drooling over the *Mexicano* she vowed to hate. I wonder how hard she'll fall on that tight white ass when I'm done with her.

I hold out my hand. "Deal."

"You gotta show proof."

I take another drag of my cigarette. "Lucky, what do you want me to do? Pluck out one of her fuckin' pubes?"

"How'd we know it's hers?" Lucky responds. "Maybe she's not a real blond. Besides, she pro'bly gets one of those Brazilian wax jobs. You know, where everythin' is—"

"Take a picture," Pedro suggests. "Or video. I bet we could make *muchos billetes* on that thing. We can title it *Brittany Goes South of the Border.*"

It's trash-talkin' times like these that give us a bad rep. Not that rich kids don't talk trash, I'm sure they do. But when my friends go at it, it's no-holds-barred. To be honest, I think my friends are damn entertaining when they're ragging on someone else. When they're ragging on me, I don't find it half as funny.

"What'cha talkin' about?" Paco asks, joining us with a plate of food from the cafeteria.

"I bet Alex my car for his motorcycle he can't get into Brittany Ellis's pants by Thanksgiving."

"You *loco*, Alex?" Paco says. "Makin' a bet like that is suicide."

"Lay off, Paco," I warn. It isn't suicide. Stupid, maybe. But not suicide. If I could handle hot Carmen Sanchez, I can handle vanilla cookie Brittany Ellis.

"Brittany Ellis is out of your league, *amigo*. You might be a pretty boy, but you're one hundred percent *Mexicano* and she's as white as Wonder Bread."

A junior named Leticia Gonzalez walks by us. "Hi, Alex," she says, flashing me a smile before sitting with her friends. While the other guys drool over Leticia and talk to her friends, Paco and I are left alone by the tree.

Paco nudges me. "Now *she's* a *bonita Mexicana*, and definitely in your league."

My eye isn't on Leticia, it's on Brittany. Now that the game's on, I'm focusing on the prize. It's time to start flirting, but no bullshit come-on lines will work with her. Somehow I think she's used to those from her boyfriend and other assholes trying to get into her pants.

I decide on a new tactic, one she won't expect. I'm going to keep riffling her feathers until I'm all she thinks about. And I'll start next period when she's forced to sit next to me. Nothing like a little foreplay in chemistry class to spark things up.

"¡*Carajo!*" Paco says, throwing down his lunch. "They think they can buy a U-shaped shell, stuff it, and call it a taco, but those cafeteria workers wouldn't know taco meat from a piece of shit. That's what this tastes like, Alex."

"You're makin' me sick, man," I tell him.

I stare uncomfortably at the food I brought from home. Thanks to Paco everything looks like *mierda* now. Disgusted, I shove what's left of my lunch into my brown paper bag.

"Want some of it?" Paco says with a grin as he holds out the shitty taco to me.

"Bring that one inch closer to me and you'll be sorry," I threaten.

"I'm shakin' in my pants."

Paco wiggles the offending taco, goading me. He should seriously know better.

"If any of that gets on me—"

"What'cha gonna do, kick my ass?" Paco sings sarcastically, still shaking the taco. Maybe I should punch him in the face, knocking him out so I won't have to deal with him right now.

As I have that thought, I feel something drop on my pants. I look down even though I know what I'll see. Yes, a big blob of wet, gloppy stuff passing as taco meat lands right on the crotch of my faded jeans.

"Fuck," Paco says, his face quickly turning from amusement to shock. "Want me to clean it off for you?"

"If your fingers get anywhere close to my dick, I'm gonna personally shoot you in the *huevos*," I growl through clenched teeth.

I flick the mystery meat off my crotch. A big, greasy stain lingers. I turn back to Paco. "You got ten minutes to get me a new pair of pants."

"How the hell am I s'posed to do that?"

"Be creative."

"Take mine." Paco stands and brings his fingers to the waistband of his jeans, unbuttoning right in the middle of the courtyard.

"Maybe I wasn't specific enough," I tell him, wondering how I'm going to act like the cool guy in chem class when it looks like I've peed in my pants. "I meant, get me a new pair of pants that will fit me, *pendejo*. You're so short you could audition to be one of Santa Claus's elves."

"I'm toleratin' your insults because we're like brothers."

"Nine minutes and thirty seconds."

It doesn't take Paco more than that to start running toward the school parking lot.

I seriously don't give a crap how I get the pants; just that I get 'em before my next class. A wet crotch is not the way to show Brittany I'm a stud.

I wait at the tree while other kids throw away their lunches and head back inside. Before I know it, music starts playing through the loudspeakers and Paco is nowhere in sight. Great. Now I have five minutes to get to Peterson's class. Gritting my teeth, I walk to chemistry with my books strategically placed in front of my crotch, with two minutes to spare. I slide onto the stool and push it as close to the lab table as possible, hiding the stain.

Brittany walks into the room, her sunshine hair falling down the front of her chest, ending in perfect little curls that bounce when she walks. Instead of that perfection turning me on, it makes me want to mess it all up.

I wink at her when she glances at me. She huffs and pulls her stool as far away from me as possible.

Remembering Mrs. Peterson's zero-tolerance rule, I pull my bandanna off and place it in my lap directly over the stain. Then I turn to the pom-pom chick sitting next to me. "You're gonna have to talk to me at some point."

"So your girlfriend can have a reason to beat me up? No thanks, Alex. I'd rather keep my face the way it is."

"I don't have a girlfriend. You want to interview for the position?" I scan her from top to bottom, focusing on the parts she relies on so heavily.

She curls her pink-frosted top lip and sneers at me. "Not on your life."

"*Mujer*, you wouldn't know what to do with all this testosterone if you had it in your hands."

That's it, Alex. Tease her into wanting you. She'll take the bait.

She turns away from me. "You're disgusting."

"What if I said we'd make a great couple?"

"I'd say you were an idiot."

9

Brittany

Right after I call Alex an idiot, Mrs. Peterson calls the class to attention. "You and your partner will pick a project from this hat," she announces. "They are all equally challenging and will require meeting with your partner outside of class."

"What about football?" Colin interjects. "No way I'm missing practice."

"Or poms," Darlene chimes in before I can say the same thing.

"Schoolwork comes first. It's up to you and your partner to find a time that works for both of you," Mrs. Peterson says as she stands in front of our table and holds out the hat.

"Yo, Mrs. P. . . . is one of them a cure for multiple sclerosis?" Alex asks with his cocky attitude that's setting my nerves on edge. " 'Cause I don't think there's enough time in the school year to complete that project."

I can see that big D on my report card right now. The Northwestern admissions counselor won't care that it was my chemistry partner who wanted to make a joke out of our project. The guy doesn't care about his own life, why should he care about chemistry class? The thought of Alex controlling the grade I receive in this class is overwhelming me. Grades to my parents are a reflection of your worth. Needless to say, a C or D means you're worthless.

I reach into the hat and pull out a little white slip of paper. I open it slowly while I bite my lower lip in anticipation. In bold letters I read HAND WARMERS.

"Hand warmers?" I question.

Alex leans over and reads the paper with a confused look on his face. "What the fuck are hand warmers?"

Mrs. Peterson shoots Alex a warning glare. "If you'd like to stay after school, I have another blue detention slip on my desk with your name already on it. Now, either ask the question again without using foul language or join me after school."

"That'd be cool to hang with you, Mrs. P., but I'd rather spend the time studyin' with my chem partner," Alex responds, then has the nerve to wink at Colin, "so I'll rephrase the question. What exactly are hand warmers?"

"Thermal chemistry, Mr. Fuentes. We use them to warm our hands."

Alex has this big, cocky grin as he turns to me. "I'm sure we can find other things to warm."

"I hate you," I say loud enough for Colin and the rest of the class to hear. If I sit here and let him get the best of me, I'll probably hear my mom tsk'ing in my head about reputations meaning everything.

I know the class is watching our interaction, even Isabel, who thinks Alex isn't as bad as everyone thinks he is. Can't she see him for what he is, or is she blinded by his chiseled face and popular status among their friends?

Alex whispers, "There's a thin line between love and hate. Maybe you're confusing your emotions."

I scoot away from him. "I wouldn't bet on it."

"I would."

Alex's gaze turns toward the door to the classroom. Through the window, his friend is waving to him. They're probably going to ditch class.

Alex grabs his books and stands.

Mrs. Peterson turns around. "Alex, sit down."

"I got to piss."

The teacher's eyebrows furrow and her hand goes to her hip. "Watch your language. And the last time I checked, you don't need your books in order to go to the restroom. Put them back on the lab table."

Alex's lips are tight, but he places the books back on the table.

"I told you no gang-related items in my class," Mrs. Peterson says, staring at the bandanna he's holding in front of him. She holds out her hand. "Hand it over."

He glances at the door, then faces Mrs. Peterson. "What if I refuse?"

"Alex, don't test me. Zero tolerance. You want a suspension?" She wiggles her fingers, signaling to hand the bandanna over immediately or else.

Scowling, he slowly places the bandanna in her hand.

Mrs. Peterson sucks in her breath when she snatches the bandanna from his fingers.

I screech, "Ohmygod!" at the sight of the big stain on his crotch.

The students, one by one, start laughing.

Colin laughs the loudest. "Don't sweat it, Fuentes. My great-grandma has the same problem. Nothing a diaper won't fix."

Now that hits home because at the mention of adult diapers, I immediately think of my sister. Making fun of adults who can't help themselves isn't funny because Shelley is one of those people.

Alex sports a big, cocky grin and says to Colin, "Your girlfriend couldn't keep her hands out of my pants. She was showin' me a whole new definition of hand warmers, *compa*."

This time he's gone too far. I stand up, my stool scraping the floor.

"You wish," I say.

Alex is about to say something to me when Mrs. Peterson yells, "Alex!" She clears her throat. "Go to the nurse and . . . fix yourself. Take your books, because afterward you'll be seeing Dr. Aguirre. I'll meet you in his office with your friends Colin and Brittany."

Alex swipes his books off the table and exits the classroom while I ease back onto my stool. While Mrs. Peterson is trying to calm the rest of the class, I think about my short-lived success in avoiding Carmen Sanchez.

If she thinks I'm a threat to her relationship with Alex, the rumors that are sure to spread today could prove deadly.

10

Alex

Oh, this is rich. Peterson and Aguirre on one side of Aguirre's office, Little Miss *Perfecta* and her dickhead boyfriend on the other . . . and me standing by myself. Nobody on my side, that's for sure.

Aguirre clears his throat. "Alex, this is the second time in two weeks you're in my office."

Yep, that about sums it up. The guy is an absolute genius.

"Sir," I say, playing the game because I'm sick of Little Miss *Perfecta* and her boyfriend controlling the entire fucking school. "There was a little mishap during lunch involving grease and my pants. Instead of missin' class, I had a friend get me these as a replacement." I gesture to my current jeans Paco managed to snatch from my house. "Mrs. Peterson," I say, turning to my chem teacher, "I wouldn't let a little stain keep me from your *brilliant* lecture."

"Don't placate me, Alex," Peterson says with a snort. "I've had it up to here with your antics," she says, her hand waving above her head. She glares at Brittany and Colin. I think she's going to let them bitch at me until I hear her say, "And don't think you two are any better."

Brittany seems stunned at the scolding. Oh, but she was perfectly content watching Mrs. P. bitch me out.

"I can't be partners with him," Little Miss *Perfecta* blurts out.

Colin steps forward. "She can partner up with me and Darlene."

I almost smile when Mrs. P.'s eyebrows rise so high I think they're about to run up her forehead and never stop. "And what makes you two so special you think you can change my class structure?"

Go, Peterson!

"Nadine, I'll take it from here," Aguirre says to Mrs. P., then points to a picture of our school framed on the wall. He doesn't let the two north siders answer Mrs. P.'s question before he says, "Our motto at Fairfield High is Diversity Breeds Knowledge, guys. If you ever forget, it's etched into the stones at the front entrance, so the next time you pass by it take a minute to think about what those words mean. Let me assure you as your new principal my goal is to bridge any gap in the school culture that negates that motto."

Okay, so diversity breeds knowledge. But I've also seen it breed hatred and ignorance. I'm not about to taint Aguirre's rosy picture of our motto, because I'm starting to believe our principal actually believes the crap he's spouting.

"Dr. Aguirre and I are on the same page. In light of that . . ." Peterson fires me a fierce look—one so convincing she probably practices it in front of a mirror. "Alex, stop goading Brittany." She fires the same look to the two on the other side of the room. "Brittany, stop acting like a diva. And Colin . . . I don't even know what you have to do with this."

"I'm her boyfriend."

"I'd appreciate it if you'd keep your relationship out of my classroom."

"But—," Colin starts.

Peterson cuts him off with a wave of her hand. "Enough. We're done here and so are all of you."

Colin grabs the diva's hand and they both file out of the room.

After I walk out of Aguirre's office, Peterson puts a hand on my elbow. "Alex?"

I stop and look at her. Into her eyes, which have sympathy written all over them. It doesn't sit well in my gut. "Yeah?"

"I see right through you, you know."

I need to wipe that sympathy off her face. The last time a teacher looked at me like that, it was in first grade right after my dad was shot. "It's the second week of school, *Nadine*. You might want to wait a month or two before you make a statement like that."

She chuckles and says, "I haven't been teaching that long, but I've already seen more Alex Fuenteses in my classroom than a lot of teachers will see in a lifetime."

"And I thought I was unique." I put my hands over my heart. "You wound me, Nadine."

"You want to make yourself unique, Alex? Finish school and graduate without dropping out."

"That's the plan," I tell her, although I've never admitted it to anyone before. I know my mom wants me to graduate, but we've never discussed it. And, to be honest, I don't know if she actually expects it.

"I'm told they all say that at first." She opens her purse and pulls out my bandanna. "Don't let your life outside of school dictate your future," she says, getting all serious on me.

I shove the bandanna into my back pocket. She has no clue how much my life outside of school leaks into the life I lead inside of school. A redbrick building can't shield me from the outside world. Hell, I couldn't hide in here even if I wanted to. "I know what you're gonna say next . . . *if you ever need a friend, Alex, I'm here.*"

"Wrong. I'm not your friend. If I were, you wouldn't be a gang member. But I've seen your test scores. You're a smart kid who can succeed if you take school seriously."

Succeed. Success. It's all relative, now, isn't it? "Can I go to class now?" I ask, because I have no comeback to that. I'm ready to accept that my chem teacher and new principal might not be on my side . . . but I'm not sure they're on the other side, either. Kinda blows my theories out of the water.

"Yeah, go to class, Alex."

I'm still thinking about what Peterson said when I hear her call after me, "And if you call me Nadine again, you'll have the pleasure of getting another detention slip *and* writing an essay on respect. Remember, I'm not your friend."

As I walk into the hallway, I smile to myself. That woman sure does wield those blue detention slips and threats of essays like weapons.

11

Brittany

There's only a half hour left in gym. As I change into my gym clothes, I think of what happened in Dr. Aguirre's office. Mrs. Peterson was blaming me as much as she blamed Alex.

Alex Fuentes is already ruining my senior year, and it's hardly even begun.

As I pull up my gym shorts, the sound of tap-tap-tapping on the hard cement floor alerts me that I'm not alone in the locker room. I clutch my gym shirt to my chest as Carmen Sanchez comes into view.

Oh no.

"It must be my lucky day," she says, staring me down and looking very much like a cougar ready to attack. Although cougars don't have long, straight brown hair . . . they sure do have claws. And Carmen's claws are painted bright red.

She steps closer.

I want to step back. Actually, I want to run. But I don't, mainly because she'd probably follow.

"You know," she says, her mouth quirked in a wicked grin. "I always wondered what color bra Brittany Ellis wore. Pink. How fitting. I bet it was as expensive as your dye job."

"You don't want to talk about bras and dye jobs, Carmen," I tell her while I pull my gym shirt over my head. I swallow hard before I add, "You want to kick my ass."

"When a *ho* moves in on my man, I get territorial."

"I don't want your man, Carmen. I have my own."

"Oh, please. Girls like you want every guy to like them, just so you can have them when you decide you want them." As she's talking, she's getting more riled up. I'm in trouble. "I heard you talkin' shit about me. You think you're all that, Miss High and Mighty. Let's see what you look like with a busted lip and a big, black eye. Would you come to school with a garbage bag over your head? Or would you stay holed up in your big house and never come out?"

I look at Carmen as she walks toward me. Really look at her. She knows deep down how much importance I put on controlling the image I portray, while she doesn't care if she's suspended . . . or expelled.

"Answer me!" she yells, then shoves my shoulder. It collides with the locker behind me.

I guess I wasn't listening because I don't know what I'm supposed to answer. The consequences of me coming home bruised and having been in a fight are insurmountable. My mom will be furious and blame the entire thing on me for not preventing it from happening. I hope to God she doesn't start talking about sending Shelley away again. When stressful stuff happens, my parents talk about sending Shelley away. As if magically all of the Ellises' external problems will be solved if Shelley disappeared.

"Don't you think Coach Bautista will come here looking for me? You want to be suspended?" I know, lame questions. But I'm trying to buy time here.

She chuckles. "You think I give a shit about being suspended?"

Not really, but it was worth a try.

Instead of cowering next to my locker, I stand tall. Carmen tries again to push my shoulder, but this time I manage to swat her arm away.

I'm about to get into my first fight. A fight I'm bound to lose. My heart feels like it's going to burst out of my chest. My whole life I've avoided situations like these, but this time I have no choice. I wonder if I can pull the fire alarm to avoid this, like I've seen in the movies. But of course I don't see one of those little red boxes anywhere near me.

"Carmen, leave her alone."

We both turn to the sound of a girl's voice. It's Isabel. A nonfriend. A nonfriend who just might save my face from getting bashed in.

"Isa, stay out of my business," Carmen growls.

Isabel comes toward us, her dark brown hair in a high ponytail that sways when she walks. *"No chingues con ella, Carmen."*

"¿Por qué no?" Carmen asks. "Because you think you're BFFs with blondie here now that you both wave stupid-ass pom-poms together?"

Isa puts her hands on her hips. "You're mad at Alex, Carmen. That's why you're acting like a *perra*."

At the mention of Alex, Carmen goes rigid. "Shut up, Isa. You don't know anything."

Carmen turns her fury on Isabel and yells at her in Spanish. Isabel doesn't back off, she stands tall in front of Carmen and spouts Spanish right back at her. Isabel is a short girl and probably weighs less than I do, so I'm shocked she's standing up to Carmen. But she's holding her own. I can tell by the way her words make Carmen back off.

Coach Bautista appears behind Carmen. "You three having a party and didn't invite the rest of the class?"

"We were having a little chat," Carmen says, not missing a beat and acting as if we're all friends hanging out.

"Well, then, I suggest you chat after school instead of during class. Miss Ellis and Miss Avila, join the rest of your classmates in the gym. Miss Sanchez, go to where you're supposed to be."

Carmen points her red-painted fingernail at me. "Later," she says, then walks out of the locker room, but not before making Isabel move out of the way for her to pass.

"Thanks," I say softly to Isabel.

Her answer is a nod.

12

Alex

"You almost done with the Honda? It's time to close up," my cousin Enrique says to me. I work at his auto body shop every day after school . . . to help my family put food on our table, to get away from the Latino Blood for a few hours, and because I'm damn good at fixing cars.

Covered in grease and oil from working on the Civic, I roll out from under the car. "It'll be done in a sec."

"Good. The guy's been on my ass to have it fixed for three days now."

I tighten the last bolt and walk over to Enrique as he wipes his dirty hands on a shop cloth. "Can I ask you somethin'?"

"Shoot."

"Can I have a day off next week? There's this chem project at school," I explain, thinking of the topic assigned to us today, "and we're supposed to meet with—"

"Peterson's class. Yeah, I remember those days. She's a real hard-ass." My cousin shudders.

"You had her?" I ask, amused. I wonder if her parents are parole officers. That woman sure likes discipline.

"How can I forget? *You're not a success unless you develop a treatment for a disease or save the earth*," Enrique says, doing a pretty decent imitation of Mrs. P. "You don't forget a nightmare like Peterson. But I'm sure havin' Brittany Ellis as a partner—"

"How'd you know?"

"Marcus came by and told me 'bout her, says he's in class with you guys. He's jealous you got a hot partner with long legs and big . . ." Enrique moves his hands in the air, mock feeling her chest. "Well, you know."

Yeah, I know.

I shift my weight from one foot to the other. "What about takin' time off Thursday?"

"*No hay problema.*" Enrique clears his throat. "You know, Hector was lookin' for you yesterday."

Hector. Hector Martinez, the guy who runs the Latino Blood from behind the scenes. "Sometimes I hate . . . you know."

"You're stuck in the Blood," Enrique says. "Like the rest of us. Never let Hector hear you question your commitment to the Blood. If he suspects you're disloyal you'll become the enemy so fast your head'll spin. You're a smart kid, Alex. Play it safe."

Enrique is an OG—an Original Gangster—because he'd proven himself to the Latino Blood a long time ago. He paid his dues, so now he can sit back while the younger LB members are on the front lines. According to him, I've just gotten my feet wet and have a long time to go before my friends and I get OG status.

"Smart? I bet my motorcycle I could get Brittany Ellis to sleep with me," I tell him.

"Scratch what I said." Enrique points to me with a smirk on his face. "You're a dumbass. And you'll soon be a dumbass without a ride. Girls like that don't look at guys like us."

I'm beginning to think he's right. How the hell did I ever think I could lure the very beautiful, very rich, and very white Brittany Ellis into my very poor, very Mexican, and very dark life?

Diego Vasquez, a guy from school, was born on the north side of Fairfield. Of course, my friends consider him a white guy even though his skin is darker than mine. They also think Mike Burns, a white guy who lives on the south side, is Mexican even though he doesn't have any Mexican blood in his body. Or Latino blood, for that matter. Yet he's considered one of us. In Fairfield, where you were born defines who you are.

A horn beeps loudly in front of the garage.

Enrique presses the button to raise the large garage door.

Javier Moreno's car screeches inside. "Close the door, Enrique," Javier orders breathlessly. "*La policía* are lookin' for us."

My cousin slams his fist on the button again and turns off the lights to the shop. "What the hell did you guys do?"

Carmen is in the backseat, her eyes bloodshot from either drugs or alcohol; I can't tell which. And she's been messing around with whoever is back there with her, because I know all too well what Carmen looks like when she's been messing around.

"Raul tried to smoke a Satin Hood," Carmen slurs, sticking her head out of the car window. "But he's got lousy aim."

Raul turns to her and yells at her from the front passenger seat, "*Puta*, you try and shoot a movin' target while Javier's driving."

I roll my eyes as Javier steps out of the car. "You dissin' my driving, Raul?" he says. "'Cause if you are, I have a fist here that I'll ram into your face."

Raul steps out of the car. "You want a piece of me, *culero*?"

I step in front of Raul and hold him back.

"Shit, guys. *La policía* are right outside." These are the first words out of Sam, the guy who Carmen must have been with tonight.

Everyone in the garage ducks as the police shine their flashlights through the windows. I crouch behind a large tool drawer, holding my breath. The last thing I need is attempted murder on my record. I've miraculously avoided getting arrested, but one day my luck is bound to run out.

A gang member rarely avoids the cops. Or jail time.

Enrique's face shows what he's thinking. He finally saved enough to open this shop, and now four high school punks could ruin his dream if anyone makes a sound. The cops will take my cousin, with his old LB tattoos on the back of his neck, in right along with the rest of us.

And he'll be out of business within a week.

The door to the shop jiggles. I wince and pray *please be locked*.

The cops give up on the door, then shine their flashlights in the garage again. I wonder who tipped them off—nobody in this neighborhood would narc. A secret code of silence and affiliation keeps families safe.

After what seems like forever, the cops drive away.

"Shit, that was close," Javier says.

"Too close," Enrique agrees. "Wait ten minutes, then get outta here."

Carmen steps out of the car—actually, trips out. "Hiya, Alex. I missed you tonight."

My gaze rests on Sam. "Yeah, I see how much you missed me."

"Sam? Oh, I don't really like him," she coos, coming close. I can smell the *mota* radiating off her. "I'm waiting for you to come back to me."

"Not gonna happen."

"Is it because of your stupid chemistry partner?" She grabs my chin, trying to force me to look at her, her long nails digging into my skin.

I grab both her wrists and pull them aside, all the time wondering how my tough-as-nails ex-girlfriend turned into a tough-as-nails bitch. "Brittany has nothin' to do with you and me. I hear you've been talkin' shit to her."

"Did Isa tell you that?" she asks, her eyes narrowed into slits.

"Just back off," I say, ignoring her question, "or you'll have a lot more to deal with than a bitter ex-boyfriend."

"Are you bitter, Alex? Because you don't act bitter. You act like you don't give a shit."

She's right. After I found her sleeping around, it took me a while to get over it, get over her. I wondered what other guys were giving her that I couldn't.

"I used to give a shit," I tell her. "I don't now."

Carmen slaps me. "Fuck you, Alex."

"Lovers' quarrel?" Javier drawls from the hood of the car.

"*Cállate*," Carmen and I say simultaneously.

Carmen whips around, stalks back to the car, and slides into the backseat. I watch as she pulls Sam's head toward her. The sounds of heavy kissing and moaning fill the auto shop.

Javier calls out, "Enrique, open the door. We're outta here."

Raul, who'd taken a leak in the bathroom, asks me, "Alex, you comin'? We need you, man. Paco and this Satin Hood are gonna fight at Gilson Park tonight. The Hood never fight fair, you know."

Paco didn't tell me about the fight, probably because he knew I'd try to talk him out of it. Sometimes my best friend gets into situations he can't get out of.

And sometimes he exposes me to situations I can't help but get into.

"I'm in," I say, then jump into the front seat so Raul is stuck in back with the two lovebirds.

We slow down a block before we reach the park. The tension in the air is thick, I can feel it in my bones. Where is Paco? Is he getting the shit kicked out of him in the back of an alley?

It's dark. Shadows move, making my hair stand on end. Everything looks menacing, even the trees blowing in the wind. During the day, Gilson Park resembles any other suburban park . . . except for the LB graffiti on the buildings surrounding the park. This is our territory. We've marked it.

We're in the Chicago suburbs, ruling our 'hood and the streets that lead here. It's a street war, where other suburban gangs fight us for territory. Three blocks away are mansions and million-dollar houses. Right here, in the real world, the street war rages on. The people in the million-dollar houses don't even realize a battle is about to begin less than a half mile from their backyards.

"There he is," I say, pointing to two silhouettes standing a few feet away from the park swings. The streetlights shining on the park are out, but I can tell which one is Paco right away because of his short body and trademark stance resembling that of a wrestler about to start a match.

As one silhouette pushes the other, I jump out of the car even though it's still moving. Because walking down the street are five more Hoods. Ready to fight with my best friend, I push away thoughts that this confrontation could end with all of us in the morgue. If I go into a fight with confidence and fire, without thinking of the consequences, I win. If I think too much about it, it'll be my doom.

I rush toward Paco and the Satin Hood before the rest of his friends reach them. Paco is putting up a good fight, but the other guy is like a worm, squirming away from Paco's grasp. I roughly grab the Hood's shirt and pull him up, then my fists do the rest.

Before he's able to stand and face me, I glare at Paco.

"I can take him, Alex," Paco says as he wipes blood off his lip.

"Yeah, but what about them?" I say, my gaze focused on the five Hoods behind him.

Now that I have a closer look, I realize these guys are all fresh. New members, full of piss and vinegar and not much else. New members I can take. But new members who pack heat are dangerous.

Javier, Carmen, Sam, and Raul stand next to me. I have to admit we're an intimidating bunch, even Carmen. Our homegirl can hold her own in a fight, and her fingernails are downright deadly.

The guy I pulled off Paco stands up and points to me. "You're dead."

"Listen, *enano*," I say. Little guys hate when you make fun of their height and I can't resist. "Go back to your own turf and leave this shit-hole to us."

Enano points to Paco. "He stole my steerin' wheel, man."

I look over at Paco, knowing it's just like him to taunt a Satin Hood by stealing something so stupid. When I glance back at *Enano*, I notice he's now wielding a switchblade in his hand. And he's aiming it right at me.

Oh, man. After I fight these Hoods, I'm gonna kill my best friend.

13

Brittany

My chemistry partner hasn't been in school since we received our projects. A week later he finally struts into class. It pisses me off, because no matter how bad my home life is, I come to school.

"Nice of you to show up," I say.

"Nice of you to notice," he says as he pulls off his bandanna.

Mrs. Peterson walks into class. When she sees Alex, I think she seems relieved. Squaring her shoulders, she says, "I was going to give you a pop quiz today. But instead I'll have you work with your partners in the library. Rough outlines are due in two weeks."

Colin and I hold hands as we walk to the library. Alex is behind us somewhere, talking with his friends in Spanish.

Colin squeezes my hand. "Wanna get together after practice?"

"I can't. After poms I have to go home."

Baghda quit on Saturday and my mom freaked out. Until she hires someone else I have to help out more.

He stops and pulls his hand from mine. "Shit, Brit. You gonna make some time for me, or what?"

"You can come over," I offer.

"So I can watch you take care of your sister? No thanks. Not to be a prick, but I want alone time . . . just you and me."

"I know. I do, too."

"What about Friday?"

I should be with Shelley, but my relationship with Colin is rocky and I can't let him think I don't want to be with him. "Friday works for me."

Before we seal our plans with a kiss, Alex clears his throat in front of us. "No PDA. School rules. Besides, she's my partner, dickhead. Not yours."

"Shut up, Fuentes," Colin mutters, then joins Darlene.

I put my hand on my hip and glare at Alex. "Since when are you so concerned with school rules?"

"Since you became my chem partner. Outside chemistry, you're his. In chemistry, you're mine."

"Want to find your club and pull me by my hair into the library?"

"I'm not a Neanderthal. Your boyfriend is the ape, not me."

"Then stop acting like one." All of the work tables in the library are taken, so we're forced to find a corner in the back of the library in the secluded nonfiction section and sit on the carpet. I set my books down and realize Alex is staring at me, almost as if he stares long enough he might be able to see the real me. No chance of that because I hide my true self from everyone.

I stare back, because two can play this game. On the surface he's impermeable, except a scar above his left brow tells the truth . . . he's human. His shirt outlines muscles you can get only from manual labor or working out regularly.

When my eyes meet his gaze as we're sitting here staring at each other, time stops. Those eyes are piercing mine, and I can swear at this moment he senses the real me. The one without the attitude, without the facade. Just Brittany.

"What would it take for you to go out with me?" he asks.

"You're not serious."

"Do I look like I'm jokin'?"

Mrs. Peterson wanders by us, saving me from answering. "I'm keeping my eyes on you two. Alex, we missed you last week. What happened?"

"I kinda fell onto a knife."

She shakes her head in disbelief, then moves away to harass other partners.

I look at Alex, wide-eyed. "A knife? You're kidding, right?"

"Nope. I was cuttin' a tomato, and wouldn't ya know the thing flung up and sliced my shoulder open. The doc stapled me back together. Wanna see?" he asks as he starts pulling up his sleeve.

I slap a hand over my eyes. "Alex, don't gross me out. And I don't believe for one second a knife flung out of your hand. You were in a knife fight."

"You never answered my question," he says, not admitting or denying my theory about his wound. "What would it take for you to go out with me?"

"Nothing. I wouldn't go out with you."

"I bet if we make out you'll change your mind."

"As if that'll ever happen."

"Your loss." Alex stretches his long legs in front of him, his chem book resting in his lap. He looks at me with chocolate brown eyes that are so intense I swear they could hypnotize someone. "You ready?" he asks.

For a nanosecond, as I'm staring into those dark eyes, I wonder what it would be like to kiss Alex. My gaze drops to his lips. For less than a nanosecond, I can almost feel them coming closer. Would his lips be hard on mine, or soft? Is he a slow kisser, or hungry and fast like his personality?

"For what?" I whisper as I lean closer.

"The project," he says. "Hand warmers. Peterson's class. Chemistry."

I shake my head, clearing all ridiculous thoughts from my overactive teenage mind. I must be sleep-deprived. "Yeah, hand warmers." I open my chem book.

"Brittany?"

"What?" I say, staring blindly at the words on the page. I have no clue what I'm reading because I'm too embarrassed to concentrate.

"You were lookin' at me like you wanted to kiss me."

I force a laugh. "Yeah, right," I say sarcastically.

"Nobody's watchin' if you want to, you know, try it. Not to brag, but I'm somewhat of an expert."

He gives me a lazy smile, one that was probably created to melt girls' hearts all over the globe.

"Alex, you're not my type." I need to tell him something to stop him from looking at me like he's planning to do things to me I've only heard about.

"You only like white guys?"

"Stop that," I say through gritted teeth.

"What?" he says, getting all serious. "It's the truth, ain't it?"

Mrs. Peterson appears in front of us. "How's that outline coming along?" she asks.

I put on a fake smile. "Peachy." I pull out the research I did at home and get down to business while Mrs. Peterson watches. "I did some research on the hand warmers last night. We need to dissolve sixty grams of sodium acetate and one hundred millimeters of water at seventy degrees."

"Wrong," Alex says.

I look up and realize Mrs. Peterson is gone. "*Excuse* me?"

Alex folds his arms across his chest. "You're wrong."

"I don't think so."

"You think you've never been wrong before?"

He says it as if I'm a ditzy blond bimbo, which sets my blood to way past boiling. "Sure I have," I say. I make my voice sound high and breathless, like a Southern debutante. "Why, just last week I bought Bobbi Brown Sandwash Petal lip gloss when the Pink Blossom color would have looked so much better with my complexion. Needless to say the purchase was a total disaster," I say. He expected to hear something like that come out of my mouth. I wonder if he believes it, or from my tone realizes I'm being sarcastic.

"I'll bet," he says.

"Haven't you ever been wrong before?" I ask him.

"Absolutely," he says. "Last week, when I robbed that bank over by the Walgreens, I told the teller to hand over all the fifties he had in the till. What I really should have asked for was the twenties 'cause there were way more twenties than fifties."

Okay, so he did get that I was putting on an act. And gave it right back to me with his own ridiculous scenario, which is actually unsettling because it makes us similar in some twisted way. I put a hand on my chest and gasp, playing along. "What a disaster."

"So I guess we can both be wrong."

I stick my chin in the air and declare stubbornly, "Well, I'm not wrong about chemistry. Unlike you, I take this class seriously."

"Let's have a bet, then. If I'm right, you kiss me," he says.

"And if I'm right?"

"Name it."

It's like taking candy from a baby. Mr. Macho Guy's ego is about to be taken down a notch, and I'm all too happy to be the one to do it. "If I win you take me and the class project seriously," I tell him. "No teasing me, no making ridiculous comments."

"Deal. I'd feel terrible if I didn't tell you I have a photographic memory."

"Alex, I'd feel terrible if I didn't tell you I copied the info straight from the book." I look at the research I'd done, then flip open to the corresponding page in my chem book. "Without looking, what does it need to be cooled at?" I ask.

Alex is a guy who thrives on challenges. But this time the tough guy is going to lose. He closes his own book and stares at me, his jaw set. "Twenty degrees. And it needs to be dissolved at one hundred degrees, not seventy," he answers confidently.

I scan the page, then my notes. Then back at the page again. I can't be wrong. Which page did I— "Oh, yeah. One hundred degrees." I look up at him in complete shock. "You're right."

"You gonna kiss me now, or later?"

"Right now," I say, which I can tell shocks him because his hands go still. At home, my life is dictated by my mom and dad. At school, it's different. I need to keep it that way, because if I have no control in every aspect of my life I might as well be a mannequin.

"Really?" he asks.

"Yeah." I take one of his hands in mine. I'd never be this bold if we had an audience, and am thankful for the privacy of the nonfiction titles surrounding us. His breathing slows as I sit up on my knees and lean into him. I'm ignoring the fact that his fingers are long and rough and that I've never actually touched him before. I'm nervous. I shouldn't be, though. I'm the one in control this time.

I can feel him restraining himself. He's letting me make the move, which is a good thing. I'm afraid of what this boy would do if he let loose.

I place his hand against my cheek so it cups my face and I hear him groan. I want to smile because his reaction proves I have the power.

He's unmoving as our eyes meet.

Time stops again.

Then I turn my head into his hand and kiss the inside of his palm.

"There, I kissed you," I say, giving him back his hand and ending the game.

Mr. Latino with the big ego got bested by a ditzy, blond bimbo.

14

Alex

"You call that a kiss?"

"Yep."

Okay, so I'm in shock the girl put my hand on her creamy cheek. Damn, you'd think I *was* on drugs by the way my body reacted.

She had me totally under her spell a minute ago. Then the pretty witch turned my game around so she was the one with the upper hand. She surprised me, that's for sure. I laugh, deliberately calling attention to us because I know it's exactly what she doesn't want.

"Shh," Brittany says, hitting me on the shoulder to shut me up. When I laugh louder, she whacks my arm with the heavy chem book.

My bad arm.

I wince. "Ow!" The cut on my biceps feels like a million little bees are stinging it. *¡Cabrón me dolio!*

She bites her Bobbi Brown Sandwash Petal'd frosted bottom lip, which in my opinion looks fine on her. Though I wouldn't mind seeing her in the Pink Blossom color, too.

"Did I hurt you?" she asks.

"Yes," I say through gritted teeth as I concentrate on her lip gloss instead of the pain.

"Good."

I lift my sleeve to examine my wound, which now (thanks to my chem partner) has blood trickling from one of the staples the doc at the free clinic put in it after the fight at the park with the Satin Hoods. Brittany's got a pretty good whack for someone who probably weighs a buck ten soaking wet.

She sucks in her breath and scoots away. "Oh my God! I didn't mean to hurt you, Alex. Really, I didn't. When you threatened to show me the scar, you lifted your left sleeve."

"I wasn't really gonna show you," I say. "I was fuckin' with you. It's okay," I tell her. Geez, you'd think the girl never saw red blood before. Then again, her blood probably runs blue.

"No, it's not okay," she insists while shaking her head. "Your stitches are bleeding."

"They're staples," I correct her, trying to lighten the mood. The girl is even whiter than she usually is. And she's breathing heavy, almost panting. If she passes out, I swear I'm losing the bet with Lucky. If she can't handle a little streak of my blood, how's she gonna handle having sex with me? Unless we're not naked, so she doesn't have to see my various scars. Or if it's dark, then she can pretend I'm someone white and rich. Fuck that, I want the lights on . . . I want to feel all of her against me and want her to know it's me she's with and not some other *culero*.

"Alex, are you okay?" Brittany asks, looking totally concerned.

Should I tell her I was spacing out while thinking about us having sex?

Mrs. P. walks up the aisle with a stern look on her face. "This is a library, you two. Keep it down." But then she notices the small line of blood snaking down my arm and staining my sleeve. "Brittany, help him to the nurse. Alex, next time come to school with that thing bandaged."

"Don't I get sympathy, Mrs. P.? I'm bleedin' to death."

"Do something to help mankind or the planet, Alex. Then you'll get my sympathy. People who get into knife fights don't earn anything from me except disgust. Now go get cleaned up."

Brittany lifts my books off my lap and says in a shaky voice, "Come on."

"I can hold the books," I tell her as I follow her out of the library. I'm pressing my sleeve against the wound, hoping to stop more blood from leaking out.

She's walking ahead of me. If I tell her I need help walking because I feel faint, will she believe me and come to my rescue? Maybe I should stumble . . . although knowing her she wouldn't care.

Right before we reach the nurse's office, she turns around. Her hands are shaking. "I'm so sorry, Alex. I di—didn't m—mean—"

She's freaking out. If she cries, I won't know what to do. I'm not used to crying chicks. I don't think Carmen cried once during our entire relationship. In fact, I'm not sure Carmen has tear ducts. That turned me on, because emotional chicks scare me.

"Um . . . you okay?" I ask.

"If this gets around, I'm never going to live it down. Oh, God, if Mrs. Peterson calls my parents I'm dead. Or at least I'll wish I was dead." She keeps talking and shaking, as if she's a car with bad shocks and no brakes.

"*Brittany?*"

". . . and my mom'll blame it on me. It's my fault, I know. But she'll freak out on me and then I'll have to explain and hope she—"

Before she can get another word out I yell, "Brittany!" The girl looks up at me with an expression so confused I don't know whether to feel sorry for her or stunned she's rambling and can't seem to stop. "You're the one freakin' out," I comment, stating the obvious.

Her eyes are usually clear and bright, but now they're dull and blank as if she's not all here.

She looks down and around and everywhere except directly at me. "No, I'm not. I'm fine."

"The hell you are. Look at me."

She hesitates. "I'm fine," she says, now focused on a locker across the hall. "Just forget everything I just said."

"If you don't look at me, I'm gonna bleed all over the floor and need a fuckin' transfusion. Look at me, dammit."

Her breathing is still heavy as she focuses on me. "What? If you want to tell me my life is out of control, I'm already aware of it."

"I know you didn't mean to hurt me," I tell her. "Even if you did, I probably deserved it." I'm hoping to lighten the mood so the girl doesn't have a complete breakdown in the hallway. "Makin' mistakes ain't a crime, you know. What's the use in having a reputation if you can't ruin it every now and then?"

"Don't try and make me feel better, Alex. I hate you."

"I hate you, too. Now please move out of the way so the janitor doesn't have to spend all day moppin' up my blood. He's a relative, you know."

She shakes her head, not believing for an instant the head janitor at Fairfield is a relative. Okay, so he isn't exactly a relative. But he does have family in Atencingo, the same small town where my mom has cousins in Mexico.

Instead of moving out of the way, my chem partner opens the door to the nurse's office for me. I think she's functioning even if her hands are still shaking.

"He's bleeding," she calls out to Miss Koto, the school nurse.

Miss Koto has me sit down on one of the examining tables. "What happened here?"

I look over at Brittany. She has a worried look on her face, as if she's concerned I might croak right here. I hope to God that's what the Angel of Death looks like before I kick the bucket. I'd be more than happy to go to hell if a face like Brittany's was greeting me.

"My staples opened up," I say. "No big deal."

"And how did that happen?" Miss Koto asks as she wets a white cloth and dabs it on my arm. I hold my breath, waiting for the stinging to recede. I'm also not about to narc on my partner, especially since I'm trying to seduce her.

"I hit him," Brittany says, her voice hitching.

Miss Koto turns around, stunned. "*You* hit him?"

"By accident," I chime in, not having a clue why I suddenly want to protect this girl who hates me and would probably rather flunk Mrs. P.'s class than have to partner with me.

My plans with Brittany are not working. The only feeling she's admitted to having toward me is hatred. But the thought of Lucky on my motorcycle is more painful than the antiseptic crap Miss Koto is now rubbing on my wound.

I've got to get Brittany alone if I'm gonna have any chance of saving face *and* saving my Honda. Does her freakout session mean she really doesn't hate me? I've never seen that girl do anything not scripted or 100 percent intentional. She's a robot. Or so I thought. She's always looked and acted like a princess on camera every time I've seen her. Who knew it'd be my bloody arm that would crack her.

I look over at Brittany. She's focused on my arm and Miss Koto's ministrations. I wish we were back in the library. I could swear back there she was thinking about getting it on with me.

I'm sporting *la tengo dura* right here in front of Miss Koto just thinking about it. *Gracias a Dios* the nurse walks over to the medicine cabinet. Where's a large chem book when you need one?

"Let's hang Thursday after school. You know, to work on the out-line," I tell Brittany for two reasons. First, I need to stop thinking about getting naked with her in front of Miss Koto. Second, I want Brittany to myself.

"I'm busy Thursday," she says.

Probably with Burro Face. Obviously she'd rather be with that *pendejo* than me.

"Friday, then," I say, testing her although I probably shouldn't. Testing a girl like Brittany could put a serious damper on my ego. Although I caught her at a time when she's vulnerable and still shaking from seeing my blood. I admit I'm a manipulative asshole.

She bites her bottom lip that she thinks is glossed with the wrong color. "I can't Friday, either." My hard-on is officially deflated. "What about Saturday morning?" she says. "We can meet at the Fairfield Library."

"You sure you can pencil me into your busy schedule?"

"Shut up. I'll meet you there at ten."

"It's a date," I say while Miss Koto, obviously eavesdropping, fin-ishes wrapping my arm with dorky gauze.

Brittany gathers her books. "It's not a date, Alex," she says over her shoulder.

I grab my book and hurry into the hallway after her. She's walking alone. The loudspeaker music isn't playing so class is still on.

"It might not be a date, but you still owe me a kiss. I always collect debts." My chem partner's eyes go from dull to shining mad and full of fire. Mmm, dangerous. I wink at her. "And don't sweat about what lip gloss to wear on Saturday. You'll just have to reapply it after we make out."

15

Brittany

One thing in life is certain—I am not making out with Alex Fuentes.

Thankfully Mrs. Peterson had us busy doing experiments all week, giving us no time to talk except about who's going to light the Bunsen burner. Although every time I looked at Alex's bandaged arm it reminded me of when I whacked him.

I'm trying not to think about him while I gloss my lips for my date with Colin. It's Friday night and we're going to dinner and a movie.

After double-checking and triple-checking myself in the mirror, and attaching the Tiffany's bracelet he gave me for our anniversary last year, I head to the backyard, where my sister is in our pool with her physical therapist. My mom, wearing her pink velour cover-up, is lounging on a chaise reading some home-design magazine.

It's pretty quiet, except for the physical therapist's voice instructing Shelley.

Mom puts down her magazine, her face tight and stern. "Brit, don't be out past ten thirty."

"We're seeing an eight-o'clock movie, Mom. We'll be home after that."

"You heard what I said. No later than ten thirty. If you have to leave the movie early to get home on time, so be it. Colin's parents won't respect a girl without a curfew."

Our doorbell rings. "That's probably him," I say.

"You better hurry up and get it. A boy like that won't wait forever, you know."

I rush to the front door before my mom does it for me and makes a fool out of both of us. Colin is standing on our front stoop with a dozen red roses in his hand.

"For you," he says, surprising me.

Wow! I'm feeling stupid for thinking about Alex so much this past week. I hug Colin and give him a kiss, a real one on the lips.

"Let me put these in water," I say, stepping back.

I hum happily as I walk to the kitchen, smelling their sweet fragrance. Putting water in a vase, I wonder if Alex ever brought his girlfriend flowers. Alex probably brings his dates sharp knives as gifts, in case she'll need one when she's out on a date with him. Being with Colin is so . . .

Boring?

No. We're not boring. We're safe. Comfortable. Cute.

After cutting the bottoms off the roses and placing them in the vase, I find Colin chatting with my mom on the patio, something I really don't want him doing.

"Ready?" I say.

Colin flashes me his super white million-dollar smile. "Yep."

"Have her back by ten thirty," my mom calls out. As if a girl with a curfew equals high morals. It's ridiculous, but I look at Shelley and swallow my argument.

"Sure thing, Mrs. Ellis," Colin responds.

When we're in his Mercedes, I ask, "What movie are we seeing?"

"Change in plans. My dad's firm got tickets to the Cubs game. In a suite right behind home plate. Baby, we're goin' to watch the Cubbies."

"How cool. Will we be back by ten thirty?" Because I know without a doubt my mom will be waiting at the door for me.

"If they don't go into extra innings. Does your mom think you'll turn into a pumpkin or something?"

I take hold of his hand. "No. It's just that, well, I don't want to upset her."

"No offense, but your mom is strange. She's a hot MILF, but totally off the wall."

I take my hand back. "Eww! Colin, you just called my mom a MILF! I'm completely grossed out."

"Please, Brit." He glances in my direction. "Your mom looks more like your twin sister than your mother. She's hot."

She works out so much, I admit her body looks more like a thirty-year-old's than a forty-five-year-old's. But to think my boyfriend is hot for my mom is plain yuck.

At the game, Colin leads me to his dad's corporate suite at Wrigley Field. The box is crowded with people from a bunch of downtown law firms. Colin's parents greet us. His mom hugs me and gives me an air-kiss before leaving us to mingle with other people.

I watch as Colin talks with the other people in the suite. He's so at home here; he's in his element. He shakes hands, smiles wide, and laughs at everyone's jokes whether they're funny or not.

"Let's watch the game in the seats over there," he says, leading me to the suite's seats after we get hot dogs and drinks from the food bar.

"I'm hoping to get an internship at Harris, Lundstrom, and Wallace next summer," he says quietly, "so I gotta get face time with these guys."

When Mr. Lundstrom appears next to us, Colin goes into full-on business mode. I watch in admiration as he talks with Mr. Lundstrom as if they're old friends. My boyfriend definitely has a knack for schmoozing people.

"I hear you want to follow in your father's footsteps," Mr. Lundstrom says.

"Yes, sir," Colin responds, then they start talking about football and stocks and whatever else Colin brings up to keep Mr. Lundstrom talking.

Megan calls on my cell and I give her highlights of the game and we talk while I'm waiting for Colin to finish talking to Mr. Lundstrom. She tells me she had the best time at this dance club called Club Mystique that will let in teens. She insists Sierra and I will love it there.

At the seventh-inning stretch, Colin and I stand and sing "Take Me Out to the Ball Game." We're totally out of tune, but it doesn't matter because right now it sounds as if the thousands of Cubs fans singing are as out of tune as we are. It feels good to be with Colin like this, having fun together. It makes me think I've been overcritical of our relationship.

At nine forty-five, I turn to Colin and tell him we need to start heading home even though the game isn't over.

He takes my hand in his. I think he's going to excuse himself from his conversation with Mr. Lundstrom. Instead, Mr. Lundstrom calls over Mr. Wallace.

As the minutes tick by, I'm getting nervous. There has been enough tension in my house. I don't want to cause more. "Colin . . . ," I say, squeezing his hand.

He puts his arm around me in response.

At the top of the ninth inning, when it's past ten, I say, "I'm sorry, but Colin has to drive me home now."

Mr. Wallace and Mr. Lundstrom shake Colin's hand, then I pull him out of the park.

"Brit, do you know how hard it is to get an internship at HL&W?"

"At this point, I don't care. Colin, I needed to be home by ten thirty."

"So you'll be home at eleven. Tell your mom we got stuck in traffic."

Colin doesn't know what my mom is like when she's in one of her moods. Thankfully I've been able to avoid bringing him around the house often and if he comes over, it's just for a few minutes or less. He has no clue what it's like when my mom goes off on me.

We pull into my driveway not at eleven, but closer to eleven thirty. Colin is still pumped about the possible internship at HL&W while listening to the after-game recap on WGN radio.

"I gotta go," I tell him, leaning over for a quick kiss.

"Stay here a few minutes," he says against my lips. "We haven't fooled around in, like, forever. I miss it."

"Me, too. But it's late." I give him a look of apology. "We'll have more nights together."

"Hopefully sooner rather than later."

I walk into my house, prepared to be yelled at. Sure enough, my mom is standing in the foyer with her arms crossed. "You're late."

"I know. I'm sorry."

"What do you think, that I make up arbitrary rules?"

"No."

She sighs.

"Mom, I really am sorry. We went to a Cubs game instead of a movie, and the traffic was terrible."

"Cubs game? All the way in the city? You could have been mugged!"

"We were fine, Mom."

"You think you know it all, Brit, but you don't. For all I know you could've been lying dead in a city alley and all along I thought you were at a movie. Check your purse to see if any money or your ID is missing."

I open my purse and check the contents of my wallet, only to appease her. I hold up my ID and cash. "It's all here."

"Consider yourself lucky. This time."

"I'm always careful when I go to the city, Mom. Besides, Colin was with me."

"I don't need excuses, Brit. Did you not think it would be nice to call and tell me about the change in plans and that you were going to be late?"

To have her yell at me over the phone, and then again when I got home? No way. But I can't tell her that. "I didn't think about it," is all I say.

"Do you ever think about this family? It's not all about you, Brittany."

"I know that, Mom. I promise next time I'll call. I'm tired. Can I just go to bed now?"

She dismisses me with a wave of her hand.

On Saturday morning I wake up to my mom's screaming. Throwing the covers back, I rush out of bed and run down the stairs to see what the commotion is all about.

Shelley is in her wheelchair, which is pushed up to the kitchen table. Food is all over her mouth and splattered on her shirt and pants. She looks like a little kid instead of a twenty-year-old.

"Shelley, if you do it again you're going to your room!" my mom yells, then places a bowl of her blended food on the table in front of her.

Shelley swipes it on the ground. My mom gasps, then narrows her eyes at Shelley.

"I'll deal with it," I say, rushing to my sister.

My mom has never hit my sister. But my mom's frustration is in overdrive, which stings just the same.

"Don't baby her, Brittany," Mom says. "If she doesn't eat, she'll be tube fed. Would you like that?"

I hate when she does this. She'll talk about the worst possible scenario and not work on fixing what's wrong. When my sister looks at me, I see the same frustration in her eyes.

My mom points her finger at Shelley, then at the food on the floor. "That's why I haven't taken you to a restaurant in months," she says.

"Mom, stop," I say. "You don't need to escalate the situation. She's already upset. Why make it worse?"

"And what about me?"

Tension starts building, beginning inside my veins and spreading to my fingertips and toes. It bubbles up and bursts with such force I can't keep it inside any longer. "This isn't about you! Why does it always go back to how everything affects you?" I scream. "Mom, can't you see she's hurting? Instead of yelling at her, why don't you spend the time figuring out what's wrong?"

Without thinking, I take a washcloth and kneel beside Shelley. I start wiping her pants clean.

"Brittany, don't!" my mom yells out.

I don't listen. I should have, though, because before I can move away Shelley's hands go in my hair and she starts pulling. Hard. With all the commotion, I forgot my sister's new thing is pulling hair.

"Ow!" I say. "Shelley, please stop!" I'm trying to reach around and push down on her knuckles like her doctor told us to do to make her release her grasp, but it's no use. I'm in the wrong position, crouched at Shelley's feet with my body twisted. My mom is swearing, droplets of food are flying, and my scalp feels raw already.

Shelley isn't loosening her hold, even though my mom is trying to pull her hands away from my hair.

"Knuckles, Mom!" I yell, reminding her what Dr. Meir suggested. Holy crap, how much hair has she pulled out? It feels like an entire section of my head is bald.

After my reminder, my mom must have pressed hard enough on her knuckles because my hair is released. Either that, or Shelley pulled out whatever chunks she'd grabbed.

Falling onto the floor, I immediately put a hand to the back of my head.

Shelley is smiling.

My mom is frowning.

And tears come to my eyes.

"I'm taking her to Dr. Meir, right now," my mom says, shaking her head at me so I'm aware she's blaming me for the situation spiraling out of control. "This has gone on long enough. Brittany, take your father's car and go to O'Hare to pick him up. His flight comes in at eleven. It's the least you can do to help."

16

Alex

I've been waiting at the library for an hour. Okay, so it's been an hour and a half. Before ten, I sat outside on the cement benches. At ten I came inside and stood looking at the display case, pretending to be interested in upcoming library events. I didn't want to look overly eager to see Brittany. At ten forty-five I sat on the couches in the teen section, reading my chem book. Okay, so my eyes skimmed the pages even if no words registered.

Now it's eleven. Where is she?

I could just go hang with my friends. Hell, I should go hang with my friends. But I have a stupid urge to know why Brittany blew me off. I tell myself it's an ego thing, but in the back of my mind I'm worried about her.

She'd hinted, during her freakout in front of the nurse's office, that her mom isn't a candidate for a Mother of the Year award. Doesn't Brittany realize that she's eighteen now and can leave home if she wanted? If it's that bad, why stay?

Because her parents are rich.

If I left home, my new life wouldn't be so different from my old one. With a girl who lives on the north side, a life lacking designer towels and a maid to pick up after you is probably worse than death.

I've had enough of standing here waiting for Brittany. I'm going to her house, to confront her on why she ditched me. Without thinking it through, I get on my motorcycle and head to the north side. I know where she lives . . . in the big honkin' white house with pillars flanking the front.

I park my bike in her driveway and ring her doorbell. I clear my throat so I don't choke on my words. *Mierda*, what am I gonna say to her? And why am I feeling all insecure, like I need to impress her because she'll judge me?

Nobody answers. I ring again.

Where's a servant or butler to answer the door when you need one? Just as I'm about to give up and slap myself with a big dose of what-the-fuck-do-I-think-I'm-doing, the door opens. Standing before me is an older version of Brittany. Obviously her mom. When she takes one look at me, her disappointing sneer is obvious.

"Can I help you?" she asks with an attitude. I sense either she expects me to be part of the gardening crew or someone going door-to-door harassing people. "We have a 'no soliciting policy' in this neighborhood."

"I'm, uh, not here to solicit anythin'. My name's Alex. I just wanted to know if Brittany was, uh, at home?" Oh, great. Now I'm mumbling *uh*'s every two seconds.

"No." Her steely answer matches her steely glare.

"Do you know where she went?"

Mrs. Ellis closes the door halfway, probably hoping I won't peek inside and see her valuables and be tempted to steal them. "I don't give out information on the whereabouts of my daughter. Now if you'll excuse me," she says, then closes the door in my face.

I'm left standing in front of the door like a complete *pendejo*. For all I know, Brittany was behind the door instructing her mom to get rid of me. I wouldn't put it past her to play games with me.

I hate games I can't win.

I walk back to my bike with my tail between my legs, wondering if I should feel like a kicked dog or an angry pit bull.

17

Brittany

"Who's Alex?"

Those are the first words my mom asks me after I arrive back home from the airport with my dad.

"He's a guy from school I'm partnered with for chemistry," I answer slowly. Wait one minute. "How do you know about Alex?"

"He was here after you left for the airport. I sent him away."

As if my brain is synapsing, reality hits me.

Oh, no!

I forgot to meet Alex this morning.

Guilt sets in as I think about him waiting for me at the library. I was the one who didn't trust him to show, but I'm the one who flaked. He must be furious. Ugh, I'm feeling sick.

"I don't want him near the house," she says. "The neighbors will start talking about you." *Just like they talk about your sister*, I know she's thinking.

One day I hope to live in a place where I don't have to worry about neighbors gossiping. "Fine," I tell her.

"Can't you change partners?"

"No."

"Did you try?"

"Yes, Mom. I did. Mrs. Peterson refuses to reassign partners."

"Maybe you didn't try hard enough. I'll call the school on Monday and make them—"

I whip my attention to her, ignoring the stinging, throbbing pain in the back of my head from where my sister ripped out the chunk of hair. "Mom, I'll handle it. I don't need you calling the school and making me feel like a two-year-old."

"Did that boy Alex teach you how to talk to your mother without respect? All of a sudden you can open a mouth to me because you're partnered with *that boy?*"

"Mom—"

I wish my dad was here to intervene. But he went directly to his study to check his e-mails right after coming home. I wish he'd act as a referee instead of sitting on the sidelines.

"Because if you start hanging out with trash like that, people will consider *you* trash. That's not how your father and I have brought you up."

Oh, no. Here comes the lecture. I'd rather eat live fish, scales and all, than hear this right now. I know the meaning behind her words. Shelley's not perfect, so I have to be.

I take a deep breath, trying to calm myself. "Mom, I get it. I'm sorry."

"I'm only trying to protect you," she says. "And you throw it back in my face."

"I know. I'm sorry. What did Dr. Meir say about Shelley?"

"He wants her to come twice a week for some evaluations. I'm going to need your help taking her."

I don't talk to her about Ms. Small's policy about missing pom practice, because there's no use in having both of us stressed. Besides, I want to know why Shelley is lashing out just as much as she does . . . if not more.

Thankfully, the phone rings and my mom turns to answer it. I hurry into my sister's room before my mom can call me back for more discussions. Shelley is sitting by her personalized computer in her room, tapping at the keyboard.

"Hi," I say.

Shelley looks up. She's not smiling.

I want her to know I'm not upset with her, because I know she didn't mean to hurt me. Shelley might not even understand her own motivations for doing things. "Want to play checkers?"

She shakes her head.

"Watch television?"

Another shake.

"I want you to know I'm not mad at you." I go closer, careful not to get my hair within reach, and rub her back. "I love you, you know."

No answer, no head nodding, no verbal approximation. Nothing.

I sit on the edge of her bed and watch as she plays with her computer. Every once in a while I make comments, so she knows I'm here. She might not need me now, but I wish she did. Because I know a time will come when she does need me and I won't be there for her. That scares me.

A little while later I leave my sister and head for my room. I search my Fairfield High student directory for Alex's phone number.

Flipping open my cell, I dial his number.

"Hello?" a boy's voice answers.

I take a deep breath. "Hi," I say. "Is Alex there?"

"He's out."

"*¿Quién es?*" I hear his mom asking in the background.

"Who is this?" the boy asks me.

I realize I'm chipping my nail polish off as I'm talking. "Brittany Ellis. I'm, uh, a friend of Alex's from school."

"It's Brittany Ellis, a friend of Alex's from school," the boy relates to his mom.

"*Toma el mensaje,*" I hear her say.

"Are you his new girlfriend?" the boy asks.

I hear a thump and an "Ow!" and then he says, "Can I take a message?"

"Tell him Brittany called. Here's my number . . ."

18

Alex

Right now I'm standing inside the warehouse where the Latino Blood hang every night. I just finished my second or third cigarette—I've stopped counting.

"Drink some beer and stop lookin' depressed," Paco says, throwing me a Corona. I told him about Brittany blowing me off this morning and all he's done is shake his head at me as if I should have known better than to go to the north side.

I catch the can in one hand, but toss it right back. "No, thanks."

"*¿Que tienes, ese?* This stuff not good enough for you?" It's Javier, probably the stupidest Latino Blood. *El büey* can control his liquor about as well as he controls his drug use, which isn't much.

I challenge him without saying a word.

"Just kiddin', man," a drunken Javier slurs.

Nobody wants to get into it with me. During my first year as a member of the Latino Blood, in a clash with a rival gang, I proved my worth.

As a little kid, I thought I could save the world . . . or at least save my family. *I'll never be in a gang,* I told myself when I was old enough to join one. *I'll protect mi familia with my two hands.* On the south side of

Fairfield, you're either in a gang or against them. I had dreams of a future then; deluded dreams that I could stay away from gangs and still protect my family. But those dreams died along with my future the night my father was shot twenty feet from my six-year-old face.

When I stood over his body, all I could see was this red spot spreading on the front of his shirt. It reminded me of a bull's-eye, except the target kept getting larger and larger. The next thing I knew, he gasped and that was it.

My dad was dead.

I never held him or touched him. I was too afraid. In the days that followed, I didn't say a word. Even when the police questioned me, I couldn't speak. They said I'd been in shock and my brain didn't know how to process what happened. They were right. I don't even remember what the guy looked like who shot him. I've never been able to seek revenge for my father's murder, even though every night I replay the shooting in my head trying to put the pieces together. If I could only remember, the fucker would pay.

My memory of today is clear, though. Being stood up by Brittany, her mother scowling at me . . . things I want to forget are stuck in my brain like glue.

Paco downs half his beer in one gulp, not even caring when it dribbles down the sides of his mouth and onto his shirt. When Javier is talking to other guys, Paco says to me, "Carmen really screwed you up, you know."

"And how's that?"

"You don't trust chicks. Take Brittany Ellis—"

I curse under my breath. "Paco, on second thought toss that Corona over here." After I catch it, I down the beer and crush the can against the wall after it's empty.

"You may not want to listen, Alex. But you're gonna hear me out no matter if you're drunk or not. Your loose-talkin', hickey-makin', sexy Latina ex-girlfriend Carmen stabbed you in the back. So you're makin' a complete U-turn by stabbin' Brittany in the back."

I'm reluctantly listening to Paco as I grab another beer. "You callin' my chem partner a U-turn?"

"Yeah. But it's gonna backfire big-time, man, 'cause you actually like the girl. Admit it."

I don't want to admit it. "I only want her for the bet."

Paco laughs so hard he stumbles and ends up sitting on the warehouse floor. He points to me with the beer still in his hand. "You, my friend, are so good at lyin' to yourself you're actually startin' to believe the bullshit comin' out of your mouth. Those two girls are total opposites, man."

I grab another beer. As I flip the top open, I think about the differences between Carmen and Brittany. Carmen's got sexy, dark, mysterious eyes. Brittany's got seemingly innocent, light blue ones you can practically see through. Will they be that way when I make love to her?

Shit. Make love? What the hell possessed me to think about Brittany and love in the same sentence? I am seriously losing it.

I spend the next half hour ingesting as much beer as possible. I'm feeling good enough to not think . . . about anything.

A familiar female voice cuts through the numbness. "Wanna party at Danwood Beach?" she asks.

I'm staring into chocolate eyes. Although my brain is clouded and I'm dizzy, I know enough to register that chocolate is the opposite of blue. I don't want blue. Blue confuses me too much. Chocolate is straightforward, easier to deal with.

There's something not right here, but I can't pinpoint it. And when Chocolate's lips are on mine, I don't care about anything except wiping Blue from my mind. Even if I remember Chocolate as being bitter.

"*Sí*," I say when my lips separate from hers. "Let's party. *¡Vamos a gozar!*"

An hour later, I'm standing in water up to my waist. It makes me long to be a pirate and sail the lonely seas. Of course in the back of my hazy mind I know I'm gazing across Lake Michigan and not an ocean. But right now I'm not thinking clearly, and being a pirate seems like a damn good option. No family, no worries, nobody with blond hair and blue eyes glaring at me.

Arms like tentacles wrap around my stomach. "What're you thinkin' about, *novio*?"

"Becoming a pirate," I murmur to the octopus who just called me her boyfriend.

The octopus's suction cups are kissing my back and moving their way around to my face. Instead of scaring me, it feels good. I know this octopus, these tentacles.

"You be a pirate, I'll be a mermaid. You can rescue me."

Somehow I think I'm the one who needs rescuing because I feel like she's drowning me with her kisses. "Carmen," I say to the brown-eyed octopus–turned–sexy mermaid, suddenly aware that I'm drunk, naked, and standing in water up to my waist in Lake Michigan.

"Shh, let go and enjoy."

Carmen knows me well enough to make me forget about real life and help me focus on the fantasy. Her hands and body wrap around me. She feels weightless in the water. My hands go to the places I've been before and my body presses against familiar territory, but the fantasy doesn't come. And when I look back at the shore, the sounds of my rowdy friends remind me we have an audience. My octopus/mermaid loves an audience.

I don't.

Grabbing my mermaid's hand, I start walking back to shore.

Ignoring the comments from my friends, I tell my mermaid to get dressed as I pull on my jeans. When we're dressed, I take her hand once again and we weave through the crowd until we find a vacant space to sit among our friends.

I lean against a big rock and stretch out my legs. My ex-girlfriend straddles me, as if we'd never broken up and she'd never cheated on me. I feel trapped, caught.

She takes a drag of something stronger than a cigarette and passes it to me. I look at the small, wrapped joint.

"This ain't amped, is it?" I ask. I'm wasted, but the last thing I need is narcs in my system on top of the marijuana and beer. My goal is to be numb, not dead.

She puts it to my lips. "It's just Acapulco gold, *novio*."

Maybe it'll work to wipe out my memory for good and make me forget shootings and ex-girlfriends and bets of having hot sex with a girl who thinks I'm the scum of the earth.

I take the joint from her and inhale.

My mermaid's hands move up my chest. "I can make you happy, Alex," she whispers, so close I can smell the alcohol and *mota* on her breath. Or it might be mine, I'm not sure. "Give me another chance."

Being high and drunk makes me confused. And when the image of Brittany and Colin with their arms around each other at school yesterday forms in my head, I pull Carmen's body closer.

I don't need a girl like Brittany.

I need hot and spicy Carmen, my lying little mermaid.

19

Brittany

I convinced Sierra, Doug, Colin, Shane, and Darlene to go to Club Mystique tonight, the club Megan told me about. It was in Highland Grove, on the beach. Colin doesn't like to dance, so I ended up dancing with the rest of the gang and even this one guy named Troy, who was an amazing dancer. I think I picked up some moves I can introduce to our pom squad.

Now we're at Sierra's, headed for the private beach behind her house. My mom knows I'm sleeping at Sierra's tonight, so I don't have to worry about checking in. While Sierra and I are setting up blankets on the sand, Darlene is lagging behind with the guys, who are unloading stashed beer and bottles of wine from the back of Colin's car.

"Doug and I had sex last weekend," Sierra blurts out.

"Seriously?"

"Yeah. I know I wanted to wait until we were in college, but it just happened. His parents were out of town, and I went over to his place and one thing led to another and we just did it."

"Wow. So, how was it?"

"I don't know. To be honest it was kinda weird. But he was really sweet afterward, asking me over and over if I was okay. And at night he came to my house and brought me three dozen red roses. I had to lie to my parents and say they were for our anniversary. I couldn't very well say the flowers were in celebration of his taking my virginity. What about you and Colin?"

"Colin *wants* to have sex," I tell her.

"Every guy over the age of fourteen *wants* to have sex," she says. "It's their job to want to do it."

"I just . . . don't want to. At least, not now."

"Then it's your job to say no," she says, as if it's that easy. Sierra isn't a virgin anymore, she'd said yes. Why is it so hard for me to say yes, too?

"How will I know when it's the right time?"

"You sure as hell won't be asking me about it. I guess when you're totally ready you'll want to do it with no reservations or questions. We *know* they want to have sex. It's up to you to make it happen. Or not. Listen, the first time wasn't fun or easy. It was kind of sloppy and most of the time I felt stupid. Opening yourself up to making mistakes and being vulnerable is what makes it beautiful and special with the person you love."

Is that why I haven't wanted to do it with Colin? Maybe deep down I don't love him as much as I thought. Am I even capable of loving someone so much that I open myself up to being vulnerable? I really don't know.

"Tyler broke up with Darlene today," Sierra whispers to me. "He started dating a girl in his dorm."

If I didn't feel sorry for Darlene before, now I do. Especially because she thrives on attention from guys. It fuels her self-esteem. It's no wonder she was totally all over Shane tonight.

I watch as the rest of the guys and Darlene come into view and set blankets down on the beach. Darlene grabs Shane's shirt and pulls him aside. "Let's go make out," she tells him. Shane is all too ready to honor her request.

Pulling her away from him, I lean close and say so only she can hear, "Don't fool around with Shane."

"Why not?"

"Because you don't like him like that. Don't use him. Or let him use you."

Darlene pushes me away. "You seriously have a demented view of reality, Brit. Or maybe you want to point out everyone else's imperfections so you stay the Queen of Perfect."

That's not fair. I don't want to point out her flaws, but if I see her going on a self-destructive path, isn't it up to me as her friend to stop her?

Maybe not. We're friends, but not super-close friends. The only one I let close enough is Sierra. How dare I give Darlene advice when she can't reciprocate?

Sierra, Doug, Colin, and I sit on blankets and talk about the last football game in front of a bonfire we make with sticks and old pieces of wood.

We laugh, remembering the missed plays and imitating the football coach who yelled at the players from the sidelines. His face gets all red and when he's really upset spit flies out of his mouth as he yells. Players get out of the way so they don't get sprayed. Doug does a hilarious imitation of him.

It feels good sitting here with my friends and Colin, and for a while I forget about my chemistry partner, who's been occupying my thoughts lately.

After a while, Sierra and Doug go for a walk and I'm leaning against Colin in front of the fire, the light giving the sand around us a bright glow. Darlene and Shane have hooked up for the night despite my advice against it and aren't back yet.

I grab the bottle of Chardonnay the guys brought. The boys have been drinking beer and the girls have been drinking wine because Sierra hates the taste of beer. I bring the bottle to my lips and finish it off. I'm feeling buzzed, but I probably need to drink an entire bottle myself in order to feel completely carefree.

"Did you miss me this summer?" I ask, leaning into Colin as he smoothes down my hair. It's probably a mess. I wish I was drunk enough not to care.

Colin takes my hand in his and leads it to his crotch. He lets out a slow, moaning breath.

"Yeah," he says into my neck. "Lots."

When I take my hand back, his arms snake around to my front. He squeezes my boobs like they're water balloons. I've never minded Colin's touch before, but now I'm annoyed and creeped out by his roving hands. I shrug out of his grasp.

"What's wrong, Brit?"

"I don't know." I really don't know. Things with Colin seem strained since school started. And thoughts of Alex keep invading my head, which is annoying me more than anything. I reach over and grab a beer. "It feels forced," I tell my boyfriend as I open the can and take a sip. "Can't we sit here without fooling around?"

Colin lets out a long, dramatic deep breath. "Brit, I want to do it."

I try and down the entire can in one gulp, but end up spewing out some of it. "You mean *now*?" Where our friends can see us if they turn around?

"Why not? We've waited long enough."

"I don't know, Colin," I say, really scared to be having this conversation although I knew it was coming. "I guess . . . I guess I thought it would happen naturally."

"What can be more natural than doing it outside, in the sand?"

"What about condoms?"

"I'll pull out."

That doesn't sound romantic *at all*. I'll be freaking out the entire time and worrying about getting pregnant. Not how I want my first time to be. "Making love means a lot to me."

"To me, too. So let's do it already."

"I feel like this summer changed you."

"Maybe it did," he says defensively. "Maybe I realized our relationship has to be more. Geez, Brit. Whoever heard of a senior being a fucking virgin? Everyone thinks we've done it, why don't we just do it? Shit, you even let that guy Fuentes think he can get into your pants."

My heart slams into my chest. "You think I'd rather sleep with Alex than you?" I ask, my eyes getting watery. I don't know if it's the alcohol making me emotional or if it's because his words hit the target. My thoughts are on my chem partner. I hate myself for having these thoughts, and hate Colin right now for pointing it out.

"What about Darlene?" I throw back. I look around, making sure Darlene is out of hearing range. "You two are like one cozy couple in chemistry class."

"Get off it, Brit. So some girl pays attention to me in chemistry. Obviously *you* don't because you're too busy arguing with Fuentes. Everyone knows it's all foreplay."

"That's not fair, Colin."

"What's going on?" Sierra says, walking up with Doug from behind a large boulder.

"Nothing," I tell her. I stand up, my sandals in hand. "I'm going home."

Sierra grabs her purse. "I'll go with you."

"No." I'm finally feeling light-headed. It's like I'm having an out-of-body experience and I want to go through it it all by myself. "I don't want or need anyone. I'll walk."

"She's drunk," Doug says, eyeing the empty bottle and beer can beside me.

"Am not," I tell them. I snatch another beer and open it as I walk down the beach. Alone. By myself. Which is how it should be.

Sierra says, "I don't want you going alone."

"I just want to be by myself right now. I need to sort things out."

"Brit, come back here," Colin says, but doesn't get up.

I ignore him.

"Don't go past the fourth pier," Sierra warns. "It's not safe."

Safe shmafe. So what if something happens to me, anyway? Colin doesn't care. Or my parents, for that matter.

Closing my eyes as the sand sinks between my toes, I breathe in the scent of the fresh, cool Lake Michigan breeze washing over my face and drink more beer. Forgetting everything except the sand and my beer, I continue walking, pausing only to look out over the dark water with moonlight shining across it like a line splitting the water in two.

I've passed two piers. Or maybe three. Anyway, it's not a long walk home. Less than a mile. When I get to the next beach entrance, I'll walk up the street and head home. It's not like I haven't done it before.

But the sand feels so good beneath my feet, like one of those squishy bean bag pillows you sink into. And I hear music up ahead. I love music. Closing my eyes, my body moves to the unfamiliar song.

I haven't realized how far I've walked and danced until the sound of laughing and voices in Spanish make me freeze. People wearing red and black bandannas in front of me are a clue I've gone past the fourth pier.

"Look everybody, it's Brittany Ellis, Fairfield High's sexiest pom-pom girl," a guy says. "Come here, *mamacita*. Dance with me."

I scan the crowd desperately for a familiar or friendly face. Alex. He's here. Sitting in his lap facing him is Carmen Sanchez.

A sobering picture.

Another guy advances on me. "Don't you know this side of the beach is for *Mexicanos* only?" he says, moving closer. "Or maybe you've come sniffin' for some dark meat. You know what they say, baby—dark meat's the juiciest."

"Leave me alone." My words are slurred.

"You think you're too good for me?" He moves toward me, his eyes full of anger. The music stops.

I stagger backward. I'm not too drunk to know I'm in danger.

"Javier, lay off." Alex's voice is low—it's an order.

Alex is caressing Carmen's shoulder, his lips mere inches from it. I sway. This is a nightmare and I need to get away, fast.

I start running, the gang members' laughter ringing in my ears. I can't run fast enough and feel like I'm in a dream where my feet are moving but I'm not going anywhere.

"Brittany, wait!" a voice calls from behind me.

I turn around and am face-to-face with the guy who's haunting my dreams . . . daydreams and night dreams.

Alex.

The guy who I hate.

The guy who I can't get out of my mind, no matter how drunk I am.

"Ignore Javier," Alex says. "Sometimes he gets carried away tryin' to be a badass." I'm stunned when he steps closer and wipes away a tear from my cheek. "Don't cry. I wouldn't let him hurt you."

Should I tell him I'm not afraid of being hurt? I'm afraid of not being in control.

Though I haven't run far, it's far enough from Alex's friends. They can't see me or hear me.

"Why do you like Carmen?" I ask as the world tilts and I stumble in the sand. "She's mean."

He holds out his hands to help me but I flinch, so he stuffs his hands in his pockets. "What the fuck do you care, anyway? You stood me up."

"I had stuff going on."

"Like washin' your hair or gettin' a manicure?"

Or having my hair ripped out by my sister and getting reamed out by my mom? I jab my finger into his chest. "You're an asshole."

"And you're a bitch," he says. "A bitch with a kick-ass smile and eyes that can seriously screw with a guy's head." He winces, as if the words slipped out and he wants to take them back.

I was expecting him to say a lot of things, but not that. Especially not that. I notice his bloodshot eyes. "You're high, Alex."

"Yeah, well you don't look too sober yourself. Maybe now's a good time to give me that kiss you owe me."

"No way."

"*¿Por qué no?* Afraid you'll like it so much you'll forget your boyfriend?"

Kiss Alex? Never. Although I've been thinking about it. A lot. More than I should. His lips are full and inviting. Oh, boy, he's right. I am drunk. And I'm definitely not feeling right. I'm past numbness and going on delirium, because I'm thinking things I have no business thinking. Like how I want to know what his lips feel like against mine.

"Fine. Kiss me, Alex," I say, stepping forward and leaning into him. "Then we'll be even."

His hands are braced on my arms. This is it. I'm going to kiss Alex and find out what it's like. He's dangerous and he mocks me. But he's sexy and dark and beautiful. Being this close to him makes my body shiver with excitement and my head spin. I loop my finger through his belt loop to steady myself. It's like we're standing on a Tilt-a-Whirl ride at the carnival.

"You're gonna be sick," he says to me.

"Am not. I'm . . . enjoying the ride."

"We're not on a ride."

"Oh," I say, all confused. I let go of his belt loop and focus on my feet. They look like they're moving off the ground, floating over the sand. "I'm dizzy, that's all. I'm fine."

"The hell you are."

"If you'd stop moving, I'd feel a lot better."

"I'm not movin'. And I hate to break the bad news, *mamacita*, but you're about to puke."

He's right. My stomach won't stop churning. He's holding me up with one hand while his other hand is wound in my hair, keeping it away from my face as I bend over and throw up.

I can't stop my stomach from roiling. I throw up and heave again. Disgusting gurgling and gagging sounds come from my mouth, but I'm too drunk to care.

"Look at that," I say between puking fits. "My dinner is all over your shoe."

20

Alex

I look down at the chunks on my shoe. "I've had worse done to me."

She straightens, so I let go of her hair, which I couldn't help but save from falling in her face during her puking episode. I'm trying not to think of how that hair felt as it slid through my fingers like silky threads.

Thoughts of being a pirate and stealing her away to my ship race across my mind. Although I'm not a pirate, and she's not my captured princess. We're just two teenagers who hate each other. Okay, so I don't really hate her.

I slide the bandanna off my head and hand it to her. "Here, wipe your face."

She takes it from me and dabs the sides of her mouth as if it's a napkin from a high-class restaurant while I clean my shoe in the cold Lake Michigan water.

I don't know what to say or do. I'm alone . . . with a very drunk Brittany Ellis. I'm not used to being alone with sloppy-drunk white chicks, especially ones who turn me on. I can either take advantage of her and win the bet, which would be a slam dunk in her condition or . . .

"Let me get someone to drive you home," I say before my fucked-up mind thinks of a million ways I could violate her tonight. I'm buzzed from alcohol and high, too. When I have sex with this girl, I want all my faculties.

She purses her lips and pouts like a kid. "No. I don't want to go home. Anywhere but home."

Oh, man.

I'm in trouble. *Tengo un problema grande.*

She looks up at me, her eyes in the moonlight sparking like rare, expensive jewels. "Colin thinks I want you, you know. He says our bickering is foreplay."

"Is it?" I ask, holding my breath to hear her response. Please, please let me remember the answer in the morning.

She puts her finger up and says, "Hold that thought."

Then she kneels on the ground and pukes her guts out again. When she's finished, she's too weak to walk. She resembles a garage-sale left-over rag doll. I carry her to where my friends have built a huge bonfire, not knowing what else to do.

When she wraps her arms around my neck, I sense she needs someone to be her champion in life. Surely Colin isn't the one. I'm not the one, either. I heard her freshman year, before Colin, she dated a junior. The girl has got to be experienced.

So how come right now she looks so innocent? Sexy as hell, but innocent.

All eyes are on me when I get close to my friends. They see a limp, rich white girl in my arms and they immediately think the worst. I didn't mention that during the walk my chem partner decided to fall asleep in my arms.

"What did you do to her?" Paco asks.

Lucky stands, totally pissed. "Shit, Alex. Did I lose my RX-7?"

"No, dumbass. I don't do passed-out chicks."

Out of the corner of my eye I see a seething Carmen. Shit. I royally screwed her over tonight and deserve her wrath.

I motion for Isabel to talk to me. "Isa, I need you."

Isa takes one look at Brittany. "What do you want me to do with her?"

"Help me get her out of here. I'm wasted and can't drive."

Isa shakes her head. "You do realize she has a boyfriend. And she's rich. And white. And wears designer clothes you'll never be able to afford."

Yeah, I know that. And I'm sick and tired of being reminded of it. "I need your help, Isa. Not a lecture. I've got Paco givin' me his crap already."

Isa holds up her hands. "I'm just pointing out facts. You're a smart guy, Alex. Add it up. No matter how much you might want her in your life, she doesn't belong. A triangle can't fit into a square. Now I'll shut up."

"*Gracias.*" I don't point out that if it's a big enough square, a small triangle can fit inside perfectly. All you have to do is make a few adjustments in the equation. I'm too drunk and high to explain it now.

"I'm parked across the street," Isa says. She lets out a big, frustrated sigh. "Follow me."

I follow Isabel to her car, hoping we can walk in silence. No such luck.

"I was in class with her last year, too," Isa says.

"Uh-huh."

She shrugs. "Nice girl. Wears too much makeup."

"Most chicks hate her."

"Most chicks wish they looked like her. And they wish they had her money and boyfriend."

I stop and regard her in disgust. "Burro Face?"

"Oh, please, Alex. Colin Adams is cute, he's the captain of the football team and Fairfield's hero. You're like Danny Zuko in *Grease*. You smoke, you're in a gang, and you've dated the hottest bad girls around. Brittany is like Sandy . . . a Sandy who'll never show up to school in a black leather jacket with a ciggie hangin' from her mouth. Give up the fantasy."

I lay my fantasy in the backseat of Isa's car and slide in next to her. She snuggles up, using me as her personal pillow, her blond curls sprawled over my crotch. I close my eyes for a second, trying to get the image out of my head. And I don't know what to do with my hands. My right one is on the door armrest. My left one hovers over Brittany.

I hesitate. Who am I kidding? I'm not a virgin. I'm an eighteen-year-old guy who can deal with having a hot, passed-out girl next to me. Why am I afraid of putting my arm where it's comfortable, right over her midsection?

I hold my breath as I settle my arm on her. She cuddles closer and I'm feeling weird and light-headed. Either it's the aftereffects from the joint or . . . I don't want to think about the "or." Her long hair is wrapped around my thigh. Without thinking, I weave my hands in her hair and watch as the silky strands slowly fall through the V's between my fingers. I stop abruptly. There's a big, irritated bald spot on her scalp in the back of her head. As if she had to have a drug test for a job or something and they ripped out a big chunk for a sample.

As Isa backs up the car, Paco stops her and jumps into the front seat. I quickly cover Brittany's bald spot, not wanting to show anyone her imperfection. I'm not about to analyze my motives for that move, since it'll cause me to think too hard. Thinking hard in my condition will hurt badly.

"Hey, guys. I thought I'd come along for the ride," Paco says.

He turns around and sees my arm on Brittany. He tsk's and shakes his head.

"Shut up," I tell him.

"I didn't say anythin'."

A cell phone rings. I can feel the vibration through Brittany's pants.

"It's hers," I say.

"Answer it," Isa instructs.

I already feel like I've kidnapped the girl. Now I'm gonna answer her cell? Shit. Rolling her a bit, I feel for the bulge in her back pocket.

"*Contesta,*" Isa whispers loudly, this time in Spanish.

"I am," I hiss, my fingers clumsy as I fumble for the phone.

"I'll do it," Paco says, leaning over the seats and reaching toward Brittany's ass.

I whack his hand away. "Get your hands off her."

"Geez, man, I was just tryin' to help."

My response is a glare.

I slide my fingers into her back pocket, trying not to think about what it would feel like without her jeans in the way. I slide the phone out inch by inch while it vibrates. When I have the phone free, I look at the caller ID.

"It's her friend Sierra."

"Answer it," Paco says.

"*Estás loco, güey?* I'm not talking to one of *them*."

"Then why'd you get it out of her pocket?"

That's a good question. One I don't know how to answer.

hat's what you get for mixing with a

sq

"We should take her home," Paco says. "You can't keep her."

I know that. But I'm not ready to give her up just yet. "Isa, take her to your house."

21

Brittany

I'm having a nightmare that a thousand little Oompa Loompas are in my head, hammering my skull. Opening my eyes to bright light, I wince. The Oompa Loompas are still in there, and I'm awake.

"You've got a hangover," a girl says to me.

When I squint, I find Isabel standing over me. We're in what looks like a small bedroom with walls painted a pastel yellow. Matching yellow curtains are billowing in the wind from the open windows. It can't be my house because we never open the windows. We always have the air-conditioning or heat on.

I squint up at her. "Where am I?"

"My house. I wouldn't move if I were you. You might puke again and my parents will freak if you mess up their carpeting," she says. "Lucky for us they're out of town, so I get the house to myself until tonight."

"How did I get here?" The last thing I remember was starting to walk home. . . .

"You passed out at the beach. Alex and I brought you here."

At the mention of Alex, my eyes open fully. I vaguely remember drinking, then walking on the sand and finding Alex and Carmen together. And then Alex and I . . .

Did I kiss him? I know I leaned in, but then . . .

I puked. I distinctly remember puking. Not the perfect image I'm trying to project. I sit up slowly, hoping sometime soon my head will stop spinning. "Did I do anything stupid?" I ask.

Isa shrugs. "I'm not sure. Alex wouldn't really let anyone get close enough to you. If you want to call passing out in his arms stupid, then I think you've managed it."

I drop my head in my hands. "Oh, no. Isabel, please don't tell anyone on the squad."

She's smiling. "Don't worry. I won't tell anyone that Brittany Ellis is in fact human."

"Why are you nice to me? I mean, when Carmen wanted to beat my face in, you defended me. And you let me sleep here last night, even though you made it very clear we're not friends."

"We're not friends. Carmen and I have a rivalry that goes way back. I'd do just about anything to piss her off. She can't stand that Alex isn't her boyfriend anymore."

"Why did they break up?"

"Ask him yourself. He's sleeping on the couch in the living room. He passed out as soon as he carried you to my bed." Oh, no. Alex is here? In Isabel's house? "He likes you, you know," Isabel says, looking at her fingernails instead of at me.

Butterflies start flittering around in my stomach. "He does not," I say, even though I'm tempted to ask for details.

She rolls her eyes. "Oh, please. You know it, even if you don't want to admit it."

"For someone who says they'll never be friends with me, you sure are sharing a lot this morning."

"I have to admit I kinda wish you were the bitch some people say you are," she says.

"Why?"

"Because it's easy to hate someone who has it all."

A short, cynical laugh escapes from my mouth. I'm not about to tell her the truth—that my life is crumbling beneath my toes just like that sand was last night. "I've got to get home. Where's my cell?" I ask, patting my back pocket.

"Alex has it, I think."

So sneaking out without talking to him isn't an option. I struggle to keep the Oompa Loompas at bay as I stagger out of the bedroom, searching for Alex.

It's not hard to find him, the house is smaller than Sierra's pool house. Alex is lying on an old sofa, wearing jeans. Nothing else. His eyes are open, but they're bloodshot and glazed with sleep.

"Hey," he says warmly while stretching.

Oh, God. I'm in big trouble. Because I'm staring. I can't keep my eyes from ogling his chiseled triceps and biceps and every other "eps" he has. The butterflies in my stomach have just multiplied tenfold as my wandering gaze meets his.

"Hey." I swallow, hard. "I, um, guess I should thank you for taking me here instead of leaving me passed out on the beach."

His gaze doesn't falter. "Last night I realized somethin'. You and I, we're not so different. You play the game just like I do. You use your looks, your bod, and your brains to make sure you're always in control."

"I'm hungover, Alex. I can't even think straight and you're getting all philosophical on me."

"See, you're playin' a game right now. Be real with me, *mamacita*. I dare you."

Is he kidding? Be real? I can't. Because then I'll start crying, and maybe freak out enough to blurt the truth—that I create a perfect image so I can hide behind it. "I better get home."

"Before you do that, you should probably go to the bathroom," he says.

Before I ask why, I catch a glimpse of my reflection in a mirror hanging on the wall. "Oh, shit!" I shriek. Black mascara is caked under my eyes and streaky lines of it are running down my cheeks.

I resemble a corpse. Hurrying past him, I find the hall bathroom and stare at myself in the mirror. My hair is a stringy bird's nest. If the mascara marring my cheeks wasn't bad enough, the rest of me is as pale as my aunt Dolores without her makeup. I have puffy bags under my eyes as if I'm storing water for the winter months.

All in all, not a pretty sight. By anyone's standards.

I wet toilet paper and rub under my eyes and on my cheeks until the streaks are gone. Okay, so I need my eye-makeup remover in order to get it completely off. And my mom warned me that rubbing under my eyes will stretch out my skin and I'll be subject to premature wrinkles. But desperate circumstances call for desperate measures. After the mascara streaks are unnoticeable, I dab cold water on my eye bags.

I'm fully aware that this is damage control. I can only bandage the imperfections and hope nobody else sees me in this condition. I use my fingers as a comb, with little results. Then I poof my hair up, hoping the poof look will be better than the ratty-nest look.

I rinse my mouth with water and rub my teeth with some toothpaste, hoping to get the worst of the night of puking and sleeping and drunkenness from my mouth until I get home.

If only I had lip gloss with me. . . .

But, alas, I don't. Squaring my shoulders and keeping my head held high, I open the door and walk back to the living room to find Isabel walking to her room and Alex standing when he sees me.

"Where's my cell phone?" I ask. "And please put a shirt on."

He reaches down and grabs my phone off the floor. "Why?"

"The reason I need my cell," I say as I take it from him, "is to call a cab and the reason I want you to put a shirt on is, well, because, um . . ."

"You've never seen a guy with his shirt off?"

"Ha, ha. Very funny. Believe me, you don't have anything I haven't seen before."

"Wanna bet?" he says, then moves his hands to the button on his jeans and pops it open.

Isabel walks in at that exact moment. "Whoa, Alex. Please keep your pants on."

When she looks over at me I put my hands up. "Don't look at me. I was just about to call a cab when he—"

Shaking her head while Alex buttons back up, she walks to her purse and picks up a set of keys. "Forget the cab. I'll drive you home."

"*I'll* drive her," Alex cuts in.

Isabel seems exhausted dealing with us, similar to how Mrs. Peterson looks during chemistry class. "Would you rather me drive you, or Alex?" she asks.

I have a boyfriend. Okay, so I admit every time I catch Alex looking at me a warmth spreads through my body. But it's normal. We're two teenagers with obvious sexual tension passing between us. As long as I never act on it, everything will be just fine.

Because if I ever did act on it, the consequences would be disastrous. I'd lose Colin. I'd lose my friends. I'd lose the control I have over my life.

Most of all, I'd lose what's left of my mother's love.

If I'm not seen as perfect, what happened yesterday with my mom would seem tame. Being perfect to the outside world equates to how my mom treats me. If any of her country club friends see me out with Alex, my mom might as well be an outcast too. If she's shunned by her friends, I'll be shunned by her. I can't take that chance. This is as real as I can afford to get.

"Isabel, take me home," I say, then look at Alex.

He gives a small shake of his head, grabs his shirt and keys, and storms out the front door without another word.

I silently follow Isabel to her car.

"You like Alex more than as a friend, don't you?" I ask.

"More like a brother. We've known each other since we were kids."

I give her directions to my house. Is she telling me the truth? "You don't think he's hot?"

"I've known him since he cried like a baby when his ice cream fell on the street when we were four years old. I was there when, well . . . just leave it at the fact that we've been through a lot of stuff together."

"Stuff? Want to elaborate?"

"Not with you."

I could almost see the invisible wall going up between us. "So our friendship ends here?"

She looks at me sideways. "Our friendship just began, Brittany. Don't push it."

We're coming up to my house. "It's the third one on the right," I say.

"I know." She stops her car in front of my house, not bothering to pull into the driveway. I look at her. She looks at me. Does she expect me to ask her in? I don't even let good friends come into my house.

"Well, thanks for the ride," I say. "And for letting me crash at your place."

Isabel flashes me a weak smile. "No problem."

I cling to the door handle. "I won't let anything happen between me and Alex. Okay?" Even if there's something going on below the surface.

"Good. Because if something does, it's going to blow up in your faces."

The Oompa Loompas start knocking again, so I can't think too hard about her warning.

In the house, my mother and father are sitting at the kitchen table. It's quiet. Too quiet. There are papers in front of them. Brochures or something. They quickly straighten, like little kids caught doing something wrong.

"I . . . I thought you were st—still . . . at Sierra's," my mom says. My senses pick up. My mom *never* stutters. And she's not giving me shit about the way I look. This is not good.

"I was, but I got a killer headache," I say, walking forward and focusing on the suspicious brochures my parents are so interested in.

Sunny Acres Home for Special People.

"What are you guys doing?"

"Discussing our options," my dad says.

"Options? Didn't we all agree that sending Shelley away was a bad idea?"

My mom turns to me. "No. *You* decided sending her away was a bad idea. We were still discussing it."

"I'm going to Northwestern next year so I can live at home and help."

"Next year you'll have to concentrate on your studies, not your sister. Brittany, listen," my dad says, standing. "We have to look into this option. After what she did to you yesterday—"

"I don't want to hear it," I tell him, cutting him off. "There is absolutely no way I'm letting you send my sister away." I snatch the brochures off the table. Shelley needs to be with her family, not in a facility with some strangers. I tear the brochures in two, toss them into the garbage can, then run to my bedroom.

"Open the door, Brit," my mom says, jiggling my bedroom doorknob a minute later.

I sit on the edge of my bed, my mind whirling with the image of Shelley being sent away. No, it can't happen. The thought makes me sick. "You didn't even train Baghda. It's like you wanted to send Shelley away all along."

"Don't be ridiculous," my mom's muffled voice comes through the door. "There's a new facility being built in Colorado. If you'd open this door we can have a civilized discussion about it."

I'll never let it happen. I'll do everything in my power to keep my sister at home.

"I don't want to have a civilized discussion. My parents want to send my sister to a *facility* behind my back and my head feels like it's about to split open. Leave me alone, okay?"

Something is sticking out of my pocket. It's Alex's bandanna. Isabel isn't a friend, yet she helped me. And Alex, a boy who cared about me last night more than my own boyfriend did, acted as my hero and is urging me to be real. Do I even know how to be real?

I clutch the bandanna to my chest.

And I allow myself to cry.

22

Alex

She called me. If it weren't for the ripped piece of paper with her name and number scribbled on it by my brother Luis, I'd never believe Brittany actually dialed my number. Grilling Luis hadn't helped because the kid has the memory of a flea and hardly remembered taking the call. The only info I got was that she wanted me to call her back.

That was yesterday afternoon, before she puked her guts out on my shoe and passed out in my arms.

When I told her to be real, I could see the fear in her eyes. I wonder what she's afraid of. Breaking down her "perfection" wall is going to be my goal. I know there's more to her than blond streaks and a killer bod. Secrets she'll take to the grave and secrets she's dying to share. Oh, man. She's like a mystery, and all I can think about is unraveling the clues.

When I told her we're similar, I wasn't bullshitting. This connection we have isn't going away, it's only getting stronger. Because the more I spend time with her, the closer I want to be.

I have the urge to call Brittany just to hear her voice, even if it's filled with venom. Flipping open my cell as I sit on the sofa in my living room, I enter her number into memory.

"Who ya' callin'?" Paco asks, barging into my house without ringing or knocking. Isa files in behind him.

I click my phone shut. *"Nadie."*

"Then get your ass off that couch and come play soccer."

Playing soccer is a helluva lot better than sitting here thinking about Brittany and her secrets, even if I'm still feeling the effects of last night's partying. We head to the park where a bunch of guys are already warming up.

Mario, a guy in my class whose brother died in a drive-by last year, slaps me on the back. "Wanna play goalie, Alex?"

"No." I have what you call an offensive personality. In soccer, and in life.

"Paco, what about you?"

Paco agrees and takes his position, which is sitting on his ass in front of the goal line. As usual, my lazy friend sits until the ball rolls to his side of the field.

Most of the guys playing are from my neighborhood. We've grown up together . . . played on this playground since we were kids and even got initiated into the Latino Blood at the same time. Before I was jumped in I remember Lucky telling us how being in a gang was like having a second family . . . a family who would be there for you when your own family wasn't. They would offer protection and security. It sounded perfect to a kid who'd lost his father.

Over the years, I've learned to block out the bad stuff. The beatings, the dirty drug deals, the shootings. And I'm not just talking about guys on the other side. I know of guys who tried to get out, guys who were found dead or beaten so badly by their own gang they probably wished they were dead.

To be honest, I block it out 'cause it scares the shit out of me. I'm supposed to be tough enough not to care, but I do.

We take our positions on the field. I imagine the ball holds a jack-pot. If I keep it away from everyone else and kick it into the goal, I'll magically transform into a rich and powerful guy who can take my family (and Paco) away from this hellhole neighborhood.

There's a lot of good players on each team. The other side has an advantage because we have Paco as our goalie, scratching his balls on the other end of the field.

"Yo, Paco. Stop playin' with yourself!" Mario yells.

Paco's answer is making a huge point of grabbing his balls and juggling them in his hands. Chris shoots the ball right past him and scores.

Mario picks up the ball from inside the goal and chucks it at Paco. "If you were as interested in the game as you are in your *huevos*, they wouldn't have scored."

"I can't help it if they itch, man. Your girlfriend must have given me crabs last night."

Mario laughs, not believing for a second his girlfriend would cheat on him. Paco tosses the ball to Mario, who passes to Lucky. Lucky brings the ball downfield. He passes it to me and I have my chance. I dribble down the makeshift field, pausing only to gauge how far I have to go before I kick it into the goal.

Faking to the left, I pass to Mario and he passes it back. With one swift kick, the ball soars right and we've scored.

"Goooaaaallll," our team sings as Mario gives me a high five.

Our celebration is short-lived, though. A blue Escalade is creeping suspiciously down the street.

"Recognize it?" Mario asks, tensing.

The game stops as guys realize there's something not cool. "Maybe it's retaliation," I say.

My eyes never leave the car window. When the car stops, we're all waiting for a glimpse of either someone or something to emerge from the car. When it does, we'll be ready.

But I'm not. My brother Carlos steps out of the car with a guy named Wil. Wil's ma is in the Blood and recruits new members. My brother better not be one of those recruits. I've worked too damn hard making sure he knows I'm in the Blood so he doesn't have to be. If one family member is in, the rest are protected. I'm in. Carlos and Luis aren't, and I'll do anything to make sure they stay that way.

I put on a game face and walk over to Wil, soccer completely forgotten. "New car?" I ask him, eyeing his wheels.

"It's my mom's."

"Nice." I turn to my brother. "Where have you guys been hangin'?"

Carlos leans against the car, as if hanging with Wil is no big deal. Wil got initiated recently and now he thinks he's the shit. "At the mall. They've got this cool new guitar store. Hector met us there and—"

Did I hear right? "Hector?" The last thing I want is my brother hanging around Hector.

Wil, with his big shirt hanging over his pants, whacks Carlos on the shoulder to shut him up. My brother closes his mouth as if something was about to fly in it. I swear I'll kick his ass from here to Mexico if he even thinks about joining the Blood.

"Fuentes, you in or out?" someone yells from the field.

Keeping my anger hidden, I turn to my brother and his friend, who's capable of luring him to the dark side. "Wanna play?"

"Nah. We're gonna hang at my house," Wil says.

I shrug nonchalantly, not feeling the least bit nonchalant. *¡Qué me importa!*

I walk to the field, even if I have the urge to grab Carlos by the ear and drag him home. I can't afford to cause a scene that might get back to Hector, who might start questioning my loyalty.

Sometimes I feel my life is one big lie.

Carlos leaves with Wil. That, combined with the fact that I can't get Brittany out of my mind, is driving me nuts. On the field, when the game starts back up, I'm restless. Suddenly, it's like the players on the other team aren't guys I know, but enemies in the way of everything I want. I charge the ball.

"Foul!" a cousin of one of my friends yells at me when I slam into him.

I put up my hands. "That was *not* a foul."

"You pushed me."

"Don't be a *panocha*," I say, knowing I'm blowing it out of proportion.

I want to get in a fight. I'm asking for it. He knows it. The guy is about my height, my weight. My adrenaline is running high.

"You want a piece of me, *pendejo*?" he says, holding his arms out wide like a bird in flight.

Intimidation doesn't work with me. "Come and get it."

Paco runs in between us. "Alex, cool down, man."

"Either fight or play!" someone shouts.

"He said I made a foul," I tell Paco, my veins pumping.

Paco shrugs casually. "You did."

Okay, now when my own best friend doesn't back me up, I know I've lost it. I look around. Everyone is waiting to see what I'm going to do. My adrenaline is in overdrive, matching their heightened anticipation. Do I want to fight? Yeah, if only to get this raw energy out of my body. And to forget, even for a minute, that my chem partner's number is cued up in my cell. And my brother is on the Blood radar to be recruited.

My best friend shoves me away from the guy wanting to rip my head off and pushes me to the side of the field. He calls out for subs to take our place in the game.

"What'd you do that for?" I ask.

"To save your hide, man. Alex, you've lost it. Completely."

"I can take that guy."

Paco looks straight at me and says, "You're the one actin' like a *panocha*."

I shrug his hands off my shirt and stalk off not knowing how, in the matter of a few weeks, I've gotten my life screwed up so badly. I need to fix it. I'll deal with Carlos when he comes home tonight. He's gonna get an earful from me. And Brittany . . .

She didn't want me to drive her home from Isa's house because she didn't want to be seen with me. Fuck that shit. Carlos isn't the only one who deserves an earful from me.

I flip open my cell and cue Brittany's number.

"Hello?"

"It's Alex," I tell her, although she has caller ID and knows damn well it's me. "Meet me at the library. Now."

"I can't."

This is not the Brittany Ellis Show. It's the Alex Fuentes Show now. "Here's the deal, *mamacita*," I say as I reach my house and straddle my motorcycle. "You either show up at the library in fifteen minutes or I'm bringin' five friends to your house and we're campin' out on your front lawn tonight."

"How dare you—" she starts to say, but I close the phone before she can finish her sentence.

Revving the engine to block out thoughts of last night when she snuggled into my lap, I realize I don't have a game plan.

I wonder if the Alex Fuentes Show will end up being a comedy or, more likely, a tragedy. Either way, it'll be a reality show worth not missing.

23

Brittany

I'm steaming mad as I pull into the library parking lot and park next to the woods at the far end of the lot. The last thing on my mind is our chemistry project.

Alex is waiting for me, leaning against his motorcycle. I take the keys out of the ignition and storm over to him. "How dare you order me around!" I yell. My entire life is full of people trying to control me. My mom . . . Colin. And now Alex. I'm done with it. "If you think you can threaten me into—"

Without saying anything Alex snatches my keys out of my hand and sits in the driver's seat of my Beemer.

"Alex, what do you think you're doing?"

"Get in."

The engine roars. He's going to drive off and leave me stranded in the library parking lot.

Clenching my fists, I stomp to the passenger side. When I'm in, Alex revs the engine.

"Where's my picture of Colin?" I ask, eyeing my dashboard. It was taped up there a minute ago.

"Don't worry, you'll get it back. I don't have the stomach to look at it while I'm drivin'."

"Do you even know how to drive a stick?" I bark out.

Without blinking or looking down, he puts the car into first gear and the car screeches out of the lot. My Beemer follows his lead as if the car and Alex are completely in sync.

"This is carjacking, you know." Silence. "And kidnapping," I add.

We're stopped at a light. I look at the cars around us, glad the top is up so no one can see us.

"*Mira*, you got in on your own free will," he says.

"It's *my* car. What if someone sees us?"

My words really piss him off, because the tires screech angrily when the light turns green. He's purposely ruining my car.

"Stop it!" I order. "Take me back to the library."

But he doesn't. He's silent as he winds my car through unknown towns and deserted roads, just like people do in the movies when they drive to meet dangerous drug dealers.

Great. I'm going on my first drug deal. If I get arrested, will my parents come bail me out? I wonder how my mom's going to explain that one to her friends. Maybe they'll send me away to some military boot camp for delinquents. I bet they'd like that . . . making Shelley go to a facility and me to boot camp.

My life would suck even more.

I will not be a part of anything illegal. I am the ruler of my destiny, not Alex. I grab the handle to the door. "Let me out of here or I swear I'm jumping out."

"You're wearin' a seatbelt." He rolls his eyes. "Relax. We'll be there in two minutes." He shifts into a lower gear and slows the car as we enter an old, deserted airport. "Okay, we're here," he says as he pulls up the parking brake.

"Yeah, okay. But where is *here?* I hate to tell you but the last inhabited place was, like, three miles back. I'm not getting out of the car, Alex. You can do your drug deals on your own."

"If I had any doubts you were a true blond, you've squelched them," he says. "As if I'd take you on a drug deal. Get out of the car."

"Give me one good reason why I should?"

"Because if you don't, I'm gonna drag you out. Trust me, *mujer.*"

He puts my keys in his back pocket and steps out of my car. Seeing no other options, I follow him. "Listen, if you wanted to discuss our hand warmers we could have done it over the phone."

He meets me around the back of my car. We're standing, toe to toe, in the middle of nowhere.

There's been something nagging at me all day. As long as I'm here with him, I might as well ask. "Did we kiss last night?"

"Yes."

"Well, it wasn't memorable because I have no recollection of it."

He laughs. "I was kiddin'. We didn't kiss." He leans in. "When we kiss you'll remember it. Forever."

Oh, God. I wish his words didn't leave my knees weak. I know I should be scared, alone with a gang member in a deserted place talking about kissing. But I'm not. Deep in my soul I know he wouldn't intentionally hurt me or force me to do anything.

"Why did you kidnap me?" I ask.

He grabs my hand and leads me to the driver's side. "Get in."

"Why?"

"I'm teachin' you how to drive this car properly, before the engine falls out from abuse."

"I thought you were mad at me. Why are you helping me?"

"Because I want to."

Oh. I wasn't expecting that at all. My heart is starting to thaw, because it's been a long time since someone cared enough to do something just to help me. Although . . . "This isn't because you want me to pay you back with favors, is it?"

He shakes his head.

"For real?"

"For real."

"And you're not mad at me because of anything I said or did?"

"I'm frustrated, Brittany. About you. About my brother. About a lot of shit."

"Then why take me here?"

"Don't ask questions you're not ready to hear the answer to. Cool?"

"Cool." I slide into the driver's seat and wait for him to sit beside me.

"You ready?" he asks when he's settled and buckled in the passenger seat.

"Yep."

He leans over and puts the keys in the ignition. When I release the parking brake and start the car, it dies.

"You didn't put it in neutral. If you don't have your foot on the clutch, it's gonna die if you're in gear."

"I knew that," I say, feeling totally stupid. "You're just making me nervous."

He puts the stick into neutral for me. "Put your left foot on the clutch, your right foot on the brake, and go into first," he instructs.

Putting my foot on the gas and letting up on the clutch, the car jerks forward.

He braces himself with his hand on the dash. "Stop."

I stop the car and put it in neutral.

"You've got to find the sweet spot."

I look at him. "The sweet spot?"

"Yeah. You know, when the clutch catches." He's using his hands when he talks, pretending his hands are the pedals. "You release it too fast. Get that balance and stay there . . . feel it out. Try again."

I put the car in first again and let up on the clutch as I press on the gas.

"Hold it . . . ," he says. "Feel the sweet spot. Linger there."

I let out the clutch and hold down the gas pedal but don't push down on it all the way. "I think I got it."

"Let go of the clutch now, but don't gun the gas."

I try, but the car jerks, then stalls.

"You popped the clutch. Don't release the clutch too fast. Try again," he says, totally unfazed. He's not upset, frustrated, or itching to give up. "You needed to give it more gas. Don't gun it, but give it enough juice to start movin'."

I do the same steps, but this time the car moves forward without jerking. We're on the runway, moving up to ten miles an hour.

"Press in the clutch," he instructs, then puts his hand over mine on the stick and helps me shift into second. I try to ignore his gentle touch and the warmth of his hand, so contradictory to his personality, and attempt to focus on the task.

He's very patient as he instructs in detail how to downshift until we've come to a stop at the end of the runway. His fingers are still wrapped around mine.

"Lesson over?" I ask.

Alex clears his throat. "Um, yeah." He takes his hand off mine, then weaves his fingers through his black mane, strands falling loosely across his forehead.

"Thanks," I say.

"Yeah, well, my ears were bleedin' every time I heard your engine rev in the lot at school. I didn't do it to be a good guy."

I cock my head to the side and try and get him to look at me. He doesn't. "Why is it so important that you're perceived as a bad boy, huh? Tell me."

24

Alex

For the first time we're having a civilized discussion. Now I've got to come up with something to break that defensive wall of hers.

Oh, man. I need to reveal something that makes me vulnerable. If she sees me as vulnerable instead of an asshole, maybe I can make some headway with her. And somehow I know she'll be able to tell if I'm bullshitting.

I'm not sure if I'm doing this for the bet, for the chemistry project, or for me. In fact, I'm totally cool with *not* analyzing that part of what's happening here.

"My dad was murdered in front of me when I was six," I tell her.

Her eyes go wide. "Really?"

I nod. I don't like talking about it, not sure I can even if I want to.

Her manicured hands cover her mouth. "I didn't know that. Oh, God, I'm so sorry. That must have been horrible."

"Yep." It feels good to let it out, to make myself talk about it out loud. My dad's nervous smile turning into shock right before he was shot.

Wow, I can't believe I remembered the expression on his face. Why would his smile be replaced by shock? That detail was totally forgotten until now. I'm still confused as I turn to Brittany. "If I care too much about shit and it's taken away, I'll feel like I did the day my dad died. I never want to feel that way, so instead I make myself care about nothin'."

Her face is full of regret, sorrow, and sympathy. I can tell it's not an act.

Her brow is still furrowed when she says, "Thanks for, you know, telling me. But I can't imagine you can actually make yourself care about nothing. You can't program yourself like that."

"Wanna bet?" Suddenly I'm desperate to change the subject. "Your turn to share."

She looks away. I don't push her to say anything for fear she'll come to her senses and want to leave.

Could it be harder for her to share even a glimpse into her world? My life has been so fucked up, it's damn hard to believe her life could possibly be any worse. I watch as a lone tear escapes from her eye and she quickly wipes it away.

"My sister—," she starts. "My sister has cerebral palsy. And is mentally delayed. 'Retarded' is the term most people use. She can't walk, she uses what's called verbal approximations and nonverbal cues instead of words because she can't talk. . . ." With that, another tear escapes. This time she lets it fall without wiping it away. I have the urge to wipe them for her but sense she needs to be left untouched. She takes a deep breath. "And she's been angry about something, but I don't know what. She started pulling hair, and yesterday she pulled mine so hard a clump came out. My head was bleeding and my mom was freaking out on me."

So that's where the mysterious patch of baldness came from. Not a drug test.

For the first time, though, I feel sorry for her. I imagined her life as a fairy tale; the worst thing that could possibly happen would be a pea under her mattress keeping her up at night.

I guess that's not the case.

Something is happening. I sense a change in the wind . . . a mutual understanding of each other. I haven't felt this way in forever. I clear my throat, then say, "Your mom probably blows up at you the most because she knows you can take it."

"Yeah. You're probably right. Better me than my sister."

"It's no excuse, though." I'm being real now, and hope she is, too. "Listen, I don't want to be an asshole to you," I say. So much for the Alex Fuentes Show.

"I know. It's your image, what Alex Fuentes is all about. It's your brand, your logo . . . dangerous, deadly, hot and sexy Mexican. I wrote the book on creating an image. I wasn't exactly aiming for the blond bimbo look, though. More like the perfect, untouchable look."

Whoa. Rewind. Brittany called me hot and sexy. I was not expecting that at all. Maybe I have a chance of winning that stupid bet. "You do realize you called me hot."

"As if you didn't know."

I didn't know *Brittany Ellis* considered me hot. "For the record, I thought you were untouchable. But now that I know you think I'm a hot, sexy, Mexican god . . ."

"I never said the word 'god.'"

I put my finger to my lips. "Shh, let me enjoy the fantasy for one minute." I close my eyes. Brittany laughs, this sweet sound that echoes in my ears.

"In some deranged way, Alex, I think I understand you. Although I'm really pissed off at you for being such a Neanderthal." When I open my eyes, I find her watching me. "Don't tell anyone about my sister," she says. "I don't like people knowing anything about me."

"We're actors in our lives, pretendin' to be who we want people to think we are."

"So you understand why I'd freak out if my parents find out we're . . . friends."

"You'd get in trouble? Shit, you're eighteen. Don't you think you can be friends with who you want to by now? The umbilical cord's been cut, you know."

"You don't understand."

"Try me."

"Why do you want to know so much?"

"Aren't chem partners supposed to know a lot about each other?"

She gives a short laugh. "I hope not."

Truth is, this girl isn't what I thought she'd be. From the moment I told her about my dad, it was as if her entire body sighed in relief. As if someone else's misery comforted her, made her feel as if she wasn't alone. I still can't understand why she cares so much, why she chooses the I-am-flawless facade to show the world.

Looming over my head is The Bet. I have to get this girl to fall for me. And while my body says *go for it*, the rest of me is thinking *You're a complete bastard because she's vulnerable.*

"I want the same things out of life you do," I admit. "I just go about them in a different way. You adapt to your environment, I adapt to mine." I put my hand back on hers. "Let me show you I'm different. *Oye*, would you ever date a guy who couldn't afford to take you to expensive restaurants and buy you gold and diamonds?"

"Absolutely." She slips her hand out from under mine. "But I have a boyfriend."

"If you didn't, would you give this *Mexicano* a chance?"

Her face turns a deep shade of pink. I wonder if Colin ever makes her blush like that. "I'm not answering that," she says.

"Why not? It's a simple question."

"Oh, please. Nothing about you is simple, Alex. Let's not even go there." She puts the car in first gear. "Can we go now?"

"Sí, if you want. Are we cool?"

"I think so."

I hold my hand out for her to shake. She eyes the tattoos on my fingers, then extends her hand toward mine and shakes it, her enthusiasm apparent. "To hand warmers," she says with a smile on her lips.

"To hand warmers," I agree. *And sex,* I add silently.

"Do you want to drive back? I don't know the way."

I drive her back in comfortable silence while the sun sets. Our truce brings me closer to my goals: graduating, the bet . . . and something else I'm not ready to admit.

As I pull her kick-ass car into the dark library parking lot, I say, "Thanks for, you know, lettin' me kidnap you. I guess I'll see you around." Taking my keys out of my front pocket, I wonder if I'll ever be able to afford a car that isn't rusted, used, or old. After I step out of her car, I pull out Colin's picture from my back pocket and toss it on the seat I just vacated.

"Wait!" Brittany calls out as I'm walking away.

I turn around and she's right in front of me. "What?"

She smiles seductively as if she's wanting something more than a truce. Way more. Shit, is she gonna kiss me? I'm taken off guard here, which usually doesn't happen. She bites her bottom lip, as if she's contemplating her next move. I'm totally game to making out with her.

As my brain goes through every scenario, she steps closer to me.

And snatches my keys out of my hand.

"What do you think you're doin'?" I ask her.

"Getting you back for kidnapping me." She steps back and with all her might whips my keys into the woods.

"You did *not* just do that."

She backs up, facing me the entire time, as she moves toward her car. "No hard feelings. Payback's a bitch, ain't it, Alex?" she says, trying to keep a straight face.

I watch in shock as my chem partner gets into her Beemer. The car drives out of the lot without a jolt, jerk, or hitch. Flawless start.

I'm pissed off because I'm going to have to either crawl around in the dark woods trying to find my keys or call Enrique to pick me up.

I'm also amused. Brittany Ellis bested me at my own game.

"Yeah," I say to her even though she's probably a mile away and can't hear me. "Payback *is* a bitch." *¡Carajo!*

25

Brittany

The sound of my sister's heavy breathing beside me is the first thing I hear as early morning sunlight pours into her room. I'd gone to Shelley's room and laid next to her for hours, watching her sleep peacefully before drifting off myself.

When I was little, I would hurry to my sister's room whenever there was a thunderstorm. Not to comfort Shelley, but so she could comfort me. I would hold Shelley's hand and somehow my fears would fade.

Watching my older sister sleep soundly, I can't believe my parents want to send her away. Shelley is a big part of who I am; the thought of living without her seems so—wrong. Sometimes I feel Shelley and I are connected in a way few people understand. Even when our parents can't figure out what Shelley is trying to say, or why she's so frustrated, I usually know.

That's why it devastated me when she pulled my hair. I never really thought she'd do it to me.

But she did.

"I won't let them take you away," I say softly to my sleeping sister. "I'll always protect you."

I ease myself off Shelley's bed. There is no way I can spend time with Shelley without her suspecting I'm upset. So I get dressed and leave the house before she wakes up.

I confided in Alex yesterday and the sky didn't fall. I actually felt better after telling him about Shelley. If I can do it with Alex, surely I can try it with Sierra and Darlene.

As I sit in front of Sierra's house in my car, my thoughts turn to my life.

Nothing is going right. Senior year is supposed to be a blast—easy and fun. So far it's been anything but. Colin is pressuring me, a guy in a gang is more than my chemistry partner, and my parents are going to send my sister far from Chicago. What else can go wrong?

I notice movement coming from Sierra's second-story window. First legs, then a butt. Oh, God, it's Doug Thompson trying to jump to the trellis.

Doug must see me, because Sierra's head pops out of the window. She waves and motions for me to wait.

Doug's foot still hasn't reached the trellis. Sierra is holding onto his hand to steady him. He finally reaches the thing, but the flowers distract him and he falls, flinging his body in all directions. He's fine, though, I realize after he gives Sierra a thumbs-up before jogging off.

I wonder if Colin would climb trellises for me.

Sierra's front door opens three minutes later and she steps out in her underwear and tank top. "Brit, what are you doing here? It's seven o'clock. In the morning. You do realize it's a teacher in-service and we have no school."

"I know, but my life is spinning out of control."

"Come inside and we'll talk," she says, opening my car door. "I'm freezing my butt off here. Oh, why don't the Chicago summers last longer?"

Inside, I take off my shoes so I won't wake up her parents.

"Don't worry, they left for the health club an hour ago."

"Then why was Doug escaping out your window?"

Sierra winks. "You know, to keep the relationship exciting. Guys love adventure."

I follow Sierra into her spacious bedroom. It's decorated in fuchsia and apple green, the colors her mother's decorator picked out for her. I plunk myself down on the extra bed as Sierra calls Darlene. "Dar, come over. Brit's in crisis mode."

Darlene, in her pj's and slippers, arrives a few minutes later since she lives only two houses down.

"Okay, spill," Sierra demands when we're all together.

Suddenly, with all eyes on me, I'm not so sure this sharing thing is such a good idea. "It's not really anything."

Darlene straightens. "Listen, Brit. You got me out of bed at seven a.m. Dish the dirt."

"Yeah," Sierra says. "We're your friends. If you can't share with your friends, who can you share with?"

Alex Fuentes. But I'd never tell them that.

"Why don't we watch old movies," Sierra suggests. "If Audrey Hepburn doesn't get you to spill your guts, nothing will."

Darlene groans. "I can't believe you got me up for a noncrisis and old movies. You guys seriously need to get a life. The least you can do is give me gossip. Anyone have any?"

Sierra leads us to the living room and we all sink into the cushions on her parents' sofa. "I heard Samantha Jacoby was found kissing someone in the custodian closet on Tuesday."

"Whoop-de-doo," Darlene says, totally unimpressed.

"Did I mention it was Chuck, one of the custodians?"

"Now *that* is good gossip, Sierra."

Is that how it's going to be if I share anything, turning my misery into gossip for everyone to laugh about?

In Sierra's living room four hours, two movies, popcorn, and a tub of Ben & Jerry's Confection Connection ice cream later, I'm feeling better. Maybe it was Audrey Hepburn as Sabrina, but somehow I think everything is possible. Which makes me think about . . .

"What do you guys think of Alex Fuentes?" I ask.

Sierra pops a piece of popcorn in her mouth. "What do you mean 'what do we think of him?' "

"I don't know," I say, unable to stop thinking about the intense, undeniable attraction that is always between us. "He's my chemistry partner."

"And . . . ?" Sierra urges, waving her hand in the air as if saying, "So what's your point?"

I grab the remote control and pause the movie. "He's hot. Admit it."

"Eww, Brit," Darlene says, pretending to stick her finger down her throat and gagging.

Sierra says, "Okay, so I admit he's cute. But he's not someone I would ever date. He's, you know, a *gang member*."

"Half the time he comes to school high," Darlene chimes in.

"I sit right next to him, Darlene, and I've never noticed him high at school."

"Are you kidding, Brit? Alex does drugs before school, and in the guys' bathroom when he ditches study hall. And I'm not just talking about pot. He's into the hard stuff," Darlene states like it's fact.

"Have you seen him do drugs?" I challenge.

"Listen, Brit. I don't have to be in the room with him to know he snorts or shoots up. Alex is dangerous. Besides, girls like us don't mix with Latino Bloods."

I lean into the plush cushions of the couch. "Yeah, I know."

"Colin loves you," Sierra says, changing the subject.

Love, I sense, is a far cry from what Colin felt for me at the beach, but I don't even want to go there.

Three times my mom tries to contact me. First on my cell, although turning it off didn't deter her because she called Sierra's house twice.

"Your mom's coming over if you don't talk to her," Sierra says, the phone dangling from her fingers.

"If she does, I'm leaving."

Sierra hands me the phone. "Me and Darlene are going outside so you can have some privacy. I don't know what this is all about, but talk to her."

I hold the phone to my ear. "Hello, Mother."

"Listen, Brittany, I know you're upset. We finalized the plans about Shelley last night. I know it's hard on you, but she's been more and more frustrated lately."

"Mom, she's twenty years old and gets upset when people can't understand her. Don't you think that's normal?"

"You're going to college next year. It's not fair to keep her home anymore. Stop being so selfish."

If Shelley is being sent away because I'm going to college, it *is* my fault. "You're going to do this no matter how I feel about it, aren't you?" I ask.

"Yes. It's a done deal."

26

Alex

When Brittany walks into Mrs. P.'s class on Friday I'm still thinking about how I'm going to get back at her for throwing my keys into the woods last weekend. It took me forty-five minutes to find the suckers, and all the while I was cursing Brittany. Okay, so I give her props for dishing it out. I also have her to thank for helping me talk about the night of my *papá's* death. Because of it, I've called older OG's in the Blood, asking them if they know who might have had a grudge against my dad.

Brittany has been wary this whole week. She's waiting for me to play a joke on her, to get her back for tossing my keys into the woods. After school, as I'm at my locker picking books to take home, she storms up to me wearing her sexy pom uniform.

"Meet me in the wrestling gym," she orders.

Now I can do two things: meet her like she told me to or leave the school. I take my books and enter the small gym. Brittany is standing, holding out her keychain without keys dangling from it.

"Where have my keys magically disappeared to?" she asks. "I'm going to be late for the game if you don't tell me. Ms. Small will kick me off the squad if I'm not at the game."

"I tossed them somewhere. You know, you should really get a purse that has a zipper. You never know when someone will reach in and grab somethin'."

"Glad to know you're a klepto. Wanna give me a hint as to where you've hidden them?"

I lean against the wall of the wrestling gym, thinking about what people would think if they caught us in here together. "It's in a place that's wet. Really, really wet," I say, giving her a clue.

"The pool?"

I nod. "Creative, huh?"

She tries to push me into the wall. "Oh, I'm going to kill you. You better go get them."

If I didn't know her better, I'd think she was flirting with me. I think she likes this game we have going on. "*Mamacita*, you should know me better than that. You're all on your own, like I was when you left me in the library parking lot."

She cocks her head, gives me sad eyes, and pouts. I shouldn't concentrate on her pouty lips, it's dangerous. But I can't help it.

"Show me where they are, Alex. *Please*."

I let her sweat it out a minute before I give in. By now most of the school is deserted. Half of the students are on their way to the football game. The other half is glad they're not on their way to the football game.

We walk to the pool. The lights are off, but sunlight is still shining through the windows. Brittany's keys are where I threw 'em—in the middle of the deep end. I point to the shiny pieces of silver under the water. "There they are. Have at it."

Brittany stands with her hands on her short skirt, contemplating how she's going to get them. She struts over to the long stick hanging on the wall that's used to pull drowning people from the water. "Piece of cake," she tells me.

But as she sticks the pole into the water, she finds out it's not a piece of cake. I suppress a laugh as I stand at the edge of the pool and watch her attempt the impossible.

"You can always strip and go in naked. I'll watch to make sure nobody comes in."

She walks up to me, the pole gripped firmly in her fingers. "You'd like that, wouldn't you?"

"Uh, yeah," I say, stating the obvious. "I have to warn you, though. If you have granny undies on, you'll blow my fantasy."

"For your information, they're pink satin. As long as we're sharing personal info, are you a boxers or briefs guy?"

"Neither. My boys go free, if you know what I mean." Okay, I don't let my boys go free. She'll just have to figure that out herself.

"Gross, Alex."

"Don't knock it till you try it," I tell her, then walk toward the door.

"You're leaving?"

"Uh . . . yeah."

"Aren't you going to help me get the keys?"

"Uh . . . nope." If I stay, I'll be tempted to ask her to ditch the football game to be with me. I'm definitely not ready to hear the answer to that question. Toying with her I can handle. Showing my true colors like I did the other day made me take my guard down. I'm not about to do that again. I push the door open after taking one last glance at Brittany, wondering if leaving her right now makes me an idiot, a jerk, a coward, or all of the above.

At home, when I'm far from Brittany and her car keys, I look for my brother. I promised myself I'd talk to Carlos this week and I've delayed it long enough. Before I know it he'll be jumped in and get the ritual beating as the initiation into the Latino Blood just like I got.

I find Carlos in our bedroom, in the process of shoving something under his bed.

"What was that?" I ask.

He sits on his bed with his arms crossed. *"Nada."*

"Don't give me that *nada* bullshit, Carlos." I push him aside and look under his bed. Sure enough, a shiny .25 Beretta is staring back at me. Mocking me. I pull it out and hold it in my hand. "Where'd you get this?"

"None of your business."

This is the first time in my life I've seriously wanted to scare the crap out of Carlos. I itch to stick that gun in between his eyes and show him what it's like for gang members all the time, to feel threatened and unsure of what day will end up being your last. "I'm your older brother, Carlos. *Se nos fue mi Papá,* so that leaves me to knock some sense into you." I look at the gun. From the weight I can tell it's loaded. Geez, if it accidentally went off, Carlos could be killed. If Luis found it . . . shit, this is bad.

Carlos attempts to stand but I push him back on the bed.

"You go around strapped," he complains. "Why can't I?"

"You know why. I'm a gangbanger. You're not. You're gonna study, go to college, and have a life."

"You think you've got our lives all planned out, don't you?" Carlos spits out. "Well, I've got a plan, too."

"It better not include gettin' jumped in."

Carlos is silent.

I think I've already lost him and my body is as tense as a steel rod. I can prevent the jumping in from happening but only if Carlos is willing to let me intervene. I look at the picture of Destiny above Carlos's bed.

He met her this summer in Chicago when we watched fireworks from Navy Pier on July Fourth. Her family lives in Gurnee and ever since they met he's been obsessed with her. They talk on the phone every night. She's smart, she's Mexican, and when she eyed me and my tattoos when Carlos tried to introduce us she got so scared her eyes darted around as if she'd get shot just being within five feet of me.

"You think Destiny'll want to date you if you're a strapped gang member?" I ask.

No response, which is good. He's thinking.

"She'll dump your ass as soon as you can say 'twenty-five caliber.'"

Carlos's gaze wanders to the picture of her on his wall.

"Carlos, ask her where she's goin' to college. I'll bet she has a plan. If you want the same plan, it's doable."

My brother looks up at me. He's waging a war within himself, choosing between what he knows is coming easy to him—the gang life—and the harder things he wants to go for, like Destiny.

"Stop hangin' around Wil. Find some new friends, and join the soccer team at school or somethin'. Start actin' like a kid and let me take care of the rest."

I stuff the Beretta in the waistband of my jeans and walk out of the house, heading for the warehouse.

27

Brittany

I was late to the football game. After Alex left, I stripped down to my bra and underwear and jumped into the pool to grab my keys. Thanks to Alex, I got a demotion. Darlene, the co-captain of the pom squad, is now officially the captain. It took me a half hour to dry my hair and reapply my makeup in the girl's changing room. Ms. Small was p.o.'d I was late to the game. She told me I should feel lucky I got a demotion instead of being suspended from the squad.

After the game, I lay down on the living room couch with my sister. My hair still smells like chlorine, but I'm too tired to care. As I watch reality shows after dinner, my eyes start to close.

"Brit, wake up. Colin is here," my mom says, shaking me.

I look up at Colin, standing over me. He puts his hands up. "You ready?"

Oh, man. I forgot about Shane's party, which was planned months ago. I'm so not in the mood. "Let's ditch it and stay home."

"Are you kidding? Everyone is expecting us to be there. There's no way you're missing the biggest bash of the year." He looks at my sweat-pants and T-shirt that says GET CHECKED, which I got when I did the

Breast Cancer Walk last year. "I'll wait while you get changed. Hurry up. Why don't you wear that black minidress I love?"

I drag myself to my closet to change. In the corner, lying next to my DKNY tank top, is Alex's bandanna. I washed it last night, but I close my eyes and bring it to my nose to see if his scent lingers in the fabric. All I smell is laundry detergent and find myself disappointed. I'm not ready to analyze my feelings right now, especially since Colin is downstairs waiting for me.

Slipping on the black minidress and fixing my hair and makeup takes a while. I hope Colin isn't pissed I'm taking so long. I have to get it right. My mom will surely comment on my appearance in front of him.

Back downstairs, I see Colin sitting on the edge of the couch ignoring Shelley. I think he's nervous around her.

My mom "the inspector" walks over to me and feels my hair. "Did you condition?"

Does she mean before or after my swim in the pool to retrieve my keys? I push her hand away. "Mom, please."

"You look amazing," Colin says, sidling up beside me.

Thankfully Mom backs away, obviously pleased and comforted by Colin's approval even if my hair isn't perfect.

During the ride to Shane's house, I study my boyfriend of two years. The first time we kissed was during a spin-the-bottle game at Shane's house our sophomore year. We made out in front of everyone, Colin taking me in his arms and kissing me for a full five minutes. Yes, the onlookers timed it. We've been a couple ever since.

"Why are you looking at me like that?" he asks, glancing my way.

"I was remembering the first time we kissed."

"At Shane's place. Yeah, we sure put on a show for everyone, didn't we? Even the seniors back then were impressed."

"Now we're the seniors."

"And we're still the golden couple, babe," he says, pulling into Shane's driveway. "Let the party start, the golden couple has arrived!" Colin yells when we walk into the house.

Colin joins the guys while I search for Sierra. I find her in the living room. Sierra hugs me, then motions to a spot on the sofa next to her. A bunch of girls from the pom squad are here, including Darlene.

"Now that Brit's here," Sierra says, "we can start playing."

"Who would you rather kiss?" Madison asks.

Sierra leans back on the couch. "Let's start easy. Pug or poodle?"

I laugh. "You mean as in dog?"

"Yeah."

"Okay," I say. Poodles are cute and cuddly, but Pugs are more masculine and have that don't-mess-with-me look. As much as I like cute and cuddly, a poodle won't cut it. "Pug."

Morgan scrunches up her face. "Ew! Poodle for sure. Pugs have that pushed-in nose and snorting problem. Not conducive to kissing."

"We're not actually going to try it, dumbass," Sierra says.

"I've got one," I say. "Coach Garrison or Mr. Harris the math teacher?"

Every girl says in unison, "Garrison!"

"He is such a hottie," Megan says.

Sierra giggles. "I hate to break the news, but I hear he's gay."

"No way," Megan says. "You sure? Well, even if he is, I'd still pick him over Harris any day."

"I've got one," Darlene chimes in. "Colin Adams or Alex Fuentes?"

All eyes turn to me. Then Sierra nudges me, giving me a hint we've got company—Colin. Why did Darlene set me up like that?

Everyone's eyes now focus on Colin, standing behind me.

"Oops. Sorry," Darlene says, covering her slip of the tongue.

"Everyone knows Brittany would choose Colin," Sierra pipes in as she pops a pretzel into her mouth.

Megan sneers. "Darlene, what's wrong with you?"

"What? It's only a game, Megan."

"Yeah, but we're playing a different game than you're playing."

"What's that supposed to mean? Just because you don't have a boyfriend—"

Colin walks past us and heads for the patio. After giving Darlene a pissed-off look and silently praising Megan for telling her off, I follow him outside.

I find Colin sitting on one of the lounge chairs by the pool.

"Did you have to fucking hesitate when Darlene asked that question?" he says to me. "You made a fool out of me back there."

"Yeah, well, I'm not very happy with Darlene right now."

He gives a short laugh. "Don't you get it? It's not Darlene's fault."

"You think it's mine? As if I asked for Alex to be my partner."

He stands. "You didn't protest too much."

"You want to fight, Colin?"

"Maybe I do. You don't even know how to be a girlfriend."

"How can you say that? Who took you to the hospital when you sprained your wrist? Who ran onto the field and kissed you after your first touchdown? Who came to visit you every day last year when you got chicken pox?"

I got driving lessons against my will. I passed out drunk in Alex's arms, but I didn't know what I was doing. Nothing happened with Alex. I'm innocent, even if I have thoughts that aren't.

"That was last year." Colin takes my hand and leads me into the house. "I want you to show me how much you care. Now."

We enter Shane's bedroom and Colin pulls me down on the bed with him.

I push him away when he nuzzles my neck.

"Stop acting like I'm going to force you, Brit," Colin slurs. The bed creaks under his weight. "Ever since school started you've been acting like a damn prude."

I sit up. "I don't want to base our relationship on sex. It's like we never talk anymore."

"So talk," he says as his hand wanders on my chest.

"You go first. You say something, then I'll say something."

"That's the stupidest fucking thing I've ever heard. I don't have anything to say, Brit. If you've got something on your mind, let it out."

I breathe deeply, chastising myself for feeling more comfortable with Alex than here in a bed with Colin. I can't let our relationship end. My mom would freak, my friends would freak . . . the solar system would go out of alignment. . . .

Colin pulls me beside him. I can't break up with him just because I'm scared of having sex. He is, after all, a virgin, too. And he's waiting for me so we could share our first time together. Most of our friends have done it; maybe I'm being silly about the whole thing. Maybe my interest in Alex is my excuse to avoid doing it with Colin.

Colin's arm snakes around my waist. We've spent two years together, why blow it all for some silly attraction to someone I shouldn't even be talking to?

When his lips are inches from mine, my gaze freezes. On Shane's dresser is a picture. Shane and Colin at the beach this summer. There are two girls with them, and Colin has his arms intimately around the cute one with brown hair and a short, shag cut. They're smiling wide, as if they have a secret they aren't about to share.

I point to the picture. "Who's that?" I ask, trying to keep the unease out of my voice.

"Just a couple of girls we met at the beach," he says, leaning back while looking at the picture.

"What's the name of the girl you have your arm around?"

"I don't know. I think it was Mia or something like that."

"You look like a couple," I say.

"That's ridiculous. Come here," he says, pushing himself up and blocking my view of the picture. "You're the one I want now, Brit."

What does he mean by *now*? As if he wanted Mia over the summer, but now he wants me? Am I overanalyzing his words?

Before I can think further, he eases my dress and bra up to my chin. I'm trying to get into the mood and convince myself my hesitation stems from my nervousness. "Did you lock the door?" I ask, filing my uneasiness into the dark recesses of my mind.

"Yeah," he says, totally concentrating on my breasts.

Knowing I need to participate but having a hard time motivating myself, I feel him through his pants.

Colin lifts himself up, pushes my hand away, and unzips himself. When he lowers his pants down to his knees he says, "Come on, Brit. Let's try something new."

It's not feeling right, it feels orchestrated. I move closer, although my mind is far away.

The door creaks open and Shane's head pokes into the room. His mouth stretches into a wide grin. "Holy shit! Where's a cell phone camera when you need one?"

"I thought you locked the door!" I say angrily to Colin as I quickly pull my bra and dress back down. "You lied to me."

Colin grabs the blanket and covers himself. "Shane, give us

some fucking privacy, will ya? Brit, stop freaking out like a psycho."

"In case you hadn't noticed, this is *my* room," Shane says. He leans against the doorway and wiggles his eyebrows at me. "Brit, tell me the truth. Are those real?"

"Shane, you're a pig," I say, then move away from Colin.

Colin reaches for me as I hop off the bed. "Come back here, Brit. I'm sorry I didn't lock it. I was caught up in the moment."

The problem is, the unlocked door is only part of the reason why I'm mad. He called me "psycho" and didn't think twice about it. And he didn't defend me to Shane. I look back at my boyfriend. "Yeah? Well right now I'm *caught up* in the act of leaving," I say.

At one thirty in the morning I'm staring at my cell phone in my bedroom. Colin has called thirty-six times. And left ten messages. Since Sierra drove me home, I've ignored him. Mostly because I need to let my anger deflate. I'm mortified Shane saw me half undressed. In the time it took me to find Sierra and asked her to take me home, at least five people were whispering about my show in Shane's room. I don't want to blow up like my mom does, and I was about to lose it on Shane and Colin back at Shane's house.

By Colin's thirty-ninth call, my heart rate is as slow as it's gonna get tonight.

I finally answer it. "Stop calling me," I say.

"I'll stop calling when you listen to what I have to say," Colin says on the other end of the line, frustration laced through his voice.

"So talk. I'm listening."

I hear him take a deep breath. "I'm sorry, Brit. I'm sorry I didn't lock the door tonight. I'm sorry for wanting to have sex. I'm sorry one of my best friends thinks he's funny when he's not. I'm sorry I can't stand watching you and Fuentes in Peterson's class. I'm sorry I changed this summer."

I don't know what to say. He has changed. Have I? Or am I the same person who he said good-bye to before he left for the summer? I don't know. There's one thing I do know, though. "Colin, I don't want to fight anymore."

"Me, neither. Can you just try to forget tonight ever happened? I promise I'll make it up to you. Remember our anniversary last year when my uncle flew us to Michigan for the day in his Cessna?"

We ended up at a resort. When we got to the restaurant for dinner that night, a huge bouquet of red roses was on our table, along with a turquoise box. Inside was a white gold bracelet from Tiffany's. "I remember."

"I'm going to buy you the earrings that match the bracelet, Brit."

I don't have the heart to tell him that it's not the earrings I want. I love the bracelet a ton and wear it all the time. But what blew me away wasn't the gift, it was that Colin went above and beyond in the planning of the day just to make it super special for us. That's what I remember when I look at the bracelet. Not the gift, but the meaning behind it. I've only seen small glimpses of that Colin since school started.

The expensive earrings would be a symbol of Colin's apology and would remind me of tonight. It might also serve to guilt me into giving something to him . . . like my virginity. He might not think of it consciously, but just the fact that the thought is lingering in my mind is a sign. I don't want that pressure. "Colin, I don't want the earrings."

"Then what do you want? Tell me."

It takes me a while to answer. Six months ago I could have written a hundred-page essay on what I wanted. Since school started, everything has turned around. "Right now I don't know what I want." I feel bad for saying it, but it's the truth.

"Well, when you figure it out will you clue me in?"

Yeah, *if* I ever figure it out myself.

28

Alex

On Monday I try not to read too much into my anticipation for chemistry. Surely it's not Mrs. P. making me crave class. It's Brittany.

She walks into class late.

"Hey," I say to her.

"Hey," she mumbles back. No smile, no bright eyes. Something is definitely bothering her.

"Okay, class," Mrs. P. says. "Get out your pencils. Let's see how well you've been studying."

While I silently curse Mrs. P. for not having a lab day with experiments so we can talk, I glance over at my partner. She looks totally unprepared. Feeling protective even though I have no right, I raise my hand.

"I'm afraid to call on you, Alex," Mrs. P. says, staring down at me.

"It's a small question."

"Go ahead. Make it quick."

"This is an open book test, right?"

The teacher glares at me over her glasses. "No, Alex, this is not an open book test. And if you didn't study, you're going to get yourself a big fat F. Understand?"

I drop my books with a loud thud onto the floor in response.

After Mrs. P. passes out the test, I read the first question. *The density of Al (aluminum) is 2.7 grams per millimeter. What volume will 10.5 grams of Al (aluminum) occupy?*

After I work out my answer, I look over at Brittany. She's staring blankly at the test.

Catching me watching her, she sneers. "What?"

"Nothin'. *Nada.*"

"Then stop staring at me."

Mrs. P. is looking right at us. Taking a deep breath to calm myself, I go back to working on the test. Does Brittany have to do that, get all hot-and-cold without warning? What sets her off?

Out of the corner of my eye, I see my chem partner grab the bathroom pass off the hook by the classroom door. Problem is, the bathroom pass can't help you escape life. It's still there when you come out. Believe me, I've tried it. Problems and crap don't go away by hiding in the can.

Back in class, Brittany lays her head on the lab table as she scribbles answers. One glance and I know she's not into it, the girl is doing a half-ass job. And when Mrs. P. orders everyone to hand in their papers, my chem partner has a blank stare on her face.

"If it makes you feel any better," I say quietly so only Brittany can hear, "I flunked health class in eighth grade for puttin' a lit cigarette in the dummy's mouth."

Without looking up she says, "Good for you."

Music pipes through the speaker, signaling the end of class. I watch Brittany's golden hair bouncing less than usual as she shuffles out of class, surprisingly not accompanied by her boyfriend. I wonder if she thinks everything is supposed to land in her lap, even good grades.

I have to work for everything I have. Nothing lands in my lap.

"Hiya, Alex." Carmen is standing in front of my locker. Okay, so some things do land in my lap.

"*¿Que pasa?*"

My ex-girlfriend leans toward me, the deep V of her shirt extra low-cut. "A bunch of us are going to hang out at the beach after school. Wanna come?"

"I've got to work," I tell her. "Maybe I'll catch up with ya later."

I think about two weekends ago. After going to Brittany's house only to be talked down to by her mother, something inside me snapped.

Getting drunk to drown my busted ego was a dumb idea. I wanted to be with Brittany, to hang out with her not only to study but to find out what's underneath those blond streaks. My chem partner blew me off. Carmen didn't. The memory is a hazy one, but I remember Carmen in the lake, wrapping her body around me. And sitting on top of me by the fire as we smoked something much stronger than a Marlboro. In my inebriated and stoned ego-busted state, any girl would have felt good to me.

Carmen was there, willing, and I owe her an apology because even if she was offering, I shouldn't have nibbled at the bait. I'll have to catch up with her and explain my dumbass behavior.

After school, there's a crowd around my motorcycle. Shit, if anything happened to Julio I swear I'm going to kick someone's ass. I don't have to push through the crowd because a path opens up when I get close.

All eyes are on me as I witness the vandalism to my motorcycle. They're expecting me to be in a rage. After all, who would dare attach a pink tricycle horn to the handlebars and tape sparkling streamers from the ends of the handles? Nobody can get away with this shit.

Except Brittany.

I scan the area, but she's not around.

"I didn't do it," Lucky is quick to say.

Everyone else murmurs they didn't do it, either.

Then murmurs of who it could be race through the crowd. "Colin Adams, Greg Hanson . . ." I'm not listening, because I know full well who the culprit is. It's my chem partner, the one who ignored me today.

I yank off the streamers with a jerk of my hand, then unscrew the pink rubber horn. Pink. I wonder if it was hers once upon a time.

"Get out of my way," I tell the crowd. They disperse pretty quick, thinking my rage level is high and they don't want to be caught in the crossfire. Sometimes playing the part of a badass does have its advantages. The truth? I'll use the pink horn and streamers as an excuse to talk to Brittany again.

After everyone is out of sight, I walk to the side of the football field. The pom squad is there, practicing as usual.

"Looking for someone?"

I turn around to Darlene Boehm, one of Brittany's friends. "Is Brittany around?" I ask.

"Nope."

"Know where she is?"

Alex Fuentes asking the whereabouts of Brittany Ellis? I expect her to say it's none of my business. Or that I should leave her alone.

Instead her friend says, "She went home."

Murmuring a "thanks," I turn and walk back to Julio while I dial my cousin's number.

"Enrique's Auto Body."

"It's Alex. I'm gonna be late for work today."

"You get another detention?"

"No, nothin' like that."

"Well, make sure you work on the Lexus for Chuy. I told him he could pick it up at seven and you know how Chuy is when you don't come through for him."

"No problem," I tell him as I think of Chuy's role in the Blood. He's the guy you never want to mess with, the guy who was born without an empathy chip in his brain. If someone is disloyal, Chuy is responsible for either making them loyal or making sure they never narc. By any means possible, even if they're screaming for their life. "I'll be there."

Knocking on the Ellises' door ten minutes later with the pink horn and streamers in hand, I try to put on the I-am-a-cool-motherfucker pose.

When Brittany opens the door wearing a baggy T-shirt and shorts, I'm floored.

Her pale blue eyes open wide. "Alex, what are you doing here?"

I hold out the horn and streamers.

She snatches them from my hand. "I can't believe you came here because of some prank."

"We've got some things to discuss. Besides pranks."

She swallows nervously. "I'm not feeling great, okay? Let's just talk at school." She tries to close the door.

Shit, I can't believe I'm going to do this like a stalker guy in the movies. I push open the door. *¡Qué mierda!*

"Alex, don't."

"Let me in. For a minute. Please."

She shakes her head, those angelic curls swaying back and forth across her face. "My parents don't like when I have people over."

"Are they home?"

"No." She sighs, then opens the door hesitantly.

I step inside. The house is even bigger than it looks from the outside. The walls are painted bright white, reminding me of a hospital. I swear dust wouldn't have the nerve to land on their floors or counters. The two-story foyer boasts a staircase that rivals the one I saw in *The Sound of Music,* which we were forced to watch in junior high, and the floor is as shiny as water.

Brittany was right. I don't belong here. It doesn't matter, because even if I don't belong in this place, she's here and I want to be where she is.

"Well, what did you want to talk about?" she asks.

I wish her long, lean legs weren't sticking out from her shorts. They're a distraction. I look away from them, desperate to keep my wits. So what if she has sexy legs? So what if she has eyes as clear as glass marbles? So what if she can take a prank like a man and give it right back?

Who am I kidding? I have no reason for being here other than the fact that I want to be near her. Screw the bet.

I want to know how to make this girl laugh. I want to know what makes her cry. I want to know what it feels like to have her look at me as if I'm her knight in shining armor.

"Bwiee!" a distant voice echoes through the house, breaking the silence.

"Wait here," Brittany orders, then hurries down a hallway to the right. "I'll be right back."

I'm not about to stand here like a jackass in the foyer. I follow her, knowing I'm about to get a glimpse into her private world.

FuKe

29

Brittany

I'm not ashamed of my sister's disability. But I don't want Alex to judge her. Because if he laughs, I couldn't take it. I whip around. "You're not good at following directions, are you?"

He grins as if saying, *I'm a gang member, what did you expect?*

"I have to check on my sister. Do you mind?"

"Nope. It'll give me a chance to meet her. Trust me."

I should kick him out, tattoos and all. I should, but I don't.

Without another word, I lead him into our dark, mahogany-paneled library. Shelley is sitting in her wheelchair, her head awkwardly slumped to the side as she watches television.

When she realizes she has company, her gaze shifts from the television to me to Alex.

"This is Alex," I explain, shutting off the TV. "A friend from school."

Shelley gives Alex a crooked smile and hits her specialized keyboard with her knuckles. "Hello," says a feminine, computerized voice. She hits another button. "My name is Shelley," the computer continues.

Alex kneels down to Shelley's level. The simple act of respect tears at something suspiciously like my heart. Colin always ignores my sister, treating her as if she's blind and deaf as well as physically and mentally disabled.

"What's up?" Alex says, taking Shelley's stiff hand in his and shaking it. "Cool computer."

"It's a personal communication device or PCD," I explain. "It helps her communicate."

"Game," the computer voice says.

Alex moves beside Shelley. I hold my breath as I watch her hands, making sure they're nowhere near his thick head of hair.

"You have games on there?" he asks.

"Yeah," I answer for her. "She's become a checkers fanatic. Shelley, show him how it works."

While Shelley slowly taps the screen with her knuckles, Alex watches, seemingly fascinated.

When the checkers screen comes up, Shelley nudges Alex's hand.

"You go first," he says.

She shakes her head.

"She wants you to go first," I tell him.

"Cool." He taps the screen.

I watch, getting all mushy inside, as this tough guy plays quietly with my big sister.

"Do you mind if I make a snack for her?" I say, desperate to leave the room.

"Nah, go ahead," he says, his concentration on the game.

"You don't have to let her win," I say before leaving. "She can hold her own in checkers."

"Uh, thanks for the vote of confidence, but I am tryin' to win,"

Alex says. He has a genuine grin on his face, without trying to act cocky or cool. It makes me even more desperate to escape.

When I walk into the library with Shelley's food a few minutes later, he says, "She beat me."

"I told you she was good. But enough games for now," I say to Shelley, then turn to Alex. "I hope you don't mind me helping to feed her."

"Go for it."

He sits in my dad's favorite leather chair as I place a tray in front of Shelley and feed her applesauce. It's a messy affair, as usual. Tilting my head, I catch Alex watching as I wipe the side of my sister's mouth with a towel.

"Shelley," I say. "You should've let him win. You know, to be polite." Shelley's response is a shake of her head. Applesauce drips on her chin. "That's the way it's going to be, huh?" I say, hoping the scene doesn't gross Alex out. Maybe I'm testing him, to see if he can handle a glimpse of my home life. If so, he's passing. "Wait until Alex leaves. I'll show you who the checkers champion is."

My sister smiles that sweet, crooked smile of hers. It's like a thousand words put into one expression. For a moment I forget Alex is still watching me. It's so weird having him inside my life and my house. He doesn't belong, yet he doesn't seem to mind being here.

"Why were you in a crappy mood in chem class?" he asks.

Because my sister is going to be sent away and yesterday I got caught with my boobs exposed while Colin had his pants down right in front of me. "I'm sure you heard the gruesome rumors."

"Nope, haven't heard a thing. Maybe you're just paranoid."

Maybe. Shane saw us, but he has a big mouth. Every time someone looked my way today, I imagined they knew. I look at Alex. "Sometimes I wish there were Do Over Days."

"Sometimes I wish there were Do Over *Years*," he responds seriously. "Or Fast Forward Days."

"Unfortunately, real life doesn't have a remote control." When Shelley is done eating, I sit her in front of the TV, then lead Alex to the kitchen. "My life doesn't seem so perfect after all, does it?" I ask while I take drinks out of the fridge for both of us.

Alex looks at me curiously.

"What?"

He shrugs. "I guess we all have stuff to deal with. I've got more demons than a horror movie."

Demons? Nothing bothers Alex. He never complains about his life. "What are your demons?" I ask.

"*Oye*, if I told you about my demons, you'd run like hell away from me."

"I think you'd be surprised what I'd run from, Alex." Chimes from our grandfather clock echo through the house. One. Two. Three. Four. Five.

"I gotta go," Alex says. "How about studying tomorrow, after school. At my house."

"Your house?" On the south side?

"I'll show you a glimpse into my life. You game?" he asks.

I swallow. "Sure." Game on.

As I lead him to the door, I hear a car drive up to my house. If it's my mom, I'm in big trouble. No matter if we had the most innocent meeting, she'll go ballistic.

I peek through the windows by the front door and recognize Darlene's red sports car. "Oh, no. My friends are here."

"Don't panic," he tells me. "Open the door. It's not like you can pretend I'm not here. My motorcycle is parked in your driveway."

He's right. I can't hide the fact that he's here.

I open the door and walk outside. Alex is right behind me as I face Darlene, Morgan, and Sierra walking up the sidewalk. "Hey, guys!" I say. Maybe if I act all innocent they won't make a big deal about Alex being here. I touch Alex's elbow. "We were just discussing our chemistry project. Right, Alex?"

"Right."

Sierra's eyebrows are raised. I think Morgan is about to pull out her cell, no doubt to inform the other M's she saw Alex Fuentes walking out of my house.

"Should we go so you guys can be alone?" Darlene asks.

"Don't be ridiculous," I say too quickly.

Alex steps toward his motorcycle, his shirt outlining his perfect, muscular back and his jeans outlining his perfect, muscular—

He points at me after putting on his helmet. "See ya tomorrow."

Tomorrow. His house.

I nod.

After Alex is out of sight, Sierra says, "What was *that* all about?"

"Chemistry," I mumble.

Morgan's mouth is open in shock.

"Were you guys doing it?" Darlene asks. "'Cause we've been friends for ten years and I can count on one hand how many times I've been invited inside your house."

"He's my chemistry partner."

"He's a *gang member*, Brit. Don't ever forget that," Darlene says.

Sierra shakes her head and says, "Are you crushing on someone other than your boyfriend? Colin told Doug you've been acting strange lately. As your friends, we're here to talk some sense into you."

I sit on the front stoop and listen to them rant about reputations and boyfriends and loyalty for a half hour. They make sense.

"Promise us there's nothing going on between you and Alex,"

Sierra says to me alone while Morgan and Darlene are waiting in the car for her.

"There's nothing going on between me and Alex," I assure her. "I swear."

30

Alex

I'm sitting in calculus when the security guard knocks on the door and tells the teacher I need to be escorted out of class. Rolling my eyes, I grab my books and let the guy have his kicks by humiliating me in front of an audience.

"What now?" I ask. Yesterday I was pulled out of class for starting a food fight in the courtyard. I didn't start it. I might have participated, but I didn't start it.

"We're taking a little trip to the basketball courts." I follow the guy to the courts. "Alejandro, vandalism to school property is very serious business."

"I didn't vandalize anything," I tell him.

"I got a tip that you did."

A tip? You know the phrase "whoever smelt it, dealt it"? Well, whoever snitched probably did it. "Where is it?"

The guard points to the gym floor, where someone spray painted a very poor replica of the Latino Blood symbol. "Can you explain this?"

"No," I say.

Another security guard joins us. "We should check his locker," he says.

"Great idea." All they'll find is a leather jacket and books.

I'm turning the combination lock when Mrs. P. passes us.

"What's the problem?" she asks them.

"Vandalism. On the basketball court."

I open my locker and stand back to let them inspect it.

"Aha," the security guy says, reaching inside and pulling out a can of black spray paint from the top shelf. He holds it out to me. "Are you still going to plead innocent?"

"I'm bein' set up." I turn to Mrs. P., who's looking at me like I killed her cat. "I didn't do it," I tell her. "Mrs. P., you've got to believe me." I can see me now, being hauled to jail because of something an idiot did.

She shakes her head. "Alex, the evidence is right there. I want to believe you, but it's really hard." The officers are on either side of me, and I know what's coming next. Mrs. P. holds up her hand, stopping them. "Alex. Help me."

I'm tempted not to explain, to let them all think I was the one who defaced school property. They probably won't listen, anyway. But Mrs. P. is looking at me like a teenage rebel who wants to prove everyone wrong.

"The symbol is all wrong," I tell her. I show her my forearm. "This is the Latino Blood symbol. It's a five-point star with two pitchforks coming out the top and LB in the middle. The one on the floor had a six-point star with two arrows. Nobody in the Blood would make that mistake."

She says to the officers, "Where's Dr. Aguirre?"

"In a meeting with the superintendent. His secretary said he doesn't want to be disturbed."

Peterson checks her watch. "I've got a class in fifteen minutes. Joe, radio Dr. Aguirre on your walkie-talkie."

Joe the security guy isn't too happy. "Ma'am, this is the sort of thing we were hired for."

"I know. But Alex is my student, and believe me when I say he can't miss class today."

Joe shrugs, then radios for Dr. Aguirre to meet him in L hall. When his secretary asks if it's an emergency, Mrs. P. takes the walkie-talkie from Joe and says she's considering it her personal emergency and Dr. Aguirre should get down to L hall right away.

Two minutes later, Aguirre with a stern look on his face comes into view. "What's this all about?"

"Vandalism in the gym," Officer Joe informs him.

Aguirre stiffens. "Dammit, Fuentes. Not you again."

"I didn't do it," I tell him.

"Then who did?"

I shrug.

"Dr. Aguirre, he's telling the truth," Peterson says. "You can fire me if I'm wrong."

He shakes his head, then turns to the security guy. "Get Chuck to the gym and see what he can do to clean that stuff off." He points the spray paint can at me. "But I warn you, Alex. If I find out it was you, you'll be not only suspended but arrested. Got it?"

When the officers leave, Aguirre says, "Alex, I didn't tell you this before, but I'm telling you now. I thought the world was my enemy when I was in high school. I wasn't that much different than you, you know. It took me a damn long time to learn that I was my own enemy. When I realized that, I turned my life around. Mrs. Peterson and I, we're not the enemy."

"I know that," I say, and actually believe it's the truth.

"Good. Now I happen to be in the middle of an important meeting. If you'll excuse me, I'll be in my office."

"Thanks for believing me," I say to Mrs. P. once he's gone.

"Do you know who vandalized the gym?" she asks.

I look her straight in the eye and tell her the truth. "I've got no idea. I'm pretty confident it's not one of my friends."

She sighs. "If you weren't in a gang, Alex, you wouldn't get yourself into these messes."

"Yeah, but I'd be in other ones."

31

Brittany

"It looks like some of you don't think my class is important," Mrs. Peterson says. She starts handing out the test from yesterday.

As Mrs. Peterson heads toward my and Alex's shared table, I sink down in my chair. The last thing I need is Mrs. Peterson's wrath.

"Nice job," the woman says as she places my paper facedown in front of me. Then the woman turns to Alex. "For someone who aspires to be a chemistry teacher, you're off to a very poor start, Mr. Fuentes. Maybe I'll think twice about sticking up for you if you don't come prepared to my class."

She drops Alex's test in front of him with her index finger and thumb, as if the paper is too disgusting to touch with the rest of her fingers. "See me after class," she tells him before passing out the rest of the tests.

I can't understand why Mrs. Peterson didn't rip me a new one. I turn my paper over to find an A on the top of it. I rub my palms over my eyes and readjust them. There must be some mistake. It takes me less than a second to realize who was responsible for my grade. The truth hits me like a hammer to my gut. I look over at Alex, tucking his flunked test into his book.

• • •

"Why did you do it?" I wait until Mrs. Peterson finishes her after-class discussion with Alex before approaching him. I'm standing beside his locker, where he's paying little, if any, attention to me. I'm ignoring the stares burning into the back of my head.

"I don't know what you're talkin' about," he says.

Duh! "You switched our tests."

Alex slams his locker shut. "Listen, it was no big deal."

Yes, it is. He walks away, as if expecting me to leave it at that. I'd watched him work diligently on his test, but when I glanced at the big red F on the front of his paper, I recognized my own test.

After school, I hurry out the front doors to catch him. He's on his motorcycle, getting ready to leave.

"Alex, wait!"

Feeling fidgety, I curl my hair behind my ears.

"Hop on," he orders.

"What?"

"Hop on. If you want to thank me for savin' your ass in Mrs. P.'s class, come home with me. I wasn't kiddin' yesterday. You showed me a glimpse into your life, I'm gonna show you a glimpse of mine. It's only fair, right?"

I scan the parking lot. Some people are looking our way, probably ready to spread the gossip that I'm talking to Alex. If I actually leave with him, rumors will fly.

The sound of Alex revving his motorcycle brings my attention back to him. "Don't be afraid of what they think."

I take in the sight of him, from his ripped jeans and leather jacket to the red and black bandanna he just tied on top of his head. His gang colors.

I should be terrified. Then I remember how he was with Shelley yesterday.

To hell with it.

I shift my book bag around to my back and straddle his motor-cycle.

"Hold on tight," he says, pulling my hands around his waist. The simple feel of his strong hands resting on top of mine is intensely inti-mate. I wonder if he's feeling these emotions, too, but dismiss the thought. Alex Fuentes is a hard guy. Experienced. The mere touch of hands isn't going to make his stomach flutter.

He deliberately brushes the tips of his fingers over mine before reaching for the handlebars. Oh. My. God. What am I getting myself into?

As we speed away from the school parking lot, I grab Alex's rock-hard abs tighter. The speed of the motorcycle scares me. I feel light-headed, like I'm riding a roller coaster with no lap bar.

The motorcycle stops at a red light. I lean back.

I hear him chuckle when he guns the engine once more as the light turns green. I clutch his waist and bury my face in his back.

When he finally stops and puts the kickstand down, I survey my surroundings. I've never been on his street. The homes are so . . . small. Most are one level. A cat can't fit in the space between them. As hard as I try to fight it, sorrow settles in the pit of my stomach.

My house is at least seven, maybe even eight or nine times Alex's home's size. I know this side of town is poor, but . . .

"This was a mistake," Alex says. "I'll take you home."

"Why?"

"Among other things, the look of disgust on your face."

"I'm not disgusted. I guess I feel sorry—"

"Don't ever pity me," he warns. "I'm poor, not homeless."

"Then are you going to invite me in? The guys across the street are gawking at the white girl."

"Actually, around here you're a 'snow girl.'"

"I hate snow," I say.

His lips quirk up into a grin. "Not for the weather, *querida*. For your snow-white skin. Just follow me and don't stare at the neighbors, even if they stare at you."

I sense his wariness as he leads me inside. "Well, this is it," he says, motioning inside.

The living room might be smaller than any room in my house, but it feels warm and cozy. There are two afghans lying on the sofa I'd love to have on top of me on cold nights. We don't have any afghans at my house. We have comforters . . . custom-designed ones to match the decor.

I walk around Alex's house, gliding my fingers over the furniture. A shelf with half-melted candles sits below a picture of a handsome man. I feel Alex's warmth as he stands behind me. "Your dad?" I ask.

He nods.

"I can't begin to imagine what it would be like to lose my dad." Even though he's not around much, I know he's a permanent fixture in my life. I always want more out of my parents. Should I feel lucky just having them around?

Alex studies the picture of his dad. "At the time, you're numb and try to block it out. I mean, you know he's gone and all, but it's like you're in this fog. Then life kind of gets into a routine and you follow it." He shrugs. "Eventually you stop thinkin' about it so much and move on. There's no other choice."

"It's kind of like a test." I catch a glimpse of myself in the mirror on the opposite wall. I absently run my fingers through my hair.

"You're always doin' that."

"Doing what?"

"Fixin' your hair or makeup."

"So, what's wrong with trying to look good?"

"Nothin', unless it becomes an obsession."

I put my hands down, wishing I could superglue them to my sides. "I'm not obsessed."

He shrugs. "Is it so important that people think you're beautiful?"

"I don't care what people think," I lie.

"'Cause you are . . . beautiful, I mean. But it shouldn't matter so much."

I know that. But expectations mean a lot where I come from. Speaking of expectations . . . "What did Mrs. Peterson say to you after class?"

"Oh, the usual. That if I don't take her class seriously she'll make my life miserable."

I swallow, not knowing if I should reveal my plan. "I'm going to tell her you switched the tests."

"Don't do that," he says, stepping away from me.

"Why not?"

"Because it doesn't matter."

"Yes, it does. You need good grades to get into . . ."

"What? A good college? Give me a fuckin' break. I'm not goin' to college and you know it. You rich kids worry about your GPA as if it's a symbol of your worth. I don't need it, so don't do me any favors. I'll get by with a C in that class. Just make sure those hand warmers kick ass."

If I have anything to do about it, we'll get an A+ on the project.

"Where's your room?" I ask, changing the subject. I drop my book bag on the living room floor. "A bedroom tells a lot about a person."

He gestures to a doorway off to one side. Three beds take up most of the small space, with enough room for one small dresser. I walk around the small room.

"I share it with my two brothers," he states. "Not a lot of privacy here."

"Let me guess which bed is yours," I say, smiling.

I scan the areas around each bed. A small picture of a pretty Hispanic girl is taped to one wall. "Hmmm . . . ," I murmur, glancing at Alex and wondering if the girl staring back at me is his ideal.

I slowly walk around him and examine the next bed. Pictures of soccer players are taped above it. The bed is messy, and clothes are strewn from the pillow to the foot of the bed.

Nothing adorns the wall by the third bed, as if the person who sleeps here is a visitor. It's almost sad, the first two walls saying so much about the people who sleep below them and this one totally bare.

I sit on Alex's bed, the hopeless and empty one, and my eyes meet his. "Your bed says a lot about you."

"Yeah? What does it say?"

"I wonder why you don't think you'll stay here long," I say. "Unless it's because you really do want to go to college."

He leans on the door frame. "I'm not leavin' Fairfield. Ever."

"Don't you want a degree?"

"Now you sound like the damn career counselor at school."

"You don't want to get away and start living your own life? Away from your past?"

"You see goin' to college as an escape," he says.

"Escape? Alex, you have no clue. I'm going to a college that's close to my sister. First it was Northwestern, now it's the University of Colorado. My life is dictated by the whims of my parents and where they want to send my sister. You want the easy way out, so you stay here."

"You think it's a breeze being the man of the house? Shit, makin' sure my mama doesn't get mixed up with some loser or that my brothers don't start shootin' shit up their arms or smokin' crack is enough to keep me here."

"I'm sorry."

"I warned you never to pity me."

"No," I say, my eyes moving up to meet his. "You feel such a family connection, yet you don't place anything permanent beside your bed, as if you're going to leave at any moment. I feel sorry for you about that."

He steps back, shutting me out. "You done with the psychoanalysis?" he says.

I follow him into the family room, still wondering what Alex wants for his future. It seems the guy is ready to leave this house . . . or this earth. Could it be in some way Alex is preparing for his death by not placing anything permanent beside him? That he's destined to end up like his father?

Is that what he meant by his demons?

For the next two hours, we sit on his family room couch and hatch a plan for our hand warmers. He's a lot smarter than I'd realized; that A on his test wasn't a fluke. He has a lot of ideas about how we can research online and get information from the library on how to construct the hand warmers and various uses for them to incorporate into our paper. We need the chemicals Mrs. Peterson will provide, Ziploc bags to enclose the chemicals, and to get extra brownie points we've decided to encase the Ziploc bags in material we'll pick out at the fabric store. I purposely keep the discussion on chemistry, careful not to touch on any subject too personal.

As I close my chemistry book, out of the corner of my eye I see Alex run his hand through his hair. "Listen, I didn't mean to be rude to you before."

"That's okay. I got too nosy."

"You're right."

I stand, feeling uncomfortable. He grabs my arm and urges me back down.

"No," he says, "I mean you're right about me. I don't place anything permanent here."

"Why?"

"My dad," Alex says, staring at the picture on the opposite wall. He squeezes his eyes shut. "God, there was so much blood." He opens his eyes and captures my gaze. "If there's one thing I learned, it's that nobody is here forever. You have to live for the moment, each and every day . . . the here, the now."

"And what do you want right now?" Right now I itch to heal his wounds and forget my own.

He touches my cheek with the tips of his fingers.

My breath hitches. "Do you want to kiss me, Alex?" I whisper.

"*Dios mío*, I want to kiss you . . . to taste your lips, your tongue." He gently traces my lips with the tips of his fingers. "Do you want me to kiss you? Nobody else would know but the two of us."

32

Alex

Brittany's tongue snakes out to wet her perfect heart-shaped lips, which are now shiny and oh, so inviting.

"Don't tease me like that," I groan, my lips inches from hers.

Her books hit the carpet. Her eyes follow, but if I lose her attention, I may never get this moment back. My fingers move to her chin, gently urging her to look at me.

She looks up at me with those vulnerable eyes. "What if it means something?" she asks.

"What if it does?"

"Promise me it won't mean anything."

I lean my head back on the couch. "It won't mean anythin'." Aren't I supposed to be the guy in this scenario, laying down the no-commitment rules?

"And no tongue," she adds.

"*Mi vida*, if I kiss you, I guarantee there's gonna be tongue."

She hesitates.

"I promise it won't mean anythin'," I assure her again.

I really don't expect her to do it. I think she's teasing me, testing to see how much I can take before I crack. But as her eyelids close and she leans closer, I realize it's going to happen. This girl of my dreams, this girl who is more like me than anyone I've ever met, wants to kiss me.

I take over control as soon as she tilts her head. Our lips touch for the briefest moment before I lace my fingers in her hair and keep kissing her soft and gentle. I cup her cheek in my palm, feeling her baby-soft skin against my rough fingers. My body urges me to take advantage of the situation, but my brain (the one inside my head) keeps me in check.

A satisfied sigh escapes Brittany's mouth, as if she's content to stay in my arms forever.

I brush the tip of my tongue against her lips, enticing her to open her mouth. She tentatively meets my tongue with her own. Our mouths and tongues mingle in a slow, erotic dance until the sound of the front door opening makes her jerk away.

Damn. I'm pissed off. First, for losing myself in Brittany's kiss. Second, for wanting that moment to last forever. Last, I'm pissed at *mi'amá* and brothers for coming home at the most awful time.

I watch Brittany trying to look busy as she bends down and picks up her books. My mother and brothers are standing in the doorway with their eyes bugged out.

"Hey, Ma," I say, more flustered than I should be.

From the stern look on *mi'amá*'s face, I know she's not pleased at catching us making out like there was a promise of more to come.

"Luis and Carlos, go to your bedroom," she orders, stepping into the room and composing herself. "Aren't you going to introduce me to your friend, Alejandro?"

Brittany stands, books in hand. "Hi, I'm Brittany." Even with her sun-kissed hair mussed from my fingers and the motorcycle ride, she's still kick-ass beautiful. Brittany extends her hand in greeting. "Alex and I were studying chemistry."

"What I saw wasn't studying," my ma says, ignoring her hand.

Brittany winces.

"*Mamá*, leave her alone," I say roughly.

"My home is not a whorehouse."

"*Por favor, Mamá*," I say, exasperated. "We were only kissin'."

"Kissing leads to making *niños*, Alejandro."

"Let's get out of here," I say, totally embarrassed. I whip my jacket off the couch and shrug into it.

"I'm sorry if I disrespected you in any way, Mrs. Fuentes," Brittany says, visibly upset.

My mother takes the groceries she's carrying, ignoring the apology as she walks into the kitchen.

When we're outside, I hear Brittany take a deep breath. I swear it sounds as if she's holding herself together by a thin thread. Not the way it's supposed to go down: bring girl home, kiss girl, mom insults girl, girl leaves crying.

"Don't sweat it. She's just not used to me bringin' girls in the house."

Brittany's expressive blue eyes appear remote and cold. "That shouldn't have happened," she says, throwing back her shoulders in a stance as stiff as a statue's.

"What? The kiss or you likin' it so much?"

"I have a boyfriend," she says as she fidgets with the strap on her designer book bag.

"You tryin' to convince me, or yourself?" I ask her.

"Don't turn this around. I don't want to upset my friends. I don't want to upset my mom. And Colin . . . I'm just really confused right now."

I hold out my hands and raise my voice, something I usually avoid because like Paco says, it means I actually care. I don't care. Why should I? My mind says to shut the fuck up at the same time words spout from my mouth. "I don't get it. He treats you like you're his damn prize."

"You don't even know what it's like with me and Colin. . . ."

"Tell me, dammit," I say, unable to hide the edge to my voice. Initially I hold myself back from what I really want to say, but I can't resist and tell it to her straight up. " 'Cause that kiss back there . . . it meant somethin'. You know it as well as I do. I dare you to tell me bein' with Colin is better than that."

She looks away hastily. "You wouldn't understand."

"Try me."

"When people see Colin and me together, they comment on how perfect we are. You know, the Golden Couple. Get it?"

I stare at her in disbelief. That is beyond fucked up. "I get it. I just can't believe I'm hearin' it. Does bein' perfect mean that much to you?"

There's a long, brittle silence. I catch a flicker of sadness in those sapphire eyes, but then it's gone. In an instant her expression stills and grows serious.

"I haven't been doing a bang-up job at it lately, but yes. It does," she finally admits. "My sister isn't perfect, so I have to be."

That is the most pathetic shit I've ever heard. I shake my head in disgust and point to Julio. "Get on and I'll take you back to school to get your car."

Silently, Brittany straddles my motorcycle. She holds herself so far away from me I can barely feel her behind me. I almost take a detour to make the ride last longer.

She treats her sister with patience and adoration. God knows I wouldn't be able to spoon-feed one of my brothers and wipe his mouth. The girl I once accused of being self-absorbed is not one-dimensional.

Dios mío, I admire her. Somehow, being with Brittany brings something to my life that's missing, something . . . right.

But how am I going to convince her of that?

33

Brittany

I'm going to forget the kiss with Alex happened even though I was up all night replaying it in my head. As I'm driving to school the day after *the kiss that never happened*, I wonder if I should ignore Alex. Although that's not an option because we have chemistry together.

Oh, no. Chemistry class. Will Colin suspect something? Maybe someone saw us drive off together yesterday and told him. Last night I turned off my cell so I didn't have to talk to anyone.

Ugh. I wish my life wasn't so complicated. I have a boyfriend. Okay, so my boyfriend's been acting pushy lately, interested only in sex. And I'm sick of it.

But Alex as my boyfriend would never work. His mom already hates me. His ex-girlfriend wants to kill me—another bad sign. He even smokes, which is totally not cool. I could make a huge list of all the negatives.

Okay, so there might be some positives. A few minor ones too insignificant to mention.

He's smart.

He has eyes so expressive they give a hint to more than what he portrays.

He's dedicated to his friends, family, and even his motorcycle.

He touched me as if I were made of glass.

He kissed me as if he'd savor it for the rest of his life.

The first time I see him is during lunch. As I'm waiting in the cafeteria food line, Alex is two people in front of me. This girl, Nola Linn, is in between us. And she's not moving down the line fast enough.

Alex's jeans are faded and torn at the knee. His hair is falling into his eyes and I'm itching to push it back. If Nola wouldn't be so wishy-washy about her choice of fruit . . .

Alex caught me checking him out. I quickly focus my attention on the soup of the day. Minestrone.

"Want a cup or bowl, hon?" Mary, the lunch lady, asks me.

"Bowl," I say, pretending to be totally interested in the way she ladles the soup into the bowl.

After she hands it to me, I hurry past Nola and stand by the cashier. Right behind Alex.

As if he knows I'm stalking him, he turns around. His eyes pierce mine and for a moment I feel as if the rest of the world is closed out and it's just the two of us. The urge to jump into his arms and feel the warmth of them surrounding me is so powerful, I wonder if it's medically possible to be addicted to another human being.

I clear my throat. "Your turn," I say, motioning to the cashier.

He moves forward with his tray, a slice of pizza on it. "I'll pay for hers, too," he says, pointing to me.

The cashier waves her finger at me, "What'd you get? Bowl of minestrone?"

"Yeah, but . . . Alex, don't pay for me."

"Don't worry. I can afford a bowl of soup," he says defensively, handing over three dollars.

Colin barges into the line and stands next to me. "Move along. Get your own girlfriend to stare at," he snaps at Alex, then shoos him off.

I pray Alex doesn't retaliate by telling Colin we kissed. Everyone in line is watching us. I can feel their stares on the back of my neck. Alex takes his change from the cashier and without a backward glance heads for the outside courtyard off the cafeteria where he usually sits.

I feel so selfish, because I want the best of both worlds. I want to keep the image I've worked so hard to create. That image includes Colin. I also want Alex. I can't stop thinking about having him hold me again and kiss me until I'm breathless.

Colin says to the cashier, "I'll pay for hers and mine."

The cashier looks at me in confusion. "Didn't that other boy pay for you already?"

Colin waits for me to correct her. When I don't, he gives me a disgusted look and stomps out of the cafeteria.

"Colin, wait!" I say, but he either can't hear me or is ignoring me. The next time I see him is in chemistry class, but Colin walks in just as the bell rings so we don't talk.

During chemistry, it's another experiment/observation. Alex swirls test tubes full of silver nitrate and potassium chloride liquids. "Looks like they're both water to me, Mrs. P.," Alex says.

"Looks are deceiving," Mrs. Peterson replies.

My gaze travels to Alex's hands. Those hands that are now busy measuring the right amount of silver nitrate and potassium chloride are the same ones that traced my lips intimately.

"Earth to Brittany."

I blink my eyes, snapping out of my daydream. Alex is holding a test tube full of clear liquid out to me.

Which reminds me I should help him pour the liquids together. "Uh, sorry." I pick up one test tube and pour it into the tube he's holding.

"We're supposed to write down what happens," he says, using the stirring rod to mix the chemicals together.

A white solid magically appears inside the clear liquid.

"Hey, Mrs. P.! I think we found the answer to our problems for the ozone layer depletion," Alex teases.

Mrs. Peterson shakes her head.

"So what do we observe in the tube?" he asks me, reading off of the sheet Mrs. Peterson handed out at the start of class. "I'd say the watery liquid is probably potassium nitrate now and the white solid mass is silver chloride. What's your assumption?"

As he hands me the tube, our fingers brush against each other. And linger. It leaves a tingling sensation I can't ignore.

I glance up. Our eyes meet, and for a minute I think he's trying to send me a private message but his expression turns dark and he looks away.

"What do you want me to do?" I whisper.

"You're gonna have to figure that one out yourself."

"Alex . . ."

But he won't tell me what to do. I guess I'm a bitch to even ask him for advice when he can't possibly be unbiased.

When I'm close to Alex I feel excitement, the way I used to feel on Christmas morning.

As much as I've tried to ignore it, I look over at Colin and know . . . I know our relationship isn't what it used to be. It's over. And the sooner I break it off with Colin, the sooner I can stop wondering why I'm still with him.

I meet Colin after school by the back door to the school. He's dressed for football practice. Unfortunately Shane is standing next to him.

Shane holds up his cell. "You two want to do a repeat performance of the other night? I can capture the moment forever and e-mail it to you. It'd be a great screen saver or, better yet, a YouTube video."

"Shane, get the fuck out of my sight before I lose it," Colin says, then gives Shane a stare until he leaves. "Brit, where were you last night?" When I don't answer, Colin says, "You can save your breath, 'cause I already have a clue."

This isn't going to be easy. I now know why people break up in e-mails and text messages. Doing it face-to-face is so hard because you have to stand in front of the person and witness their reaction. Face their wrath. I've spent so much time avoiding arguments and smoothing relationships with the people around me, this confrontation is painful.

"You and I both know this isn't working," I say as gently as I can.

Colin narrows his eyes at me. "What are you saying?"

"We need a break."

"A break, or a breakup?"

"Breakup," I say gently.

"This is because of Fuentes, isn't it?"

"Since you came back from summer break, our entire relationship is about fooling around. We never talk anymore, and I'm sick of feeling guilty for not ripping my clothes off and spreading my legs to prove I love you."

"You don't want to prove *anything* to me."

I keep my voice low so other students can't hear me. "Why would you want me to? Just the fact that you need me to prove I love you is probably a clue it isn't working."

"Don't do this." He tosses his head back and moans. "*Please* don't do this."

We filled the football star/pom-pom captain stereotypical box everyone put us in. For years we fit the mold. Now we're going to be under a microscope for the breakup, with rumors swirling around us. Just the thought of it makes my skin crawl.

But I can't pretend it's working anymore. The decision will probably haunt me. If my parents can send my sister away because it's good for them, and Darlene can fool around with every guy she comes in contact with because it makes her feel better, why can't I do what's right for me?

I put my hand on Colin's shoulder, trying not to focus on his watering eyes. He shrugs my hand off.

"Say something," I urge.

"What do you want me to say, Brit? That I'm thrilled you're breaking up with me? Sorry, but I'm not feeling it."

He wipes his eyes with his palms. It makes me want to cry, too, and my eyes start tearing. It's the end of something we thought was real but ended up being just another one of the roles we were thrust into. That's what makes me so sad. Not the breakup, but what our relationship stood for . . . my weakness.

"I had sex with Mia," he blurts out. "This summer. You know, that girl in the picture."

"You're saying that to hurt me."

"I'm saying it because it's the truth. Ask Shane."

"Then why did you come back here and pretend we were still the Golden Couple?"

"Because that's what everyone expected. Even you. Don't deny it."

His words sting, but they're the truth. Now I'm done playing the "perfect" girl and living by everyone else's rules, including my own.

It's time I start getting real. The first thing I do after Colin and I part is tell Ms. Small I need to take time off from poms. It feels like a weight is lifted off my shoulders. I go home, spend time with Shelley, and do homework. After dinner I call Isabel Avila.

"I should be surprised you're calling me. But I'm not," she says.

"How was practice?"

"Not great. Darlene isn't a great captain, and Ms. Small knows it. You shouldn't quit."

"I'm not. I'm just taking a break for a little while. But I didn't call to talk about poms. Listen, I wanted you to know I broke up with Colin today."

"And you're telling me because . . ."

That's a good question, one I normally wouldn't have answered. "I wanted to talk with someone about it, and I know I have friends who I can call, but I kinda wanted to go to someone who wouldn't gossip about it. My friends have big mouths."

Sierra is the one person I'm closest to, but I lied to her about Alex. And her boyfriend, Doug, is best friends with Colin.

"How do you know I won't blab?" Isabel asks.

"I don't. But you didn't tell me stuff about Alex when I asked, so I figure you're good at keeping secrets."

"I am. So shoot."

"I don't know how to say this."

"I haven't got all day, you know."

"I kissed Alex," I blurt out.

"Alex? *¡Bendita!* Was that before or after the Colin breakup?"

I wince. "I didn't plan it."

Isabel laughs so hard and loud, I have to take the phone away from my ear. "You sure *he* didn't plan it?" she asks once she can get words out.

"It just happened. We were at his house and then we were inter-rupted when his mom came home and saw us—"

"What? His ma saw you guys? In his house? *¡Bendita!*" She goes off in Spanish, and I have no clue what the hell she's saying.

"I don't speak Spanish, Isabel. Help me out here."

"Oh, sorry. Carmen is gonna shit a brick when she finds out."

I clear my throat.

"I won't tell her," Isabel is quick to say. "But Alex's mom is one tough woman. When Alex dated Carmen, he kept her far away from his *mamá*. Don't get me wrong, she loves her sons. But she's overprotective, just like most Mexican mothers. Did she kick you out?"

"No, but she pretty much called me a whore."

More laughing from the other end of the line.

"It wasn't funny."

"I'm sorry." More laughing. "I would have loved to be a fly on the wall when she walked in on you two."

"Thanks for your compassion," I say dryly. "I'm hanging up now."

"No! I'm sorry for laughing. It's just that the more we talk, the more I see you as a totally different person than I thought you were. I guess I can understand why Alex likes you."

"Thanks, I think. Remember when I told you I wouldn't let anything happen between me and Alex?"

"Yeah. Just so I get my timetable straight, that was before you kissed him. Right?" She chuckles, then says, "I'm just kidding, Brittany. If you like him, girl, go for it. But be careful, because even if I think he likes you more than he'll admit, you should keep your guard up."

"I won't stop it if something happens between me and Alex, but don't worry. I always have my guard up."

"Me, too. Well, except for the night you slept at my house. I kinda fooled around with Paco. I can't tell *my* friends 'cause they'd give me shit."

"Do you like him?"

"I don't know. I never thought about him that way before, but being with him was kinda nice. How was the kiss with Alex?"

"Nice," I say, thinking about how sensual it was. "Actually, Isabel, it was more than nice. It was *fucking* incredible."

Isabel starts laughing, and I laugh right along with her this time.

34

Alex

Brittany flew out of school today, following Burro Face. Before I left I saw them together in an intimate conversation by the back field. She picked him over me, which really shouldn't surprise me. When she asked me in chemistry what she should do, I should have told her to dump that *pendejo*. Then I'd be happy instead of pissed off. *¡Es un carbón de mierda!*

He doesn't deserve her. Okay, so I don't, either.

After school, I hung out at the warehouse to see if I could get information about my dad. It was no use, though. The guys who knew *mi papá* back then didn't have much to say except he never stopped talking about his sons. All conversation stopped when the Satin Hood sprayed the warehouse with gunfire, a sign they're out for revenge and won't stop until they get it. I don't know if I should be thankful or worried that the warehouse is in a secluded back lot behind the old railroad station. Nobody knows we're here, not even the cops. Especially not the cops.

I'm resistant to the *Pop! Pop! Pop!* of gunfire. In the warehouse, at the park . . . I expect it. Some streets are safer than others, but here, in the warehouse, rivals know it's our sacred turf. And they expect retaliation.

It's the culture. You disrespect our turf, we disrespect yours. Nobody was hurt this time, so it's not retaliation against a killing. But there will be retaliation. They expect us to come. And we won't disappoint them.

On my side of town the circle of life is dependent on the circle of violence.

Taking the long way home after it's all clear, I find myself driving past Brittany's house. I can't help it. As soon as I cross the tracks, a cop car stops me and two uniformed guys step out.

Instead of informing me why I'm being pulled over, one of the cops orders me off my motorcycle and asks me for my license.

I hand it to him. "Why am I bein' pulled over?"

The guy who has my license examines it, then says, "You can ask questions after I ask mine. You have any drugs in your possession, Alejandro?"

"No, sir."

"Any weapons?" the other officer asks.

There's a slight hesitation before I tell the truth. "Yes."

One cop takes the gun out of his holster and points it at my chest. The other one tells me to keep my hands up, then orders me to lie on the ground while he calls for backup. Fuck. I'm busted, big time.

"What kind of weapon? Be specific."

I wince before saying, "A Glock nine millimeter." Thankfully I gave Wil the Beretta back or I'd be caught double-strapped.

My answer makes the cop a little nervous and his trigger finger shakes a bit. "Where is it?"

"On my left leg."

"Don't move. I'm going to disarm you. If you stay still, you won't get hurt."

After he removes my gun the second cop puts on rubber gloves and says to me in an authoritative voice Mrs. P. would be proud of, "You have any needles on you, Alejandro?"

"No, sir," I say.

He knees my back and handcuffs me. "Get up," he orders, hauling me to my feet, and makes me lean over the hood of the car. I feel humiliated as the guy pats me down. Shit, as much as I knew getting arrested was inevitable, I'm not ready for it. He shows me my gun. "You can assume this is why we pulled you over."

"Alejandro Fuentes, you have the right to remain silent," one of the officers recites. "Anything you say can and will be used against you in a court of law. . . ."

The holding cell smells like piss and smoke. Or maybe the guys who are unlucky enough to be locked in this cage with me are the ones who smell like piss and smoke. Either way, I can't wait to get the hell out of here.

Who am I gonna call to bail me out? Paco doesn't have any money. Enrique put all his money into the auto shop. My mother will kill me if she finds out I was arrested. I lean my back against the iron bars of the cell, thinking, even though it's close to impossible in this stinkin' place.

The police call it a holding cell, but it's just a glorified way of saying "cage." Thank *Dios* it's the first time I've been here. And, damn it, I pray it's my last. *¡Lo juro!*

That thought is disturbing because I've always known I've sacrificed my life for my brothers. Why would it matter if I'm locked up for the rest of my life? Because deep down I don't want this life. I want my mother to be proud of me for being something other than a gang member. I want a future to be proud of. And I desperately want Brittany to think I'm one of the good guys.

I bang the back of my head against the steel bars, but the thoughts won't go away.

"I've seen you around Fairfield High. I go there," says a short white guy, about my age. The dork is wearing a coral-colored golf shirt and white pants, as if he came from a golf tournament with a bunch of senior citizens.

White Guy tries to look cool, but with that coral shirt . . . man, looking cool is the least of his problems.

The guy might as well have "another rich kid from the north side" tattooed on his forehead.

"What'cha in for?" White Guy asks as if it's an ordinary question between two ordinary people on an ordinary day.

"Carryin' a concealed weapon."

"Knife or gun?"

I shoot him a glare. "Does it fuckin' matter?"

"I'm just trying to make conversation," White Guy says.

Are all white people like this—talking to hear what their voice sounds like? "What are you in for?" I ask.

White Guy sighs. "My dad called the cops and told them I stole his car."

I roll my eyes. "Your old man put you in this hellhole? On purpose?"

"He thought it would teach me a lesson."

"Yeah," I say. "The lesson is that your old man's an asshole." The dad should have taught his son how to dress better instead.

"My mom'll bail me out."

"You sure?"

White Guy straightens. "She's a lawyer, and my dad's done this before. A few times. I think to piss off my mom and get her attention. They're divorced."

I shake my head. White people.

"It's true," White Guy says.

"I'm sure it is."

"Fuentes, you can make your call now," the cop on the other side of the bars barks out.

Mierda, with all of White Guy's blabberin' I still haven't decided who to call to bail me out.

It hits me like that big, fat red F on my chemistry exam. There's only one person with the money and means to get me out of this mess—Hector. The head of the Blood.

I've never called in a favor from Hector. Because you never knew when Hector would call in a favor of his own. And if I owe Hector, I owe more than money.

Sometimes in life there are no desirable choices.

Three hours later, after a judge lectures me until my ears almost bleed then sets my bail, Hector picks me up from the courthouse. He's a powerful man, with slicked-back hair darker than my own and a look about him that says he takes no shit.

I have a lot of respect for Hector because he's the guy who initiated me into the Latino Blood. He grew up in the same town as my dad, had known him since they were kids. Hector kept an eye out for me and my family after my dad died. He taught me new phrases like "second generation" and sprouted words like "legacy." I'll never forget it.

Hector thumps me on the back as we walk to the parking lot. "You got Judge Garrett. He's a tough son of a bitch. You're lucky the bail wasn't higher."

I nod, wanting nothing more than to go home. When we're driving away from the courthouse, I say, "I'll pay you back, Hector."

"Don't worry about it, man," Hector says. "Brothers help each other out. To tell you the truth, I was surprised it was your first time getting arrested. You stay cleaner than anyone in the Blood."

I stare out the window of Hector's car, the streets as calm and dark as Lake Michigan.

"You're a smart kid, smart enough to move up in the Blood," Hector says.

I would die for some of the guys in Latino Blood, but to move up? Selling drugs and guns are a few of the illegal dealings going on at the top. I like it where I am, riding the dangerous wave without actually plunging headfirst into the water.

I should be happy Hector is contemplating giving me more responsibility in the LB. Brittany and all she stands for is a fantasy.

"Think about it," Hector says as he pulls up to my house.

"I will. Thanks for bailin' me out, man," I say.

"Here, take this." Hector pulls a pistol out from under his car seat. "*El policía* confiscated yours."

I hesitate, remembering when the police asked me if I had any weapons on me. *Dios mío*, it was humiliating having a gun pointed at my chest as they removed the Glock. But refusing Hector's gun would be considered disrespectful, and I'd never dis Hector. I take the gun and stick it in the waistband of my jeans.

"I heard you've been asking questions about your *papá*. My advice is to let it go, Alex."

"I can't. You know that."

"Well, if you find anything out, let me know. I always have your back."

"I know. Thanks, man."

It's quiet in the house. I walk into my bedroom, where both of my brothers are sleeping. Opening my top drawer, I bury the gun under the wooden board where nobody can accidentally find it. It's a trick Paco taught me. I lie on my bed and cover my eyes with my forearm, hoping I can get some sleep tonight.

Yesterday flashes before my eyes. The image of Brittany, her lips on mine, her sweet breath mixed with my own, is the only picture that lingers in my mind.

As I drift off, her angelic face is the only image that keeps the nightmare of my past away.

35

Brittany

Rumors are flying furiously through Fairfield that Alex got arrested. I have to find out if it's true. I find Isabel between first and second period. She's talking with a bunch of her friends but leaves them and pulls me aside.

She tells me Alex was arrested yesterday but made bail. She has no clue where he is, but she'll ask around and meet me between third and fourth period at my locker. I hurry to my locker between third and fourth, craning my neck in anticipation. Isabel is waiting for me.

"Don't tell anyone I gave this to you," she says, and slips me a folded sheet of paper.

Pretending to look in my locker, I unfold it. It has an address on it.

I've never ditched school before. Of course a boy I kissed has never been arrested before, either.

This is about me being real. To myself. And now I'm going to be real to Alex, like he's always wanted. It's scary, and I'm not convinced I'm doing the right thing. But I can't ignore this magnetic pull that Alex has over me.

I plug in the address on my GPS. It leads me to the south side, to a place called Enrique's Auto Body. A guy is standing in front. His mouth drops open the minute he sees me.

"I'm looking for Alex Fuentes."

The guy doesn't answer.

"Is he here?" I ask, feeling awkward. Maybe he doesn't speak English.

"What do you want with Alejandro?" the guy finally asks.

My heart is pumping so hard I can see my shirt move with each beat. "I need to talk to him."

"He'll be better off if you leave him alone," the guy says.

"*Está bien*, Enrique," a familiar voice booms. I turn to Alex, leaning against the auto body's front door with a shop towel hanging out of his pocket and a wrench in his hand. The hair peeking out of his bandanna is mussed and he looks more masculine than any guy I've ever seen.

I want to hold him. I need him to tell me it's okay, that he's not going to jail ever again.

Alex keeps his eyes fixed on mine.

"I guess I'll leave you two alone," I think I hear Enrique say, but I'm too focused on Alex to hear clearly.

My feet are glued to the same spot so it's a good thing he saunters toward me.

"Um," I start. *Please let me get through this.* "I, uh, heard you got arrested. I had to see if you're okay."

"You ditched school to see if I was okay?"

I nod because my tongue won't work.

Alex steps back. "Well, then. Now that you've seen I'm *okay*, go back to school. I gotta, you know, get back to work. My bike was impounded last night and I need to make money to get it back."

"Wait!" I yell. I take a deep breath. This is it. I'm going to spill my guts. "I don't know why or when I started falling for you, Alex. But I did. Ever since I almost ran over your motorcycle that first day of school I haven't been able to stop thinking about what it would be like if you and I got together. And that kiss . . . God, I swear I never experienced anything like that in my life. It *did* mean something. If the solar system didn't tilt then, it never will. I know it's crazy because we're so different. And if anything happens between us I don't want people at school to know. Not that you'll agree to have a secret relationship with me, but I at least have to find out if it's possible. I broke up with Colin, who I had a very public relationship with and I'm ready for something private. Private and real. I know I'm babbling like an idiot, but if you don't say something soon or give me a hint of what you're thinking then I'll—"

"Say it again," he says.

"That whole drawn-out speech?" I remember something about a solar system, but I'm too light-headed to recite the entire thing all over again.

He steps closer. "No. The part about you fallin' for me."

My eyes cling to his. "I think about you all the time, Alex. And I really, really want to kiss you again."

The sides of his mouth turn up.

Unable to face him, I look at the ground. "Don't make fun of me." I can take anything but that right about now.

"Don't turn away from me, *mamacita*. I'd never make fun of you."

"I didn't want to like you," I admit, looking back up at him.

"I know."

"This probably won't work," I tell him.

"Probably not."

"My home life's not so perfect."

"That makes two of us," he says.

"I'm willing to find out what this thing is going on between us. Are you?"

"If we weren't outside," he says, "I'd show you—"

I cut him off by grabbing the thick hair at the base of his neck and pulling that gorgeous head of his down. If we can't exactly have privacy right now, I'll settle for being real. Besides, everyone who we need to keep this a secret from is in school.

Alex keeps his hands at his side, but when I part my lips, he groans against my mouth and his wrench drops to the ground with a loud clink.

His strong hands wrap around me, making me feel protected. His velvet tongue mingles with mine, creating an unfamiliar melting sensation deep within my body. This is more than making out, it's . . . well, it feels like a lot more.

His hands never stop moving; one circles my back while the other plays with my hair.

Alex isn't the only one exploring. My hands are roving all over him, feeling his muscles tense beneath my hands and heightening my awareness of him. I touch his jaw and the roughness of a day's growth scratches my skin.

A loud clearing of Enrique's throat tears us apart.

Alex looks at me with intense passion. "I have to get back to work," he says, his breathing ragged.

"Oh. Well, sure." Suddenly embarrassed at our PDA, I step back.

"Can I see you later today?" he asks.

"My friend Sierra is coming over for dinner."

"The one who looks in her purse a lot?"

"Um, yeah." I need to change the subject or I'll be tempted to invite him, too. I can see it all now—my mom seething in disgust at Alex and his tattoos.

"My cousin Elena is gettin' married on Sunday. Go with me to the wedding," he says.

I look at the ground. "I can't have my friends know about us. Or my parents."

"I won't tell 'em."

"What about people at the wedding? They'll all see us together."

"Nobody from school will be there. Except my family, and I'll make sure they keep their mouths shut."

I can't. Lying and sneaking around has never been my strong point. I push him away. "I can't think when you're standing that close."

"Good. Now about that wedding."

God, looking at him makes me want to go. "What time?"

"Noon. It'll be an experience you won't forget. Trust me. I'll pick you up at eleven."

"I didn't say 'yes' yet."

"Ah, but you were about to," he says in his dark, smooth voice.

"Why don't I meet you here at eleven," I suggest, gesturing to the body shop. If my mom finds out about us, all hell will break loose.

He lifts my chin up to face him. "Why aren't you afraid of bein' with me?"

"Are you kidding? I'm terrified." I focus on the tattoos running up and down his arms.

"I can't pretend to live a squeaky-clean life." He holds up my hand so it's palm against palm with his. Is he thinking about the difference in the color of our skin, his rough fingers against the nail polish on the tips of mine? "In some ways we're so opposite," he says.

I thread my fingers through his. "Yeah, but in other ways we're so similar."

That gets a smile out of him, until Enrique clears his throat again.

"I'll meet you here at eleven on Sunday," I say.

Alex backs away, nods, and winks. "This time it's a date."

36

Alex

"Man, she was kissin' you like it was the last kiss of her life. If she kisses like that, I wonder how she—"

"Shut up, Enrique."

"She's gonna ruin you, Alejo," Enrique continues, calling me by my Spanish nickname. "Look at you already, spendin' time in jail last night and cuttin' school to get your motorcycle back. Granted, she's got a *buena torta*, but is she worth it?"

"I gotta get back to work," I say, my mind whirling with Enrique's words. And as I work under a Blazer for the remainder of the evening, all I want to do is make out with my *mamacita* again and again.

Yes, she's definitely worth it.

"Alex, Hector is here. With Chuy," Enrique says at six o'clock when I'm ready to head home.

I wipe my hands on my work pants. "Where are they?"

"In my office."

A feeling of dread washes over me as I approach the room. When I open the door, Hector stands there as if he owns the place. Chuy is in the corner, a not-so-innocent bystander.

"Enrique, this is a private matter."

I hadn't noticed Enrique behind me, acting as my ally should I need one. I give a nod to my cousin. I've been loyal to the Blood, there's no reason Hector should doubt my commitment. Chuy's presence makes this meeting a big deal. If it was just Hector, I wouldn't be this tense.

"Alex," Hector says the moment Enrique is out of sight. "Ain't it good to meet here instead of the courthouse?"

I give him a weak smile and shut the door.

Hector motions to the small, ripped couch on the far side of the room. "Sit down." He waits until I take a seat. "I need you to do me a favor, *amigo*."

There's no use in delaying the inevitable. "What kind of favor?"

"A shipment needs to be delivered October thirty-first."

That's over a month and a half away. Halloween night. "I don't deal drugs," I cut in. "You knew that from day one."

I eye Chuy like a pitcher in baseball does when a guy leads too far off base.

Hector stands over me and puts his hand on my shoulder. "You've got to get over what happened to your old man. If you want to lead the Blood, you've got to deal drugs."

"Then count me out."

Hector's hand tightens and Chuy steps forward. A silent threat.

"I wish it were that simple," Hector says. "I need you to do this for me. And, quite honestly, you owe me."

Shit. If I hadn't gotten arrested in the first place, I wouldn't owe this debt to Hector.

"I know you won't disappoint me. By the way, how's your mother? I haven't seen her in a while."

"She's fine," I say, wondering what *mi'amá* has to do with this conversation.

"Tell her I said hello, will ya?"

What the hell does that mean?

Hector opens the door, motions for Chuy to follow him, and leaves me to stew over it.

I sit back, staring at the closed door, and wonder if I have it in me to do a drug deal. If I want to keep my family safe, my choice has been made for me.

37

Brittany

"I can't believe you broke up with Colin." Sierra is painting her nails on my bed after dinner. "I hope you don't live to regret your decision, Brit. You two have been together for so long. I thought you loved him. You broke his heart, you know. He called Doug crying."

I sit up. "I want to be happy. Colin doesn't make me happy anymore. He admitted to cheating on me over the summer with some girl he met. He had sex with her, Sierra."

"What? I can't believe it."

"Trust me. Colin and I were over when he went away for the summer. It just took me a while to realize we couldn't fake it anymore."

"So, did you move on to *Alex*? Colin thinks you're mixing more than just test tubes with your chem partner."

"No," I lie. Even though Sierra is my best friend, she holds the belief there's a definite social divide. While I want to tell her the truth, I can't. Not now.

Sierra closes the bottle of nail polish and huffs. "Brit, I'm your best friend whether you want to believe it or not. You're lying to me. Admit it."

"What do you want me to say?" I ask.

"Try the truth, for once. Geez, Brit. I understand you don't want Darlene to know shit because she's gone off the deep end emotionally. And I can understand you not wanting the triple M-factor knowing everything. But this is me. Your best friend. You know, the one who knows about Shelley and who has seen your mom go off on you."

Sierra grabs her purse and shoves it onto her shoulder.

I don't want her mad at me, but I want her to know where I'm coming from. "What if you want to tell Doug stuff? I don't want to put you in a situation where you have to lie to him."

Sierra gives me a sneer that resembles the one I use all the time. "Screw you, Brit. Thanks for making me feel like my best friend doesn't trust me." Before she leaves my room she turns back and says, "You know how people have selective hearing? You have selective disclosure. I saw you having a major conversation with Isabel Avila today in the hall. If I didn't know better, I'd say you were sharing secrets with her." She throws up her hands. "Okay, so I admit I was jealous that my best friend is obviously sharing stuff with another friend and not me. When you realize I'm rooting like hell for you to be happy, call me."

She's right. But this thing with Alex is so new, and I'm feeling vulnerable about it. Isabel is the only one who knows both me and Alex, so I went to her. "Sierra, you're my best friend. You know that," I say, hoping she knows it's the truth. I might have trust issues, but that doesn't negate the fact that she's the closest friend I have.

"Then start acting like it," she says before leaving.

I wipe a bead of sweat slowly dripping from my brow as I drive to meet Alex for the wedding.

I picked a cream-colored, fitted sundress with spaghetti straps. My parents will be home when I get back, so I put a change of clothes inside my workout bag. My mom will see the Brittany she expects to see when I get home—a perfect daughter. Who cares if it's a facade as long as it keeps her happy. Sierra was right; I do have selective disclosure.

My car rounds the corner, riding the path to the body shop. When I spot Alex leaning on his motorcycle waiting for me in the parking lot, my pulse skips a beat.

Oh, boy. I'm in trouble.

Gone is his ever-present bandanna. Alex's thick black hair rests on his forehead, daring to be swept back. Black pants and a black silk shirt have replaced his jeans and T-shirt. He looks like a young Mexican daredevil. I can't help but smile as I park next to him.

"*Querida*, you look like you've got a secret."

I do, I think as I step out of my car. *You.*

"*Dios mío*. You look . . . *preciosa*."

I turn in a circle. "Is this dress okay?"

"Come here," he says, pulling me against him. "I don't want to go to the wedding anymore. I'd rather have you all to myself."

"No way," I say, running a slow finger along the side of his jaw.

"You're a tease."

I love this playful side of Alex. It makes me forget all about those demons.

"I came to see a Latino wedding, and I expect to see one," I tell him.

"And here I thought you were comin' to be with me."

"You've got a big ego, Fuentes."

"That's not all I've got." He backs me against my car, his breath warming my neck more than the midday sun. I close my eyes and expect his lips on mine, but instead I hear his voice. "Give me your keys," he says, reaching around and taking them from my hand.

"You're not going to throw them into the bushes, are you?"

"Don't tempt me."

Alex opens my car door and slides into the driver's seat.

"Aren't you going to invite me in?" I ask, confused.

"No. I'm parkin' your car in the shop so it doesn't get jacked. This is an official date. I'm drivin'."

I point to his motorcycle. "Don't think I'm getting on that thing."

His left eyebrow raises a fraction. "Why not? Julio's not good enough for you?"

"Julio? You named your motorcycle Julio?"

"After my great uncle who helped my parents move here from Mexico."

"I like Julio just fine. I just don't want to ride on him wearing this short dress. Unless you want everyone riding behind us to see my undies."

He rubs his chin, thinking about it. "Now that would be a sight for sore eyes."

I cross my arms over my chest.

"I'm jokin'. We're takin' my cousin's car." We get in a black Camry parked across the street.

After driving a few minutes he pulls a cigarette from a pack lying on the dashboard. The click of the lighter makes me cringe.

"What?" he asks, the lit cigarette dangling from his lips.

He can smoke if he wants. This might be an official date, but I'm not his official girlfriend or anything. I shake my head. "Nothing."

I hear him exhale, and the cigarette smoke burns my nostrils more than my mom's perfume. As I lower my window all the way, I suppress a cough.

When he stops at a stoplight, he looks over at me. "If you've got a problem with me smokin', tell me."

"Okay, I've got a problem with you smoking," I tell him.

"Why didn't you just say so?" he says, then smashes it into the car's ashtray.

"I can't believe you actually like it," I say when he starts driving again.

"It relaxes me."

"Do I make you nervous?"

His gaze travels from my eyes to my breasts and down to where my dress meets my thighs. "In that dress you do."

38

Alex

If I keep looking at her long legs I'm gonna have an accident. "How's that sister of yours?" I ask, changing the subject.

"She's waiting to beat you again at checkers."

"Is that right? Well, tell her I was goin' easy on her. I was tryin' to impress you."

"By losing?"

I shrug. "It worked, didn't it?"

I notice her fidgeting with her dress as if she needs to fix it to impress *me*. Wanting to ease her anxiety, I slide my fingers down her arm before capturing her hand in mine.

"You tell Shelley I'll be back for a rematch," I say.

She turns to me, her blue eyes sparkling. "Really?"

"Absolutely."

During the drive, I try and make small talk. It doesn't work. I'm not a small talk kind of guy. It's a good thing Brittany seems content without talking.

Before long I park in front of a small, two-story brick house.

"Isn't the wedding at a church?"

"Not for Elena. She wanted to get married at her parents' house."

I rest my hand on the small of her back as we walk up to the house. Don't ask me why I feel a need to claim her as mine. Maybe deep down I *am* a Neanderthal.

When we enter the house, Mariachi music blares from the back-yard and people fill up almost every inch of space. I check out Brittany's reaction, wondering if she feels like she's been magically transported to Mexico. My family doesn't live in big houses with swimming pools like she's used to.

Enrique and a bunch of my other cousins yell greetings to us. They all speak Spanish, which would seem normal except that my date only speaks English. I'm used to being kissed to death by my aunts and given hearty slaps on the backs by my uncles. I'm not sure she is, though. I nudge Brittany closer to me as a sign that I haven't forgotten her, and attempt to introduce her to my family but give up when I realize there's no way she'll remember all their names.

"*¡Ese!*" comes a voice from behind us.

I turn to Paco. "What's up?" I say, slapping my friend on the back. "Brittany, I'm sure you've seen *mi mejor amigo* around school. Don't worry, he knows not to tell anyone he saw you here."

"My lips are sealed," he says, then like a dork pretends to lock his mouth and toss the key away.

"Hi, Paco," she says, laughing.

Jorge sidles up to us, wearing a white tuxedo and a red rose in his lapel.

I slap my cousin-to-be on the back. "Yo, man, you really do clean up nice."

"You don't look too bad yourself. You gonna introduce me to your friend, or not?"

"Brittany, this is Jorge. He's the poor guy . . . I mean, lucky guy, marrying my cousin Elena."

Jorge hugs her. "Any friend of Alex's is a friend of ours."

"Where's the bride?" Paco asks.

"She's upstairs in her parents' bedroom, crying."

"From happiness?" I guess.

"No, man. I went in there to give her a kiss and now she's thinkin' of callin' it off, says it's bad luck to see the groom before the wedding," Jorge adds, shrugging.

"Good luck," I say. "Elena is superstitious. She'll probably make you do some crazy shit to make the bad luck go away."

As Paco and Jorge contemplate what Elena will make him do to erase the bad luck, I take Brittany's hand and lead her outside. A live band is playing. Even though we're *pochos*, we definitely keep our traditions and culture close. Our food is spicy, our families are big and close, and we like to dance to music that makes our bodies move.

"Is Paco your cousin?" Brittany asks.

"No, he just likes to think he is. Carlos, this is Brittany," I say when we reach my brother.

"Yeah, I know," Carlos says. "Remember I saw you two swapping spit."

Brittany is stunned into silence.

"Watch your mouth," I say, slapping Carlos on the back of the head.

Brittany puts her hand on my chest. "It's okay, Alex. You don't have to protect me from everyone."

Carlos takes on a cocky stance. "That's right, bro. You don't have to protect her. Well, maybe except from *Mamá*."

That's it. I exchange heated words with Carlos in Spanish so Brittany can't understand. *"Vete, cabrón no molestes."* Is he trying to make my date have a shitty time? With a huff, Carlos heads for the food.

"Where's your other brother?" Brittany asks.

We sit at one of the many small rented tables in the middle of the yard. I drape my arm over the back of her chair.

"Luis is right there." I point to the corner of the yard, where my little brother is the center of attention doing imitations of barnyard animals. I have yet to inform him that talent isn't as much of a chick magnet when you get into junior high.

Brittany's eyes are focused on my cousin's four little kids, all under the age of seven, running around. Two-year-old Marissa has decided her dress isn't comfortable and has tossed it in the corner of the yard.

"They probably all look like a bunch of rowdy *mojados* to you."

She smiles. "No. They look like a bunch of people having fun at an outdoor wedding. Who's that?" she asks as a guy in a U.S. military uniform walks past us. "Another cousin?"

"Yep. Paul just came back from the Middle East. Believe it or not, he used to be in the Python Trio, a Chicago gang. Man, before the Marines he was really fucked up with drugs."

She flashes me a look.

"I told you before, I don't mess with drugs. Not anymore, at least," I say firmly, wanting her to believe me. "Or deal them."

"Promise?"

"Yeah," I say, remembering at the beach when I got fucked up with Carmen. That was the last time. "No matter what you've heard, I stay away from the *coca*, 'cause that stuff ain't no joke. Believe it or not, I'd like to keep all the brain cells I was born with."

"What about Paco?" she asks. "Does he do drugs?"

"Sometimes."

She watches Paco, laughing and joking with my family, desperately trying to be a part of it, instead of his own. His ma left a few years ago, leaving him in a crap situation at home with his dad. I don't blame him for wanting an escape.

My cousin Elena finally appears in a lacy white dress and the wedding starts.

While the vows are recited, I stand behind Brittany and gather her into my arms, holding her snugly. I wonder what she'll be wearing at her wedding. She'll probably have professional photographers and videographers capturing the moment for eternity.

"Ahora los declar. Marido y Mujer," the priest says.

The bride and groom kiss and everyone applauds.

Brittany squeezes my hand.

39

Brittany

I can tell Jorge and Elena are madly in love with each other and it makes me wonder if I'll be as in love with my future husband.

I think about Shelley. She'll never have a husband, never have children. I know my own kids will love her as much as I do; she'll have no lack of love her entire life. But will she ever internally yearn for something she'll never have—a husband and family of her own?

Looking back at Alex, I can't see myself involved in gangs and who knows what else. It isn't me. But this guy, smack dab in the middle of everything I'm against, is connected to me like nobody else. It's my mission to make him change his life so, one day, people might say we're a perfect couple.

As music fills the air, I wrap my arms around Alex's waist and lay my head on his chest. He pushes stray tendrils away from my neck and holds me as we sway to the music.

A guy approaches the bride with a five-dollar bill.

"It's a tradition," Alex explains. "He's payin' to dance with the bride. They call it the prosperity dance."

I observe, fascinated, as the guy attaches the five-dollar bill to the train of the bride's dress with a safety pin.

My mother would be horrified.

Someone yells to the guy dancing with the bride and everyone laughs.

"What's so funny?"

"They're sayin' he pinned the bill close to her ass."

I study the couples on the dance floor and try to replicate their moves as I get into the music. When the bride stops dancing, I ask Alex if he's going to dance with her, too.

When he says yes, I push him forward. "Go dance with Elena. I'm going to talk to your mom."

"You sure you want to do that?"

"Yeah. I saw her when we first walked in, and I don't want to ignore her. Don't worry about me. I need to do this."

He takes a ten-dollar bill out of his wallet. I try not to notice, but it's now empty. He's about to give all the money he has on him to the bride. Can he afford it? I know he works at the auto body shop, but the money he makes probably goes directly to his family.

I step back until our hands separate. "I'll be back soon."

At the row of tables where the women are setting out platters of food, I walk up to Alex's mom. She's wearing a red wraparound dress and looks younger than my mom. People think my mom is pretty, but Mrs. Fuentes has the timeless beauty of a movie star. Her eyes are big and brown, her eyelashes touch her eyebrows, and her skin is slightly bronzed and flawless.

I tap her on the shoulder as she's setting the napkins on the table. "Hi, Mrs. Fuentes," I say.

"Brittany, right?" she asks.

I nod. *Re-introduction over, Brittany. Stop stalling.* "Umm, I've wanted to say something to you since I got here. And now seems like as good a time as any, but now I seem to be rambling and not getting to the point. I do this when I'm nervous."

The woman is looking at me like I have a screw loose. "Go on," she urges.

"Yes, well, I know we got off on the wrong foot. And I'm sorry if you felt disrespected in any way the last time we met. I just wanted you to know that I didn't go to your house with the intention of kissing Alex."

"Forgive me if I'm curious, but what *are* your intentions?"

"Excuse me?"

"What are your intentions with Alex?"

"I . . . I'm just not sure what you want me to say. To be honest, we're figuring it out as we go along."

Mrs. Fuentes puts a hand on my shoulder. "The dear Lord knows I'm not the best mother in the world. But I care about my sons more than life itself, Brittany. And I'll do anything to protect them from harm. I see the way he looks at you, and it scares me. I can't bear to see him hurt one more time by someone he cares about."

Hearing Alex's mom talk about him makes me yearn for a mother who cares and loves me as much as Alex's mom loves him.

Trying to swallow what Mrs. Fuentes said is close to impossible; her words leave a lump the size of a golf ball in my throat.

The truth is, lately I don't even feel like a part of my own family. I'm someone who is expected by my parents to do and say the right things all the time. I've played the role for so long to help my parents concentrate on Shelley, who truly needs their undivided attention.

It's so hard sometimes, trying desperately to make up for being the "normal" kid. Nobody told me I didn't have to be perfect all the time. Truth is, my life is filled with never-ending, humongous amounts of guilt.

Guilt for being the normal child.

Guilt for feeling that I have to make sure Shelley is loved as much as I am.

Guilt for fearing that my own children might be like my sister.

Guilt for being embarrassed when people stare at Shelley in public places.

It'll never stop. How can it when I was born with guilt right up to my ears? To Mrs. Fuentes, family means love and protection. To me, family equals guilt and conditional love.

"Mrs. Fuentes, I can't promise not to hurt Alex. But I can't stay away from him, even if that's what you want. I already tried that." Because being with Alex takes me away from my own darkness. I can feel tears welling in the corners of my eyes and falling down my face. I push my way through the crowd to find a bathroom.

Paco is walking out of the bathroom and I rush past him.

"You might want to wait before you—" Paco's voice fades as I close the door, locking myself in. Wiping my eyes, I gaze into the mirror. I'm a complete mess. My mascara is dripping and . . . oh, it's no use. I slide down and sit on the cold tile floor. Now I realize what Paco was about to tell me. The place stinks; it really reeks . . . almost to the point where I want to throw up. I put my hand over my nose, trying to ignore the offending smell as I think about Mrs. Fuentes's words.

I sit on the bathroom floor, wiping my eyes with toilet paper and doing my best to cover my nose.

A loud knock interrupts my crying fit. "Brittany, you in there?" Alex's voice comes through the door.

"No."

"Please come out."

"No."

"Then let me in."

"No."

"I want to teach you somethin' in Spanish."

"What?"

"No es gran cosa."

"What does it mean?" I ask, the tissue still on my face.

"I'll tell you if you let me in."

I turn the knob until it clicks.

Alex steps inside. "It means it's not a big deal." After locking the door behind him, he crouches beside me and takes me in his arms, pulling me close. Then he sniffs a few times. "Holy shit. Was Paco in here?"

I nod.

He smoothes my hair and mutters something in Spanish. "What did my mother say to you?"

I bury my face in his chest. "She was just being honest," I mumble into his shirt.

A loud knock at the door interrupts us.

"Abre la puerta, soy Elena."

"Who's that?"

"The bride."

"Let me in!" Elena commands.

Alex unlocks the door. A vision in white ruffles with dozens of dollar bills safety-pinned to the back of her dress squeezes her way into the bathroom, then shuts the door behind her.

"Okay, what's goin' on?" She, too, sniffs a bunch of times. "Was Paco in here?"

Alex and I nod.

"What the fuck does that guy eat that it comes out his other end smelling so rotten? Dammit," she says, wadding up tissue and putting it over her nose.

"It was a beautiful ceremony," I say through my own tissue. This is the most awkward and surreal situation I've ever been in.

Elena grabs my hand. "Come outside and enjoy the party. My aunt can be confrontational, but she doesn't mean any harm. Besides, I think deep down she likes you."

"I'm taking her home," Alex says, playing the role of my hero. I wonder when he'll get sick of it.

"No, you're not takin' her home or I'll lock both of you in this stinkin' smelly room so you'll stay."

Elena means every word.

Another knock at the door. *"Vete vete."*

I don't know what Elena said, but she sure said it with gusto.

"Soy Jorge."

I shrug and look to Alex for an explanation.

"It's the groom," he says, clueing me in.

Jorge slips in. He isn't as crude as the rest of us because he ignores the fact that the room smells like something died. But he sniffs loudly a few times and his eyes start to water.

"Come on, Elena," Jorge says, trying to cover his nose inconspicuously but doing a poor job of it. "Your guests are wondering where you are."

"Can't you see I'm talkin' to my cousin and his date?"

"Yeah, but—"

Elena holds up a hand to silence him while holding the tissue over her nose with the other. "I said, I'm talkin' to my cousin and his date," she declares with attitude. "And I'm not finished yet."

"You," Elena says, pointing directly at me. "Come with me. Alex, I want you and your brothers to sing."

Alex shakes his head. "Elena, I don't think—"

Elena holds up a hand in front of Alex, silencing even him. "I didn't ask you to think. I asked you to join your brothers in singin' to me and my new husband."

Elena opens the door and yanks me through the house, stopping only when we reach the backyard. She lets me go only to grab the microphone from the lead singer.

"Paco!" she announces loudly. "Yeah, I'm talkin' to you," Elena says, pointing to Paco talking to a bunch of girls. "Next time you want to take a dump, do it in someone else's house."

Paco's entourage of girls backs up and giggles, leaving him alone.

Jorge rushes to the stage and attempts to pick up his wife. The poor man struggles while everyone laughs and claps.

When Elena is finally off the stage and Alex talks to the band leader, the guests cheer for Alex and his brothers to sing.

Paco sits next to me.

"Uh, sorry about the bathroom thing. I tried to warn you," he says sheepishly.

"It's okay. I think Elena embarrassed you enough." I lean over to Paco and ask, "Seriously, what do *you* think of Alex and me together?"

"Seriously, you're pro'bly the best thing that's ever happened to the guy."

40

Alex

After my dad died, our ma tried to cheer me, Carlos, and Luis with music. We'd dance around the house, taking turns singing with her. I think it was her way to forget her sorrow, at least for a little while. At night I used to hear her sobbing in her room. I never opened the door, but I itched to break into song and make all of her hurt go away.

I talk to the band before taking the microphone. "I wouldn't make a fool out of myself by doin' this, but the Fuentes brothers can't ignore this special request from the bride. Elena can be pretty persuasive."

"Yeah, I know!" Jorge yells back.

Elena punches him in his arm. He winces. Elena knows how to land a punch. Jorge kisses his bride, too happy to care.

My brothers and I start to sing. It isn't a serious song. We ad lib songs by Enrique Iglesias, Shakira, and even my favorite, Maná. When I crouch down to sing to my little cousins, I wink at Brittany.

That's when I notice a hush in the crowd and whispers of shock. It's Hector. He made an appearance, which is rare. He winds his way through the yard wearing an expensive suit while everyone stares at him.

I finish the song and take my place at Brittany's side. I have an urge to protect her.

"Want a smoke?" Paco asks me as he pulls Marlboros out of his back pocket.

I briefly glance at Brittany before answering, "No."

Paco looks at me curiously, then shrugs and takes one for himself. "Great singin', Alex. If you would've given me a few more minutes I'd have your *novia* in the palm of my hand."

He called her my girl. Is she my girl?

I lead her to a cooler full of drinks, Paco in tow. I'm careful not to steer her toward Hector.

Mario, a friend of one of my cousins, is standing over the cooler sporting Python Trio gang colors and big, baggy jeans that hang off his ass. The Python Trio are our allies, but if Brittany saw him on the street, she'd probably run in the opposite direction.

"Hey Alex, Paco," Mario says.

"I see you dressed up for the wedding, Mario," I mutter.

"*Cabrón*, monkey suits are for white guys," Mario says, ignoring the fact that my date is in fact white. "You suburban gangstas are too soft. In the city are the real broth'as."

"Okay, tough guy," Paco says with pure attitude. "Tell that to Hector."

I glare at Mario. "Mario, you keep talkin' shit like that and I'll give you firsthand proof of how tough we are . . . *never* underestimate the LB."

Mario backs up. "Well, I've got a date with a bottle of Corona. Catch you later, *güey*."

"It looks like he's carryin' a load in those pants," Paco says, staring at Mario from behind.

I look over at Brittany, who looks paler than she usually is. "You okay?"

"You threatened that guy," she whispers. "I mean, *seriously* threatened him."

Instead of answering her, I take her hand and lead her to the edge of the makeshift dance floor, which is really a section of grass. Slow music is playing.

When I pull her close, she backs away. "What are you doing?"

"Dance with me," I order. "Don't argue with me. Put your arms around me and dance." I don't want to hear about how I'm in a gang, and how it scares her, and how she wants me to be out of the gang in order for her to date me.

"But—"

"Don't think about what I said to Mario," I say close to her ear. "He was feelin' us out, checkin' how loyal we are to Hector. If he senses any dissension, his gang might take advantage. You see, all gangs are separated into Folks or People. Every gang is affiliated with one or the other, and those affiliated with Folks are rivals with those affiliated with People. Mario is affiliated—"

"Alex," she interrupts.

"Yeah."

"Assure me nothing's going to happen to you."

I can't. "Just dance," I say quietly as I guide her arms around me and we dance.

Looking over Brittany, I see Hector and my mother in an intense conversation. I wonder what they're talking about. She starts walking away from him, until he grabs her arm and pulls her back and says something in her ear. Just when I'm about to stop dancing to find out what the hell is going on, *mi'amá* smiles at Hector playfully and laughs at something he said. I'm obviously being paranoid.

Hours pass and darkness falls on the city. The party is still going strong when we walk to the car. On the drive back to Fairfield, we're both quiet.

"Come here," I say softly when I park in the auto body's back lot.

She leans over the middle console, closing the distance between us. "I had an amazing time," she whispers. "Well, besides when I hid in the bathroom . . . and you threatened that guy."

"Forget about that and kiss me," I say.

I weave my hands in her hair. She wraps her arms around my neck as I trace the valley between her lips with my tongue. Parting her lips, I deepen the kiss. It's like a tango, first moving slow and rhythmic and then, when we're both panting and our tongues collide, the kiss turns into a hot, fast dance I never want to end. Carmen's kisses may have been hot, but Brittany's are more sensual, sexy, and extremely addictive.

We're still in the car, but it's cramped and the front seats don't give us enough room. Before I know it, we've moved to the backseat. Still not ideal, but I hardly notice.

I'm so getting into her moans and kisses and hands in my hair. And the smell of vanilla cookies. I'm not going to push her too far tonight. But without thinking, my hand slowly moves up her bare thigh.

"It feels so good," she says breathlessly.

I lean her back while my hands explore on their own. My lips caress the hollow of her neck as I ease down the strap to her dress and bra. In response, she unbuttons my shirt. When it's open, her fingers roam over my chest and shoulders, searing my skin.

"You're . . . perfect," she pants.

Right now I'm not gonna argue with her. Moving lower, my tongue follows a path down to her silky skin exposed to the night air. She grabs the back of my hair, urging me on. She tastes so damn good. Too good. *¡Caramelo!*

I pull away a few inches and capture her gaze with mine, those shining sapphires glowing with desire. Talk about perfect.

"I want you, *chula*," I say, my voice hoarse. She presses against my erection, the pleasure/pain almost unbearable. But when I start to pull her panties down, she stills my hand and pushes it away.

"I . . . I'm not ready for that. Alex, stop."

I move off her and sit back in the seat, waiting for my body to cool down. I can't look at her as she adjusts her straps, covering her body again. Shit, I went too fast. I told myself not to get too excited, to keep my wits when I'm with this girl. Raking my hand through my hair, I let out a slow breath. "I'm sorry."

"No, I'm sorry. It's not your fault. I urged you on and you have every right to be pissed off. Listen, I just got out of a relationship with Colin and I've got a lot of stuff going on at home." She puts her face in her hands. "I'm so confused." She grabs her purse and opens the door.

I follow her, my black shirt open and flying in the wind behind me like a vampire's cape. Either that or the grim reaper's. "Brittany, wait."

"Please . . . open the door to the garage. I need my car."

"Don't go."

I press the keypad code.

"I'm sorry," she says once more.

"Stop sayin' that. Listen, no matter what happened, I'm not with you just to get into your pants. I got carried away with the way we clicked tonight, your vanilla scent that I wanted to keep inhalin' forever and . . . shit, I really messed this up, didn't I?"

Brittany climbs inside her car. "Can we take it slow, Alex? This is going way too fast for me."

"Yeah," I say, nodding. I keep my hands in my pockets, resisting the urge to pull her out of the car.

And dammit if Brittany doesn't drive away.

I'd been caught up in her exploring eager hands and went overboard. I forget about everything except her when her body is close.

The bet.

This thing with Brittany is supposed to be about a bet, not falling for a north sider. I have to keep in mind that I'm only interested in Brittany because of the bet, and I better ignore what I suspect are real feelings.

Feelings can't be a part of this game.

41

Brittany

I pull into a McDonald's where I can be anonymous, change into jeans and a pink wrap-around sweater, and drive home.

I'm scared because with Alex, it feels too raw. When I'm with Alex, everything is way more intense. My feelings, my emotions, my desire. I was never addicted to Colin, never wanted to be with him twenty-four/seven. I crave Alex. Oh, God. I think I'm falling in love with him.

But I know loving someone means losing a part of myself. And tonight, in the car when Alex reached under my dress, I was afraid of losing control. My entire life is about staying in control, so this is not good. It scares me.

I walk through the front door of my house, ready to sneak up to my room and put the dress in my closet. Unfortunately, my mom is standing in the foyer, waiting for me.

"Where were you?" my mother asks sternly while holding up my chemistry book and folder. "You said you were working out, then *studying* with that Hernandez boy."

Busted. Time to either shut up or fess up. "His last name is Fuentes, not Hernandez. And yes, I was with him."

Silence.

My mother's lips are in a tight, thin line. "It's obvious you weren't studying. What do you have in that gym bag?" she demands. "Drugs? Are you hiding drugs in there?"

"I don't do drugs," I respond sharply.

She cocks an eyebrow and points to my bag. "Open it," she orders.

I huff and kneel down to unzip it. I feel like a jail inmate. Pulling out my dress, I hold it up.

"A dress?" my mother asks.

"I went to a wedding with Alex. His cousin got married."

"That boy made you lie to me. He's manipulating you, Brittany."

"He didn't make me lie, Mom," I say, exasperated. "Give me a little credit, would you? I did it all on my own."

Her anger is in full swing, I can tell by the way her eyes are blazing and her hands are shaking. "If I ever . . . EVER find you were out with that boy again, I'll have no problem convincing your father that you should be sent to boarding school the rest of your senior year. Don't you think I have enough to worry about with Shelley? Promise me you'll have no other contact with him outside of school."

I promise, then run to my room and call Sierra.

"What's up?" she says.

"Sierra, I need a best friend right now."

"And you chose me? Gee, I'm flattered," she says dryly.

"Okay, I lied to you. I like Alex. Big-time."

Silence.

Silence.

"Sierra, are you there? Or are you ignoring me?"

"I'm not ignoring you, Brit. I'm just wondering why you chose to tell me now."

"Because I need to talk about it. With you. Do you hate me?"

"You're my best friend," she says.

"And you're mine."

"Best friends are still best friends even though one decides to abandon all reason and date a gangbanger. Right?"

"I hope so."

"Brit, don't lie to me ever again."

"I won't. And you can share the info with Doug as long as he promises to keep it to himself."

"Thanks for trusting me, Brit. You may not think it means a lot, but it does."

After I finish the entire story and I hang up with Sierra feeling really good that things are back to normal with her, my phone rings. It's Isabel.

"I have to talk to you," Isabel says when I answer.

"What is it?"

"Did you see Paco today?"

Umm . . . so much for secrets. "Yeah."

"Did you mention me?"

"No. Why? Did you want me to?"

"No. Yes. Oh, I don't know. I'm so confused."

"Isabel, just tell him how you feel. It worked for me with Alex."

"Yeah, but you're Brittany Ellis."

"You want to know what it's like being Brittany Ellis? I'll tell you. I'm insecure, just like anyone else. And have more pressure on me to put on an act, so people's image of me isn't shattered and they don't see that I'm really just like anyone else. And that makes me more vulnerable, and more scrutinized, and more susceptible to gossip."

"So I guess you probably won't be happy about the rumors

spreading about you and Alex within my group of friends. Do you want to know what they are?"

"No."

"You sure?"

"Yeah. If you consider yourself my friend, don't tell me."

Because if I know the rumors, I'll feel like I have to confront them. And right this second I want to live in ignorant bliss.

42

Alex

After having Brittany speed out of the body shop to get away from me, I'm not feeling like talking and hope to avoid *mi'amá* when I get home. But one glance at the living room sofa puts that wish to rest.

The television is off, the lights are low, and my brothers have probably been sent to our bedroom.

"Alejandro," she starts. "I didn't want this life for us."

"I know."

"I hope Brittany doesn't put ideas in your head that shouldn't be there."

I shrug. "Like what? That she hates I'm in a gang? You may not have chosen this life for me, but you sure as hell didn't protest when I got jumped in."

"Don't talk like that, Alejandro."

"Because the truth is too painful? I'm in a gang to protect you and my brothers, *Mamá*. You know that, even though we don't talk about it," I say, my voice getting louder to match my frustration. "It's a choice I made a long time ago. You can pretend you didn't encourage me, but," I pull off my shirt, revealing my Latino Blood tattoos, "look at me real good. I'm a gangbanger, just like *Papá*. You want me to deal drugs, too?"

Tears stream down her face. "If I thought there was another way—"

"You were too scared to leave this shithole, and now we're stuck. Don't put your guilt on me, or my girl."

"That's not fair," she says, rising.

"What's not fair is you livin' like a widow in perpetual mourning since *Papá* died. Why don't we move back to Mexico? Tell Uncle Julio he wasted his life's savings sendin' us to America. Or are you afraid to go back to Mexico and tell your family that you failed here?"

"We are not having this discussion."

"Open your eyes." I stretch my arms out wide. "What do you have here worth stayin' for? Your sons? 'Cause that's a copout. Is this the image of the American Dream to you?" I point to the shrine of my father. "He was a gangbanger, not a saint."

"He had no choice," she cries. "He protected us."

"And now I'm protectin' us. You gonna have a shrine of me when I get whacked? And Carlos? Because he's next in line, you know. And Luis after him."

Mi'amá slaps me hard, then backs away. *Dios mío*, I hate that I upset her. I reach out to her, my fingers wrapping around her arm to hug her and apologize, but she winces. *"Mamá?"* I question, wondering what's wrong. I wasn't rough with her, but she's acting like I was.

She wrenches herself out of my grasp and turns away, but I can't let it go. I step forward and lift up the sleeve of her dress. To my horror I find a nasty bruise on her upper arm. Its purple, black, and blue hues stare back at me, and my mind rushes back to the wedding when I saw my mom and Hector in a private discussion.

"Hector did this to you?" I question softly.

"You have to stop asking questions about your *papá*," she tells me, quickly pulling down her sleeve to cover the bruise.

Rage rumbles in my gut and spreads as I realize *mi'amá* got bruised as a warning to me. "Why? Who is Hector trying to protect?" Is he protecting someone in the LB, or another gang member affiliated with the LB? I wish I could just ask Hector. Even more, I'd like to retaliate and kick his ass for hurting my mom, but Hector is untouchable. We all know if I challenge Hector, it'll be as if I'm turning on the Blood.

She glares at me. "Don't question me on this. There are things you don't know, Alejandro. Things you should never know. Just let it go."

"You think living in ignorance is a good thing? *Papá* was a gang member who dealt drugs. I'm not afraid of the truth, dammit. Why is everyone around me covering up the truth?"

My hands feel clammy as I hold them stiffly at my sides. A sound from the hallway catches my attention. I turn to see my two brothers, their eyes wide in confusion.

Fuck.

As soon as she sees Luis and Carlos, she sucks in a breath. I'd do anything to take the hurt away from her.

I step toward her and put my hand gently on her shoulder. *"Perdón, Mamá."*

She swipes my hand away as she suppresses a sob and runs to her room, slamming the door behind her.

"Is it true?" Carlos asks, his voice as tight as a noose.

I nod. "Yeah."

Luis shakes his head and furrows his brows in confusion. "What are you two saying? I don't understand. I thought *Papá* was a good man. *Mamá* always said he was a good man."

I walk over to my little brother and pull his head into my chest.

"It's all lies!" Carlos blurts out. "You, him. It's all lies. ¡*Mentiras!*"

"Carlos . . . ," I say, releasing Luis and grabbing Carlos's arm.

Carlos looks at my hand in disgust, his temper seething. "And all along I thought you joined the Latino Blood to protect us. But you're just following in *Papá's* footsteps. Screw being a hero. You like being an LB, but you forbid me to join. Isn't that a bit hypocritical, brother?"

"Maybe."

"You're a disgrace to this family, you know that, don't you?"

As soon as I lessen my grip on him, Carlos punches open the back door and storms out.

Luis's quiet voice breaks the silence. "Sometimes good men need to do things that aren't good. Right?"

I ruffle his hair. Luis is way more innocent than I was at his age. "You know, I think you're gonna be the smartest Fuentes yet, little bro. Now go to bed and let me talk to Carlos."

I find Carlos sitting on our back stoop, which faces our neighbor's yard.

"Is that how he died?" he asks as I sit beside him. "In a drug deal?"

"Yeah."

"He took you along?"

I nod.

"You were only six years old, the bastard." Carlos cynically blows out a breath. "You know, I saw Hector today at the basketball courts on Main Street."

"Stay away from him. Truth is, I had no choice after *Papá* died, and now I'm stuck. If you think I'm in the LB 'cause I like it, guess again. I don't want you jumped in."

"I know."

I give him a stern look like our mother used to give me when I put tennis balls in her panty hose and flung them to see how high they'd fly. "Listen to me, Carlos, and listen good. Concentrate on school so you can go to college. Make somethin' of yourself." Unlike me.

There's a long silence.

"Destiny doesn't want me to join, either. She wants to go to some university and get a nursing degree." He chuckles. "She said it would be great if we went to the same university." I listen, because he needs me to stop giving advice and let him figure the rest out on his own. "I like Brittany, you know," he says.

"Me, too." I think of earlier, when we were in the car. I got carried away, big-time. I hope I haven't screwed everything up with her, too.

"I saw Brittany talkin' to *Mamá* at the wedding. She held her own."

"To tell you the truth, she kind of had a meltdown in the bathroom."

"For someone so smart, you're *loco* if you think you can handle everything."

"I'm tough," I tell Carlos. "And always prepared for danger."

Carlos pats my back. "Somehow, brother, I think dating a girl from the north side is tougher than being in a gang."

It's the perfect opening to tell my brother the truth. "Carlos, you see guys in the LB who talk of brotherhood and honor and loyalty and it sounds great. But they're not family, you know. And the brotherhood lasts only as long as you're willing to do what they want you to do."

My mom opens the door and looks down at us. She looks so sad. I wish I could change her life and take the hurt away, but I know I can't.

"Carlos, let me talk to Alejandro alone."

When Carlos is inside the house, out of hearing range, my mom sits beside me. She has a cigarette in her hand, the first one I've seen her smoke in a long time.

I'm waiting for her to talk first. I've said enough tonight.

"I've made a lot of mistakes in my life, Alejandro," she says as she blows cigarette smoke up at the moon. "And some of them can't be undone no matter how much I pray to the Lord above." She reaches out and tucks my hair behind my ears. "You're a teenager who has the responsibilities of a man. I know it's not fair to you."

"*Está bien.*"

"No, it's not. I grew up too fast, too. I didn't even graduate high school because I got pregnant with you." She looks at me, as if seeing herself as a teenager not that long ago. "Oh, I wanted a baby so bad. Your father wanted to wait until after high school, but I was going to make it happen sooner. All I wanted in this world was to be a mom."

"You regret it?" I ask.

"Being a mom? Never. Seducing your father and making sure he didn't use a condom, yes."

"I don't want to hear this."

"Well, I'm gonna tell it to you whether you want to hear it or not. Be careful, Alex."

"I am."

She takes another drag of her cigarette while shaking her head. "No, you don't get it. You might be careful, but girls won't be. Girls are manipulative. I should know, I'm one of them."

"Brittany is—"

"The kind of girl who can make you do things you don't want to do."

"Believe me, Mom. She doesn't want a kid."

"No, but she'll want other things. Things you can never give her."

I look up at the stars, the moon, the universe that I know doesn't end. "But what if I want to give them to her?"

She lets out a slow breath, the action causing cigarette smoke to fly out of her mouth in one long stream. "At the age of thirty-five I'm old enough to have seen people die thinking they can change the ways of the world. No matter what you think, your father died trying to fix his life.

Your facts are distorted, Alejandro. You were just a little boy, too young to understand."

"I'm old enough now."

A tear escapes from her eye and she wipes it away. "Yes, well, now it's too late."

43

Brittany

"Brit, please tell me again why we're picking up Alex Fuentes and taking him with us to Lake Geneva," Sierra says to me.

"My mom threatened me if I saw him outside of school, so going to Lake Geneva is a perfect place to hang out with him. Nobody will know us there."

"Except us."

"And I know you guys won't rat on me. Right?"

I catch Doug rolling his eyes. It seemed like a good idea at the time. Going to Lake Geneva for the day on a double date is sure to be fun. Well, once Sierra and Doug get over the initial shock of the two of us as a couple. "Please don't give me more shit about this."

"The guy's a loser, Brit," Doug says as he drives to the school parking lot where Alex should be waiting for us. "She's your best friend, Sierra. Talk some sense into her."

"I tried, but you know her. She's stubborn."

I sigh. "Can you please stop talking about me like I'm not even here? I like Alex. And he likes me. I want to give this thing a chance."

"And you're going to do that how? By keeping him a secret forever?" Sierra asks.

Thank goodness we reach the parking lot so I don't have to respond. Alex is sitting on the curb beside his motorcycle, his long legs stretched in front of him. I chew my bottom lip anxiously as I open the door to the backseat.

When he sees Doug driving and Sierra next to him, a muscle in his jaw tenses.

"Come on in, Alex," I say, and slide over.

He leans into the car. "I don't think this is a good idea."

"Don't be silly. Doug promised to be nice. Isn't that right, Doug?" I hold my breath for the answer.

Doug gives an impersonal nod. "Sure," he says, totally monotone.

Any other guy would leave, I'm sure of it. But Alex slides in beside me. "Where we goin'?" he asks.

"Lake Geneva," I say. "Ever been there before?"

"No."

"It's about an hour away. Doug's parents have a cabin there."

As we drive, you'd think we were in a library instead of a car. Nobody says a word. When Doug stops for gas, Alex gets out, walks off, and lights a cigarette.

I sink lower in my seat. So far, this is not how I'd envisioned the day turning out. Sierra and Doug are usually hilarious together, but this is about as much fun as a funeral.

"Can you at least try and make conversation?" I ask my best friend. "I mean, you can spend hours talking about what kind of dog you'd rather kiss but you can't even put two words together in front of a guy I like."

Sierra turns around in her seat to face me. "I'm sorry. It's just that . . . Brit, you can do better. A LOT better."

"Like Colin, you mean."

"Like anyone." Sierra huffs and turns back around.

Alex gets into the car and I give him a weak smile. When he doesn't smile back, I take his hand in mine. He doesn't return the hold, but he doesn't pull away. Is that a good sign?

When we drive from the station, Alex says, "You've got a loose tire. Hear that noise comin' from the left rear?"

Doug shrugs. "It's been like that for a month. No biggie."

"Pull over and I'll fix it," Alex says. "If it falls off on the highway, we're toast."

I can tell Doug doesn't want to rely on Alex's assessment, but after about a mile he grudgingly stops on the side of the road.

"Doug," Sierra says, pointing to the adult bookstore we're in front of. "Do you know what kind of people go in there?"

"Right now, sweetheart, I really don't give a shit." He turns to Alex. "Okay, big shot. Fix the car."

Alex and Doug step out. "I'm sorry I bitched at you," I say to Sierra.

"I'm sorry, too."

"Do you think Doug and Alex will start fighting?"

"Maybe. We better get out there and distract them."

Outside, Alex takes tools out of the trunk.

After jacking up the car, Alex holds the tire iron in his hands. Doug has his hands on his hips and his jaw thrust forward in defiance.

"Thompson, what's up your ass?" Alex asks.

"I don't like you, Fuentes."

"You think you're my favorite person?" Alex snaps back as he kneels beside the tire and tightens the lug nuts.

I look over at Sierra. Should we intervene? Sierra shrugs. I shrug. It's not as if they've come to blows . . . yet.

A car screeches beside us. Four Hispanic guys are inside, two in the front and two in back. Alex ignores them as he lowers the jack and returns it to the trunk.

"Hey, *mamacitas*! How about you ditch those losers and come with us. We'll show you a real good time," one of them shouts through the window.

"Fuck off," Doug shouts.

One of the guys stumbles out of the car and advances on Doug. Sierra yells something but I'm not paying attention. Instead, I'm watching Alex tear off his jacket and block the guy's path.

"Get out of my way," the guy orders. "Don't lower yourself by protecting this white dick."

Alex stands toe to toe with the guy, the tire iron gripped tightly in his hand. "You fuck with the white dick, you fuck with me. It's that simple. *Comprendes, amigo?*"

Another guy steps out of the car. We are in some serious trouble.

"Girls, take the keys and get in the car," Alex orders, his tone precise.

"But . . ."

There's a lethal calmness in his eyes. Oh, boy. He's dead serious.

Doug tosses Sierra his car keys. Now what? Are we supposed to sit in the car and watch them fight? "I'm not going anywhere," I tell him.

"Me, either," Sierra says.

A guy in the other car sticks his head out of the window. "Alejo, that you?"

Alex's stance relaxes. "Tiny? What the hell you doin' with these *pendejos*?"

The guy named Tiny says something in Spanish to his buddies and they jump back into the car. They almost seem relieved they won't have to fight Alex and Doug.

"I'll tell you as soon as you tell me what you're doin' with a bunch of *gringos*," Tiny says.

Alex chuckles. "Get out of here."

When we're all back in the car, I hear Doug say, "Thanks for having my back."

Alex mumbles, "Don't sweat it."

Nobody speaks again until we reach the outskirts of Lake Geneva. Doug parks in front of a sports bar for lunch. Inside, Sierra and I order chopped salads while Doug and Alex order burgers.

In the booth while we're waiting for food, nobody is talking. I kick Sierra under the table.

"So, um, Alex," she starts. "See any good movies lately?"

"Nope."

"Apply to any colleges?"

Alex shakes his head.

Surprisingly, Doug sits up and takes over. "Who taught you so much about cars?"

"My cousin," Alex says. "On weekends I'd hang at his house and watch him bring cars back from the dead."

"My dad has a '72 Karmann Ghia sitting in our garage. He thinks it'll magically start running."

"What's wrong with it?" Alex asks.

As Doug explains, Alex listens intently. While they discuss the pros and cons of buying refurbished engine parts off of eBay, I sit back and relax. The tension from earlier seems to disintegrate the longer they talk.

After we finish eating, we walk down Main Street. Alex takes my hand in his, and I can't think of anything I'd rather do than be here with him.

"Ooh, there's that new gallery," Sierra says, pointing across the street. "Look, they're having a grand opening. Let's go in!"

"Cool," I say.

"I'll hang outside," Alex says as we follow Sierra and Doug across the street. "I'm not a gallery kind of guy."

That's not true. When is he going to realize that he doesn't have to live up to the stereotype everyone else has placed on him? Once he goes inside, he'll realize he's as welcome in a gallery as he is in the auto body. "Come on," I say, pulling him inside. I smile inwardly as we enter the gallery.

A huge spread of food is laid out. About forty people are milling about, observing the artwork.

I tour the gallery with Alex, who's walking stiffly at my side. "Loosen up," I tell him.

"Easy for you to say," he mumbles.

44

Alex

Bringing me into a gallery wasn't the best idea she's ever had. When Sierra pulled Brittany away from me to show her a painting, I've never felt more out of place.

I wander around and scan the food table, thankful we already ate. You can't really call this stuff food, actually. Sushi, which I'm tempted to nuke in order to make edible. Then there are sandwiches the size of a quarter.

"We're out of wasabi."

I'm still concentrating on identifying the assortment of food when someone taps me on the back.

I turn around to a short, blond white guy. He reminds me of Burro Face and I immediately want to push him away.

"We're out of wasabi," he says again.

If I knew what the fuck wasabi was, I could respond. But I don't, so I don't. And it makes me feel stupid.

"Don't you speak English?"

My hand balls into a fist. *Yes, I speak English, you dumbass. But the last time I was in English class the word "wasabi" wasn't on a fucking spelling test.* Instead of responding, I ignore the guy and walk away to look at one of the paintings.

The one I stop at shows a girl and a dog walking on what looks like a sloppy imitation of the Earth.

"There you are," Brittany says, coming to my side. Doug and Sierra are right behind her.

"Brit, this is Perry Landis," Doug says, pointing to the Colin look-alike. "The artist."

"Omigod, your work is amazing!" Brittany says, gushing at him.

She said "omigod" as if she really is an airhead. Is she kidding me?

The guy looks over her shoulder at his painting. "What do you think of this one?" he asks her.

Brittany clears her throat. "I think it shows great insight to the relationship between man, animal, and Earth."

Oh, please. What bullshit.

Perry puts his arm around her and I'm tempted to pick a fight in the middle of the gallery. "I can tell you're very deep."

Deep, my ass. He wants to get into her pants . . . pants he's never going near if I have anything to say about it.

"Alex, what do you think?" Brittany asks, turning to me.

"Well . . ." I rub my chin as I stare at the painting. "I think the entire collection is worth a buck fifty, two tops."

Sierra's eyes go wide and her hand covers her mouth in shock. Doug is coughing up his drink. And Brittany? I look at my "let's see what happens" girlfriend.

"Alex, you owe Perry an apology," Brittany says.

Yeah, right after he apologizes for asking me about wasabi. Not a chance in hell. "I'm outta here," I say, then turn my back on all of them and walk out the gallery door. *Me voy.*

Outside, I bum a cigarette from a waitress across the street who's on break. All I can think about is how Brittany looked as she ordered me to apologize.

I do not take orders well.

Damn, I hated watching that asshole artist put his arm around my girl. I'm sure every guy wants to put his hands on her in some way, to claim they've touched her. I want to touch her, too, but I also want her to want only me. Not order me around like some puppy dog and only hold hands with me when she's not putting on a show.

This is definitely not turning out like it's supposed to.

"I saw you come out of the gallery. Only hoiteys go in there," the waitress says after I hand back her lighter.

Wasabi. Now hoiteys. Seriously, you'd think I really didn't know English. "Hoiteys?"

"Hoitey-toitey types. You know, white-collar stiffs."

"Yeah, well, I'm definitely not one of those. More like a blue collar who followed a bunch of hoiteys in there." I take a long drag, thankful for nicotine. I feel calmer immediately. Okay, so my lungs are probably shriveled up, but I have a good idea I'll probably die before my lungs decide to quit on me.

"I'm Blue-Collar Mandy," the waitress says, holding out her hand and flashing me a smile. She's got light brown hair streaked with purple. She's cute, but she's no Brittany.

I shake her hand. "Alex."

She eyes my tattoos. "I've got two. Wanna see?"

Not really. I have a feeling she got drunk one night and tattooed her chest . . . or ass.

"Alex!" Brittany yells my name from the front of the gallery.

I'm still smoking and trying to forget that she brought me here because I'm her dirty little secret. I don't want to be a fucking secret anymore.

My pseudo-girlfriend crosses the street. Her designer shoes click on the pavement, reminding me she's a class above. She eyes Mandy and me, the two blue collars, smoking together.

"Mandy here was about to show me her tattoos," I tell Brittany to piss her off.

"I'll bet she was. Were you going to show her yours, too?" She eyes me accusingly.

"I'm not into drama," Mandy says. She throws down her cigarette and smashes it with the tip of her gym shoe. "Good luck, you two. God knows you need it."

I take another drag while wishing Brittany didn't tempt me like she does. "Go back to the gallery, *querida*. I'll take a bus home."

"I thought we'd have a *nice* day together, Alex, in a town where nobody knows us. Don't you want to be anonymous sometimes?"

"You think it's *nice* havin' that little piece of shit artist thinkin' I'm the busboy? I'd rather be known as the gangbanger than the immigrant busboy."

"You didn't even give it a chance. If you'd relax and take that chip off your shoulder, you could fit in. You can be one of them."

"Everyone is plastic in there. Even you. Wake up, Miss *Omigod!* I don't *want* to be one of them. Get it? *¿Entiendes?*"

"Loud and clear. For your information, I am not plastic. You can call it that, but we call it considerate and polite."

"In your social circles, not mine. In my circles, we tell it like it is. And never, ever order me to apologize like you're my mother. I swear, Brittany, the next time you do that we're done."

Oh, man. Her eyes are getting all glassy. She turns her back to me and I want to kick myself for hurting her.

I put out my cigarette. "I'm sorry. I didn't mean to be a dickhead. Well, I did. But that's 'cause I didn't feel comfortable in there."

She's not looking at me. Reaching out to rub her back, I'm thankful she doesn't shy away from me.

I continue talking. "Brittany, I love hangin' with you. Shit, when I get to school I scan the halls lookin' for you. As soon as I catch sight of these angelic streaks of sunshine," I say, fingering her hair, "I know I can make it through the day."

"I'm no angel."

"You are to me. If you forgive me, I'll go back and apologize to that artist guy."

She opens her eyes. "Really?"

"Yeah. I don't want to do it. But I will . . . for you."

Her mouth curves into a small smile. "Don't do it. I appreciate you saying you'll do it for me, but you're right. His art did suck."

"There you guys are," Sierra says. "We've been looking all over for you lovebirds. Let's hit the road and get to the cabin already."

At the cabin, Doug claps his hands together. "Hot tub or movie?" he asks.

Sierra walks over to the window overlooking the lake. "I'll fall asleep if we put a movie on."

I'm sitting with Brittany on the couch in the living room, reeling over the fact that this huge house is Doug's second home. It's bigger than the one house I live in. And a hot tub? Jeez, rich people have it all. "I don't have a bathin' suit," I tell them.

"Don't worry," Brittany says. "Doug probably has one in the pool house you can wear."

In the pool house, Doug looks through a drawer searching for suits.

"There's only two here." Doug picks up a skimpy Speedo and holds it out to me. "This okay for you, big guy?"

"That wouldn't fit my right testicle. Why don't you wear it and I'll take this one," I say, reaching around Doug and grabbing a boxer-type suit. I notice the girls are gone. "Where'd they go?"

"To change. And to talk about us, I'm sure."

In the small changing room as I strip and get into the suit, I think about my life back home. Here, in Lake Geneva, it's easy to forget about home life for a while. Not having to worry about who's got my back.

When I step out of the changing room, Doug says, "She'll take a lot of shit by being with you, you know. People are already starting to talk."

"Listen, Douggie. I like that girl more than I can remember likin' anything in my life. I'm not about to give her up. I'll start carin' about what other people think when I'm six feet under."

Doug smiles and holds out his arms. "Ah, Fuentes, I think we just had a male bonding moment. Wanna hug?"

"Not on your life, white boy."

Doug slaps me on the back, then we walk to the hot tub. Despite everything, I think we do have, if not a bonding, then at least an understanding. Either way, I'm still not hugging him.

"Very sexy, babe," Sierra says, eyeing Doug's Speedo.

Doug is walking like a penguin, waddling while trying to get comfortable. "I swear to God I'm taking these off as soon as I get in the hot tub. They're choking my balls."

"TMI," Brittany chimes in, covering her ears with her palms. She's wearing a yellow bikini, leaving very little to the imagination. Does she realize she looks like a sunflower, ready to rain sunshine on all who look down upon her?

Doug and Sierra climb into the tub.

I hop into the tub and sit beside Brittany. I've never been in a hot tub before, and am not sure about hot-tub protocol. Are we going to sit here and talk, or do we break off into couples and make out? I like the second option, but Brittany looks nervous.

Especially when Doug tosses his Speedo out of the tub.

I wince. "Come on, man."

"What? I want to be able to have kids one day, Fuentes. That thing was cutting off my circulation."

Brittany hops out of the tub and pulls a towel around her. "Let's go inside, Alex."

"You guys can stay in here," Sierra says. "I'll make him put the marble bag back on."

"Forget it. You two enjoy the tub. We'll be inside," Brittany says.

When I'm out of the tub, Brittany hands me an extra towel.

I put my arm around her as we walk to the cabin. "You okay?"

"Absolutely. I was thinking *you* were upset."

"I'm cool. But . . ." Inside, I pick up a blown-glass figurine and study it. "Seein' this house, this life . . . I want to be here with you, but I look around and realize this will never be me."

"You're thinking too much." She kneels on the carpet and pats the floor. "Come here and lie on your stomach. I know how to give Swedish massages. It'll relax you."

"You're not Swedish," I say.

"Yeah, well, neither are you. So if I do it wrong you'll never know the difference."

I lie next to her. "I thought we were gonna take this relationship slow."

"A back rub is harmless."

My eyes roam over her kick-ass bikini-covered bod. "I'll have you know I've been intimate with girls wearin' a lot more."

She slaps me on the butt. "Behave yourself."

When her hands move over my back, I let out a groan. Man, this is torture. I'm trying to behave, but her hands feel too damn good and my body has a mind of its own.

"You're tense," she says in my ear.

Of course I'm tense. Her hands are all over me. My answer is another groan.

After a few minutes of Brittany's mind-numbing massage, loud moaning, groaning, and grunting from the hot tub floats into the room. Doug and Sierra have obviously skipped the back rub portion of the evening.

"Do you think they're doing *it*?" she asks.

"Either that, or Doug's a very religious guy," I say, referring to the guy screaming *Oh, God!* every two seconds.

"Does it make you horny?" she sings quietly into my ear.

"No, but you keep massagin' me like that and you can forget about that goin' slow bullshit." I sit up and face her. "What I can't figure out is if you know you're a tease and are fuckin' with me or whether you really are innocent."

"I'm not a tease."

I cock an eyebrow, then look down at my upper thigh where she's parked her hand. She snatches it away. "Okay, I didn't mean to put my hand there. Well, I mean, not really. It just kinda . . . wh . . . what I mean to say is—"

"I like it when you stutter," I say as I pull her down next to me and show her my own version of a Swedish massage until we're interrupted by Sierra and Doug.

Two weeks later, I get word that I have a court date for my gun possession charge. I hide the info from Brittany, because she'd freak out. She'd probably go on and on about how a public defender isn't as good as a private lawyer. The thing is, I can't afford a fancy lawyer.

As I'm worrying about my fate while I'm hanging by the front doors before school, I'm suddenly sideswiped by someone and almost lose my balance.

"What the hell?" I push back.

"Sorry," the guy says nervously.

I realize the guy is none other than White Guy from the jail cell.

"Come and fight me, geek," Sam calls out.

I step forward, getting in the middle. "Sam, what's your problem?"

"This *pendejo* took my parkin' spot," Sam says, pointing past me to White Guy.

"So what? Did you find another spot?"

Sam stands stiffly, ready to kick White Guy's ass. Sam can do it, no problem.

"Yeah, I found another spot."

"Then leave the guy alone. I know him. He's cool."

Sam raises an eyebrow. "You *know* this guy?"

"Listen," I say, taking one look at White Guy and am glad he's wearing a blue button-down instead of his coral shirt. It's still geek city, but at least I can keep a straight face when I say, "This guy's been in jail more times than me. He might look like a complete *pendejo*, but under-neath that fucked-up hair and lame shirt he's a complete badass."

"You're fuckin' with me, Alex," Sam says.

I step out of the way and shrug. "Don't say I didn't warn you."

White Guy steps forward, attempting to look tough. I bite my lower lip to keep from laughing and cross my arms around my chest as if waiting for the ass-kicking to start. My LB buddies also wait, ready to see Sam get his ass kicked by a white geek.

Sam looks from Alex to White Guy and back. "If you're fuckin' with me, Alex—"

"Check his police record. Grand theft auto is his specialty."

Sam contemplates his next move. White Guy doesn't wait. He walks over to me, holding out his fist. "You need anything, Alex, you know who's got your back."

My fist connects with White Guy's. He's gone a second later and I'm thankful nobody noticed his fist shaking in fear.

I catch White Guy at his locker between first and second period. "Did you mean it? That if I needed anythin' you'd help?"

"After this morning, I owe you my life," White Guy says. "I don't know why you stuck up for me, but I was scared shitless."

"That's rule number one. Don't let them see you scared shitless."

White Guy snorts. I guess it's his laugh—either that or he has a really bad sinus infection. "I'll try and remember that the next time a gang member threatens my life." He holds out his hand for me to shake. "I'm Gary Frankel."

I grab his hand and give it a shake. "Listen, Gary," I say. "My court date is next week and I'd rather not rely on a public defender. You think your mom can help?"

Gary smiles. "I think so. She's really good. If it's your first offense, she could probably get you a short probation."

"I can't afford—"

"Don't worry about the money, Alex. Here's her card. I'll tell her you're a friend of mine and she'll do it pro bono."

As Gary walks down the hallway, I think of how funny it is that the most unlikely person sometimes becomes your ally. And how a blond girl can make you think futures are something to look forward to.

45

Brittany

After the game on Saturday afternoon, a game we won due to Doug's touchdown pass with four seconds to go in the game, I'm talking to Sierra and the M-factors on the side of the field. We're trying to figure out where we want to go celebrate the victory.

"How about Lou Malnati's?" Morgan calls out.

Everyone agrees, because it's the best pizza place in town. Megan is on a diet and is craving their special house salad, so it's a done deal.

As we're figuring out the logistics, I look over at Isabel talking to Maria Ruiz. I walk over to them. "Hey, guys," I say. "You want to come to Lou Malnati's with us?"

Maria's eyebrows are furrowed in confusion. Isabel's aren't, though. "Sure," Isabel says.

Maria looks from Isabel to me, then back. She says something to Isabel in Spanish, then says she'll meet us at the restaurant.

"What did she say?"

"She wanted to know why you'd ask us to hang with you and your friends."

"What did you tell her?"

"I told her that I'm one of your friends, although as a hint my friends call me Isa, not Isabel."

I lead her over to the rest of my friends, then look over at Sierra, who admitted to being jealous of my friendship with Isabel not too long ago. But instead of acting cold, she smiles at Isabel and asks her to show her how she does the double back flip in one of our routines. It just reinforces why she's my best friend. Madison seems as stunned as Maria was when I inform everyone that Maria and Isabel will be joining us at Lou Malnati's, but she doesn't say anything.

Maybe, just maybe, this is a small step toward what Dr. Aguirre calls "bridging the gap." I'm not naive enough to think I can change Fairfield overnight, but over the past weeks my perceptions of certain people have changed. I hope their perceptions of me have changed, too.

At the restaurant, I'm sitting next to Isabel. A bunch of guys from the football team have come in, so the restaurant has been taken over by Fairfield High students. Darlene walks in with Colin. He's got his arm around her as if they're a couple.

Sierra, on the other side of me, says, "Tell me she doesn't have her hand in his back pocket. That is so lame."

"I don't care," I tell her, easing any worries she might have about me being upset. "If they want to date, all the more power to them."

"She's only doing it because she wants everything you had. It's a competition thing with her. First taking your position on the squad, now putting her claws into Colin. Next thing you know she'll want to change her name to Brittany."

"Very funny."

"You say that now," she says, then moves in close and whispers, "it won't be so funny if she wants Alex next."

"Now that's *not* funny."

Doug walks in and Sierra waves him over. He can't squeeze into a chair so Sierra gives up her seat then sits on his lap. They start making out, and that's my cue to turn away and talk to Isabel.

"How are things progressing with you-know-who?" I ask, knowing I can't bring up Paco's name because she doesn't want Maria to know she has the hots for him.

She sighs. "They're not."

"Why not? Didn't you have the talk with him like I told you to?"

"No. He's been acting like a *pendejo*, completely ignoring the fact that we got together that one night. I'm thinking he doesn't bring it up because he doesn't want it to go farther."

I think of me breaking up with Colin and going for it with Alex. Every time I break out of what is expected of me and finally do what feels right, I feel stronger. "Take a risk, Isa. I guarantee it's worth it."

"You just called me Isa."

"I know. Is that okay?"

She pushes my shoulder playfully. "Yeah, *Brit*. It's fine."

Talking to Isa about Paco makes me feel adventurous, and feeling adventurous makes me think of Alex. As soon as we're done eating, and everyone starts leaving, I call Alex on my cell as I'm walking to my car. "Do you know where Club Mystique is?"

"Yeah."

"Meet me there tonight at nine."

"Why? What's up?"

"You'll see," I say, then hang up but realize Darlene is right behind me. Did she hear me talking to Alex?

"Hot date tonight?" she asks.

That answers my question. "What have I done to you to make you hate me so much? We're friends one minute, and the next I feel you're plotting against me."

Darlene shrugs, then flips her hair back. The gesture alone is a sign

I can no longer consider her my friend. "I guess I'm sick of living in your shadow, Brit. It's time to give up your reign. You've played Fairfield High's princess for so long. It's time to give someone else a chance to be in the spotlight."

"You can have the spotlight. Enjoy it," I tell her. She has no clue I never wanted it in the first place. If anything, I just used the spotlight to enhance the show I put on for everyone else.

When I get to Club Mystique at nine, Alex sneaks up behind me outside. I turn around and wrap my arms around his neck.

"Whoa, girl," he says, taken aback. "I thought we were keepin' this thing between us a secret. I hate to tell you, but a bunch of north siders from Fairfield are right over there. And they're starin' at us."

"I don't care. Not anymore."

"Why?"

"You only live once."

He seems to like my answer, because he takes my hand in his and leads me to the back of the line. It's cold outside, so he opens his leather jacket and envelopes me in his warmth while we wait to get in.

I look up at him, our bodies pressed together. "Are you going to dance with me tonight?" I ask.

"Hell, yeah."

"Colin never wanted to dance with me."

"I'm not Colin, *querida*, and never will be."

"Good. I've got you, Alex. I realize it's all I need and I'm ready to share it with the world."

Inside the club, Alex immediately heads for the dance floor with me. I ignore the gawking stares from Fairfield students from my side of town as I pull Alex close to me and we move as one to the beat.

We move together as if we've been a couple forever, every movement in sync with each other. For the first time I'm not afraid of what people think of me and Alex together. Next year, in college, it won't matter who came from what side of town.

Troy, a boy I danced with the last time I came to Club Mystique, taps me on the shoulder as the music makes the dance floor vibrate. "Who's the new stud?" he asks.

"Troy, this is my boyfriend, Alex. Alex, this is Troy."

"Hey, man," Alex says as he holds out his hand and quickly shakes Troy's.

"I have a feeling this guy won't make the same mistake the other one did," Troy says to me.

I don't answer, because I feel Alex's hands around my waist and back and it feels so right to have him here with me. I think he liked me calling him my boyfriend, and it felt so good to say it out loud. I lean my back against his chest and close my eyes, letting the rhythm of the music and the movement of our bodies mold together.

After we've been dancing awhile and need a breather, we walk off the dance floor. I whip out my cell and say, "Pose for me."

The first picture I take is of him trying to pose like a cool bad boy. It makes me laugh. I take another one before he can strike a pose this time.

"Let's take one of the both of us," he says, pulling me close. I press my cheek against his while he takes my cell and puts it as far away as he can reach, then freezes this perfect moment with a click. After the picture is taken, he pulls me into his arms and kisses me.

Leaning against Alex, I scan the crowd. On the first floor, right by the balcony, is Colin—the last person I thought would be here. Colin hates it here; he hates to dance.

His angry eyes meet mine, then he makes a big show of kissing the girl standing next to him. It's Darlene. And she's kissing him back with all she's got while he grabs her butt and grinds against her. She knew I'd be here tonight with Alex, and she obviously planned this.

"You want to go?" Alex asks as he catches sight of Colin and Darlene.

I turn to face him and once again I'm breathless just looking at his beautiful, strong features. "Nope. But it's so hot in here. Take off your jacket."

He hesitates before saying, "I can't."

"Why not?"

He winces.

"Tell me the truth, Alex."

He tucks a loose strand of hair that's fallen in my face behind my ear. "*Mujer*, this isn't Latino Blood turf. It's the Fremont 5's territory, a rival of the Latino Blood. Your friend Troy is one of them."

What? When I suggested we come here, I never thought about territory or gang affiliation. I just wanted to dance. "Oh, God. Alex, I put you in danger. Let's get out of here!" I say frantically.

Alex pulls me close and whispers in my ear, "You only live once, isn't that what you said? Dance with me again."

"But—"

He cuts me off with a kiss so powerful I forgot what I was supposed to be upset about. And as soon as I come to my senses, we're back on the dance floor.

We beat the odds and dance dangerously close to the sharks, but come out without a scratch. The danger lurking around ends up heightening our awareness of each other.

In the girls' restroom, Darlene is fixing her makeup in the mirror. I see her. She sees me.

"Hi," I say.

Darlene walks past me without a word. It's a taste of what it's like to be a north sider outcast, but I don't care.

At the end of the night, as Alex is walking me to my car, I take his hand in mine and look up at the stars. "If you could wish on a star right now, what would you wish for?" I ask him.

"For time to stop."

"Why?"

He shrugs. " 'Cause I could live forever at this moment. What would you wish for?"

"That we'd go to college together. While you want to stop the future from happening, I look forward to it. Wouldn't it be great if we went to the same school? I mean it, Alex."

He pulls away from me. "For someone who wanted to take things slow, you sure are plannin' far in advance."

"I know. I'm sorry. I can't help it. I applied early decision to the University of Colorado to be close to my sister. That place my parents are sending her is a few miles away from the campus. It wouldn't hurt to apply, would it?"

"I guess not."

"Really?"

He squeezes my hand. "Anything to make you smile like that."

46

Alex

"I need an update on the Brittany situation," Lucky says while I'm hanging outside the warehouse. "Guys are makin' side bets, and most of them are bettin' on you. They know somethin' I don't?"

I shrug, then look over at Julio, shiny from my wash earlier. If my motorcycle could talk, he'd beg me to save him from Lucky. But I'm not about to spill any info about Brittany. Not yet, at least.

Hector walks up to us and waves Lucky away. "We need to talk, Fuentes," Hector says in a tone that means business, "about that favor we were talking about. On Halloween night, you'll take a rental car, drive it to the drop-off, and exchange the goods for the green. Think you can handle that?"

My brother is right. I do have my *papá*'s blood running through my veins. By doing the drug deal, I'll secure my future in the Blood, which is my birthright. Other kids inherit money or a family business from their parents. I inherited the Latino Blood.

"There's nothin' I can't handle," I tell Hector, even as I feel the pit of my stomach lurch. I knowingly lied to Brittany. Her face lit up when she talked about possibly going to college together. I couldn't tell her the truth, that not only am I staying in the Latino Blood, I'm about to *exchange goods for the green.*

Hector pats me on the back. "That's my loyal brother. I knew the Blood would come before your fear. *Somos hermanos, c'no?*"

"*¡Seguro!*" I answer so he knows I'm loyal to him and the Blood. It isn't the drug deal I fear. It's that the drug deal signifies the end of any dreams I had. By doing it, I'll cross over the line. Like my *papá.*

"Yo, Alex."

Paco is standing a few feet away. I hadn't even noticed Hector left.

"Wha's up?"

"I need your help, *compa*," Paco says.

"You, too?"

He gives me that I-am-Paco-and-I-am-exasperated look. "Just take a ride with me."

Three minutes later I'm in the passenger seat of a borrowed red Camaro.

I sigh. "You gonna tell me what you want help with or are you keepin' me in suspense?"

"Actually, I'm gonna keep you in suspense."

I read the WELCOME TO sign on the side of the road. "Winnetka?" What does Paco want in this wealthy suburban town?

"Trust," Paco says.

"What?"

"Best friends need to trust each other."

I lean back, totally aware I'm brooding like one of those guys in a bad Western movie. I agreed to do a drug deal and now I'm heading into upper-class suburbia for apparently no reason.

"Ah, here it is," Paco says.

I look up at the sign. "You've got to be kiddin'."

"Nope."

"If you're plannin' to rob the place, I'll stay in the car."

Paco rolls his eyes. "We're not here to rob a bunch of golfers."

"Then why drag me all the way out here?"

"My golf swing. Come on, get off your ass and help."

"It's fifty-five degrees outside and the middle of October, Paco."

"It's all a matter of priority and perception."

I sit in the car, contemplating how to get home. Walking will take too long. I don't know where the closest bus stop is and . . . and . . . and I'm going to kick Paco's ass for bringing me to a fuckin' golf range.

I stalk over to where Paco is setting down a basket of balls. Man, there are probably a hundred of them.

"Where'd you get that club?" I ask.

Paco swings it in the air like a propeller. "From the guy who rents the balls. You want one so you can hit a few?"

"No."

Paco points the end of the golf club at a green wooden bench situated behind him. "Then sit over there."

As I sit, my gaze wanders to the other guys hitting balls in their little sections, warily eyeing us out of the corners of their eyes. I'm all too aware Paco and I look and dress drastically different from the rest of the guys at the range. Jeans, T-shirts, tattoos, and bandannas on our heads make us stick out while most of the golfers are wearing long-sleeve golf shirts, Dockers, and no distinguishing marks on their skin.

I don't normally care, but after the talk with Hector, I want to go home, not be a spectacle. I rest my elbows on my knees, watching Paco make a complete fool of himself.

Paco takes a little white golf ball and places it on top of a rubber circle inserted into the fake grass. When he swings the golf club, I wince.

The club misses the ball and connects with the fake grass instead. Paco swears. The guy next to Paco takes one look at him and moves to another section.

Paco tries again. This time the club connects, but his ball only rolls along the grass in front of him. He keeps trying, but each time Paco swings, he makes a complete ass out of himself. Does he think he's hitting a hockey puck?

"You done?" I ask once he's gone through half the basket.

"Alex," Paco says, leaning on the golf club like it's a cane. "Do ya think I was meant to play golf?"

Looking Paco straight in the eye, I answer, "No."

"I heard you talkin' to Hector. I don't think you were meant to deal, either."

"Is that why we're here? You're tryin' to make a point?"

"Hear me out," Paco insists. "I've got the keys to the car in my pocket and I'm not goin' nowhere until I finish hittin' all of these balls, so you might as well listen. I'm not smart like you. I don't have choices in life, but you, you're smart enough to go to college and be a doctor or computer geek or somethin' like that. Just like I wasn't meant to hit golf balls, you weren't meant to deal drugs. Let me do the drop for you."

"No way, man. I appreciate you makin' an ass out of yourself to prove a point, but I know what I need to do," I tell him.

Paco sets up a new ball, swings, and yet again the ball rolls away from him. "That Brittany sure is hot. She goin' to college?"

I know what Paco is doing; unfortunately my best friend is nothing less than obvious. "Yep. In Colorado." To be close to her sister, the person she cares for more than herself.

Paco whistles. "I'm sure she'll meet a lot of guys in Colorado. You know, real guys with cowboy hats."

My muscles tense. I don't want to think about it. I ignore Paco until we're back in the car. "When are you going to stop stickin' your ass into my business?" I ask him.

He chuckles. "Never."

"Then I guess you won't mind me bargin' into yours. What happened between you and Isa, huh?"

"We fooled around. It's over."

"You might think it's over, but I don't think she does."

"Yeah, well, that's her problem." Paco turns the radio on and blasts the music loud.

He's never dated anyone because he's scared of getting close to someone. Even Isa isn't aware of all the abuses he's endured at home. Believe me, I understand the reasons behind his keeping a distance from a girl he cares about. Because the truth is, sometimes getting close to the fire does actually burn you.

47

Brittany

"Paco, what are you doing here?" The last person I expected to see at my house is Alex's best friend.

"I kinda need to talk to you."

"Want to come in?"

"You sure it's okay?" he asks nervously.

"Of course." Well, it probably isn't okay with my parents, but it is to me. It's not like my parents will suddenly decide not to send Shelley away. I'm tired of pretending, of being afraid of my mom's wrath. This guy is Alex's best friend, and he accepts me. I'm sure it wasn't easy for him to come here. Opening the door wide, I let Paco in. If he asks me about Isabel, what do I say? She swore me to secrecy.

"Who's at the door, Brit?"

"This is Paco," I explain to my mom. "He's a friend of mine from school."

"Dinner's on the table," my mother hints not too subtly. "Tell your friend it's not polite to visit during dinner hours."

I turn to Paco. "Want to eat over?" I'm being rebellious and it feels good. Cathartic.

I hear my mom's footsteps stomping to the kitchen.

"Uh, no thanks," Paco says, stifling a laugh. "I thought maybe we could talk, you know, about Alex."

I don't know if I'm relieved he's not asking what I know about Isabel, or nervous because if Paco came here it's serious.

I lead Paco through the house. We pass Shelley in the family room looking at some magazine. "Shelley, this is Paco. He's Alex's friend. Paco, this is my sister, Shelley."

At the mention of Alex's name, Shelley gives a happy squeal.

"Hey, Shelley," Paco says.

Shelley smiles wide.

"Shell-bell, I need you to do me a favor." Shelley bobs her head in response as I whisper, "I need you to keep Mom occupied while I talk to Paco."

Shelley grins, and I know my sister will come through for me.

My mother pops into the room, ignoring me and Paco as she wheels Shelley into the kitchen.

I look at Paco warily as I lead him outside so we can have privacy from eavesdropping mothers. "What's up?"

"Alex needs help. He won't listen to me. A big drug deal is goin' down and Alex is the *elmero mero*, the key guy runnin' the show."

"Alex wouldn't do a drug deal. He promised me."

The look on Paco's face tells me he knows otherwise.

"I've tried to reason with him," Paco says. "This thing . . . it's with big-time dealers. Somethin' doesn't feel right about it, Brittany. Hector's makin' Alex do this and for the life of me I don't know why. Why Alex?"

"What can I do?" I ask.

"Tell Alex to find a way out. If anyone can get out of it, it's him."

Tell him? Alex resents being told to do anything. I can't imagine he would agree to do a drug deal.

"Brittany, dinner is already cold!" my mother yells from the kitchen window. "And your father just got home. Let's sit down as a family for once."

The sound of crashing dishes brings my mother back in the house. Shelley's brilliant move, no doubt.

But it really isn't Shelley's job to keep me from telling my parents the truth. "Wait here," I say. "Unless you want to witness an Ellis family argument."

Paco rubs his hands together. "This has got to be better than my family fights."

I walk into the kitchen and give my dad a peck on the cheek.

"Who's your friend?" my dad asks warily.

"Paco, this is my dad. Dad, this is my friend Paco."

Paco says, "Hey." My dad nods. My mom grimaces.

"Paco and I need to go."

"Where?" my dad asks, totally confused.

"To see Alex."

"No you're not," my mom says.

My dad holds up his hands, clueless. "Who's Alex?"

"That *other* Mexican boy I was telling you about," my mom says tightly. "Don't you remember?"

"I don't remember anything these days, Patricia."

My mom stands, her plateful of food in hand, and tosses it into the sink. The dish breaks and the food flies all over. "We've given you everything you want, Brittany," my mother says. "A new car, designer clothes—"

My patience snaps. "That's totally superficial, Mom. Sure, on the outside everyone sees you guys as successful, but as parents you really suck. I'd give you both a C minus on parenting and you're lucky it isn't Mrs. Peterson grading you or you'd flunk. Why are you afraid of being seen as having problems like the rest of the world?"

I'm on a roll and can't stop. "Listen, Alex needs my help. One of the things that makes me who I am is the loyalty I have to people I hold close to my heart. If that hurts or scares you, I'm sorry," I say.

Shelley makes a commotion and we all turn to her. "Brittany," comes a computer voice from the PCD attached to my sister's wheelchair. Shelley's fingers are busy punching in the words: "Good. Girl."

I wrap my fingers around my sister's hand before I talk to my parents again. "If you want to kick me out, or disown me for being who I am, then do it and get it over with."

I'm done being scared. Scared for Alex, Shelley, and myself. It's time to face all my fears, or I'll lose myself in grief and guilt my entire life. I'm not perfect. It's time the entire world realizes it, too.

"Mom, I'm going to see the social worker at school."

My mom scrunches up her face in disgust. "That's asinine. It'll be in your school records the rest of your life. You don't need a social worker."

"Yes, I do." I steel myself and add, "You do, too. We all do."

"Listen to me, Brittany. If you walk out that door . . . don't come back."

"You're being rebellious," my dad interjects.

"I know. And it feels so good." I grab my purse. It's all I have, unless you include the clothes on my back. I put on a huge smile and hold my hand out to Paco. "Ready to go?"

He doesn't miss a beat as he takes my hand. "Yep." When we're in his car he says, "You are one tough chick. I never thought you had the fight in you." Paco drives me to the darkest part of Fairfield. He leads me to a large warehouse on a secluded back road. As if Mother Nature is sending us a warning, menacing dark clouds fill the sky and a chill fills the air.

A burly guy stops us. "Who's the snow girl?" he asks.

Paco says, "She's clean."

The guy eyes me up and down suggestively before opening the door. "She starts sniffin' around and it'll be on your head, Paco," he warns.

All I want to do is take Alex away from here, away from what feels like danger all around. "Hey," a gravelly voice from beside me calls out. "If you want something to pick you up, come to me, *si*?"

"Follow me," Paco says, grabbing my arm and pulling me straight ahead through a corridor. Voices come from the opposite side of the warehouse . . . Alex's voice.

"Let me go to him myself," I say.

"That's not such a hot idea. Wait until Hector's done talkin' to him," Paco says, but I don't listen.

I walk toward Alex's voice. He's talking with two other guys. They're obviously having a serious conversation. One of the guys pulls out a sheet of paper and hands it to Alex. That's when Alex notices me.

Alex says something to the guy in Spanish before folding the paper and shoving it into his jeans pocket. His voice is hard and tough, like his expression right now. "What the hell are you doin' here?" he asks me.

"I just—"

I can't finish my sentence because Alex grabs hold of my upper arm. "You *just* are leavin' here this instant. Who the fuck brought you here?"

I'm trying to think of a response when Paco appears out of the darkness.

"Alex, please. Paco might have brought me here, but it was my idea."

"You *culero*," Alex says, letting go of me while facing Paco.

"Isn't this your future, Alex?" Paco asks. "Why are you ashamed to show your *novia* your home away from home?"

Alex throws a punch, connecting with Paco's jaw. Paco goes down. I run to him, then give Alex a sharp, warning look. "I can't believe you did that!" I scream. "He's your best friend, Alex."

"I don't want you seein' this place!" A trickle of blood streams down Paco's mouth. "You shouldn't have brought her," Alex says, calmly this time. "She doesn't belong here."

"Neither do you, bro," Paco says quietly. "Now take her away. She's seen enough."

"Come with me," Alex orders, holding out his hand.

Instead of coming to him, I cup Paco's face with my hands and inspect the damage. "My God, you're bleeding," I say, starting to freak out. Blood is enough to make me sick. Blood and violence always push me over the edge.

Paco gently pushes my hand away. "I'll be fine. Go with him."

A voice booms from the darkness, speaking Spanish to Alex and Paco.

I shiver at the authority in the guy's voice. I wasn't scared before, but I definitely am now. The guy had been talking to Alex earlier. He's dressed in a dark suit with a stark white dress shirt underneath. I saw him briefly at the wedding. His jet black hair is slicked back and his complexion is dark. One look and I know this is someone very powerful in the Latino Blood. Two large, mean-looking guys stand on either side of him.

"*Nada*, Hector," Alex and Paco say in unison.

"Take her somewhere else, Fuentes."

Alex takes my hand and hurries me out of the warehouse. When we're finally outside, I exhale deeply.

48

Alex

"Let's get out of here. You and me, *mi amor. ¡Vamos!*"

I breathe a sigh of relief as I straddle Julio and Brittany hops on behind me. She wraps her arms around my waist, holding on tight as I speed out of the parking lot.

We fly through the streets; which eventually become a blur. I don't even stop when rain starts pouring down.

"Can we stop now?" she yells through the deafening storm.

I park under an old abandoned bridge by the lake. Heavy rain pounds the cement surrounding us, but we have our own secluded place.

Brittany hops to the ground. "You're a stupid jerk," she says. "You can't deal drugs. It's dangerous and stupid, and you promised me. You'll risk going to jail. *Jail*, Alex. You may not care, but I do. I won't let you ruin your life."

"What do you want to hear?"

"Nothing. Everything. Say *something* so I don't stand here feeling like a complete idiot."

"The truth is . . . Brittany, look at me."

"I can't," she says as she stares at the pouring rain. "I'm so tired of thinking of every scary scenario."

I pull her against me. "Don't think, *muñeca*. Everything will work itself out."

"But—"

"No buts. Trust me." My mouth closes over hers. The smell of rain and cookies eases my nerves.

My hand braces the small of her back. Her hands grip my soaked shoulders, urging me on. My hands slide under her shirt, and my fingers trace her belly button.

"Come to me," I say, then lift her until she's straddling me over my bike.

I can't stop kissing her. I whisper how good she feels to me, mixing Spanish and English with every sentence. I move my lips down her neck and linger there until she leans back and lets me take her shirt off. I can make her forget about the bad stuff. When we're together like this, hell, I can't think of anything else but her.

"I'm losing control," she admits, biting her lower lip. I love those lips.

"*Mamacita*, I've already lost it," I say, grinding against her so she knows exactly how much control I've lost.

She moves her hips in a slow rhythm against me, an invitation I don't deserve. My fingertips graze her mouth. She kisses them before I slowly slide my hand down her chin to her neck and in between her breasts.

She catches my hand. "I don't want to stop, Alex."

I cover her body with mine.

I can easily take her. Hell, she's asking for it. But God help me if I don't grow a conscience.

It's that *loco* bet I made with Lucky. And what my mom said about how easy it is to get a girl pregnant.

When I made the bet, I had no feelings for this complex white girl. But now . . . shit, I don't want to think about my feelings. I hate feelings; they're only good for screwing up someone's life. And may God strike me down right now because I want to make love to Brittany, not fuck her on my motorcycle like some cheap whore.

I move my hands away from her *cuerpo perfecto*, the first sane thing I've done tonight. "I can't take you like this. Not here," I say, my voice hoarse from emotion overload. This girl was going to gift me with her body, even though she knows who I am and what I'm about to do. The reality is hard to swallow.

I expect her to be embarrassed, maybe even mad. But she curls into my chest and hugs me. *Don't do this to me,* I want to say. Instead I wrap my arms around her and hold on tight.

"I love you," I hear her say so softly it might have been her thoughts.

Don't, I'm tempted to say. ¡No! ¡No!

My gut twists and I hold her tighter. *Dios mío,* if things were different I'd never give her up. I burrow my face in her hair and fantasize about stealing her away from Fairfield.

We stay that way for a long time, long after the rain stops and reality sets in. I help her off the motorcycle so she can put her shirt back on.

Brittany looks up at me, a hopeful look on her face. "Are you going to do this drug deal?"

I get off Julio and walk over to the end of the tunnel. Sticking my hand in the water still dripping down the sides, I let the cold water fall through my fingers.

"I've got to," I say, my back to her.

She steps beside me. "Why? Why do you have to do something that might end up with you in jail?"

I put her soft, pale cheek in my palm and give her a wistful smile. "Didn't you know gang members deal drugs? It's part of the job."

"So quit. Surely there's some way. . . ."

"You want to quit, they give you a challenge. Sometimes it's torture, sometimes a beating. If you live, you get out. Let me tell you, *preciosa*, only once have I seen anyone come out of a challenge alive. The guy still wishes he was dead, he got beat up so bad. God, you'll never understand, my family needs this."

"For the money?"

My hand leaves her. "No, not for the money." I throw my head back and wince in frustration. "Can we *please* change the subject?"

"I'm against you doing anything illegal."

"*Querida*, you need a saint. Or at least a minister. And I'm neither of those."

"Aren't I important to you?"

"Yes."

"Then prove it to me."

I pull my bandanna off my head, then rake my fingers through my hair. "Do you know how hard it's been for me? *Mi madre* expects me to protect the family by being in the Blood but is in total denial, Hector wants me to prove I'm dedicated to the Blood, and you . . . the one person who I feel like I can start a life with someday, you want me to prove I love you by doin' somethin' that could put my family in danger. I *have* to do this, you know. And nobody, not even you, is gonna change my mind. *Olvídalo*."

"You'll risk what we have?"

"Dammit, don't do this. We don't have to risk anythin'."

"If you start dealing drugs, it's over. I've jeopardized everything for you . . . for us. My friends. My parents. Everything. Can't you do the same?"

I toss my jacket to her when her teeth start chattering. "Here. Put this on."

And that's it. This is my life. If she can't handle it, she can go back to Colin Adams. Or whoever she can mold into her own Ken doll.

She tells me to take her to her friend Sierra's house. "I think we should work separately on the chemistry project," Brittany says. She hands me back my jacket when we reach the big house on the beach. "Do you want to put the hand warmers together or would you rather write the paper?"

"Whatever you want."

"Well, I'm a pretty good writer. . . ."

"Fine. I'll do the rest."

"Alex, it doesn't have to end like this."

I watch as tears well in her eyes. I've got to get out of here before they start falling down her face. That will definitely be my undoing.

"Yeah, it does," I say, then drive off.

49

Brittany

After I used two boxes of tissues, Sierra gave up on trying to cheer me up and let me cry myself to sleep. In the morning, I beg her to keep her curtains closed and shades down. There's nothing wrong with staying in bed all day, is there?

"Thanks for not saying *I told you so*," I say as I scan her closet for something to wear after she forces me to get up.

She's standing by her dresser, putting on makeup. "I'm not saying it, but I sure am thinking it."

"Thanks," I say dryly.

Sierra pulls a pair of jeans and a long-sleeve shirt out of her closet. "Here, wear these. You won't look half as good in my clothes as you do in yours, but you'll still look better than any girl at Fairfield."

"Don't say that."

"Why? It's true."

"No, it's not. My top lip is too fat."

"Guys think it's sexy. Movie stars pay big bucks for big lips."

"My nose is crooked."

"Only from a certain angle."

"My boobs are lopsided."

"They're big, Brit. Guys are obsessed with big boobs. They could care less if they're lopsided." She pulls me in front of the mirror. "Face it, you're model-gorgeous. Okay, so your eyes are bloodshot and you've got bags from crying all night. But all in all, you've got it goin' on. Look in the mirror, Brit, and say out loud *I'm the bomb.*"

"No."

"Come on. It'll make you feel better. Look right in the mirror and yell *my boobs rock!*"

"Nuh-uh."

"Can you at least admit you've got good hair?"

I look at Sierra. "You talk to yourself in front of a mirror?"

"I do. Wanna see?" She pushes me aside and moves up close to the mirror. "Not half-bad, Sierra," she tells herself. "Doug is one lucky guy." She turns to me. "See, it's easy."

Instead of laughing, I start to cry.

"Am I that ugly?"

I shake my head.

"Is it because I don't have clothes with bling? I know your mom kicked you out, but do you think she'll let us go over and raid your closet? I don't know how long you'll be able to stand wearing my size-eight clothes on your size-four body."

My mom didn't call here last night looking for me. I kind of expected her to, but then again she rarely meets my expectations. And my dad . . . well, he probably doesn't know I didn't sleep at home. They can keep my clothes. I'll probably sneak in during the day to check up on Shelley, though.

"You want my advice?" Sierra asks.

I look at her warily. "I don't know. You hated the idea of Alex and me together from the beginning."

"That's not true, Brit. I didn't tell you this, but he's actually a nice guy when he loosens up. I had fun the day we all went to Lake Geneva. Doug did, too, and even said Alex was cool to hang with. I don't know what happened between the two of you, but either forget about him, or give him everything you've got in your arsenal."

"Is that what you do with Doug?"

She smiles. "Sometimes Doug needs a wake-up call. When our relationship starts getting comfortable, I do something to switch it up. Don't interpret my advice as an excuse to go after Alex. But if he's what you really want, well, then, who am I to tell you not to go for it? I hate seeing you sad, Brit."

"Was I happy with Alex?"

"Obsessed is more like it. But yeah, I saw you happy. Happier than you've been in a really, really long time. With someone you like that much, the lows are as low as the highs are high. Does that make sense?"

"It does. It also makes me sound bipolar."

"Love will do that to a person."

50

Alex

I'm eating breakfast the morning after Brittany's warehouse visit when I glimpse a shaved head peeking through my front door.

"Paco, if that's you I'd stay the hell away from me," I call out.

Mi'amá slaps me on the back of my head. "That's no way to treat your friends, Alejandro."

I go back to eating while she opens the door for that . . . traitor.

"You're not still mad at me, Alex," Paco says, "are you?"

"Of course he's not mad at you, Paco. Now sit down and eat. I've made some *chorizo con huevos.*"

Paco has the gall to pat me on the shoulder. "I forgive you, man."

I look up then, first at *mi'amá* to make sure she isn't paying attention, then at Paco. "*You* forgive *me?*"

"You've got yourself a real fat lip, Paco," she says, examining the damage I'd done to it.

Paco touches his lip lightly. "Yeah, I fell onto a fist. You know how it is."

"No, I don't. You fall onto too many fists you're going to end up in the hospital one day," she warns, shaking her finger at him. "Well, I'm going to work. And Paco, keep away from fists today, *si*? Lock up before you go out, Alejandro, *porfis*. . . ."

I glare at Paco.

"What?"

"You know *what*. How could you have brought Brittany to the warehouse?"

"I'm sorry," Paco says as he chows down on our food.

"No, you're not."

"Okay, you're right. I'm not."

I watch in disgust as he uses his fingers to scoop food up and shove it into his mouth.

"I don't know why I put up with you," I say.

"So what happened with you and Brittany last night?" Paco asks while following me outside.

My breakfast is threatening to come up, and it's not due to Paco's eating habits. I grab his collar. "It's over between Brittany and me. I don't even want to hear her name again."

"Speak of the devil," he says, craning his neck. I release Paco and turn around, expecting to see Brittany. But she isn't there and the next thing I know Paco's fist is in my face.

"Now we're even. And boy, have you got it bad for Miss Ellis if you're threatenin' me if I use her name. I know you could kill me with your two hands," Paco says, "but I got to admit . . . I don't think you'd do it."

As I test my jaw, I taste blood. "I wouldn't be too sure of that. Tell you what. I won't kick your ass if you stop interferin' in my life. That means with Hector *and* Miss Ellis."

"I got to tell ya, interferin' in your life is what keeps me goin'. Hell, even the beatin' my old man gave me last night when he was shit-faced drunk doesn't give me as much entertainment as your life."

I lower my head. "I'm sorry, Paco. I shouldn't have hit you. You get it enough from your old man."

Paco murmurs a "don't sweat it."

Last night was the first time I've regretted using my fists on anyone. Paco has gotten beat up so many times by his old man, he probably has permanent scars on his body. I'm a complete asshole for hitting him. In a way I'm glad it's over between me and Brittany. I'm unable to control my feelings or emotions when she's near.

My only hope is that outside of chemistry I can avoid her. Yeah, right. Even if she's not with me, thoughts of her are always in my head.

One good thing about my breakup with Brittany—it's given me time these last two weeks to think about my father's murder. The night is starting to come back to me in flashes. Something doesn't fit, but I can't figure it out. My dad smiled, talked, and was shocked and nervous when the gun was pulled on him. Shouldn't he have been wary all along?

Tonight is Halloween, the night Hector chose for the drug deal to go down. All day I've been restless. I've worked on seven cars today, from giving an oil change to replacing worn-out, leaky gaskets.

I left Hector's gun in my bedroom drawer, not wanting to pack heat until I absolutely have to. Which is actually stupid because this will be the first of many drug deals I'll be doing in my lifetime.

You're like your old man. I shrug off the voice inside my head that's been plaguing me all day. *Como el Viejo.*

I can't help it. I remember all the times my *papá* said *Somos cuates, Alejandro. You and me are the closest.* He always spoke Spanish, as if he was still in Mexico. *Someday you gonna be strong like your padre?* he'd ask in Spanish. I always looked up to my father as if he was a deity. *Claro, Papá. I want to be like you.*

My father never said to me I could be better or do better than him. But tonight I'll prove I'm a carbon copy of my old man. I tried to be different by telling Carlos and Luis they can have a different path. I'm an idiot to think I've been a role model to them.

My thoughts drift to Brittany. I've tried to forget Brittany will be going with someone else to the Halloween dance. I heard she was going with her old boyfriend. I try to push out of my mind the fact that another guy will have his hands on her.

Her date will kiss her tonight, I'm sure of it. Who wouldn't want to kiss those sweet, soft, frosted lips?

I'm going to work tonight until I have to leave for the deal. Because if I was home alone, I'd go nuts thinking about everything.

My grip on the riveter in my hand loosens and it drops smack in the middle of my forehead. I don't get pissed off at myself, I blame Brittany. And by eight o'clock I'm as angry as anything with my little chem partner, whether it's warranted or not.

51

Brittany

I'm standing in front of Enrique's Auto Body, doing deep-breathing exercises to keep from being nervous. Enrique's Camry is nowhere in sight, so I know Alex is alone.

I'm going to seduce Alex.

If what I'm wearing doesn't capture his attention, nothing will. I'm giving this my all . . . bringing out all the artillery. I rap on the door, then close my eyes tight and pray this goes as planned.

I open my long, silver satin jacket and the cool night air rushes onto my exposed skin. When the creak of the door alerts me to Alex's presence, I slowly open my eyes. But it's not Alex's black eyes staring at my scantily clad body. It's Enrique—who's staring at my pink lace bra and pom-pom skirt as if he's won the lottery.

Ripped with embarrassment, I wrap my coat around myself. If I could wrap it around twice, I would.

"Uh, Alex," Enrique laughs. "There's a trick-or-treater here to see you."

My face is probably beet red, but I'm determined to see this through. I'm here to show Alex I'm not going to desert him.

"Who is it?" comes Alex's voice from somewhere inside the garage.

"I was just leavin'," Enrique says, slipping past me. "Tell Alex to lock up. *Adiós.*"

Enrique walks across the darkened street, humming to himself.

"Yo, Enrique. *¿Quién está ahí?*" Alex's voice fades when he reaches the front of the shop. He looks at me with contempt. "Need directions or your car fixed?"

"None of the above," I say.

"Trick-or-treatin' on my side of town?"

"No."

"It's over, *mujer. ¿Me oyes?* Why do you keep droppin' into my life and fuckin' with my head? Besides, aren't you supposed to be at the Halloween dance with some college guy?"

"I blew him off. Can we talk?"

"Listen, I've got a shitload of work that still needs to get done. What did you come here for? And where's Enrique?"

"He, uh, left," I say nervously. "I think I scared him away."

"You? I don't think so."

"I showed him what I was wearing under my coat."

Alex's eyebrows shoot up.

"Let me in before I freeze out here. Please." I look behind me. The darkness seems inviting right now as my blood pumps harder. Pulling the coat tighter around me, my skin puckers with goose bumps. I shiver.

Sighing, he leads me into the body shop and locks the door. There's a space heater in the middle of the shop, thank goodness. I stand by it and rub my hands together.

"Listen, truth is I'm glad you're here. But didn't we break up?"

"I want to give us another try. Pretending we're just chemistry partners in class has been torture. I miss you. Don't you miss me?"

He looks skeptical. His head is cocked to the side, as if he's not quite sure he's hearing correctly. "You know I'm still in the Blood."

"I know. I'll take whatever you can give me, Alex."

"I'll never be able to meet your expectations."

"What if I tell you I won't have any expectations?"

He takes a deep breath and lets it out slowly. I can tell he's thinking hard about this, because his expression turns serious. "I'll tell you what," he says. "You keep me company while I finish my dinner. I won't even ask you what you have . . . or don't have . . . under that coat. Deal?"

I smile tentatively and smooth down my hair. "Deal."

"You don't have to do that for me," he says, gently taking my hand away from my hair. "I'll get a blanket so you don't get dirty."

I wait until he pulls a clean light green fleece blanket out of a closet.

We sit on the blanket and Alex looks at his watch. "Want some?" he asks, pointing to his dinner.

Maybe eating will calm my nerves. "What is it?"

"Enchiladas. *Mi'amá* makes kick-ass enchiladas." He stabs a small portion with a fork and holds it out to me. "If you're not used to this kind of spicy food—"

"I love spicy," I interrupt, taking it into my mouth. I start chewing, enjoying the blend of flavors. But when I swallow, my tongue slowly catches on fire. Somewhere behind all the fire there's flavor, but the flames are in the way.

"Hot," is all I can say as I attempt to swallow.

"I told you." Alex holds out the cup he'd been drinking from. "Here, drink. Milk usually does the trick, but I only have water."

I grab the cup. The liquid cools my tongue, but when I finish the water it's as if someone stokes it again. "Water . . . ," I say.

He fills another cup. "Here, drink more, though I don't think it'll help much. It'll subside soon."

Instead of drinking it this time, I stick my tongue in the cold liquid and keep it there. Ahhh . . .

"You okay?"

"To I wook otay?" I ask.

"With your tongue in the water like that, actually, it's erotic. Want another bite?" he asks mischievously, acting like the Alex I know.

"Mo mank ooh."

"Your tongue still burnin'?"

I lift my tongue from the water. "It feels like a million soccer players are stomping on it with their cleats."

"Ouch," he says, laughing. "You know, I heard once that kissin' reduces the fire."

"Is that your cheap way of telling me you want to kiss me?"

He looks into my eyes, his dark gaze capturing mine. "*Querida*, I always want to kiss you."

"I'm afraid it won't be that easy, Alex. I want answers. Answers first, then kissing."

"Is that why you came here naked underneath that jacket?"

"Who says I'm naked underneath?" I say, leaning close.

Alex sets down his plate.

If my mouth is still burning, I hardly notice. Now is my time to get the upper hand. "Let's play a game, Alex. I call it Ask a Question, Then Strip. Every time you ask a question, you have to remove an article of clothing. Every time I ask, I have to remove one."

"I figure I can ask seven questions, *querida*. How many you got?"

"Take it off, Alex. You asked your first question."

He nods in agreement and kicks off his shoe.

"Why don't you start with your shirt?" I ask.

"You do realize you asked a question. I think that's your cue—"

"I did *not* ask a question," I insist.

"You asked me why I don't start with my shirt." He grins.

My pulse quickens. I pull down my pom skirt, keeping my long jacket tightly closed. "Now it's four."

He's trying to stay aloof, but his eyes show a hunger I've seen before. And that silly grin is definitely gone as he licks his lips.

"I need a cigarette bad. It's too bad I quit again. Four you say?"

"That sounded suspiciously like a question, Alex."

He shakes his head. "No, smart-ass, that wasn't a question. Nice try, though. Um, let's see. What's the real reason you came here?"

"Because I wanted to show you how much I love you," I say.

Alex blinks a couple of times, but beyond that he shows me no emotion. This time he lifts his shirt over his head. He flings it to the side, baring his bronzed, washboard stomach.

I kneel next to him, hoping to tempt him and throw him off balance. "Do you want to go to college? The truth."

He hesitates. "Yes. If my life was different."

I kick off a sandal.

"Did you ever have sex with Colin?" he asks.

"No."

He takes off his right shoe, his eyes never leaving mine.

"Did you ever do it with Carmen?" I ask.

He hesitates. "You don't want to hear this."

"Yes, I do. I want to know everything. How many people you've been with, the first person you slept with . . ."

He rubs the back of his neck, as if there's a tension knot there he's trying to relieve. "That's a lot of questions." He hesitates. "Carmen and I . . . so, um, yeah, we had sex. The last time was in April, before I found out she was sleepin' around. Before Carmen is a bit of a blur. That's when I went through a year-long period where it felt like I dated a different girl every few weeks. And slept with most of 'em. It was fucked up."

"Did you always use protection?"

"Yeah."

"Tell me about the first time?"

"My first time was with Isabel."

"Isabel Avila?" I ask, totally stunned.

He nods. "It's not what you think. It happened the summer before freshman year and we both wanted to get the virgin thing over with and find out what all the hype about sex was. It sucked. I fumbled around while she laughed most of the time. We both agreed doin' it with a friend who you treated like a sibling was the worst idea. Okay, I've told you everythin'. Now please take that jacket off."

"Not yet, *muchacho*. If you've slept with so many people, how do I know you didn't catch a disease? Tell me you got tested."

"At the clinic when I got the staples in my arm, they tested me. Trust me, I'm clean."

"I am, too. Just in case you were wondering." I remove my other sandal, glad he didn't make me feel stupid or give me crap for asking more than one question. "Your turn."

"Do you ever think about makin' love to me?" He slides off a sock before I even answer his question.

52

Alex

"Yes," she answers. "Do you think about making love with me?"

I lie awake most nights, fantasizing about sleeping next to her . . . loving her. "Right now, *muñeca*, makin' love to you is the only thing on my mind." I check my watch. I've got to go soon. Drug dealers don't give a shit about your personal life. I can't be late, but I want Brittany so damn bad. "Your coat's next. You sure you want to keep goin'?"

I slip off my other sock. The only things preventing me from being naked are my jeans and briefs.

"Yes, I want to keep going." She smiles wide, her beautiful pink lips glistening in the light. "Turn off the lights before I . . . take my coat off."

I turn off the shop lights, watching as she stands on the blanket and unbuttons her coat with trembling fingers. I'm in a trance, especially when she looks at me with those clear eyes shining with desire.

As she opens her coat slowly, my eyes are fixed on the present inside. She walks toward me, then trips on a discarded shoe.

I catch her, then place her on the soft blanket and settle atop her.

"Thanks for breaking my fall," she says breathlessly.

I brush a strand of hair from her face, then move beside her. When she wraps her arms around my neck, all I want to do is protect this girl for the rest of my life. I ease her jacket open and lean away. A pink lace bra stares back at me. Nothing else.

"*Como un ángel,*" I whisper.

"Is our game over?" she asks nervously.

"It's definitely over, *querida*. 'Cause what we're gonna do next is no game."

Her manicured fingers are on my chest. Can she feel my heart beating against her palm? "I brought protection," she says.

If I'd known . . . if I had any idea tonight would be "the night" . . . I would have been prepared. I guess I never wholeheartedly thought this would be a reality with Brittany. She reaches into her coat pocket and a dozen condom packages spill onto the blanket.

"You plannin' on makin' this an all-nighter?"

Embarrassed, she puts her hands over her face. "I just grabbed a bunch."

I remove her hands and touch my forehead to hers. "I'm jokin'. Don't be shy with me."

Slipping the jacket off her shoulders, I know I'm going to hate leaving her tonight. I wish we could have an all-nighter. But wishes are only granted in fairy tales.

"Aren't . . . aren't you going to take your jeans off?" she asks.

"Soon." I wish I could take my time and make this night last forever. It's like being in heaven and knowing the next stop is hell. I slowly trace kisses down her neck and shoulders.

"I'm a virgin, Alex. What if I do everything wrong?"

"There is no *wrong* here. This isn't a test in Peterson's class. This is you and me. The rest of the world is shut out right now, okay?"

"Okay," she says softly. Her eyes are glistening. Is she crying?

"I don't deserve you. You know that, *querida*, don't you?"

"When are you gonna realize you're one of the good guys?" When I don't answer, she pulls my head down to hers. "My body is yours tonight, Alex," she whispers against my lips. "Do you want it?"

"God, yes." As we make out, I shrug off my jeans and briefs and hug her tight, devouring the softness and warmth of her body against mine. "Are you scared?" I whisper in her ear when she's ready and I'm ready and I can't wait any longer.

"A little, but I trust you."

"Relax, *preciosa*."

"I'm trying."

"This won't work unless you relax." I pull away and reach for a condom, my hands shaking. "You sure about this?" I ask.

"Yes, yes, I'm sure. I love you, Alex," she says. "I love you," she says again, saying it almost desperately this time.

I let her words seep into my body and hold myself back, not wanting to hurt her. Who am I kidding? The first time for a girl hurts, no matter how careful a guy is.

I want to tell her how I feel, tell her how much she's become the center of my being. But I can't. The words won't come.

"Just do it," she says, sensing my hesitation.

So I do, but when she sucks in a breath, I just wish I could take the pain away from her.

She sniffs and wipes a tear that's running down her cheek. Seeing her that emotional is my undoing. For the first time since I saw my dad lying dead in front of me, a tear drops from my eye.

She holds my head in her hands and kisses my tear away. "It's okay, Alex."

But it's not. I need to make this perfect. Because I may never get another chance and she needs to know how good it can be.

I focus on her completely, desperate to make it special. Afterward, I pull her close. She nestles into me while I stroke her hair, both of us content to stay in our private world for as long as possible.

I can't believe she shared her body with me. I should feel victorious. Instead, *me siento una mierda.*

It'll be impossible to protect Brittany for the rest of her life from all the other guys who want to be near her, to see her as I've seen her. Touch her as I've touched her. Man, I never want to let her go.

But it's too late. I can't waste more time. After all, she isn't mine forever and I can't pretend she is. "You okay?" I ask her.

"I'm fine. More than fine."

"I really gotta go," I say, glancing at the digital clock sitting crooked on one of the tool carts.

Brittany rests her chin on my chest. "You're going to quit the Blood now, right?"

My body stiffens. "No," I say, my voice filled with torment. Hell, why'd she go and ask me that?

"Everything's different now, Alex. We made love."

"What we did was great. But it doesn't change anythin'."

She stands, collects her clothes, and starts dressing in the corner. "So I'm just another girl you can add to the list of girls you've slept with?"

"Don't say that."

"Why not? It's true, isn't it?"

"No."

"Then prove it to me, Alex."

"I can't." I wish I could tell her something different. She has to know it'll always be like this, I'll have to leave her for the Blood time and time again. This white girl who loves with her heart and soul so intensely is like an addictive drug. She deserves better. "I'm sorry," I say after I step into my jeans. What else is there to say?

She averts her eyes and walks to the garage's exit like a robot.

When I hear tires screeching, my protective senses kick in. A car is heading our way . . . Lucky's RX-7.

This is not good. "Get in your car," I order.

But it's too late; Lucky's RX carrying a bunch of guys from the Blood comes to a screeching halt in front of us.

"*No lo puedo creer, ganaste la apuesta!*" Lucky yells out the window.

I attempt to hide Brittany behind me, but it's no use. Plain as day they can spot her sexy, bare legs sticking out of her coat.

"What is he saying?" she asks.

I have the urge to take my pants off and give them to her. If she finds out about the bet, she'll think that's why I slept with her. I have to get her out of here fast.

"Nothin'. He's trash talkin'," I say. "Get in the car. 'Cause if you don't I'm gonna put you in there."

I hear the creak of Lucky's car door at the same time Brittany opens hers.

"Don't be mad at Paco," she says, then slides into the driver's seat.

What is she talking about? "Go," I order, not having time to ask what she means. "We'll talk later."

She speeds away.

"Shit, man," Lucky says, eyeing the back of her BMW with appreciation. "I had to find out if Enrique was shittin' me. You really did screw Brittany Ellis, didn't you? Did you videotape it?"

My answer is a savage punch to Lucky's gut, making him fall to his knees. I straddle my motorcycle and rev the engine. When I see Enrique's Camry, I stop by his car.

"Listen, Alejo," Enrique says to me through the open window. "*Lo siento mucho—*"

"I quit," I interrupt before throwing the keys to the shop at Enrique and riding away.

As I drive home, my thoughts turn to Brittany and how much she means to me.

The reality hits me.

I'm not doing the drug deal.

Now I understand all those chick flicks I make fun of. 'Cause now I'm the sappy dork willing to risk it all for the girl. *Estoy enamorado . . .* I'm in love.

Fuck the Blood. I can protect my family and be true to myself first. Brittany was right. My life is too important to throw away on a drug deal. The truth is, I want to apply to college and make something good out of my life.

I'm not like my father. My father was a weak man who took the easy way out. I'll take the challenge required to leave the Blood, forget the risk. And if I survive, I'll go back to Brittany a free man. *¡Lo juro!*

I'm not a drug dealer. I'm letting Hector down, but my reasons for being in the gang were to help protect my neighborhood and family, not deal drugs. Since when did dealing become a necessity?

Since I got pulled over, it snowballed from there. I got arrested, then Hector bailed me out. Right after I asked questions of other OG's about the night my father died, Hector and my mom got in a heated discussion. She had bruises on her. After that, Hector was all over me about the drug deal.

Paco tried to warn me; he was convinced something wasn't right.

Racking my brain, the pieces slowly come together. *Dios*, was the truth right in front of my face? There's one person who can tell me the truth about the night my dad died.

I storm into my house and find *mi'amá* in her room. "You know who killed *Papá*."

"Alejandro, don't."

"It was someone in the Blood, wasn't it? The night at the wedding, Hector and you were talkin' about it. He knows who it is. You know, too."

Tears start welling in her eyes. "I'm warning you, Alejandro. Don't do this."

"Who was it?" I ask, ignoring her plea.

She looks away from me.

"Tell me!" I scream at the top of my lungs. My words make her flinch.

For so long I just wanted to take the hurt away from her, I didn't think to ask what she knew about my father's murder. Or maybe I didn't want to know, because I was afraid of the truth. I can't let it go any longer.

Her breathing is slow and jerky as she puts her hand to her mouth. "Hector . . . it was Hector." While the truth sinks in, dread, shock, and pain spread through my body like wildfire. My mom looks up at me with sad eyes. "I just wanted to protect you and your brothers. That's all. Your *papá* wanted out of the Blood, and got killed for it. Hector wanted you to replace him. He threatened me, Alejandro, and said if you didn't get jumped in, the whole family would end up like your father—"

I can't listen anymore. Hector set me up to get arrested so I'd owe him. And he set up the drug deal, duping me to think it's a step up when it was only a step into his trap. He probably suspected someone would spill the truth, and soon. I hurry to my dresser, my mind set on what I need to do—confront my father's killer.

The gun is gone.

"Did you go in my drawer?" I growl at Carlos, grabbing him by the collar as he's sitting on the living room couch.

"No, Alex," Carlos says. "*¡Créeme!* Paco was here earlier, and he went to our room, but he said it was just to borrow one of your jackets."

Paco took my gun. I should have known. But how did Paco know I wouldn't be home to catch him?

Brittany.

Brittany stalled me tonight on purpose. She said not to be mad at Paco. They were both trying to protect me, because I was too stupid and cowardly to stick up for myself and face the facts that were right in front of my face.

Brittany's words as she got in her car ring in my ears. *Don't be mad at Paco.*

I hurry to *mi'amá*'s room. "If I don't come back tonight, you've got to take Carlos and Luis to Mexico," I tell her.

"But, Alejandro—"

I sit on the edge of her bed. "*Mamá*, Carlos and Luis are in danger. Save them from my fate. Please."

"Alex, don't talk like that. Your father talked like that."

I'm just like Papá, I want to say, and made the same mistakes. I won't let it happen to my brothers. "Promise me. I need to hear you say it. I'm dead serious."

Tears are streaming down her face. She kisses my cheek and hugs me tight. "I promise . . . I promise."

I hop on Julio and call someone I never thought I'd call for advice—Gary Frankel. He urges me to do something I'd never thought I'd do—call the cops and inform them what's going down.

53

Brittany

I've been sitting in Sierra's driveway for five minutes. I still can't believe Alex and I did it. I don't regret a single minute of it, but I still don't believe it.

Tonight I sensed desperation in Alex, though, as if he wanted to prove something to me through actions instead of words. I'm mad at myself for getting emotional, but I couldn't help it. The tears streamed out from joy, happiness, love. And when I saw a tear escape from his eye, I kissed it. . . . I wanted to save that tear forever because it was the first time Alex let me see him like that. Alex doesn't cry; he doesn't let himself get that emotional about anything.

Tonight changed him, whether he wants to face that fact or not.

I've changed, too.

I walk into Sierra's house. Sierra is sitting on her living room couch. My father and mother are sitting across from her.

"This looks suspiciously like an intervention," I tell them.

Sierra says, "Not an intervention, Brit. A talk."

"Why?"

"Isn't it obvious?" my dad says. "You're not living at home."

I stand in front of both my parents, wondering how we got to this point. My mother is in a black pants suit and her hair is in a bun, as if she's dressed for a funeral. My dad is wearing jeans and a sweatshirt, and his eyes are bloodshot. He's been up all night, I can tell. And maybe my mom has, too, but she'd never show it. She'd put in Visine to mask it all.

"I can't play the perfect daughter anymore. I'm not perfect," I say calmly and evenly. "Can you accept that?"

My dad's eyebrows come together, as if he's struggling to keep his composure. "We don't want you to be perfect. Patricia, tell her how you feel."

My mom shakes her head, as if she can't comprehend why I'm making a big deal about this. "Brit, this has gone on long enough. Stop pouting, stop rebelling, stop being selfish. Your father and I don't want you to be perfect. We want you to be the best you can be, that's all."

"Because Shelley, no matter how hard she tries, can't possibly live up to your expectations?"

"Don't bring Shelley into this," my dad says. "It's not fair."

"Why not? This is *all* about Shelley." I'm feeling defeated, like no matter how many words come out of my mouth to try and explain it, it'll never come out right. I plop myself down in one of the plush, velvet chairs in front of them. "For the record, I didn't run away. I'm staying at my best friend's house."

My mom brushes away a piece of lint on her thigh. "Thank goodness for her. She's been telling us what's been going on with you, giving us daily reports."

I look over at my best friend, still sitting in the corner as a witness to the Ellises' meltdown. Sierra puts her hands up guiltily as she heads for the door to hand out candy to late trick-or-treaters who just rang the bell.

My mom sits up straight on the edge of the couch. "What will it take for you to come home?"

I want so much from my parents, probably more than they're capable of giving. "I don't know."

My dad puts his hand on his forehead, as if he has a headache. "Is it *that* bad at home?"

"Yeah. Well, not bad. But stressful. Mom, you stress me out. And Dad, I hate it when you come and go like the house is your hotel. We're all strangers living in the house. I love you both, but I don't want to always be 'the best I can be.' I just want to be me. I want to be free to make my own decisions and learn from my mistakes without freaking out, feeling guilty, or worrying that I'm not living up to your expectations." I choke back tears. "I don't want to let you two down. I know Shelley can't be like me. I'm so sorry . . . please don't send her away because of me."

My dad kneels beside me. "Don't be sorry, Brit. We're not sending her away because of you. Shelley's disability isn't your fault. It's nobody's fault."

My mom is silent and still, staring at the wall as if she's in a trance. "It's my fault," she says.

Everyone focuses on my mom because those are the last words we expected to come out of her mouth.

"Patricia?" my dad says, trying to get her attention.

"Mom, what are you talking about?" I ask.

She's looking straight ahead. "All these years I've blamed myself."

"Patricia, it's not your fault."

"When I had Shelley, I took her to playgroups," my mom says in a soft voice as if she's talking to herself. "I admit I envied the other moms with the normal kids who could keep their heads up on their own and grasp things. Most of the time I got the pity stares. I hated that. I became obsessed with thinking I could've prevented her from being disabled by eating more vegetables and exercising more—I blamed myself for her condition even when your father insisted it wasn't my fault." She looks at me and smiles wistfully. "Then you came along. My blond-haired, blue-eyed princess."

"Mom, I'm no princess and Shelley's not someone to pity. I'm not always going to date the guy you want me to date, I'm not always going to dress the way you want me to dress, and I'm definitely not always going to act the way you want. Shelley isn't going to live up to your expectations either."

"I know."

"Will you ever be okay with it?"

"Probably not."

"You're so critical. Oh, God, I'd do anything for you to stop blaming me for every little thing that goes wrong. Love me for who I am. Love Shelley for who she is. Stop focusing on the bad stuff because life is just too damn short."

"You don't want me being concerned because you've decided to date a gang member?" she asks.

"No. Yes. I don't know. If I didn't feel like you'd be judgmental, I'd share it with you. If you could meet him . . . he's just sooo much more than people see on the outside. If you want me to sneak around just so I can be with him, I'll do it."

"He's a gang member," my mom says dryly.

"His name is Alex."

My dad leans back. "Knowing his name doesn't change the fact that he's in a gang, Brittany."

"No, it doesn't. It's a step in the right direction, though. Would you rather have me be truthful, or sneaking around?"

It took us an hour until my mom agreed to try and stop hovering so much. And for my dad to agree to come home twice a week from work before six.

I agreed to have Alex come by the house so they could meet him. And to tell them where I'm going and who I'm going with. They haven't agreed to approve or like my choice in boyfriends, but it's a start. I want to try making things right because picking up the pieces is way better than leaving them the way they are.

54

Alex

The deal is supposed to happen here, at the forest preserve in Busse Woods.

The parking lot and area beyond are dark, with a sliver of moonlight to guide me. The place is deserted, except for a blue sedan with its lights on. I walk farther into the woods and catch a glimpse of a dark figure lying on the ground.

I run while dread washes over me. I recognize my jacket the closer I get. It's like seeing my own death in front of me.

Kneeling on the ground, I slowly turn the body over.

Paco.

"Oh, shit," I cry as I feel his hot, wet blood soak my hands.

Paco's eyes are glazed, but he moves his hand slowly and grabs onto my arm. "I fucked up."

I rest Paco's head on my thighs. "I told you to stop interferin' with my life. Don't die on me, you better not die on me," I choke out. "Holy shit, you're bleedin' all over."

Bright red blood streams out of his mouth.

"I'm scared," he whispers, then winces in pain.

"Don't leave me. Hold on and it'll be fine." I hold Paco tightly, knowing I just lied to him. My best friend is dying. There's no going back. I feel his pain as if it's my own.

"Lookie here, it's pretend Alex and his sidekick, the real Alex. Some Halloween night, ain't it?"

I turn to the sound of Hector's voice.

"It's too bad I couldn't tell it was Paco I was shooting at," he continues. "Man, you two look so different in daylight. I guess I should get my eyes checked." He pulls a gun on me.

I'm not scared. I'm angry. And I need answers. "Why did you do this?"

"If you must know, it's your father's fault. He wanted out of the Blood. But there is no out, Alex. He was the best we had, your *padre*. Right before he died, he tried to quit. That last drug deal was his challenge, Alex. Father-son drug deal. You both make it out alive, he wins." He laughs, a cackling sound reverberating in my ears. "The stupid motherfucker never had a chance. You're too much like your old man. I thought I could train you to take his place as a great drug and gun dealer. But no, you really are like your old man. A quitter . . . *un rajado.*"

I look down at Paco. He's hardly breathing, the air barely making it out of his lungs. Looking down at his blood-stained chest, the growing red bull's-eye reminds me of my *papá*. This time, though, I'm not six years old. Everything is crystal clear.

My eyes meet Paco's for an intense second.

"The Latino Blood betrayed us both, man," are the last words Paco says before his eyes glaze over and he falls limp in my arms.

"Put him down, already! He's dead, Alex. Just like your old man. Get up and face me!" Hector yells, waving his gun in the air like a lunatic.

I gently lay Paco's lifeless body on the ground and stand, ready to fight.

"Put your hands on your head so I can see 'em. You know, when I killed *el viejo* you ~~cried like an~~ *escuincle*, a baby, Alex. You cried in my arms, the guy who killed him. Ironic, huh?"

I was only six. If I'd known it was Hector, I wouldn't have joined the Blood. "Why'd you do it, Hector?"

"Boy, you'll never learn, will you? You see, *tu papá* thought he was better than me. I showed him, didn't I? He bragged that the south side of Fairfield was a cut above since the high school was in a rich hood. Said in Fairfield there were no gangs. I changed that, Alex. Got my guys to go in and make every household belong to me. It was either come to me, or lose everything. That, my boy, is what makes me *el jefe*."

"It makes you a madman."

"Madman. Genius. Same thing." Hector pushes me with the gun. "Now get on your knees. I think this is a good place for you to die. Right here in the woods, like an animal. You want to die like an animal, Alex?"

"You're the animal, asshole. You could at least look me in the eye when you murder me, like you did to my father."

When Hector walks around me, I finally have a chance. Grabbing Hector's wrist, I force him to the ground.

Hector swears and is fast to his feet, the gun still in his hand. I use his disorientation to my advantage and kick him in the side. Whirling around, Hector knocks the side of my head with the butt of his gun. I fall on my knees, cursing the fact that I'm not invincible.

Thoughts of *mi papá* and Paco give me the strength to fight back through the blur. I'm all too aware Hector is trying to get a good shot at me.

When I kick Hector back, I scramble to my feet. Hector's Glock is pointed directly at my chest.

"This is the Arlington Heights police! Drop your weapons and put your hands in the air where we can see them!"

Through the woods and the haze, I can barely see red and blue lights flashing in the distance.

I raise my hands. "Drop it, Hector. The game is over."

Hector holds the gun steady, aimed at my chest.

"Put the gun down," the police call out. "Now!"

Hector's eyes are wild. I feel his rage from the five feet separating us.

I know he's going to do it. *Es un cabrón.*

He's going to pull the trigger.

"You're wrong, Alex," he says. "The game has just begun."

The whole thing happens fast. I move to the right as the shots ring out.

Pop. Pop. Pop.

Stumbling backward, I know I'm hit. The bullet burns through my skin as if someone is pouring Tabasco on it.

Then my world goes black.

55

Brittany

At five in the morning, my ringing cell phone wakes me up. It's Isabel, probably wanting advice about Paco.

"Do you know what time it is?" I ask when I answer the call.

"He's dead, Brittany. He's gone."

"Who?" I ask frantically.

"Paco. And . . . I didn't know if I should call you, but you'll find out eventually that Alex was there also and—"

My fingers tighten on the phone. "Where's Alex? Is he okay? Please tell me he's okay. I beg of you, Isa. Please."

"He was shot."

For a second, I wait for her to say the dreaded words. He's dead. But she doesn't. "He's in surgery at Lakeshore Hospital."

Before she finishes the sentence, I'm ripping off my pj's and frantically throwing on clothes. Grabbing my keys, I head out the door still holding my cell phone tight as Isabel relays all of the details she knows.

The drug deal went bad and Paco and Hector are dead. Alex was shot, and is in surgery. That's all she knows.

"Oh my God, oh my God, oh my God," I chant throughout the

ride to the hospital after I hang up with Isabel. When I spent the eve-ning with Alex last night, I was sure he would choose me over the drug deal. He might have betrayed our love, but I can't.

Deep sobs rack me. Paco assured me yesterday he was going to make sure Alex didn't do the drug deal but . . . oh, God. Paco took Alex's place and ended up dead. Poor, sweet Paco.

I'm trying to drown out the images of Alex not making it through the surgery. A part of me will die with him.

I ask the hospital receptionist where I should wait for updates on Alex's condition.

The lady asks me to spell his name, then types it on her keyboard. The sound is making me crazy. She's taking so long I want to grab her shoulders and shake her into going faster.

The woman looks at me with curious eyes. "Are you family?"

"Yes."

"Relation?"

"Sister."

The lady shakes her head in disbelief, then shrugs. "Alejandro Fuentes was brought in with a gunshot wound."

"He's going to be okay, right?" I cry.

The lady punches her keyboard again. "It looks like he's been in surgery all morning, *Miss Fuentes*. The waiting room is the orange room down the hall on the right. The doctor will inform you of your *brother's* prognosis after surgery."

I clutch the counter. "Thank you."

At the waiting room, I freeze as soon as I see Alex's mother and two brothers huddled in the corner, sitting on orange-colored hospital chairs. His mother looks up first. Her eyes are bloodshot and tears stream down her face.

My hand goes to my mouth and I can't help a sob from escaping;

I can't hold it in. Tears well in my eyes, and through the blurriness I see Mrs. Fuentes open her arms to me.

Overwhelmed with emotion, I run into her embrace.

His hand twitched.

I lift my head from Alex's hospital bed. I've sat beside him through the night waiting for him to wake up. His mother and brothers haven't left his side, either.

The doctor said it could be hours before he's conscious.

I wet a paper towel from the hospital room sink and touch it to Alex's forehead. I've done this throughout the night as he sweated and thrashed in a restless sleep.

His eyes flutter. I can tell he's fighting the sedation as he forces them open. "Where am I?" His voice is scratchy and faint.

"The hospital," his mom says as she rushes to his side.

"You were shot," Carlos adds, his voice full of agony.

Alex's brows draw together in confusion. "Paco . . . ," he says, his voice hitching.

"Don't think about that right now," I say, trying to hold my emotion in with little success. I need to be strong for him now and I won't let him down.

I think he's about to reach for my hand, but a pained expression crosses his face and he pulls back. I have so much to tell him, so much to say. I wish I could have a Do Over Day and change the past. I wish I could have saved Paco and Alex from their fates.

His eyes are still glassy from drowsiness when he looks at me and says, "Why are you here?"

I watch as his mom rubs his arm, trying to lend him comfort. "Brittany stayed all night, Alex. She's worried about you."

"Let me talk to her. Alone," he says weakly.

His brothers and mother exit the room, giving us privacy.

When we're alone, he winces in pain as he adjusts his position. Then he glares at me. "I want you to leave."

"You don't mean that," I say, reaching for his hand. He can't mean it.

He jerks his hand away, as if my touch burned him. "Yes. I do."

"Alex, we'll get through this. I love you."

He turns his head and focuses on the floor. He swallows and clears his throat. "I fucked you because of a bet, Brittany," he says softly, but his words come out crystal clear. "It didn't mean anythin' to me. You don't mean anythin' to me."

I step back as Alex's hurtful words seep into my brain. "No," I whisper.

"You and me . . . it was a game. I bet Lucky his RX-7 that I could fuck you before Thanksgiving."

When Alex referred to our lovemaking as a "fuck," I cringed. Calling it sex would have left a bitter taste in my mouth. Calling it a "fuck" makes my stomach churn. I keep my hands limp at my sides. I want to make him take back his words. "You're lying."

He turns his gaze from the floor and looks right into my eyes. Oh, God. There's no emotion there. His eyes are as steely as his words. "You're pathetic if you think this thing between us was real."

I shake my head violently. "Don't hurt me, Alex. Not you. Not now." My lips are trembling as I mouth a silent but pleading, "Please." When he doesn't respond I take another step back, almost stumbling as I think about me, the *real* me only Alex knows. In a pitiful whisper I tell him, "I trusted you."

"That was your mistake, not mine."

He touches his left shoulder and winces in pain before a group of his friends file into the room. They offer him condolences and sympathy while I stand frozen in the corner, completely unnoticed.

"Was it *all* for the bet?" I say above the commotion.

The six or so people in the room stare at me. Even Alex. Isabel steps toward me, but I hold up a hand and stop her.

"Is it true? Did Alex make a bet to have sex with me?" I say, because I still can't wrap my brain around Alex's hurtful words. It can't be true.

All eyes drift to him, but Alex's eyes penetrate my own.

"Tell her," Alex orders.

A guy named Sam lifts his head up. "Well, uh, yeah. He won Lucky's RX-7."

I back up to the hospital room door, trying to hold my head high. A cold, hard expression settles on Alex's face.

My throat threatens to close as I say, "Congratulations, Alex. You win. I hope you like your new car."

As I grab the door handle to leave, Alex's steely glare turns to relief. I calmly walk out of the room. I hear Isabel come up behind me when I'm in the hallway, but I run away from her, the hospital, and Alex. Unfortunately, I can't run from my heart. It hurts, deep inside my body. And I know I'll never be the same.

56

Alex

I've been in the hospital a week. I hate nurses, doctors, needles, tests . . . and especially hospital gowns. I think the longer I've been in this place, the crabbier I've gotten. Okay, so I probably shouldn't have sworn at the nurse who took out my catheter. It was her cheery disposition that pissed me off.

I don't want to see anyone. I don't want to talk to anyone. The less people involved in my life, the better. I shoved Brittany away and it killed me to hurt her. But I had no choice. The closer she got to me, the more her life was in danger. I couldn't let what happened to Paco happen to the girl I . . .

Stop thinking about her, I tell myself.

The people I care about die, it's as simple as that. My dad. Now Paco. I was an idiot to think I could have it all.

When there's a knock at my door, I scream, "Go away!"

The knock gets more persistent.

"Fuckin' leave me alone!"

As the door creaks open, I hurl a cup at the door. The cup doesn't hit a hospital employee; it hits Mrs. P. squarely in the chest.

"Oh, shit. Not you," I say.

Mrs. P.'s got new glasses, with rhinestones on them. "That's not exactly the greeting I expected, Alex," she says. "I can still give you a detention for cussing, you know."

I turn on my side so I don't have to look at her. "Did you come here to give me detention slips? 'Cause if you did, you can forget it. I'm not goin' back to school. Thanks for visitin'. Sorry you have to leave so soon."

"I'm not going anywhere until you hear me out."

Oh, please no. Anything except having to listen to her lecture. I push the button that calls the nurse.

"Can we help you, Alex?" a voice bellows through the speaker.

"I'm bein' tortured."

"I beg your pardon?"

Mrs. P. walks over to me and pulls the speaker out of my hand. "He's joking. Sorry to bother you." She puts the remote speaker on the nightstand, deliberately out of my reach. "Don't they give you happy pills in this place?"

"I don't want to be happy."

Mrs. P. leans forward, her straight bangs brushing the top of her glasses. "Alex, I'm sorry about what happened to Paco. He wasn't a student of mine, but I heard how close you two were."

I look out the window to avoid her. I don't want to talk about Paco. I don't want to talk about anything. "Why'd you come here?"

I hear the rustling as she pulls something from her bag. "I brought you some work to do, to catch up until you come back to class."

"I'm not comin' back. I already told you, I'm droppin' out. It shouldn't surprise you, Mrs. P. I'm a gang member, remember?"

She walks around the bed, coming into my line of vision. "I guess

I was wrong about you. I would have bet you'd be the one to break the mold."

"Yeah, well, maybe that was before my best friend got shot. It was supposed to be me, you know." I'm looking at the chemistry book in her hand. All it does is remind me of what was, and what can never be. "He wasn't supposed to die, dammit! I was!" I yell.

Mrs. P. doesn't flinch. "But you didn't. You think you're doing Paco a favor by quitting school and giving up? Consider it a gift he gave you, Alex, instead of a curse. Paco isn't coming back. You can." Mrs. P. places the chem book on the window ledge. "I've had more students die than I ever thought possible. My husband urges me to quit Fairfield and teach at some school without gang members who live their lives only to die or end up as drug dealers."

Sitting on the edge of my bed, she looks down at her hands. "I stay at Fairfield hoping I can make a difference, be a role model. Dr. Aguirre believes we can bridge the gaps, and so do I. If I can just change one of my students' lives, I can—"

"Change the world?" I interject.

"Maybe."

"You can't. It is what it is."

She looks up at me, totally undefeated. "Oh, Alex. You're so wrong. It is what you make it. If you think you can't change the world, then go on and follow the path already carved out for you. But there are other roads to choose, they're just harder to trudge through. Changing the world isn't easy, but I sure as hell am going to keep trying. Are you?"

"No."

"That's your prerogative. I'm going to keep trying anyway." She pauses, then says, "Do you want to know how your chemistry partner is holding up?"

I shake my head. "Nope. Don't care." The words almost get stuck in my throat.

She sighs in frustration, then walks over to the window ledge and picks up the chemistry book. "Should I take this back with me, or leave it here?"

I don't answer.

She puts the book back on the ledge and heads for the door.

"I wish I'd chosen biology instead of chemistry," I say as she opens the door to leave.

She winks at me knowingly. "No, you don't. And just so you know, Dr. Aguirre will be coming to visit later today. I'd advise against throwing things at him as he walks through the door."

When I got out of the hospital after two weeks, my mom took us to Mexico. A month later I got a job as a valet at a hotel in San Miguel de Allende, near my family's house. A nice hotel, with whitewashed walls and pillars in the front entrance. I acted as an interpreter when needed, since my English was better than most of the employees'. When I went out with the guys after work, they tried to set me up with Mexican girls. The girls were beautiful, sexy, and definitely knew how to tempt a guy. The problem was, they weren't Brittany.

I needed to get her out of my head. And fast.

I tried. One night an American girl staying at the hotel brought me up to her room. At first I thought it would take having sex with another blond girl to erase that one night I had with Brittany. But once I was about to do it, I froze.

I realized then that Brittany had ruined every other girl for me.

It's not Brittany's face, not her smile, not even her eyes. All of that surface stuff made the world see her as beautiful, but it was the deeper stuff that made her different. It was the gentle way she wiped her sister's face, the way she took chemistry so seriously, the way she showed her love even when she knew what and who I was. I was about to do a drug deal, something she was adamantly against, and she still loved me.

So now, three months after the shooting, I'm back in Fairfield about to face what Mrs. P. would call my greatest fear.

Enrique is sitting at his desk at the auto body shop, shaking his head. We talked about Halloween night and I forgave him for whatever involvement he'd had in letting Lucky know I'd been with Brittany.

Enrique lets out a long, slow breath after I tell him what I'm going to do. "You could die," he says, looking up at me.

I nod. "I know."

"I won't be able to help you. None of your friends in the Blood can help you. Reconsider, Alex. Go back to Mexico and enjoy the rest of your life."

I've made my choice and have no intention of backing down. "I'm not gonna be a coward. I need to do this. I need to quit the Blood."

"For her?"

"Yeah." And for my *papá*. And for Paco. And for me and my family.

"What good is quitting the Blood if you end up dead?" Enrique asks. "Your jumping in will seem like a holiday party compared to this. They'll even make OG's participate."

Instead of answering, I hand him a piece of paper with a phone number on it. "If anythin' happens to me, call this guy. He's the only friend I've got who's not connected." Not connected to the Blood, or Brittany.

That night I'm facing a warehouse full of people who consider me a traitor. I've been called a bunch of other things tonight, too. An hour ago I told Chuy, who'd taken over Hector's position, I wanted out—a clean break from the Latino Blood. Just one little hitch . . . in order to do that I need to survive their gauntlet—a 360 violation.

Chuy, stiff and stern, steps forward with a Latino Blood bandanna. I scan the onlookers. My friend Pedro is standing in the back, his eyes averted. Javier and Lucky are there, too, their eyes blazing with excitement. Javier is a crazy motherfucker and Lucky is not happy he lost the bet even though I never collected. Both will enjoy being able to beat the shit out of me while I can't fight back.

Enrique, my cousin, is leaning against the wall in the corner of the warehouse. He'll be expected to participate in the challenge, to aid in breaking whatever bones possible until I pass out. Loyalty and commitment mean everything to the LB. You break that loyalty, you break that commitment . . . you're as good as an enemy in their eyes. Worse even, because you *were* one of them. If Enrique steps forward to protect me, he's toast.

I stand proud while Chuy covers my eyes with the bandanna. I can do this. If it brings me to Brittany in the end, it's all worth it. I'm not gonna even think about the other option.

After my hands are bound behind my back, I'm led to a car and pushed into the backseat while two people flank me. I have no clue where we're headed. Since Chuy is in charge now, anything is possible.

A note. I never wrote a note. What if I die and Brittany never knows how I feel about her? Maybe it's a good thing. She'll be able to get on with her life easier thinking I'm a prick who betrayed her and never looked back.

Forty-five minutes later the car is off-road. I can tell by the gravel crunching under the tires. Maybe knowing where I am would take the edge off, but I can't see a damn thing. I'm not nervous. More like anxious to know if I'll be one of the lucky ones to survive. And even if I do survive, will someone find me? Or will I die alone in some barn, warehouse, or abandoned building? Maybe they're not going to beat me. Maybe they'll take me to the roof of a building and just push me off. *Se acabó.*

Nah, Chuy wouldn't like that. He likes to hear the screaming and pleas of strong guys brought down to their knees.

I'm not going to give him the satisfaction.

I'm led out of the car. From the sound of my feet against gravel and stones, we're in the middle of nowhere. I hear more cars parking, more feet following behind us. A cow moos in the distance.

A warning moo? Truth is, I want to do this. If it's interrupted, it will postpone the inevitable. I'm willing. I'm ready. Let's get it on.

I wonder if I'll be hung by my hands to a branch of a tree, strung up like a whipping boy.

Oh, man, I hate the unknown. *Estoy perdido.*

"Stay here," I'm instructed.

As if I have anywhere to go.

Someone is walking toward me. I can hear the gravel crunch with each step. "You are a disgrace to this brotherhood, Alejandro. We protected you and your family, and you've decided to turn your back on us. Is that right?"

I wish my life was a John Grisham novel. His heroes always seem to be one step away from death but come up with a brilliant plan. It usually includes hiding information that will ruin the bad guy, and if the hero ends up dead, the bad guy will be ruined for life. Unfortunately, real life can't be wrapped up with a nice little bow.

"Hector was the one who betrayed the Blood," I respond. *"El traidor."*

The response to my calling Hector a traitor is a hard fist to my jaw. Shit, I wasn't ready for that because I can't see a fucking thing with this blindfold on. I try not to wince.

"You understand the consequences of leaving the Blood?"

I work my jaw back and forth. "Yes."

I hear crunching stones as a circle of people close in. I'm the bull's-eye this time.

An eerie silence settles over the crowd. Nobody laughs; nobody makes a sound. Some of the guys surrounding me have been my friends all my life. Like Enrique, they're waging a war inside themselves. I don't blame them. The lucky ones haven't been chosen to fight today.

Without warning, I get punched in my face. Attempting to keep myself upright is hard, especially because I know more hits are coming. It's one thing to be in a fight you could possibly win, but it's another to know you've got zero chance.

Something sharp slashes my back.

Then I get punched in the ribs.

Each blow is connecting with my upper body—no inch is left untouched. A slice here, a fist there. I stagger a few times, only to be pulled upright and slammed into another hard fist.

I've got a gash in my back and it stings as if flames are licking at my skin. I can tell Enrique's punches because they don't pack as much fury as the others.

Memories of Brittany keep me from crying out in pain. I'm going to be strong for her . . . for us. I'm not going to let them control whether I live or die. I'm in charge of my destiny, not the Blood.

I have no clue how much time goes by. A half hour? An hour? My body is weakening. I'm having trouble standing. I smell smoke. Are they going to push me into a fire? The bandanna is still secured over my eyes, but it doesn't matter because I'm pretty sure my eyes are swollen shut.

I feel like caving and falling to the ground but force myself to stand tall.

I'm probably unrecognizable now, hot blood streaming from gashes in my face and body. I can feel my shirt being ripped open and it's falling off in pieces, exposing the scar where Hector shot me. A fist punches me right there. It's too much pain.

I slump to the ground, my face scraping the gravel.

At this point, I'm not sure I can make it. *Brittany. Brittany. Brittany.* As long as I repeat the mantra in my head, I know I'm still alive. *Brittany. Brittany. Brittany.*

Is the smell of smoke real, or is it the smell of death?

Through the thick haze in my mind I think I hear someone saying, "Don't you think he's had enough?"

I hear a distant but distinct "No."

Protests follow. If I could move, I would. *Brittany. Brittany. Brittany.*

More protests. Nobody protests during these challenges. It's not allowed. What's happening? What's next? It must be worse than the beating, because I hear a lot of arguing.

"Hold him facedown," Chuy's voice rings out. "Nobody betrays the Latino Blood on my watch. Let this be a lesson to anyone else who tries to betray us. Alejandro Fuentes's body will always be marked, a reminder of his betrayal."

The burning smell gets closer. I have no clue what's about to happen until my upper back is touched with what feels like hot coals.

I think I groaned. Or growled. Or screamed. I don't know anymore. I don't know anything anymore. I can't think. All I can do is *feel*. They might as well have thrown me into the fire, this is a torture worse than anything I could have imagined. The smell of burning skin sears my nostrils as I realize the coals aren't coals at all. The bastard is branding me. *El dolor, el dolor . . .*

Brittany. Brittany. Brittany.

57

Brittany

It's April first. I haven't seen Alex in five months, since the day after the shooting. The gossip about Paco and Alex finally died down and the extra psychologists and social workers have left the school.

Last week I told the school social worker I slept more than five hours, but that was a lie. Since the shooting I've had trouble sleeping, always waking in the middle of the night because my mind won't stop analyzing that awful conversation Alex and I had in the hospital. The social worker said it'll take a long time to let go of my feelings of betrayal.

The problem is, I don't feel betrayed. More like sad and deflated. After all this time, I still go to bed staring at the pictures of him in my cell phone from the night we went to Club Mystique.

After being released from the hospital, he quit school and disappeared. He may be out of my life physically, but he'll always be a part of me. I can't let go even if I wanted to.

One positive thing that came from all of the craziness is that my family took Shelley to Colorado to see Sunny Acres, and my sister really liked it. They have activities every day, play sports, and even have celebrities visit every three months. When Shelley heard they have famous people come visit and do concerts and benefits, if she hadn't been strapped in she would have fallen out of her wheelchair.

Letting my sister choose her own path was hard, but I did it. And I didn't freak out. Knowing it was Shelley's choice made me feel so much better.

But now I'm alone. Alex took a piece of my heart with him when he left. I'm guarding what I have left with a vengeance. I've come to the conclusion that the only life I'm going to control is my own. Alex chose his path. It didn't include me.

I ignore Alex's friends at school, and they ignore me. We all pretend the beginning of senior year didn't actually happen. Except Isabel. We talk sometimes, but it's painful. We have a silent understanding between us, and it's helped make me feel like I have someone going through the same sort of pain I'm dealing with.

Opening my locker before chemistry class in May, I notice a pair of hand warmers hanging on the hooks inside. The worst night of my life comes crashing back to me full force.

Has Alex been here? Did he place the hand warmers in the locker himself?

As much as I want to forget him, I can't. I read that goldfish have a memory of five seconds. I envy them. My memory of Alex, my love for him, will last my lifetime.

I clutch the soft hand warmers to my chest and kneel beside my locker, crying. Ugh. I'm a shell of a person.

Sierra stands at my feet. "Brit, what's wrong?"

I'm unable to move. Unable to pull myself together.

"Come on," Sierra says, pulling me up. "Everybody's watching."

Darlene walks by us. "Seriously, isn't it time you got over your gang-banger boyfriend who dumped you? You're starting to look pathetic," she says, making sure the crowd gathering around us hears her.

Colin appears beside Darlene. He scowls at me. "Alex deserved what he got," he hisses.

Whether it's right or wrong, fight for what you believe in. My hands are already in fists when I swing at him. He dodges the punch, then grabs my wrist and twists it behind my back.

Doug steps forward. "Let her go, Colin."

"Stay out of this, Thompson."

"Dude, humiliating her because she dumped you for another guy is plain lame."

Colin pushes me aside and pulls up his sleeves.

I can't allow Doug to fight my battle. "If you want to fight him, you'll have to get past me first," I say.

To my surprise, Isabel steps in front of me. "And you'll have to get past me to get to her."

Sierra takes a place beside Isabel. "And me, too."

A Mexican guy named Sam pushes Gary Frankel next to Isabel. "This guy can break your arm with one snap, asshole. Get out of my sight before I sic him on you," Sam says.

Gary, who's wearing a coral shirt and white pants, growls to look tough. It doesn't work.

Colin looks left and right for support but can't find any.

I blink in disbelief. Maybe the universe was in disarray before, but now it's back in alignment.

"Come on, Colin," Darlene orders. "We don't need these pathetic lame-o's anyway." They walk off together. I almost feel sorry for them. Almost.

"I'm so proud of you, Douggie," Sierra says, throwing herself on him. They start making out immediately, not caring who's watching or about Fairfield's PDA policy.

"I love you," Doug says when they come up for air.

"I love you, too," Sierra coos in a baby voice.

"Get a room," another classmate calls out.

But they keep kissing until music plays from the loudspeakers. The crowd disperses. I'm still clutching the hand warmers.

Isabel kneels next to me. "I never told Paco how I felt, you know. I never took the risk, and now it's too late."

"I'm so sorry, Isa. I took the risk and lost Alex anyway, so maybe you're better off."

She shrugs, and I know she's trying to keep it together so she doesn't break down at school. "I suppose I'll get over it one day. It's not likely, but I can hope, can't I?" She straightens her shoulders and stands, putting on a brave front. I watch as she walks to class, wondering if she talks about it with her other friends or if she confides only in me.

"Come on," Sierra says, unlocking herself from Doug's embrace and pulling me toward the school exit. I wipe my eyes with the back of my hand and sit on the curb beside Sierra's car, not caring that I'm ditching class. "I'm fine, Sierra. Really."

"No, you're not fine. Brit, I'm your best friend. I'll be here before and after your boyfriends. So spill your guts. I'm all ears."

"I loved him."

"No shit, Sherlock. Tell me something I don't know."

"He used me. He had sex with me to win a bet. And I *still* love him. Sierra, I *am* pathetic."

"You had sex and didn't tell me? I mean, I thought it was a rumor. You know, of the untrue kind."

I lean my head in my hands in frustration.

"I'm just kidding. I don't even want to know. Okay, I do, but only if you want to tell me," Sierra says. "Forget about that now. I saw the way

Alex always looked at you, Brit. That's why I laid off you for liking him. There was no way he was acting. I don't know who told you about a supposed bet—"

I look up. "He did. And his friends confirmed it. Why can't I let him go?"

Sierra shakes her head, as if erasing the words I've said. "First things first." She grabs my chin and forces me to look at her. "Alex had feelings for you, whether he admitted it to you or not, whether there was a bet or not. You know that, Brit, or you wouldn't be clutching those hand warmers like that. Second of all, Alex is out of your life and you owe it to yourself, to his goofy friend Paco, and to me to keep plugging along even if it's not easy."

"I can't help but think he pushed me away on purpose. If I could only talk to him, I can get answers."

"Maybe he doesn't have the answers. That's why he left. If he wants to give up on life, to ignore what's right in front of him, so be it. But you show him that you're stronger than that."

Sierra is right. For the first time I feel I can make it through the rest of senior year. Alex took a piece of my heart that night we made love, and he'll forever hold it. But that doesn't mean my life has to be on hold indefinitely. I can't run after ghosts.

I'm stronger now. At least, I hope I am.

Two weeks later I'm the last one in the locker room to change for gym. The click of heels makes me look up. It's Carmen Sanchez. I don't freak out. Instead, I stand and look right at her.

"He was back in Fairfield, you know," she tells me.

"I know," I say, remembering the hand warmers in my locker. But he left. Like a whisper, he was there and then disappeared.

She looks almost nervous, vulnerable. "You know those giant stuffed-animal prizes at the carnival? The kind practically nobody wins, except the lucky few? I've never won one."

"Yeah. I've never won one, either."

"Alex was my giant prize. I hated you for taking him away," she admits.

I shrug. "Yeah, well, stop hating me. I don't have him, either."

"I don't hate you anymore," she says. "I've moved on."

I swallow and then say, "Me, too."

Carmen chuckles. Then, just as she walks out of the room, I hear her mumble, "Alex sure as hell hasn't."

What's that supposed to mean?

Brittany

FIVE MONTHS LATER

The smell of August in Colorado is definitely different from the smell in Illinois. I shake out my new, short hairstyle, not even bothering to smooth the frizzies down as I attempt to unpack boxes in my dorm room at the university.

My roommate, Lexie, is from Arkansas. She's like a little pixie, short and sweet; she could definitely pass for one of Tinkerbell's descendents. I swear I've never seen her frown. Sierra, at the University of Illinois, wasn't so lucky with her roommate, Dara. The girl has divided the closet and room into separate quarters and gets up at 5:30 a.m. every day (even weekends) to work out in their dorm room. Sierra is miserable, but she's spending most of her time in Doug's dorm room so it's not too bad.

"Ya sure you don't want t'go with us?" Lexie asks me, her Southern drawl flowing from each word. She's going with a bunch of other freshman girls to the quad, where there's some kind of welcome party.

"I've got to finish unpacking, then I'm going to see my sister. I promised her I'd visit as soon as I unpacked."

"Okay," Lexie says, pulling out and trying on clothes to get the "perfect look" for tonight. When she finds an outfit, she fixes her hair and touches up her makeup. It makes me think of the old me, the one who tried so hard to meet everyone's expectations.

When Lexie leaves a half hour later, I sit on my bed and pull out my cell phone. Flipping it open, I stare at the picture of Alex and me. I hate myself for having the urge to look at it. So many times I've tried to force myself to delete the pictures, erase the past. But I can't.

I reach into my desk drawer and pull out Alex's bandanna, fresh and clean and folded up neatly into a square. I touch the smooth material, remembering when Alex gave it to me. To me, it doesn't represent the Latino Blood. It represents Alex.

My cell rings, bringing me back to the present. It's someone from Sunny Acres. When I answer it, a woman's voice is on the other end of the line.

"Is this Brittany Ellis?"

"Yes."

"This is Georgia Jackson, from Sunny Acres. Everything is just fine with Shelley, but she wanted to know if you'd be here before or after dinner."

I look at my watch. It's four thirty. "Tell her I'll be there in fifteen minutes. I'm leaving now."

After I hang up, I place the bandanna back in my desk drawer and shove the phone into my purse.

Taking the bus to the other side of town doesn't take long, and before I know it I'm walking toward the lounge at Sunny Acres where the receptionist said my sister was.

I spot Georgia Jackson first. She's been the link between Shelley and me when I call to ask about her every few days. Her friendly and warm welcome greets me.

"Where's Shelley?" I ask, scanning the room.

"Playing checkers, as usual," Georgia says, pointing to the corner. Shelley isn't facing me, but I recognize the back of her head and her wheelchair.

She's squealing, a hint that she won the game.

As I get closer to her, I catch a glimpse of who's playing against her. The dark hair should have been a clue that my life is about to be turned upside down, but it doesn't fully register. I freeze.

It can't be. My imagination must be going berserk.

But when he turns around and those familiar dark eyes pierce mine, reality zings up my spine like a lightning bolt.

Alex is here. Ten steps away from me. Oh, God, every feeling I've ever had for him comes rushing back like a tidal wave. I don't know what to do or say. I turn back to Georgia, wondering if she knew Alex was here. One look at her hopeful face tells me she did.

"Brittany's here," I hear him tell Shelley before he stands and carefully turns her wheelchair around so she can face me.

Like a robot, I walk toward my sister and wrap her in a hug. When I release her, Alex is standing in front of me, wearing khaki chinos and a blue-checkered button-down shirt. I can only stare at him, my stomach doing weird flip-flops, making me queasy. The world recedes at the edges, and all I can see is *him*.

I finally find my voice. "A-Alex . . . ? W-what are you doing here?" I ask, all tongue-tied.

He shrugs. "I promised Shelley a rematch, didn't I?"

We stand here, staring at each other, some invisible force keeping me from looking away. "You came all the way to Colorado to play checkers with my sister?"

"Well, that's not the only reason. I'm goin' to college here. Mrs. P. and

Dr. Aguirre helped me get a GED after I quit the Blood. I sold Julio. I'm workin' at the student union and takin' out loans."

Alex? In college? His shirtsleeves, neatly buttoned at his wrists, hide most of his Latino Blood tattoos. "You quit? I thought you said it was too dangerous to quit, Alex. You said people who try to get out die."

"I almost did. If it weren't for Gary Frankel, I probably wouldn't have made it. . . ."

"Gary Frankel?" The nicest, geekiest guy in school? For the first time I scan Alex's face and see a faint, new scar above his eye and nasty ones by his ear and neck. "Oh, God! W-what did they d-do to you?"

He takes my hand and places it on his chest. His eyes are intense and dark, like they were the first time I noticed him in the parking lot that first day of school senior year. "It took me a long time to realize I needed to fix everythin'. The choices I made. The gang. Bein' beaten to within an inch of my life and branded like cattle was nothin' compared to losin' you. If I could take back every word I said in the hospital, I would. I thought if I pushed you away, I'd be protectin' you from what happened to Paco and my dad." He looks up and his eyes pierce mine. "I'll never push you away again, Brittany. Ever. I swear."

Beaten? Branded? I'm feeling sick to my stomach and tears sting my eyes.

"Shh." He puts his arms around me, rubbing his hands across my back. "It's all right. I'm okay," he chants over and over again, his voice catching.

He feels good. This feels good.

He rests his forehead against mine. "You need to know somethin'. I agreed to the bet because deep down I knew that if I got emotionally involved, it'd kill me. And it nearly did. You were the one girl who made me risk everythin' for a future worth havin'." He straightens and takes one step back to look me in the eye. "I'm so sorry. *Mujer*, tell me what you want and I'll give it to you. If it'll make you happy for me to leave you alone for the rest of your life, say the word. But if you still want me, I'll do my best to be *this*. . . ." He gestures to his clothes. "How can I prove to you I've changed?"

"I've changed, too," I tell him. "I'm not the girl I was before. And I'm sorry, but those clothes . . . they're not you."

"It's what you want."

"You're wrong, Alex. I want *you*. Not a fake image. I definitely prefer you in jeans and a T-shirt, because that's who you are."

He looks down at his attire and chuckles. "You're right." He looks back up at me. "You once said you loved me. Do you still?"

My sister is watching this exchange between us. She smiles warmly at me, giving me the strength to tell him the truth. "I never stopped loving you. Even when I tried desperately to forget you, I couldn't."

He lets out a long, slow breath and rubs his forehead in relief. His eyes look glassy, filled with emotion. I feel my own eyes welling up again and I gather a handful of his shirt in my fist. "I don't want to fight all the time, Alex. Dating should be fun. Love should be good." I'm pulling him toward me. I want his lips on mine. "W-will it ever be good for us?"

Our lips almost touch before he pulls away from me, but then he—

Oh. My. God.

He kneels on one knee before me, holds my hands in his, and my heart skips more than a few beats. "Brittany Ellis, I'm goin' to prove to you I'm the guy you believed in ten months ago, and I'm gonna be the successful man you dreamed I could be. My plan is to ask you to marry me four years from now, the day we graduate." He cocks his head as his voice takes on a more playful tone. "And I guarantee you a lifetime of fun, probably one with no lack of fightin', for you are one passionate *mamacita* . . . but I definitely look forward to some great make-up sessions. Maybe one day we can even go back to Fairfield and help make it the place my dad always hoped it would be. You, me, and Shelley. And any other Fuentes or Ellis family member who wants to be a part of our lives. We'll be one big, crazy Mexican-American family. What do you think? *Mujer*, you own my soul."

I can't help but smile as I swipe a lone tear trailing down my cheek. How can I not be crazy in love with this guy? Time away from him didn't change anything. I can't deny him another chance. That would be denying myself.

Time to take the risk, to trust once again.

"Shelley, you think she'll take me back?" Alex asks her, his hair dangerously close to her fingers. She doesn't pull his hair . . . just pats his head gently. I feel the tears running down my cheeks at full speed.

"Yeah!" Shelley yells with a goofy, gummy grin. She looks happier and more content than she's been in a long time. Both of my favorite people are with me right here; what more could I ask for?

"What's your major?" I ask.

Alex flashes me his you-can't-resist-me smile. "Chemistry. And yours?"

"Chemistry." I wrap my arms around his neck. "Kiss me so we can see if we still have it. 'Cause you own my heart, my soul, and everything else in between."

His lips finally sear mine, more powerful than ever before.

Wow. The solar system *is* finally in alignment, and I got my Do Over without even asking for it.

Epilogue

Mrs. Peterson closes the door to her classroom. "Good afternoon and welcome to senior chemistry." She walks to her desk, leans on the edge, and opens her class folder. "I appreciate you picking your own seats, but since this is my class, I make the seating arrangements . . . alphabetically."

Groans erupt from the students, the same sound that has greeted her on the first day of school for over thirty years at Fairfield High.

"Mary Alcott, take the first seat. Your partner is Andrew Carson." Down the list Mrs. Peterson goes, students reluctantly sitting in their assigned seats next to their chemistry partners.

"Paco Fuentes," Mrs. Peterson says, pointing to the table behind Mary.

The handsome young man with pale blue eyes like his mother's and smoky black hair like his father's takes his assigned seat.

Mrs. Peterson regards her new student over the glasses perched on her nose. "Mr. Fuentes, don't think this class will be a piece of cake because your parents got lucky and developed a medication to halt the progression of Alzheimer's. Your father never did finish my class and he flunked one of my tests, although I have a feeling your mother was the one who should have failed. But that just means I'll expect extra from you."

"*Sí, señora.*"

Mrs. Peterson looks down at her notebook. "Julianna Gallagher, please take your seat next to Mr. Fuentes."

Mrs. Peterson notices Julianna's blush as she sits on her stool and Paco's cocky grin beside her. Maybe the tide was starting to shift after thirty years of teaching, but she wasn't taking any chances.

"And for those of you who want to start any trouble, I have a zero tolerance policy. . . ."

ACKNOWLEDGMENTS

There are so many people I have to thank for helping me with this book. First I need to send out a big thank-you to Dr. Olympia González and her students at Loyola University, Eduardo Sanchez, Jesus Aguirre, and Carlos Zuniga for spending endless hours helping me flavor my book with Spanish and Mexican culture. I take full credit for any mistakes I've made, as they are purely my own, but I hope I've made you proud.

I've been blessed with a friend like Karen Harris, who is always there for me personally and professionally on a daily basis. Since the beginning of my career, Marilyn Brant has encouraged and supported me endlessly and I am so grateful for her friendship. I would not be where I am today without these two ladies. Other friends and family who have been instrumental to my career and this book are Alesia Holliday, Ruth Kaufman, Erika Danou-Hasan, Sara Daniel, Erica O'Rourke, Martha Whitehead, Lisa Laing, Shannon Greenland, Amy Kahn, Debbie Feiger, Marianne To, Randi Sak, Wendy Kussman, Liane Freed, Roberta Kaiser, and of course Dylan Harris (and Jesus and Carlos) for teaching me some teen slang—your mothers must be so proud.

Big appreciation goes to my agent, Kristin Nelson, and to my editor, Emily Easton, for wanting to see this book in print as much as I did.

Fran, Samantha, and Brett are riding this roller coaster with me, and I want them to know they are my inspiration. And to my sister, Tamar, who has taught me to never give up.

My dear friend Nanci Martinez has dedicated her life to people with special needs, and I want to thank her for letting me spend time with her residents. They are the most cared for and happy group of people.

My blog sisters at www.booksboysbuzz.com are a group of YA writers of whom I've loved being a part. You ladies are hilarious. I am so grateful for the Romance Writers of America and especially the Chicago-North and Windy City chapters of RWA.

Thanks to Sue Heneghan from the Chicago Police Department, not only for being a police officer and dedicating her life to public service, but for teaching me about gangs and challenging me as I wrote this book.

Last, I'd like to thank my fans. They are the best part of writing novels, and I never get tired of reading fan mail they send and e-mail to me. I want to thank some fans who have really helped me—Lexie, who moderates my fan discussion group; and Susan and Diana, who have been the definition of SuperFans.

I love to hear from my readers. So don't forget to visit me at www.simoneelkeles.net!

SIMONE ELKELES was born and raised in the Chicago area. The author of *Leaving Paradise, How to Ruin a Summer Vacation,* and *How to Ruin My Teenage Life,* she was honored to be named Illinois Author of the Year by the Illinois Association of Teachers of English. Fairfield, the town featured in *Perfect Chemistry,* is loosely based on a suburb near Simone's home—where two very different communities come together in one high school. Simone lives in Illinois with her family.

www.simoneelkeles.net

Can't get enough of the Fuentes brothers?
The chemistry continues with Carlos and Kiara ...

Read on for a sneak peek
of the hot new romance by Simone Elkeles

1

CARLOS

I want to live life on my own terms. But I'm Mexican, so *mi familia* is always there to guide me in everything I do—whether I want them to or not. Well, "guide" is too weak of a word. "Dictate" is more like it.

Mi'amá didn't ask if I wanted to leave Mexico and move to Colorado to live with my brother Alex for my senior year of high school. She made the decision to send me back to America "for my own good"—her words, not mine. When the rest of *mi familia* backed her up, it was a done deal.

Do they really think sending me back to the U.S. will prevent me from ending up six feet under or in jail? Ever since I got fired from the sugar mill two months ago, I've lived *la vida loca*. Nothing is ever gonna change that.

I look out the small window as the plane soars above the snow-capped Rockies. I'm definitely not in Atencingo anymore . . . and I'm not in the suburbs of Chicago either, where I lived my entire life before *mi'amá* made us pack up and move to Mexico during my freshman year of high school.

When the plane lands, I watch other passengers scramble to get off. I hold back and let this whole situation sink in. I'm about to see my brother for the first time in more than two years. Hell, I'm not even sure I *want* to see him.

The plane is almost empty now so I can't stall anymore. I grab my backpack and follow the signs for the baggage claim area. As I exit the terminal, I see Alex waiting for me beyond the barricade. I thought I might not recognize him, or feel like we were strangers instead of family. But there's no mistaking my brother . . . his face is as familiar to me as my own. I get a little satisfaction that I'm taller than him now, and I don't look anything like that scrawny little brother he left behind.

"*Ya estás en* Colorado," he says as he pulls me into a hug.

When he releases me, I notice faint scars above his eyebrows and by his ears that weren't there the last time I saw him. He looks older, but he's missing that guarded look he always carried with him like a shield. I think I inherited that shield.

"*Gracias*," I say flatly. He knows I don't want to be here. Uncle Julio stayed at my side until he forced me on the plane. Then threatened to stay at the airport until he knew my ass was off the ground.

"You remember how to speak English?" my brother asks as we walk to the baggage claim.

I roll my eyes. "We only lived in Mexico two years, Alex. Or should I say me, *Mamá*, and Luis moved to Mexico. You ditched us to follow Brittany to Colorado."

"I didn't ditch you. I'm goin' to college so I can actually do somethin' productive with my life. You should try it sometime, you know."

"No, thanks."

I grab my duffle off the carousel and follow Alex out of the airport.

"Why are you wearin' that around your neck?" my brother asks me.

"It's a rosary." I finger the black-and-white beaded cross. "I turned religious since I saw you last."

"Religious, my ass. I know it's a gang symbol," he says as we reach a silver Beemer convertible. My brother couldn't afford a rich car like that; he must have borrowed it from his girlfriend, Brittany.

"So what if it is?" He was in a gang back in Chicago. *Mi papá* was a gang member before him. Whether he wants to admit it or not, being a badass is my legacy. I tried living by the rules. I never complained when I worked like a dog after school at the sugar mill and made less than fifty pesos a day. After I got canned and started running with the *Guerreros del barrio*, I made over a thousand pesos in one day. It might have been dirty money, but it kept food on our table.

"Didn't you learn anything from my mistakes?" he asks.

Shit, when Alex was in the Latino Blood back in Chicago, I worshipped him. "You don't want to hear my answer to that."

Shaking his head, Alex grabs my suitcase out of my hand and tosses it in the backseat. So what if he got jumped out of the Latino Blood? He'll wear his tattoos the rest of his life. He'll always be associated with the LB whether he's active in the gang or not.

I take a long look at my brother. He's definitely changed. I sensed it from the minute I saw him. He might look like Alex Fuentes, but I can tell he doesn't have that internal fighting spirit he once did. Now that he's in college, he thinks he can play by the rules and make the world a shinier place to live. It's amazing how quickly he's forgotten that not too long ago we lived in the slums of the Chicago suburbs. Some parts of the world can't shine, no matter how much you try to polish off the dirt.

"*¿Y Mamá?*" Alex asks.

"She's fine."

"And Luis?"

"The same. Our little brother is almost as smart as you, Alex. He thinks he's gonna be an astronaut like José Hernández."

Alex nods like a proud papa, and I think he really does believe Luis can live his dream. The two of them are delusional . . . both my brothers are dreamers. Alex thinks he can save the world by creating cures for diseases, and Luis thinks he can leave this world to explore new ones.

As we turn onto the highway I see the wall of mountains in the far distance. It reminds me of Mexico.

"It's called the front range," Alex tells me. "The university is at the base of the mountains." He points off to the left. "Those are the flatirons 'cause the rocks are flat like ironing boards. I'll take you there sometime. Brit and I take walks there when we want to get away from campus."

When he glances at me, I'm looking at my brother like he's got two heads.

"What?" he questions.

Is he kidding?—¿*Me esta tomando los pelos?* "I'm just wondering who you are and what the hell you did with my brother. My brother Alex used to be tough, and now he's talkin' about mountains, ironin' boards, and takin' walks with his girlfriend."

"You'd rather I talked about getting drunk and fucked up?"

"Yes!" I say, acting like I'm excited. "And then you can tell me where I can get drunk and fucked up, 'cause I won't last here five days if I don't get some kind of illegal substance in my system," I lie. *Mi'amá* probably told him she suspects I'm into drugs, so I might as well play the part.

"Brother, I don't fall for your bullshit any more than you do."

I put my feet up on the dash. "You have no clue."

Alex shoves them down. "Do you mind? It's Brittany's car."

"You are seriously whipped, man. When are you gonna dump that *gringa* and start bein' a normal college guy who hooks up with multiple girls?"

"Brittany and I don't date other people."

"Why not?"

"It's called being boyfriend and girlfriend."

"It's called bein' a *panocha*. It's not natural for a guy to be with just one girl, Alex. I'm a free agent and I intend to stay one forever."

"Just so you and I are clear right from the start, *Señor Free Agent*, you're not screwin' anyone in my apartment."

He might be my older brother, but our father has been dead and buried a long time. I don't want or need his bullshit rules, but it's time I set my own. "Just so we're clear right from the start, I plan on doin' whatever the hell I want while I'm here."

"Just do us both a favor and listen to me. You might actually learn somethin'."

I give a short laugh. Yeah, right. What am I gonna learn from him—how to fill out college applications? Do thermal chemistry experiments? I don't plan on doing either.

We're both silent as we drive for another forty-five minutes, the mountains getting closer and closer with each mile. We pass right through the University of Colorado–Boulder campus. Redbrick buildings jut out of the landscape and college students with backpacks are scattered everywhere. Does Alex think he can beat the odds and actually find a high-paying job so he won't be poor the rest of his life? Fat chance. People will take one look at him and his tattoos and throw his ass out the door.

"I've got to be at work in an hour, but I'll get you settled in first," he says as he pulls into a parking space.

I know he got a job working at some auto body shop to help him pay off a shitload of school and government loans.

"This is it," he says as he points to the building in front of us. "*Tu casa.*"

This round, eight-story eyesore of a building resembling a giant corncob is the farthest thing from being a home, but whatever. I pull my duffle out of the trunk and follow Alex inside.

"I hope this is the poor side of town, Alex," I say. " 'Cause I get hives around rich people."

"I'm not livin' in luxury, if that's what you mean. It's subsidized student housing."

We ride the elevator to the fourth floor. The hallway smells like stale pizza, and stains scatter the carpet. Two hot girls in workout clothes pass us. Alex smiles at them, and from their dreamy reaction I wouldn't be surprised if they suddenly kneel down and kiss the ground he walks on.

"Mandi and Jessica, this is my brother Carlos," Alex says.

"Hel-*lo*, Carlos . . ." Jessica scans me up and down. I have definitely reached horny college central. And I'm definitely feelin' it. "Why didn't you tell us he was so hot?"

"He's in high school," he says.

What is he, my cock-blocker?

"A senior," I blurt out, hoping that'll lessen the blow that I'm not a college guy. "I'll be eighteen in a couple months."

"We'll throw you a birthday party," Mandi says.

"Cool," I say. "Can I have you two as my presents?"

"If Alex doesn't mind," Mandi says.

Alex walks away and threads a hand through his hair. "I'm gonna get myself in trouble if I get into this discussion."

This time, the girls laugh. Then they head down the hall, but not before looking back and waving bye.

We enter Alex's apartment and I immediately agree he's not living in luxury. A twin bed with a thin, black fleece blanket is off to the side of the room, a table and four chairs is on the right, and a small kitchen that two people would have a hard time fitting in together is by the front door. This isn't a one-bedroom apartment. It's a studio. A *small* studio.

Alex points to a door next to his bed. "There's the bathroom. And here's the closet where you can put your clothes."

I toss my duffle in the closet. "Um, Alex . . . where do you expect me to sleep?"

"I borrowed a blow-up bed from Mandi."

"*Está buena*, she's cute." I check out the room again. In our house back in Chicago, I shared a much smaller room with Alex and Luis. "Where's the TV?" I ask.

"Don't have one."

Shit. That's not good. "What the hell am I supposed to do when I'm bored?"

"Read a book."

"*Estás chiflado*—you're crazy. I don't read."

"Starting tomorrow you do," he says as he opens the window to let in the crisp, fresh air. "I've already had your transcripts sent, and they're expectin' you at Flatiron High tomorrow."

School? *My brother is talkin' about school?* Man, that's the last thing a seventeen-year-old guy wants to think about. I thought he'd give me a week at least to adjust to living in the U.S. again. Time to change course.

"Where do you stash your weed?" I say, knowing I'm pushing his patience to the limit. "You should prob'ly tell me now so I don't have to go rummagin' through your place tryin' to find it."

"I don't have any."

"Who's your dealer?"

"You don't get it, Carlos. I don't do that shit anymore."

"You said you work. Don't you make money?"

"Yeah, so I can afford to eat, go to college, and send whatever's left to *Mamá*."

Just as that news is sinking in, the apartment door opens. I recognize my brother's blond girlfriend immediately, her keys to his apartment and her purse in one hand and a big brown paper bag in the other. She looks like a Barbie doll come to life. My brother takes the bag from her and they kiss like a married couple. "Carlos, you remember Brittany."

She opens her arms out wide and pulls me close. "Carlos, it's so great to have you here!" Brittany says in a cheery voice. I almost forgot she used to be a cheerleader back in high school, but as soon as she opens her mouth I can't help but remember.

"For who?" I say stiffly.

She pulls back. "For you. And for Alex. He misses having family around."

"I bet."

She clears her throat and looks a little uneasy. "Um . . . okay, well, I brought you guys some Chinese food for lunch. I hope you're hungry."

"We're Mexican," I tell her. "Why didn't you get Mexican food?"

Brittany's perfectly shaped eyebrows furrow. "That was a joke, right?"

"Not really."

She turns toward the kitchen. "Alex, want to help me in here?"

Alex follows and then reappears with paper plates and plastic utensils. "Carlos, what's your problem?"

I hold my hands up. "No problem. I was just askin' your girlfriend why she didn't get Mexican food. She's the one who got all defensive."

"Have some fuckin' manners and say thank you instead of making her feel like shit."

It's crystal clear whose side my brother is on. At one time Alex said he joined the Latino Blood to protect our family, so Luis and I didn't have to join. But I can see now that family means crap to him.

Brittany holds her hands up. "I don't want you two getting in a fight because of me." She pushes her purse farther up her shoulder and sighs. "I think I better go and let you get reacquainted."

"Don't go," Alex says.

Dios mio, I think my brother lost his balls somewhere between here and Mexico. Or maybe Brittany has them locked in a drawer at her place. "Alex, let her go if she wants." It's time to break the leash she's got him on.

"It's okay. Really," she says, then kisses my brother. "Enjoy the lunch. I'll see you tomorrow. Bye, Carlos."

"Uh-huh." As soon as she's gone, I grab the brown bag off the kitchen counter and bring it to the table. I read the words on each container. Chicken chow mein . . . beef chow fun . . . pupu platter. "Pupu platter?"

"It's a bunch of appetizers," Alex explains.

I'm not goin' near anything with the name "pupu" on it, and I'm annoyed that my brother actually knows what a pupu platter is. I leave that container alone as I scoop myself a plateful of the identifiable Chinese food and start chowing down. "Aren't you gonna eat?" I ask Alex.

He's looking at me as if I'm some stranger.

"*¿Que pasa?*" I ask.

"Brittany's not goin' anywhere, you know."

"That's the problem. Can't you see it?"

"No. What I see is my seventeen-year-old brother actin' like he's five. It's time to grow up, *mocoso*."

"So I can be as boring as shit like you? No thanks."

Alex grabs his keys.

"Where you goin'?"

"To apologize to my girlfriend, then to work. Make yourself at home," he says, tossing me a spare set of keys. "And stay out of trouble."

"As long as you're talkin' to Brittany," I say as I bite off the end of an egg roll, "why don't you ask her for your *huevos* back."

2

Kiara

"Kiara, I can't believe he text-dumped you," Tuck says, reading the three sentences on my cell phone screen as he sits at the desk in my room. *It's nt wrkg out. Sry. Don't h8 me.* He tosses the phone on my bed. "The least he could have done is spell it out. *Don't h8 me?* The guy's a joke. Of course you're gonna hate him."

I lay back on my bed and stare at the ceiling, remembering the first time Michael and I kissed. It was at the outdoor summer concert in Niwot behind the ice-cream vendor. "I liked him."

"Yeah, well, I never did. Don't trust someone you meet in the waiting room at your therapist's office."

I turn around and prop myself up on my elbows. "It was *speech* therapy. And he just drove his brother for sessions."

Tuck, who has never liked any guy I've dated, pulls a pink skull-and-crossbones notebook from my desk drawer. He shakes his index finger at me. "Never trust a guy who tells you he loves you on the second date."

"Why? Don't you believe in love at first sight?"

"No. I believe in *lust* at first sight. And attraction. But not love.

Michael told you he loved you just so he could get into your pants."

"How do you know?"

"I'm a guy, that's how." Tuck frowns. "You didn't do *it* with him, did you?"

"No." I shake my head to emphasize my answer. We fooled around, but I didn't want to take it to the next level. I just, I don't know . . . I wasn't ready.

I haven't seen or talked to him since school started two weeks ago. Sure, we texted a few times, but he said he was always busy and would call when he got a minute. He's a senior in Longmont, twenty minutes away, and I go to school in Boulder, so I just thought he was busy with school stuff. But now I know the reason we hadn't talked had nothing to do with him being busy. It was because he wanted to break up.

Was it because of another girl?

Was it because I wasn't pretty enough?

Was it because I wouldn't have sex with him?

It can't be because I stutter. I've been working on my speech all summer and haven't stuttered once since school let out in June. Every week I go to speech therapy; every day I practice speaking in front of a mirror; every minute I'm conscious of the words that come out of my mouth.

Tuck knows this is the year I'm determined to show my confident side—the side I've been keeping hidden from kids at school. I was shy and introverted in my first three years of high school because I had an intense fear of people making fun of my stuttering. But I don't stutter anymore, unless I get really emotional. Instead of Kiara Westford being remembered as shy, they're going to remember me as the one who wasn't afraid to speak up.

I didn't count on Michael breaking up with me. I thought we'd go to homecoming together, and prom . . .

"Stop thinking about Michael," Tuck tells me.

"He was cute."

"So is a hairy ferret, but I wouldn't want to date one. You could do better than him. Don't sell yourself short."

"Look at me," I tell him. "Face reality, Tuck. I'm no Madison Stone."

"Thank God for that. I hate Madison Stone."

"She's popular."

"And a stuck-up bitch." Tuck starts scribbling words in my notebook, then hands it to me. "Here," he says, tossing me a pen.

I stare at the page. *RULES OF ATTRACTION* is written at the top, and a big line runs down the center of the page.

"What is this?"

"In the left column, write down all the great things about you."

Is he kidding me? "No."

"Come on, start writing. Consider this a self-help exercise for you to realize that girls like Madison Stone aren't even attractive. Finish the sentence *I, Kiara Westford, am great because . . .* "

I know Tuck isn't going to let up, so I write something stupid and hand it back to him.

He reads my words and cringes. "*I, Kiara Westford, am great because I know how to throw a football, change the oil in my car, and hike a Fourteener.* Ugh, guys don't care about this stuff." He grabs the pen from me, sits on the edge of my bed, and starts writing furiously. "Let's get the basics down. You've got to measure attractiveness in three parts to get the full result."

"Who made up those rules?"

"Me. These are Tuck Reese's Rules of Attraction. First, we start with personality. You're smart, funny, and sarcastic," he says, listing each one in the notebook.

"I'm not sure all of those are good things."

"They are. But wait, I'm not done. You're also a loyal friend, you love a good challenge, and you're a great sister to Brandon." He looks up when he's done writing. "The second part is your skills. You know about fixing cars, you're athletic, and you know when to shut up."

"That last one isn't a skill."

"Honey, trust me. It's a skill."

"You forgot my Special Spinach and Walnut Salad." I can't cook, but that salad is an all-time favorite.

"You do make a killer salad," he says, adding that to the list. "Okay, on to the last part of my scale—physical traits." Tuck looks me up and down, assessing me.

I moan, wondering when this humiliation will end. "I feel like I'm a steer about to be auctioned."

"Yeah, yeah, whatever. You've got flawless skin and a perky nose to match your tits. If I wasn't gay I might be tempted to—"

"Eww." I slap his hand away from the paper so he doesn't write the word. "Tuck, can you please not say or write that word in my notebook?"

"What, *tits*?"

"Ugh. Yes, that one. Just say boobs or breasts, please. The *T* word just sounds so . . . vulgar."

Tuck snorts and rolls his eyes. "Okay, perky . . . *breasts*." He laughs, totally amused. "I'm sorry, Kiara, that just sounds like something you're gonna barbecue for lunch or order off a menu." He pretends my notebook is a menu as he recites in a fake English accent, "Yes, waiter, I'd like the barbecued perky breasts with a side of coleslaw."

I throw Mojo, the big blue teddy bear my parents gave me in the hospital when I accidentally burned myself with scalding water when I was three, aiming for Tuck's head. "Just call 'em privates and move on."

Mojo bounces right off him and lands on the floor.

My best friend doesn't miss a beat. *"Perky tits*, scratch. *Perky breasts*, scratch." He makes a big deal of crossing both out. "Replace with . . . *perky privates*," he says, writing each word down as he says it. "Long legs, long eyelashes. No offense, but you could use a manicure."

"Is that it?" I ask.

"I don't know. Can you think of anything else?"

I shake my head.

"Okay, so now that we know how fabulous you are, we need to make a list of what type of guy you should be looking for. We'll write this on the right side of the page. Let's start with personality. You want a guy who is . . . fill in the blank."

"I want a guy who's confident. Really confident."

"Good," he says, writing it down.

"I want a guy who's nice to me."

Tuck continues writing. "Nice guy."

"I'd like a guy who's smart," I add.

"Street smarts or book smarts?"

"Both?" I question, not knowing if it's the right or wrong answer.

Tuck pats me on the head like I'm a little kid. "Good. Let's move on to skills." He holds up his hand, stopping me from contributing. "I'll write this part for you. You want a guy who has the same skills you have, and then some. Someone who likes sports, someone who can at least appreciate your interest in fixing up that stupid old car of yours, and—"

"Oh, shoot." I jump off my bed. "That reminds me, I have to go into town and pick up something from the auto body."

"Please don't tell me it's fuzzy dice to hang on your rearview mirror."

"It's not fuzzy dice. It's a radio. A vintage one."

"Oh, goodie! A vintage radio, to match your vintage car!" Tuck says sarcastically, then claps a bunch of times in fake excitement.

"Wanna come with?"

He closes my notebook and shoves it back in my desk. "The last thing I want to do is hang around and listen to you talk about cars with people who actually care."

It takes me fifteen minutes to get to Finney's Auto Body after I drop off Tuck at his house. Alex, one of the guys who works at the shop, was a student of my dad's. After a study session last year, my dad found out that Alex works on cars. He told Alex about this 1972 Monte Carlo I've been restoring, and Alex has been helping me get parts for it ever since.

I pull my car into the shop and find Alex bent over the engine of a VW Beetle.

"Hey, Kiara," Alex says. He wipes his hands on a shop cloth, then tells me to wait while he gets my radio. "Here it is," he says, opening the box.

I know I shouldn't be so excited about a radio, but the dash wouldn't be complete without it.

He pulls out the radio from the box and removes the bubble wrap. Wires stick out of the back like spindly legs, but it's just perfect. The one that came with my car never worked and the front plastic was cracked, so Alex had been looking online to find me an authentic replacement.

"I didn't get a chance to test it, though," he says as he wiggles each wire to make sure the connections are solid. "I had to pick up my brother at the airport so I couldn't come in early."

"Is he visiting from Mexico?" I ask.

"Yeah, but he's not visitin'. He'll be a senior at Flatiron startin' tomorrow," he says as he fills out an invoice. "You go there, right?"

I nod.

He puts the radio back in the box. "Do you need help installin' it?" he asks.

I thought so before I saw it up close, but now I'm not so sure. "Maybe," I tell him. "Last time I soldered wires, I messed them up."

"Then don't pay for it now," he says. "If you've got time tomorrow after school, stop by and I'll put it in. That'll give me time to test the thing." He looks up from the invoice and taps his pen on the counter. "I know this is gonna sound *loco*, but can you help show my brother around school? He doesn't know anyone."

"We have a peer outreach program at school," I say proudly. "I can meet you in the principal's office in the morning and sign up to be his peer guide." The old Kiara would be too shy and would never offer to be a peer guide at school, but not the new Kiara.

"I've got to warn you . . . ," he says.

"About what?"

"My brother can be tough to deal with."

My lips turn into a wide grin, because as Tuck pointed out . . . "I love a good challenge."

There's more
Perfect Chemistry online

www.perfectchemistrythebook.com

- Watch the *Perfect Chemistry* book trailer
- Read an interview with the author
- Find out if you and your crush have perfect chemistry with an online quiz
- Listen to the *Perfect Chemistry* playlist
- And more!

 www.bloomsburyteens.com

Lights, camera, action!
¡Luces, cámara, acción!

Check out Simone's funny, original trailers for *Perfect Chemistry* and *Rules of Attraction*, then tap into your creative talents, make your own trailer, and enter the *Perfect Chemistry* Trailer Contest!

Announcing the *perfect* contest for fans of Simone Elkeles

The first 100 people who enter will receive a sneak peek of Simone's next novel (coming in 2011), and if your entry is selected as a Judge's Favorite, you could win a Flip Mino camcorder or other cool prizes.

Grand prize winners will be selected by Simone from entries received between May 1, 2010, and December 31, 2010.

HOW DO YOU ENTER? ·

1. Create a book trailer based on *Perfect Chemistry* and/or *Rules of Attraction*. There's no official limit to the length, but we suggest you not go over two minutes. You can submit more than one trailer, if you're feeling extra inspired. Check out the Official Rules on www.perfectchemistrythebook.com for more information.

2. This is important! Register by e-mailing teen.publicity@bloomsburyusa.com, listing your full name, age, YouTube link, and what inspired you to create your trailer.

3. Upload your book trailer to YouTube and add it to the "Rules of Attraction Trailer Contest Group" at http://www.youtube.com/group/RoATrailerContest.

The first 100 entrants will receive a sneak peek of the third book in the Perfect Chemistry series; three Judge's Favorites will win a signed copy of *Rules of Attraction*; and two lucky grand prize winners will receive a Flip Mino camcorder as well as a signed copy of each of Simone's novels published by Walker.

For official contest rules (and lots of other cool stuff), visit www.perfectchemistrythebook.com